Broo crew 2009-11,

to the biggest

mate I've

ever known.

you've an
absolute legend.

Love your friend,

David

COINCI**DATE**

COINCI**DATE**

a novel

DAVID R. LOW

Kharms & Bowler Publishing

CoinciDATE

Copyright © 2020 David R. Low

Kharms & Bowler Publishing

ISBN: 978-1-7362773-0-0

First Edition, 2020

Cover design by Alfred Obare (Behance)
Book design by Jonas Perez Studio

For M.S.

Incels (/ˈɪnsɛlz/ *IN-selz*): a portmanteau of **involuntary celibates**, are members of an online subculture who define themselves as unable to find a romantic or sexual partner despite desiring one. Discussions in incel forums are often characterized by resentment, misogyny, misanthropy, self-pity and self-loathing, racism, a sense of entitlement to sex, and the endorsement of violence against sexually active people.

Chad (/tʃæd/): in incel terminology, a sexually active alpha male.

"I've come to the realization that I hate women. They give pussy to almost everyone except me. At the club, I get no pussy. At school, no pussy. Dating apps? No pussy. I'm fucking sick of it all. All I want is to build a rotation of bitches I can fuck. I don't give a fuck about how females feel, and I don't want them as friends. Just for sex. I hate my life."

— Incel on the internet

PART I

Chapter 1

Kenneth

A gentleman shouldn't have been disturbed by such things, yet they were becoming the bane of his existence. The numbers appeared everywhere, and they were mocking him. There they were, floating among soggy bits of cereal in his morning bowl. He saw them on peoples' faces and in the sky. They appeared in his notebook and syllabus and eventually etched on his arms and legs. Each day he wrote them down and added to them.

7,366 days without having touched a woman. Calling it 280 months didn't hit the nail on the head nearly hard enough, which was why it seemed so important to Kenneth to count it in days. The number, which he woke up repeating to himself every morning, was only likely to grow. Today wasn't the day to do *it* (not touch a woman; the other *it*). Today would have been a good day. Yesterday would have worked as well, but like everything in his life, Kenneth was burdened with bad timing and even worse luck.

To exacerbate matters, he had let himself down that

morning. Walking along the pavement toward his classroom, there was room enough for only one to pass, and like clockwork he moved out of the way to let the androgynous-looking male in skinny jeans take the opening. Not once and not even twice had he submitted to the male in the skinny jeans, but three times. He told himself this morning he wouldn't move out of the way for him. He'd stand his ground. But he'd only been lying to himself. That notion, that not only did the male in the skinny jeans make no attempt to give Kenneth passage, he more than likely believed the passage was his by right, and it was Kenneth who was obligated to move out of the way. A gentleman, one so well-dressed and with tastes so refined and who referred to cinema as kino, should have been above such trifle, but it made him sick. More so, he was sick that he had lied to himself. He knew damn well he was going to give passage to the male in the skinny jeans the moment he saw him. Worst of all, the male in the skinny jeans likely didn't realize that it had been Kenneth sacrificing the walking space on all three occasions. Just his luck that it would happen again on a day like today.

On that front, he walked into class three minutes late, and his entrance caught the attention of Mr. Sandoval, who would surely go down in history as the most unqualified history teacher ever.

"Why are you late, Kenneth?" Mr. Sandoval asked. "Making sure your hair looked pretty?" He laughed.

Everyone laughed at Kenneth—fat, thin, hot, ugly—but they all seemed to like Mr. Sandoval. Kenneth didn't get it. He'd had a hundred teachers in high school like Mr. Sandoval, guys who had been jackasses their whole lives, guys who had married women born to be ex-wives, guys who were eventually left by their wives for being such jackasses. They spent as much class time yelling at their ex-wives on the phone as they did teaching. For whatever reason, only Kenneth seemed able to discern this awfulness, even as the rest of his classmates ate up every one of Mr. Sandoval's inane jokes. At five foot three, Sandoval was almost as round as he was tall. Coupled with his black blazer and white dress shirt, he resembled a penguin.

Kenneth's hair had been subject to ridicule his entire life. His mother had insisted on cutting it herself, which meant a bowl cut through sophomore year of high school. It didn't take his peers long to catch on to the fact that his skinny body, even skinnier neck, perfectly round head, and bowl cut leant him the appearance of an erect dick.

"I've never seen a bigger dickhead in my life," classmates would say with laughter.

"Look at his shadow! I swear it looks like a cock!"

"If I rub your head, will white goo shoot out of it?"

At fifteen, he'd finally had enough. He left school during PE, called his mom an ignorant whore, and took twenty dollars from her wallet. He went to a barber for the first time in his life and exited wishing he'd left himself looking like a dickhead. It turned out he had the worst series of cowlicks imaginable, and try as he might, the barber could do nothing to tame them. Kenneth refused to show his face at school. After the third day of staying home, his mother used her enormous arms to drag Kenneth's gangly body into the car and drive him to school.

At least the nicknames bestowed upon his previous haircut had been consistent. Instead of calling him "dickhead," his classmates were then forced to call him "faggot," "pussy," "permanent virgin," and "male lesbian."

Kenneth was civilized, polite, and dressed nice, just as

a proper gentleman should be. The same could not be said for so many of his peers. But at a certain point during his lifetime, without his consent or involvement, society decided that the only thing that mattered was having won the genetic lottery. He'd reached this realization when he had bought $300-sunglasses, wore them for a week straight, and not one female commented on them. All the other boxes were checked, but due to the unfortunate nature of his face, nice clothes and immaculate taste could not save him.

Kenneth had been led to believe that college would be different, a place where he could reinvent himself and become a brand-new man. No one would know about his previous life as a dickhead. But he'd been wrong.

Getting to his seat was no easy feat, as this class had recently merged with another, making for twice as many students in too small a space. Each outer desk ended mere centimeters from the wall. To his dismay, his usual desk was occupied. Getting to an available chair meant squeezing his body through the narrow aisle, inadvertently bumping into other students, and therefore making his presence known to everyone. He typically arrived early precisely to avoid such entanglements, but that day his mom had decided to yell at him about leaving the kitchen light on all night as he was on his way out.

His whole trip to campus was filled with nothing but thoughts about how he'd berate his mom, both for humiliating him and causing future humiliation. Once he was seated, he'd write down the thoughts in a numbered list accompanied by bullet points. The list would start with her atrocious cooking. He'd fill in the details later. The second bullet point would be about how he'd now require her to ask his permission before she cleaned his room and changed his linens. Nothing would be left up in the air, and his mom would find his arguments so compelling that she'd have no choice but to apologize to her son.

"What's up, Kenneth?" Derek whispered, sticking out his hand for Kenneth to shake. He indicated an empty seat next to him.

Kenneth took it, still disturbed that his usual spot was taken. A month into the semester, it should have been obvious which seat belonged to whom, and that whether a person was late or not, that didn't give someone the right to take a seat established as belonging to another. He couldn't believe he had submitted once again to the male in the skinny jeans.

His friend Barry, who suffered from Mariko Aoki's disease, wasn't in his seat, either. Kelly, a beautiful, doe-eyed female with light brown hair, was sitting in it instead. For weeks, Kenneth had tried to figure out Kelly's last name, but hours of searching for her on Facebook and googling her name plus the name of their college provided no results. Barry would freak when Kenneth told him who was sitting in his chair, but Kenneth was also extremely pissed at Barry. For three weeks, Barry had been skipping a day of class a week. He'd never warn Kenneth beforehand what day it would be, and, more importantly, he never invited Kenneth to play hooky with him.

Derek pointed at the page and paragraph in the book the class was discussing. Kenneth gave a weak nod of gratitude. *Derek, you son of a bitch*, he wanted to tell him. *Do you think shaking my hand in the morning and telling me what page we're on makes up for the fact that you used to take so much joy in calling me dickhead? I remember it all, you cocksucker.*

The fact that Derek was now suddenly nice made

Kenneth abhor him all the more. At least back when Derek was being a cocky prick, Kenneth knew where they stood. How was he to interpret this newfound niceness?

Kenneth had thought college would be different, but in just this class were five people he had graduated with. Most of them were Chads just like Derek. One of them was even named Chad. The graduating high school class had merely relocated to this campus, and those who were Chads then were Chads now, and the girls who adored and admired those Chads then did so now as well. But there also were new girls to give their adoration to the Chads.

One Chad—Tommy—had introduced himself to Kelly on the first day, not allowing Kenneth or any other guy in the class a chance to make a first impression. That selfish prick had swooped in before anyone else had a fair chance. From then on, Kelly would laugh at every inane, unclever Chad joke Tommy told her. It was amazing that even in college girls could be as dimwitted and simpleminded as to think that someone like Tommy was interesting or funny. Kenneth knew for a fact he was a million times funnier than Tommy. His friends continuously praised him for his humor, and he knew he made them laugh more than anyone else in his inner circle. Just once, someday, right as Tommy reached the middle of a lame joke, Kenneth would be ready to jump in, steal the moment, and show Kelly who was truly funny.

The least-funny person Kenneth had ever encountered was his own father. Kenneth Senior was a dentist who lost another morsel of whatever little humor he had with each tooth he pulled. Worse than being unfunny was an unfunny person believing in his own comedic capabilities. To add insult to injury, Kenneth Senior always insisted on some sort of father-son bonding time in which they'd talk about nothing Kenneth cared about at all.

"Do we have to do this in public?" Kenneth would ask his dad.

"What's wrong? I thought you liked the food here."

"Can't we talk about this stuff at home?"

Living in a small town sandwiched somewhere between Los Angeles and Santa Barbara, Kenneth dreaded going out in public with his father because that always meant seeing former high school classmates out with their friends and partners. If he saw them, they certainly saw him, and out with his balding father besides.

The only silver lining to these ventures was that at least Kenneth didn't have to be seen with his mother, who was the ugliest woman who'd ever lived. Kenneth's father was no Chad, but he was certainly a league above whatever hell pit Mrs. Kenneth Senior had crawled out of. Mrs. Kenneth Senior was the type of ugly that even if she lost weight, she'd still look like a four-year-old's drawing of a human. In a way, the misfortune that was the physical appearance of Kenneth's parents gave him a sliver of comfort—it meant he never had a choice about his lot in life and therefore stood blameless.

Kenneth belonged to the incel community, and like all incels, he didn't find himself there by choice. He'd become an unwilling member of this brotherhood when his own member kept getting harder and harder, but no females proved willing to do anything about it. There wasn't a single Stacey on Earth who'd wrap her lips around his shaft and please him. No Stacey would ever ride him hard until his creaky old bed caved in. No Stacey would ever sit on his face and suffocate him with her ass. Both Kenneth and his member cried as this thought crept into his mind, whether he was in class listening to Sandoval spout his ill-informed bullshit, or ferociously pounding his member and thinking about Kelly. Thinking about Kelly always did more harm than good, because right before completion, the moment he'd been building toward, he'd think about how she was more than likely sitting on Tommy's face and sucking Tommy's perfectly long and girthy cock, and then his joy at the prospect of climaxing would turn into a mixture of sorrow and anger.

"Why would you want someone to sit on your face?" Barry would ask as though they hadn't had this conversation a dozen times.

"Not just someone," Kenneth would retort. "A super-hot female like Kelly."

"Okay. I don't see how that's desirable. I mean, isn't that kind of disgusting? Having your nose so close to a butthole?"

"What? You're crazy. There isn't anything better. Puritan."

"I just don't find the prospect of sniffing a butt all that appealing."

"Dude, you're nuts. Females don't shit. That's first of all. Second, if you have good hygiene like a decent human being, then imagine how much better a slut like Kelly's hygiene would be. Besides, I won't have enough time to sniff it. I'll be too busy licking it."

Kenneth hadn't been sure if the nerve he'd struck in his friend was due to his explicit description of his sexual fantasy or mentioning hygiene. Barry, while not exactly fat, still had that distinct fat-person smell about him.

When they'd met two years prior, it was immediately evident that Barry was incel. If one were to line up a group of ten men and point out which one personified the word *virgin*, it was Barry. Unlike Kenneth, Barry didn't need a Stacey to be happy. He would have settled for literally any girl, no matter how fat, ugly, or hideously deformed. Settling was what had led Kenneth Senior to Mrs. Kenneth Senior, and Kenneth would have none of that. What was the point of a woman if she wasn't fuckable?

Having a foul odor that perpetually leaked from his body wasn't Barry's only defining characteristic. He also was the first person who ever admitted to Kenneth that he was a virgin. Most of Kenneth's non-virtual friends (and Kenneth himself) didn't dare reveal that they were virgins. Instead, they hid the fact behind detailed stories of their sexual conquests. Kenneth had even come up with a list of names for the girls he supposedly bedded. When he finished the list, he wrote down bullet points detailing how he'd met each girl, the places they'd gone, and what their sexual encounters had consisted of. The list originally had six names before Kenneth considered how young he was and, facing reality, that he was a beta. He crossed out three. He was satisfied with what remained: two white girls and, to his friends' delight, one Asian.

Once he became accustomed to Barry's openness and honesty, Kenneth no longer felt the need to hide his virginity. *Incel* had the word *involuntary* built right into it, so being one meant his virginity was no fault of his own. The fault lay instead with the world and all the bitches in it.

Barry was one of those Jews who pretended to be Italian. Kenneth never let on that he knew his friend was a non-gentile. Barry's life was embarrassing enough, but Kenneth was certain everyone knew. Poor Barry didn't have the sex appeal of an Italian, nor the intelligence of a Jew.

"Why have you been missing class so much?" Kenneth asked at the bookstore, where they had come to stare at the cute girl they'd discovered working there a month ago. It was a Thursday, so they weren't sure if she'd be there, as the only time they knew for sure she worked was Monday between noon and five p.m. They'd seen her working on a Thursday once at this time, so the gamble seemed worth it. Due to Barry's disease, he ran straight to the restroom before he could answer Kenneth's question.

"I went to the movies," Barry said.

"And the other five times?" Kenneth asked.

"Movies."

"What the fuck, man? Why didn't you tell me? I would've gone."

"It was just some foreign movie. I don't even remember what language it was in."

"Most of the movies I watch are foreign!"

"Oh, I didn't know you would want to go. I always go to the movies by myself."

"You're not embarrassed?"

"Embarrassed? What for? Why do people feel they need friends with them when they go to the movies? Do they plan on talking? Okay, one of those five times I went with my mom. Dad doesn't like going to the movies."

"Bastard. Let me know next time you plan on going, so I can go with you."

"All right, all right."

When Kenneth got home, he was ready to snap as the smell of Hamburger Helper wafted from the kitchen.

"For fuck's sake, Mom!" he screamed. "This is the third

time this week you've made Hamburger Helper! Learn how to make something else, you useless bitch!" He climbed the stairs and slammed his bedroom door.

"What was that, hon?" his mom called from the kitchen.

Several tabs on his laptop had been left open. Panic struck as he realized that his mom, being the nosy bitch she was, could have walked into his bedroom at any point and seen them. He looked around to make sure that his socks and underwear were where he'd left them on the floor. Thank God they were. If his mom had walked in, she would have seen the tabs of various porn sites with pending downloads filling the screen. That wouldn't have been the worst part either. The other tabs included the profiles of whores from Nevada bordellos. Looking at the women in their brochures usually inspired a lot of anger, as most of them were sixes at best, and Kenneth couldn't believe they were charging such exorbitant prices.

The other tabs were websites for mail-order brides, one a site for Ukrainian girls and the other for Filipinas. Just sending messages to these women cost money. Kenneth had had a decent back and forth going with a female named Lucy from Manila that lasted ten messages, but he'd been forced to cut it short when funds ran out. He still looked at her picture daily and was always on the verge of tears knowing that soon enough she'd be married off to some asshole.

He would have paid any price in the world for a girl like Lucy, but he'd already spent the last of his savings on something of great value.

More disappointment was to come when one of the porn videos that had been downloading since morning was finally ready. He'd only looked at the thumbnail, which featured an Asian girl with a big ass. The video promised both ass eating and ass fucking. When he clicked the video to watch it, it turned out that the thumbnail had cleverly hidden her flabby belly. He couldn't jerk off to that. He wasn't in the mood for any of the other videos, so he succumbed to jerking off to Lucy's picture for the thousandth time. There was no satisfaction to be had. All he felt was spite, the only passion he understood. Allowing these females to be a source of pleasure, but only a simulated version of it, enraged him. Each time he groped himself, thinking of females and hating himself for thinking of them, he grew ever more spiteful.

Once his boxers were filled with cum, he closed all his old tabs and opened new ones, which included Facebook and various message boards. There were no message notifications on Facebook, but he had received a friend request. As with every new friend request, his heart raced as he convinced himself that this time it would be a babe, a chick who had finally noticed him and wanted to get to know him. He clicked the icon, only to see that it was Derek.

As he stared at Derek's page, he heard his mom yelling from the kitchen.

"What?" he shouted as angrily as possible, making it clear that his mother was disturbing something of the utmost importance.

She yelled again, followed by the mumbled but still distinct sound of, "Could you please come here?" Why couldn't she just text him like a normal person? She'd have to wait. No text or knock on the door came, so as with everything she wanted to talk with her son about, it was clearly of no importance.

Why did Derek want to add him to his friends list

now? He'd had ample opportunity throughout high school. As expected, nearly every photo of Derek featured him posing side by side with some bombshell. There were rarely two photos with the same female in them. Most of the time, they were together in bathing suits on some kind of pristine Hawaiian beach.

You've already won, you prick. Why do you have to flaunt it? Just to make guys like me even more infuriated? When the alpha wolf took its mate, did it force the rest of the pack to watch as it screwed her brains out?

After scrolling through all of Derek's photo albums, Kenneth took the next logical leap and went to check on his listed interests. As expected, Derek had the kino taste of a troglodyte. Nearly every Adam Sandler movie was there, along with the *Transformers* franchise and the occasional random progressive movie directed by a woman or a gay to show how in touch he was. By contrast, Kenneth's kino collection was of the highest quality. He had his *Rick and Morty* collection, a show only people of a certain level of wit and intelligence could comprehend. His shelf also contained the works of Takashi Miike and Dario Argento, along with all of the most highly renowned anime, which simple-minded fucks like Derek had never even heard of.

A message box popped up on Kenneth's desktop. It was from Derek.

> Hey Kenneth! How's it going, man? We have several classes together this semester, but you always seem to be really busy, so we haven't gotten a chance to talk much. It would be cool to catch up with you though, man! Remember all the shit we used to talk

in shop class? Guess what? I found Mr. Wooton's Facebook profile! Anyway, on Saturday, a bunch of friends are coming over for drinks. You should come along, man. It would be nice to catch up.

What was this bullshit? Why was he bringing up Mr. Wooton? Why was he writing now? If the friends he'd mentioned were those Kenneth assumed, then whatever would take place on Saturday night at Derek's house sounded like a nightmare.

Upon clicking on Derek's information, two things struck Kenneth. First, they shared the same birthday. Second, Derek was Jewish. Due to people like Barry, Kenneth had viewed Jews as natural allies, as they were born betas. The fact that Derek was such an alpha in every sense of the word but was somehow Jewish hurt Kenneth's head.

Kenneth's fingers eventually clicked on to Derek's friends list, and almost immediately he found what he both desired and dreaded. Kelly. Her last name was Del Rey? Had to be fake. More and more often, he noticed girls using fake last names on social media. But if they wanted to avoid creepy guys stalking them, why did they post such provocative pictures? Granted, Kenneth had spent ages searching for her, and never got the last name, but that didn't stop any random Joe Schmoe from stumbling on her page and creeping on her pictures. In every picture, her doe eyes beamed. Doe-eyed or not, she was no innocent. A female like her never could be.

Her profile showed she was in a relationship with Wallace B. Jordan. Before even clicking on his link, Kenneth knew his worst fears had been confirmed: her boyfriend was a Tyrone! A goddamn black Chad. He'd expected a Chad, but the fact that he was a Tyrone broke Kenneth's very soul. Once a girl dated a Tyrone, even most Chads didn't have a chance. It meant Kenneth was the biggest fool on Earth to even make a fantasy out of it. All those times he'd written down the scenarios in which she'd be sitting alone and notice the book he was reading, or perhaps even the clever shirt he wore. She'd come over to him, impressed by his selection, strike up a conversation, and become enamored by his wit and intelligence. But her dating a Tyrone threw all that in the trash.

Like most Tyrones, Wallace's profile was filled with pictures of him flashing his bling, showing off shoes named after some useless basketball player, and standing next to cars that he had probably spent his welfare checks on. Kenneth found himself on the verge of crying and vomiting simultaneously.

If she was in love with this Tyrone, then why was she always flirting with Tommy? Was she so insatiable that even a big Tyrone cock couldn't satisfy her?

Kenneth entered his group chat to share his discovery with his fellow incel brothers. The group used to meet regularly on various subreddits, but eventually they were all shut down. The banning of the easily accessible Reddit forums, while an annoyance, didn't put an end to their correspondence. It only made their resolve and bond stronger. They used the app Discord, often while playing video games. A few of them used WhatsApp, although some of the brothers weren't willing to give out their phone numbers. But all of them found themselves on Incel.me, a site only for them, where nothing but the truth would be posted and support shared.

The forums of Incel.me both worked as therapy and rage fuel for Kenneth. Therapy, because it was the only place where he could find truth shared by like-minded individuals. It was fuel for rage for the exact same reason. The enlightened always had been subject to deep and dark despair. Only the ignorant and the foolish ever experienced happiness—not happiness in the same realm as that of the Chads and Staceys, who were born with unfair advantages, but rather, a happiness born of the ignorance and dimwittedness of those too dumb to know how miserable they should be.

The more Kenneth scrolled through these forums and saw things he agreed with, or things that he'd always thought but couldn't articulate as well as his brothers, the more they added fuel to the fire of his anger and hatred for the unfairness bestowed upon him.

The most enlightened of these enlightened young minds was a poster who went by the name of Enlightened Celestial. Enlightened Celestial wasn't just highly intelligent, he was extremely conscientious. He could never be accused of having made a typo or a grammatical error. Kenneth wasn't exactly sure about the minute details of the rules of punctuation, but he was certain that Enlightened Celestial had never broken them. Even during intense arguments with other members, where fast typing to get your reply in before the other could strike back at you meant sacrificing precision in order to get the response out there first, Enlightened Celestial's ability to impress was never impaired.

Kenneth had been unable to finish the post from Enlightened Celestial he'd started reading at school, as the teacher had insisted he participate in his group project. So now that he finally had a moment to get back to it, he continued where he had left off.

We can learn a great deal from the way roles
and relationships are formed in the religions
of Islam and Mormonism. Western society,
for all of its supposed progress, has failed its
male population. All this talk about progress,
equality, equal opportunity, and equality of
outcome has done nothing more than hurt
those who built this world in the first place:
men. Women are the only ones benefiting
from this. This is why we really need to look
at how Islam treats females because there is
a lot we can learn from our Muslim brothers.

Kenneth took a moment to pause as conflict arose
within him. Just yesterday, he'd read a post from another
respected poster, ThugLyfe69, about how Islam was the most
detrimental thing to happen to Western society, and how it
needed to be ousted. Yet Enlightened Celestial was on the
opposite end of the spectrum, telling Kenneth to follow its
lead instead. Kenneth carried on reading.

The role of females in societies that abide
by the rules of Islam is simple, strict, and
not up for debate. There is a reason you will
never find an incel living in Saudi Arabia
or Iran but will find many incels of Arab
and Persian background among our ranks
here in the States. Islamic women living in
their home countries please their men. They
listen to them, they obey them, they satisfy
their sexual desires, and their minds aren't
corrupted with thoughts of feminism or

equal pay.

Until recently, Mormons had been able to live with nine wives happily. Do you, my brothers, know anyone happier than Mormons? Then the people promoting feminism and destroying the world of men intervened and put an end to this. The world we live in only benefits the Chads and females. Females cry about equal pay and sexism in the workplace, yet they reject every gentleman who is actually out there helping them and respecting them. These same feminist bitches become shameless sluts the moment they see a Chad. Their panties fall off at the drop of a hat.

How can we take these females who demand equality seriously when they act in such horrendously slutty and shameful ways? They say they want equal pay but fill up their Instagram pages with nothing but pictures of their asses to please the Chads and mock the incels.

Kenneth felt the warmth of blood rushing to his head, and then, to his great surprise, back to his penis. He'd only pleasured himself a couple of minutes earlier, but his member was telling him the time had come for another go.

Kenneth entered another thread where poor Barry was making a fool of himself. Barry was one of the few naïve enough to use his real name on the message board. He'd committed the mortal mistake of writing about a nice girl he'd met in one of his classes and was excited at the prospect of getting to know her. It contained the typical warning signs of disaster, such as mentioning how nice she was and that she smiled at him, but the biggest warning sign of all was when Barry had uttered the forbidden phrase: *she's different*.

Enlightened Celestial immediately jumped in to save Barry's soul.

> Listen, Barry, she's not your friend. Men and females can never be friends. That's one. Second, if this girl is as cute as you say she is, then she's doing what women of her ilk have been doing since that devious bitch Eve plucked the apple from the tree. She's using you as a means to an end. Whenever she smiles, bats her eyes, leans in close, laughs at your joke, or says those sweet phrases that guys like you let affect them so profoundly, it's all part of her deceitful and malicious game.

> Let's entertain the idea that she actually hangs out with you, lets you take her to the café, or hang out at her place. It's all simply a time-waster for her. It's her doing what she wants while feeling the compliment of your desire as it boosts her ego. All the while, she's thinking about that big Chad dick. Trust me, Barry, there's always a Chad lurking. There's either a current Chad, a past Chad, or five potential Chads on her horizon. You're merely a time-filler for her.

You said you're in a group project? That's third. She's being nice to you because she expects you to put in all the hard work.

This has happened to all of us, but only those of us who are strong enough can do anything about it. I see it now: you lie awake at night remembering how she smiled at you in class. You remember those sweet words she said to you. But those aren't validation of your greatness or worthiness in her eyes. It's nothing more than manipulation from a bitch. As she said those words, she was thinking about a big cock she's going to suck that isn't yours.

Females like her—who are twenty, for argument's sake, and look like she does— have already had a dozen cocks in them. For a female to get a cock in her requires no skill, effort, talent, or charm. She merely has to look the way she does. Yet we're supposed to treat her like an equal, and not a slut.

Remember, when you're lying there at night thinking about your interaction with her, she's not thinking about you.

It was truth bombs like those that enraged Kenneth. He had to stop reading or he was likely to break something. Instead, he went to one of his favorite forums. Another member of the site, one who went by the name Evil Genius, was truly a genius. He'd started a series of videos in which he'd film himself meeting Tinder dates. These women were unwilling victims of the trap he'd set for them.

Evil Genius was filming inside a mall, in a food court next to some shitty place like Sbarro. A short and squat Hispanic woman walked by. She was most likely in her twenties, but ugly women always looked older. Evil Genius approached her, not taking the camera off her face.

"Hi," he said.

"Hi," she responded, not looking at him but noticing being filmed.

"How ya doing?" he asked with a slight hiccup in his voice, trying to not let any laughter escape.

"I'm fine. Just waiting for my boyfriend."

"Just waiting for your boyfriend, huh?" The laughter tried ever harder to punch its way out of him. "Are you sure you're not waiting for Jason, a twenty-four-year-old fitness instructor from Camarillo, California?" The laughter poured out of him maniacally.

The girl turned white and red all at once.

"That's right! Look at the camera! You thought Jason the fitness instructor wanted to go out with *you*? Let me read some of the messages we shared together."

She ran off through the minefield of tables and customers in the food court, so he never got to read their intimate conversation aloud to her. The conversations already could be found on Incel.me anyway.

Evil Genius had amassed dozens of such videos in which he used the Tinder profile of Jason the fitness instructor to lure idiotic women into coming out in public with the hope of meeting their dream man for a date. Evil Genius made it a point to only target unattractive women, as it taught them a valuable lesson and also revealed a sickening truth to society.

Dating apps were the worst thing to ever happen to guys like Kenneth. Chads already dominated the dating market in the real world, and now that dating had come to the digital world, it only gave the Chads more room to flex their muscles and dominate. Guys like Kenneth would be judged solely on the merit of one photo before some tramp decided he was unworthy of her time without even reading a single word he'd written in his profile. Tinder only made it even easier for Chads and Staceys to fuck one another.

Even worse, ugly girls were doing extremely well on Tinder, too, because most Chads would fuck any female that moved and breathed, whether she was a Stacey or not. So while they were fucking Staceys on Fridays and Saturdays, their weekdays consisted of fucking any chick who was willing. Tinder benefited ugly females miraculously, and once more left the Kenneths of the world in the shadows. The Chads were taking all the women with a simple swipe of a thumb on a mobile screen.

Kenneth had texted Barry as soon as he got home, and two hours had passed with no reply. So he did something he nearly couldn't bear and dialed Barry's number.

"Yeah?"

"What do you mean *yeah*? Why didn't you answer my text?"

"Oh, my bad. I'm hanging out with my friend Daniel."

Christ, thought Kenneth. He couldn't stand Daniel, who was one of the biggest normies he'd ever met.

"Oh, I see. So you guys are probably gonna be hanging out for a while then?"

"Yeah, I think so."

"Okay, I'll see ya later then."

That weekend would be added to the long list of lonely weekends. Barry was spending all his time with Daniel, and Kenneth was fed up with always having to initiate conversation with his fat and smelly friend. Kenneth Senior had suggested going to the zoo as a family, an idea that embarrassed Kenneth just to hear about it, let alone actually be seen in public with his father.

~~~

Saturday came, and Kenneth reread Derek's invitation several times. He confided in his brothers online, asking for guidance. Almost immediately came a response from Enlightened Celestial.

> Going to this hangout is the worst thing you could do. Trust me, I know what's going through your head. You think this is an opportunity to interact with some Chads and Staceys, and possibly get to know some attractive women. The problem, though, is that from the sounds of it, these are people who have been in your class for quite some time already, and if they've made no effort to notice you before, then it's too late to change that now. Their impression of you is already set in stone. This Derek only invited you because he knows you don't pose any threat to him. He's simply looking for bodies

to take up space and drink his beer. If you do go, you'll only come home disappointed, thinking of that one girl who was nice to you but would never give you the time of day.

That settled it. Kenneth did the one thing he thought he'd never do and went to the movies by himself, as though he were Barry. The posters near the box office shoved nothing but romcoms in his face. Beautiful females with beautiful men. Men whose daily dilemma was deciding between the beautiful blonde female or the beautiful brunette female. Either way, his problems were beautiful.

When Kenneth bought his ticket, he hadn't realized the film was in Spanish. He settled into a seat in the last row with a large popcorn with extra butter, hoping that way he'd remain unseen. Besides himself, there were several old people scattered about the place either in couples or alone. He wondered if the old men sitting alone were widowers or lifelong incels. The latter idea nearly made him cry.

As the trailers ended and the lights fully dimmed, Kenneth was nearing the end of his popcorn. The prospect of watching the movie without it gnawed on him, but what gnawed on him even more was the group of five people who came in as the movie was starting. They didn't just come in; they came in and had a full conversation as they decided where they'd sit, finally landing directly next to Kenneth.

Kenneth sank down into his chair, but it didn't matter. They'd already seen him. In a nearly empty theater, why did these assholes have to sit next to him? How could Barry bear this torment and shame? Though determined to look straight at the screen, he couldn't shake the feeling that those next to him had their eyes on him the whole time, judging him and wondering what motivated such a loser to commit such an egregious act as going to the movies alone.

This would have been the perfect place to do *it*, Kenneth thought, but that thought didn't matter, as Kenneth didn't have the tools to implement *it*.

After enduring the cinematic torment, Kenneth went home to torment himself even further. On Derek's Instagram page, several photos and videos of his party had been uploaded. The faces Kenneth had expected to see were all there: Tommy, Kelly, and the rest. But there were also a half-dozen or so gorgeous girls he'd never seen. They were all drinking, dancing, having a great time, jumping into the pool and emerging with soaking wet bodies, and then eventually and inevitably pleasing some asshole out there.

That settled it. Monday would be the day.

Kenneth remained in his room all of Sunday, going over the plan in his head.

As the sun was going down, he decided to give Barry a call. Barry answered with his typical confusion. "Hello?"

"Hey, are you planning on going to Sandoval's class tomorrow?"

Barry hesitated. "I don't know. Why do you ask?"

"Well, you're always going to the movies by yourself. Let's go tomorrow. I'll join you."

"I don't know. I'm not sure if anything really looks all that appealing."

Kenneth suggested a movie he'd read about.

"That's really good, I've heard," Barry said. "Fuck Sandoval. Let's go see it. Is it at that place in the mall?"

"Yes."

"You meeting me there?"

"Yes, I'll meet you there at ten."

"All right."

That was settled. Barry would be waiting for him at the movies on Monday.

~~~

Kenneth woke earlier than usual on Monday because his stomach was upset, and he had to take a giant shit. He showered, only to have to run to the toilet to shit again. In total, he shat three times before leaving his house. Once on campus, he shat another time.

No one paid him any attention as he walked across the quad carrying his black Fender guitar case. He'd never once expressed any interest in guitar or been seen with a guitar, yet nonetheless, no one noticed him and his guitar case. Aside from the big case, he'd brought his backpack with him, for reasons he wasn't quite sure of.

Sandoval's classroom was located in one of the buildings farthest from the entrance and parking lot. From the quad where the cafeteria was located, it would be a little over a three-minute walk.

As usual, the front of the cafeteria was filled with students who didn't seem to ever go to class or exist outside of their permanent spots in front of the cafeteria. Whatever they or their parents were spending untold amounts of dollars on, it certainly wasn't an education. They were busy laughing at one another's jokes.

On the hill that contained the student administration

building and separated the cafeteria from the rest of the campus, Kenneth found each upward footstep slower and heavier. The laughter had died down. The only sounds that remained were the beats of his own heart.

The hill took twenty lifetimes to cross, and the instrument in his Fender carrying case weighed heavily on him. The other side of the hill showed that the campus was mostly empty, with only the occasional students talking on their phones or trying to cram in some last-minute studying before heading to class.

At the top of the hill, almost as if acting as its guardian, the creepy foreign guy who stared at people appeared. His body was covered in leather. Leather gloves and a leather jacket. His skin shone bright in the early-morning sunlight. Barry believed him to be French, but Kenneth didn't buy it. Barry had given him some stupid nickname—the Lustful Frenchman, or something along those lines. Truth be told, he didn't look like any recognizable ethnicity. He was creepy and looked creepy, and that was the only thing Kenneth had ever paid attention to. When Kenneth walked passed him, the mysterious foreigner removed his Ray-Bans to get a better look at Kenneth. This gesture was an allowance of passage to the other side of campus.

The K building was in sight, the final steps in reach. All he had to do was traverse the patch of brush and palm trees that he and his friends had nicknamed Jurassic Park. Upon setting foot in Jurassic Park, his stomach began to rumble and creak. Did he dare stop in the middle of his trek so he could detour to the bathroom? No, he was too committed at this point.

He imagined the expressions on all their faces. Mr. Sandoval would look both scared and remorseful. He'd apologize for every transgression, while knowing deep down that he held the blame for everything about to rain down on his class. Derek would have that same look.

The expression that mattered most, though, was Kelly's. Right before it was her turn, her face would give away her feelings of regret as she realized she'd been a fool her entire life and would do anything at that moment to make amends.

The windows of the K building were open. Anyone in Sandoval's class could have lifted their head and seen Kenneth's approach. He'd come to the conclusion much earlier that he'd remove the instrument from its case before entering the classroom. The door was mere inches away. Would he open it slowly and quietly, or would he kick it open forcefully? If he took one more step, shit was bound to fall out of his ass, as the tension that had begun in his stomach was now threatening to explode out of his sphincter. Sweat was forcing his bangs to stick to his eyes. He wiped them several times and pulled his instrument out of the guitar case.

The instrument was not one of music, but of death: an AR-15. He'd used all his savings to purchase it legally at a gun show. Not in California, of course. He had to go out of state. It was the only road trip he'd ever taken. When he returned from Texas, his mother had only asked him how his weekend with Barry had gone.

Kenneth hadn't been sure when he'd use the AR-15, but he always knew the day was bound to come. Now he wished he'd brought music along to accompany his grand entrance and martyrdom. There were so many choice tracks he could have selected.

Locked and loaded, he held the rifle in his right hand as he pushed the door to the classroom open with his left.

Sandoval was in the middle of a lecture, which meant jokes and anecdotes as opposed to teaching. The class was smaller than usual, with at least six people absent, including Barry.

Only when the door closed behind Kenneth did Sandoval turn to face him. The professor was nothing more than a penguin. "Are you gonna stand there all day, son, or are you gonna j—" Then his eyes locked on Kenneth's weapon. Most of the students weren't aware of what was transpiring. Several were typing away on their phones, while the rest looked lazily at their professor.

Kenneth was breathing rapidly, sweat pouring down his face, his hands shaking. He had to act quickly before Sandoval could raise an alarm—or before he lost his nerve.

Too late to turn back now. If you do, for the rest of your life you'll be seen as the guy who couldn't do it because he was too weak. No one will think about how good you were to change your mind and see the light. They'll remember you as the weak freak they already thought you were, but who didn't have the guts to do what was necessary. Do what's necessary. There's no going back. The hard part's over. Pulling the trigger is the easy part. Remember, not one person among them respects you, so pay them in kind.

Kenneth pulled the trigger.

Nothing happened. His hand shook. By then, all eyes were on him. He locked eyes with Kelly, and as if by telepathy, her gaze caught sight of the gun's safety. He switched the safety off and fired three rounds directly into Sandoval's gut. Sandoval crashed right onto the laptop on his desk, smashing it with a loud thud. Whether anyone screamed or not, Kenneth couldn't be sure, because his heartbeats were coming out of his ears, and the only thing that made any sense was pointing the gun at the next target.

It was a fat kid named Gerry. Kenneth had never spoken to him but was certain Gerry was incredibly lonely, as he never interacted with any of the other students. Showing him mercy was only a passing thought, because his pathetic nature and his useless fat existence sealed his fate. Kenneth put a round in his chest. The sound of Gerry's collapsed lung inducing a fit of wheezing managed to overpower the drum of Kenneth's own heartbeat. Kenneth shot the fat boy again in the head. He died just as he'd lived, fat and clumsy. His graceless body took out a table on the way down.

Targets were beginning to run, skip, jump, and trip over their desks. The inconveniently set up room created a perfect death trap, as it was difficult to make it to the exit. Kenneth had twenty-five rounds left and only thirteen bodies to use them on. In theory, he could have taken them all out with rounds to spare, but he knew he was in a risky position. The room was tight, and if he focused on one student, others would have enough time to run up on one of his flanks and attack him. He'd have to choose his targets carefully.

Instead, he fired madly and wildly into the crowd. One of the bullets scraped Derek's shoulder. Three hit nothing but wall and desk, while one got Kelly in the head, killing her instantly. He never got to have the satisfaction of looking her in her doe eyes as she knew she was about to die without his forgiveness.

Kenneth turned and ran for the door, firing wildly behind him, not looking to see who was hit. He lost focus on keeping his sphincter tightened, and warm shit began to slide down his leg.

He ran off, not thinking about direction. All he knew was that he had to run. He ran faster than he thought he could. The

K building had faded away, as did the screams of Sandoval's students. He ran.

Soon he was over the hill, and the cafeteria came into view. He began laughing. He was going to make it. It hadn't all gone according to plan, but he still got several of the people who needed getting, and now he'd be on his way to freedom and a new life. He didn't even mind the shit lingering in his pants and running down his leg.

He regretted not seeing the male in the skinny jeans. He'd love to see the look on his face when not only did he not step aside, but he filled his face full of lead. Dare he go on the hunt for him? A passing student gave him a startled look, and in response, Kenneth let off a round. The student fell and rolled down the hill.

Several campus police officers appeared out of thin air, guns drawn. Kenneth pulled his trigger at the officer nearest him. The gun responded with a quiet click. The three officers stared at him in awe. Did they know they were in the presence of a martyr?

Then he saw muzzle flashes an instant before a barrage of bullets slammed into his chest. He didn't have time for the pain to register, but he did have time for one final thought: *It is accomplished!*

Capitolo 2

Miranda

The broken coffeemaker had caused a lot of drama and stress at work. There was only an hour remaining on her shift, but the last hour was always the most miserable, as the number of inane and rude customers always multiplied tenfold.

Miranda hated how exposed her position at work made her. She envied her colleagues who could hide among the different shelves and aisles in the store or stand behind a stack of boxes in the warehouse and remain unseen. The building itself was large, a two-story bookstore in a shopping center. If one were to walk two minutes, they'd find themselves at the police station. Two minutes in the opposite direction, they'd reach a residential area. The bookstore was the last of its kind in the county. All the others Miranda had spent her childhood in had closed.

On the first floor of this bookstore was a café. Miranda was the first thing a customer saw upon walking into the café, and she remained visible from nearly every point in the store.

Miranda was the only member of the Santillano family to go to college besides her mother, a cause of immense joy for her father. But when she'd come out to him as an English major, he felt only intense fear and sorrow.

"*Mi flaca*," Papa Enrique said (not "honey," not "sweetie," or "buttercup," and not "muffin," or sometimes, to her annoyance "*güera*," but always "mi flaca.") "Mi flaca, your mother and I are so proud. So proud that you aren't a dumb bastard like your brother."

"Dad!"

"He's a good kid, but I never met a boy more stupid than *Gordito*. We always knew you were smart, but is becoming an English major really something a smart person does?"

"Dad, it's what I want. Do you really want me to waste my time and money doing something that doesn't interest me?"

"You mean waste *my* time and *my* money? Look, your mother and I will help you as much as possible, but I need to know what your plan is. If you think we're going to spend forty grand to send you to school just to fart around and talk about metaphors in books, then you're going to have to find financial aid elsewhere."

"I've already applied for financial aid."

"That's not what I meant. I mean this. It's great you like to read and talk about reading, but you can do that here. Even your brother can do that. This is four years of your life and a lifetime of savings. What kinds of jobs will be lined up for you?"

"Author."

His eyebrows shot up. "Oh really? You want to be an author?"

"Dad!" she said, growing frustrated. "That's not what I'm saying. I'm saying things aren't so cut and dry. Picking a major doesn't automatically mean you're going to find a career in that field. How many film majors are working in Hollywood right now? I picked English because it's what I like, but who knows what opportunities there will be once I graduate? Having a degree will look a lot better than not having one when I start filling out job applications. Don't you agree?"

"Well, if that's the case, mi flaca . . . " He paused, rummaging through the fridge and pulling out a beer. "If that's the case, why don't you study engineering? The world is never going to stop needing engineers, and there will definitely be jobs lined up for you, and all the while, you can read your little books and talk about them while working toward a major that's actually useful."

Miranda hadn't listened to her father back then, and while being yelled at by a customer for not leaving enough room for cream in their Americano, she wondered if perhaps she should have. She'd excelled at school and was on the dean's list every quarter. She'd worked part-time campus jobs to help pay her tuition, and she understood the value of a dollar.

When she'd returned home after graduation, her dad gave her a grace period of one day before saying, "You need to find a job."

"I will, Dad."

"I know what that means. It means you'll sit on your ass for five months while your student loan bills add up."

"Dad, I'll . . . "

"So you had four years to come up with careers to pursue. What do you have, Miranda?"

"What happened to 'mi flaca'?"

"Are you working on the next great American novel? Are you going to be an English teacher?"

"Papa, please, I've just gotten home. Give me time to think, please."

"You're going to get a job. You're going to prove to me that those four years weren't one big waste."

"Papa, it's not as easy as that. I want a job more than anyone, and more than you can know. Do you think I like borrowing money from my parents? I feel horrible about it, but you need to give me a little more time. Times have changed. Just because I want a job doesn't mean I'll get it. There isn't some magical building called 'Job Office' where I just walk in, say, 'I want a job,' and *bam*, they give it to me. It's hard for everyone. Look at the neighborhood. How many of the kids who I grew up with are working dream jobs, or jobs in their field of study?"

He lifted his hands, palms up. "What was this all for?"

"I—"

"Was all this just you farting around for four years? I don't care where it is. You're getting a job by the end of the week."

By the end of that week, Miranda was working at the café. A year and a half later, she was still there.

On campus, she'd worked at a small café in one of the student service centers, where a busy day consisted of ten students ordering espresso shots to help them stay awake. Most of her workday had consisted of listening to music, reading, and chatting with classmates. The most difficult part of her day was seeing a classmate she'd have preferred to avoid, but those awkward encounters never lasted more than a couple of minutes, and she could laugh about them later with her friends.

In the bookstore café, there was nowhere to hide. On this day, the line of customers wound out the door, and she couldn't even see the end. There was no rhyme nor reason to when the café would be busy. Everyone somehow seemed to desire coffee at the same time and appeared in the store.

Her school had been full of beautiful people who all had perfect bodies, chiseled chests and biceps, toothpaste-commercial-worthy teeth, and perfectly proportioned tits. The number of fat people who wandered into her current place of work frightened her in the beginning, but it didn't take her long to remember that's how things actually were, and the models she used to call classmates were a relic of her past.

These fat and angry automatons always found something to complain about. The coffee was either too hot or not hot enough, too strong or not strong enough. They wanted five smoothies but would complain if it took more than five minutes to make them. They'd moan when their Starbucks gift cards didn't work even though signs reading: *This is not a Starbucks; we just serve Starbucks drinks* were posted in half a dozen locations.

If the cashier said, "Have a good day," instead of, "Thank you," customers complained. If they had an expired coupon that wasn't accepted, they complained. If Miranda ever dared to have a mind of her own and show that she was a human being, they complained.

The only comfort came from three small images on her phone: Cinque Terre, the Colosseum, and the Amalfi Coast. Long ago in her dreams, those photos had been taken by her and not downloaded from Google. On the beaches of the Amalfi Coast, no fat, red-faced customer could reach her.

How could people be so petty, cheap, awful, and ugly when such beautiful places existed in the world? She made sure not to look at the pictures longer than fifteen seconds. Anything longer made her depressed.

"*Vaffanculo*," she'd told the last customer in a whisper. Like most learners of a foreign language, the first thing she did was go straight to the bad words. Italy . . . It wasn't fair.

Miranda complained, too, but not as much as her coworker David. David was one of those creatures who only existed inside the bookstore. He'd been working there for months or years when Miranda had started. She couldn't conceive of what kind of person he was outside the walls of work in the real world. Was he in his twenties or his thirties? Depending on the day, it could have gone either way. He was thin but not quite tall, and his dark hair contrasted with his pale complexion. She had fun talking to him often enough, but as a worker, he was devious, unreliable, and lazy. David had volunteered to take out the trash twenty minutes earlier and hadn't been seen since. Miranda secretly envied him because, despite being the worst worker in the world, there wasn't an ounce of stress in him. He could break as many rules, steal as many donuts, and upset as many customers as possible without receiving any punishment. Guilt never haunted his conscience. Miranda was always plagued by a guilty conscience. So she did her job.

On days like that day, when the coffeemaker was busted and she had to explain to each customer that there was no coffee, but that an Americano was basically the same thing, David's presence only annoyed her.

Even more annoying than David was Rudy.

No one who knew Miranda had ever accused her of

being rude. As the customers didn't know her, they often accused her of things much worse, but she was proud of her kind and respectful demeanor. Rudy had tested the limits of her kindness. As far as she knew, the young man had been hired about two months before the coffeemaker broke down. Seeing as he worked at the far end of the bookstore, she might never have met him at all if he hadn't stopped by the café for drinks.

She became aware of his presence when she was cleaning up a spill on a table and felt something stinging the back of her neck. It wasn't a physical feeling, or even painful. It was the feeling of watchful eyes piercing through the air and making contact with her body.

She looked up to see Rudy standing, not working. Rudy, with his baggy shorts and round head. It was possible he'd been in her graduating class. Many of her colleagues were. His eyes darted down to his shoes, and then he walked off to the left before correcting his position and walking to the right.

The second time she experienced the sensation, it felt like a bullet to the back of the neck. She nearly shook from convulsions and spun around to find Rudy standing half-concealed behind a shelf. That time, he didn't dart his eyes at all. After staring for several seconds, he pulled out his phone and pretended to type.

From that moment, every time Miranda felt a pain in her neck, she took it as a signal not to look up and not to react. She had enough crappy people to deal with in the form of customers and David's incompetence—she didn't feel like adding a stalker to the list.

~~~

On one of those mornings when the sun was shining and the birds were singing, Miranda woke up full of hope. There was nothing concrete to be optimistic about, but the universe was in good spirits, and who was she not to join in? Even the traffic was light.

When she arrived at work, the first thing she noticed was David behind the counter, deep in conversation with Rudy. More accurately, Rudy was deep in conversation, whereas David barely appeared conscious.

Miranda clocked in.

"Well, looks like I should, like, go," Rudy said when he noticed her. "I'm pretty busy. I'm Rudy, by the way." He barely lifted his eyes to look up at Miranda.

"Hi," Miranda said. She thought that was the end of it, and that Rudy would be on his way, but his pigeon-toed feet made no move to leave.

"So, like, what's your name, you know, by the way?" he asked, shifting his eyes left to right and then up and down before finally meeting Miranda's own.

"I'm Miranda."

He stuck out his hand to shake hers, and she offered it lightly.

"Oh yeah, that's cool, a cool name. Anyways, I gotta go, but I'll, you know, catch you around."

Once Rudy had gone, Miranda turned to David. "What was that all about?"

David immediately interpreted her gaze and question to be accusing him of some sort of heinous crime. "What the fuck did I do?"

"Calm down. I meant, what was that all about? You guys seemed pretty deep in conversation."

"Who?"

"You."

"With who?"

"Rudy."

"You and Rudy?"

"No, *you* and Rudy."

"Who's that?"

Miranda felt a blood vessel pulsing at her temple. "The guy you were deep in conversation with."

"Are you writing his biography or something? You seem obsessed with this guy."

"You were the one talking to him!"

"He wandered over here and started jabbering about God knows what. I asked if he wanted to order something so I could go grab you to take his order. He said no, so I walked away, but as I walked away, he kept talking. Seeing as it killed time, I humored the kid."

"What did you guys talk about?"

David shrugged. "I don't know. I was reading about this new local cult. He mostly talked about himself. Really, I was only half listening. I heard a couple of things about a studio. It was either a pet studio or a TV studio. I really don't remember. Kid garbled his words a bunch when he talked. Then he asked me about my coworkers and what they're like."

"Jesus Christ."

"What?"

"Nothing."

"Can you watch the counter? I have to return these books." He walked away, not carrying any books.

Miranda longed for the days when Rudy would simply stare at her and she wasn't subjected to the sound of his voice, but once they were introduced, he came to the café daily. The first time was during a busy rush. The endless line consisted of customers and store employees.

"Where's David?" one of the department supervisors asked.

"No clue," Miranda said, juggling a thousand things at once. David always found ways to disappear during the busiest rushes, only to return when every trace of customer had been removed from the store.

"Damn!" the supervisor said. "I like his sandwiches better. No offense, but he hooks it up. You guys put way too little cheese on those bitches."

"Are you going to order something?"

He gave his order, but she didn't take in a single word of it, because standing in that endless sea of customers was Rudy, staring directly at her. The grin on his face suggested that he thought she should be happy for his imminent arrival at her counter. She damned David to hell.

When it was Rudy's turn to order, he gave a big yawn, looked down at his shoes, and then at Miranda. "So, your name is like, Marisa or something, right?"

"Yeah, sure."

"I'm kidding. I know it's Miranda."

She didn't say anything.

"So, how's it going?"

"Pretty busy."

"Oh yeah, that's pretty cool. Yeah, I'm pretty busy, too, but not with this." He gestured vaguely back at the store. "You know, this is, like, a side gig for me. No big deal whatever. I'm a filmmaker."

"Are you going to order something?"

"What do you recommend, Miranda?" His mouth was twitching, trying to force a smile that wasn't too eager.

"Black coffee."

"You know, usually when I'm working, not, like, here, but my real job, you know, I'm a filmmaker, and a cameraman, and an editor. I drink Red Bull with a little bit of gin. Do you have any gin? Haha, I know you don't have gin. Let me get a green tea."

"Okay." Miranda got to work making it. Seeing as David had abandoned her, she was forced to ring up customers while simultaneously making their drinks and sandwiches. Rudy followed her every step.

"Yeah so, I have, like, a studio. It's pretty cool, a good gig, I have a crew."

He said all this as she scooped up rock-hard chunks of ice cream to throw into a blender for an impatient customer. She saw David's head peek from behind a shelf. He took one look at the line and was about to dart his head back in like a whack-a-mole, but she yelled his name. His cover blown, he had no choice but to step forward.

"Great, you're here. I'm going on break. Get this man a green tea."

That night, lying in bed, no sleep would come for her. She closed her eyes and saw flashes of *Car payments - $200*, only to open her eyes to see *Student loan payments - $250*. On top of that, Papa Enrique was on the verge of charging her rent. She was already working full-time at the café. There were no more hours to be given. If Papa began charging rent, he'd be forcing her to find a second job.

The week of the broken coffeemaker had driven her close to the edge of quitting. She'd have preferred to be homeless than to deal with any more rude, self-entitled customers who couldn't live another second without their precious coffees.

She'd been at work for only two minutes when a fat, red-faced woman began yelling at her. "This is an Americano!"

"Excuse me?"

"This is a goddamn Americano!"

"Oh, okay. Is something wrong with it?"

"I asked for a drip coffee, and that stupid punk working behind the counter said no problem, handed me this, and it's a goddamn Americano."

"Ma'am, our coffeemaker is broken at the moment. An Americano is basically the same thing—espresso with hot water."

"I know what a goddamn Americano is! You're just as stupid as the guy who gave this to me. I want a refund." She set the paper cup down on the counter.

Miranda grabbed it and was surprised to find it empty. "Ma'am, you drank all of it."

"And what's your point, smart ass?"

"It's just . . . you can't really finish the whole thing and then ask for your money back."

"I demand a supervisor at once."

As Miranda sat in the café on her lunch break, not the slightest bit hungry, she dreaded the remaining six hours of her shift. Behind the counter, David was handing out Americanos to customers who had ordered coffees, and more than half of them returned almost immediately to complain.

Unlike David, Miranda had never mastered the art of hiding her emotions from the customers. David was impossible to read—possibly because he had no emotions at all. Miranda became visibly distressed when customers laid into her. Worse, her visible distress gave the customers fuel to go off on her even more, because they knew she'd have to bite her tongue and do her job. It never entered her darkest dreams to defend herself, not as an employee but as a human being. No one stood lower on the societal totem pole than a retail worker.

The pain in Miranda's neck returned, and before she could look up, the sound of a chair being pulled against tiled floor made the whole café go deaf. She opened her eyes to see Rudy sitting across the table from her.

"Mind if I sit?"

"You already are sitting."

He stared at her, befuddled.

She flicked a hand. "Be my guest."

"Working hard or hardly working?"

"Good one."

"So, like, what's your deal?"

She was struck by the perfect roundness of his head. It also was quite large. She told herself that perhaps it wasn't abnormally large but merely looked so due to his short frame. He couldn't have been more than five foot six, whereas she stood five foot eight. She'd always been self-conscious about her lankiness.

Rudy had continued talking while she pondered the

shape of his head and the awkwardness of her height.

"I'm sorry," she said. "What was your question?"

"Oh, I was just saying, what's your deal? Is this, like, your dream job?"

"Yeah, it's every little girl's dream to work in a café."

"Well, you know that company I told you about? It's getting pretty big. Check it out." He pulled out his wallet and handed her a business card.

She held the card in her hand. *Bad PR Studios* was front and center, with an email and a phone number underneath.

"What's this?"

"My business card."

"What do you want me to do with it?"

"Oh, you know, it's just, like, if you're interested in collaborating on a project, or if you need something to be filmed."

"Well . . . what, exactly, do you guys do?"

"Film production studio."

"Yes, I get that. But are you guys, like, a YouTube channel? Do you make feature lengths, documentaries?"

"Yeah, we dabble in all those."

"So business is good?"

"Yeah, we're pretty big, getting bigger. Got a couple of investors interested, but I'll probably turn them down because I'm into doing things my own way, you know? I've got a solid crew, and we like our kind of guerilla-style approach."

"Well, good luck in your ambitions," she said, handing back his card.

"Oh, no, that's yours. Keep it. Do you have a card?"

"Why would I have a card?"

"Oh, well. If you ever need anything filmed, contact info is there."

"Okay." Miranda had no more fight left in her, so she put the card in her pocket as Rudy walked away.

She heard someone approaching from behind, followed by, "Hey." She turned and saw Rachel, a short, pleasant girl who worked at the store. She and Miranda had spoken several times.

"What were you talking to Rudy about?" Rachel asked.

"Basically nothing."

"Did he give you a card?"

"He did. How did you know?"

"Oh my God. He's given every girl in our department one of his fucking business cards. It's so goddamn weird. He keeps going around telling us he's this bigshot filmmaker, but he works here, and he rides a skateboard to work. He doesn't even have a car. So I asked him, 'What the fuck do you want me to do with this business card? Why would I need filming done? Did Spielberg start off offering freelance work to girls he worked with at the pet store?'"

"Maybe he's actually good."

"He isn't," David said, coming out of nowhere. "I just looked up Bad PR on YouTube. They should change the name to Bad Videos, or Bad Channel. He and his *crew* have about fifty videos uploaded, none of them longer than two minutes, no real common thread between any of them. I don't get it." He brought out his phone and showed them a short clip.

"David," Miranda said, "that's not him."

"It isn't?"

"These guys are Indian. They aren't even speaking

English. Does Rudy look Indian to you?"

"Oh." David sighed and walked off.

"Whoa, he's cute," Rachel said.

"Who, David?" Miranda asked, perturbed that anyone could find her useless coworker attractive.

"No, not him. *Him.*" Rachel pointed toward the entrance.

At the door stood a man in a blue business suit. He was at least six foot two, with dirty blond hair and bright blue eyes. He was thin—almost too thin—but had the looks to pull it off and avoid looking gangly. His face was handsome but boyish. He looked like a model from a JC Penney catalog. On his wrist was a Rolex, or some variation of expensive watch that resembled a Rolex. In his right hand, he clutched a briefcase as though it contained the most important documents known to man.

He noticed Miranda staring at him, and he started toward the café. She wasn't positive whether he was coming specifically toward her or just in the general direction of the café, but all the same, she wished she'd had time to make herself look more presentable. For reasons beyond her, the café had enacted a new policy several weeks earlier requiring all employees to wear hats. The hat only drew more attention to her ears, which stuck out way too much. More than that, she hated how the green hat contrasted with her dark red hair. It made her feel like Poison Ivy.

The boy-playing-adult stopped at her table. She wasn't sure where to put her hands or what to do with them, so she put them on her knees.

"Miranda Santillano?"

"Yes?"

"You probably don't remember me," he said, smiling. "I'm Alexei."

It took a moment, but eventually it hit her who he was. "Oh my God!" she said, taking her hands off her knees and putting them on the table. "Alexei Chonkin? No way!" She smiled, doing her best to contain it so it didn't scare him off.

He smiled. "Oh wow, you do remember. It's been a while, so I'd take no offense if you didn't."

"Look at you." She realized she'd said it out loud.

"Yeah, I finally grew out of all my acne."

He had indeed. He'd never been unattractive but was always a tad on the goofy side. He'd gone through a huge transformation since high school. Not just his physical appearance, but his wardrobe and his entire demeanor had changed. Gone were his nervous, shifty eyes. Gone were his bad haircuts and heavy metal T-shirts. Gone was his pimple-covered face. He looked like someone who had listened to his father and majored in something that came with a guaranteed job and a six-figure salary.

"I'm Alexei," he said, extending his hand to Rachel.

"Rachel," she said, "and I was just leaving."

"I'd love to catch up with you," Alexei said to Miranda once they were alone. "I imagine you've done a lot of amazing things since high school."

"Hey, Miranda!" David yelled. "Clock back in already. I'm hungry."

"So, working here, huh?" Alexei asked, as if prior to this moment he'd assumed that her uniform and hat were fashion choices.

"Yes, I work here." She noticed how her uniform smelled

strongly of quiche. The entire café smelled of quiche—just another dish added to the long list of foods she'd previously liked but could no longer stomach.

"Oh, cool." His phone rang, but he stopped the call and didn't check the number. "I swear, I never get a moment's peace."

"You could answer that," Miranda said. "I have to go back to work anyway."

"Miranda," he said, "I don't mean to be presumptuous, and it seems like you're doing extraordinarily well here, but I'm doing well for myself, and seeing you here again, I'm reminded of how clever you were back in the day. If you ever get tired of the whole coffee thing, consider this." Alexei pulled a card from his wallet and handed it to Miranda.

Alexei's card was much thicker than Rudy's. As she glanced at it, she felt a pain in the back of her neck. Out of instinct, she jumped and looked around, but saw no trace of Rudy.

"I should be going as well," Alexei said. "But if you ever tire of it here, give me a call. I could always use more workers like you."

"Thanks."

Alexei picked up his briefcase, threw one last smile in Miranda's direction, and exited the store. He hadn't even bought anything.

"Another brilliant filmmaker?" David asked after Miranda had clocked back in and joined him behind the counter.

"I don't even know what this is," she said, holding the card in her hand. Along with Alexei's name, email, and phone number, the card bore the word *CoinciDATE*.

Chapter 3

Barry

Barry was twenty-one years old and had never touched a woman. More importantly, a woman had never touched him, and that was far and away the bigger tragedy. Technically speaking, any man could touch a woman, but making a woman have that desire in her heart to reach out and touch you was something far more magical.

Barry had given up any hope of Tinder solving his life's problems. When he'd signed up three months earlier, he was convinced he'd finally be able to meet a girl who would judge him on his merits and interests, and not purely on his looks. As quickly became apparent, Tinder only made beta men look worse while helping alphas who already had no problem getting laid push that number up tenfold.

The eternal optimist, Barry hadn't deleted the app yet, as it had become his go-to tool to help pass time while taking care of business in the bathroom.

Worse than being ignored were the rare occasion he'd

receive a notification that a girl whose profile he'd liked had returned the gesture. They'd matched, which meant either she'd seen something in him, or her big thumbs had clicked his profile by accident. Nonetheless, he'd find himself a step closer.

Of all the girls he'd matched with—there had been three in as many months—not one responded to his opening message. Was there a special trick or code of conduct he was unaware of? Was writing, *Hello, how are you?* and then commenting on an interest of hers and asking her to elaborate on it not the proper way to start a conversation on the app? He didn't think simply saying *Hi* could possibly be any better. Should he have acted too cool for them and typed some sort of backhanded compliment? Whatever the answer, he still hadn't discovered it. Whatever he typed remained either unread or unanswered, and then the match would disappear.

If Barry couldn't get a girl to like him in either the real world or the digital one, then the remaining options seemed slim.

He was unable to quit the app, just as he was unable to stop clicking on the profiles of girls who'd never give him the time of day, or girls who smiled at him one moment, only to go home and make love to some other guy, never thinking about him again.

Barry was in the bathroom, and for once not to take a shit while scrolling through the countless girls who might as well have been figments of his imagination. He was in the movie theater bathroom because the button on his shirt had popped off, and he was trying desperately to find a way to salvage the situation, as he hadn't brought a sweater or backup shirt.

He'd made a conscious decision to buy clothes several sizes too small in order to motivate him to work on his body. He also bought shirts he couldn't afford, but figured the nicer his clothing, the more girls might notice him. So far, the only result was that he now owned a lot of shirts with missing buttons or shirts that revealed his stomach rolls every time he sat down.

Kenneth was late. This didn't bother Barry, as he held a lax attitude on punctuality, but it did concern him because Kenneth didn't share that attitude. Kenneth always arrived far too early and then chastised Barry for not arriving on the dot.

"You fat asshole," Barry said to himself, looking in the mirror after the second button from the bottom of his shirt had given way to the lowermost roll of his fat.

He told himself that as long as he kept his arm on his stomach, no one would notice, especially in a dark theater. But the bus ride home worried him. There would be no hiding it there.

He left the bathroom, bought a large bucket of popcorn with extra butter—making sure to complete the transaction with his left hand as his right covered his stomach—and proceeded to the movie.

Lately, Barry found himself coming to the theater more for the popcorn than for the movie itself. Often he went to foreign films at the art house theater because they usually featured foreign actresses taking off their clothes. He usually didn't know or care what language the film was in. He was only passively watching the film as he munched on the buttery popcorn with just the right amount of salt. Realizing that popcorn was doing nothing to help his body fit into his new clothes, he made a new rule that if he were to eat popcorn, he couldn't also get a Coke. But today would be a cheat day because Kenneth had bailed without telling him, so he left the movie five minutes in to buy a large Coke.

There was a girl sitting by herself three rows in front of Barry. For some reason, Barry felt that a girl going to the movies alone wouldn't be as looked down upon as much as a man going to the movies alone. She looked about three to four years older than he was. She had curly hair and a squat little body. Perhaps he could talk to her after the movie, get her thoughts on it, and ask what motivated her to come alone. Then he caught sight of his belly and remembered he couldn't do it that day.

His phone vibrated several times during the film. It was persistent, but seeing *Mom* pop up on the screen let him know that, whatever it was, it could wait.

Once out of popcorn and on the verge of falling asleep, he pulled out his phone to scroll through Tinder, thinking perhaps the girl with the curly hair would appear.

He only had three usable pictures to choose from and only one angle that didn't reveal the neck fat hanging below his chin. His usable pictures contained images of him wearing the only two shirts that fooled people into thinking he wasn't fat. As long as he wore those shirts, the exact curvature and shape of his belly remained hidden. The only thing he couldn't hide was his bulbous butt. No shirt or pants could disguise his backside, so he'd just have to go about life walking around with a behind that drew attention to itself.

Barry wondered long and hard if he should get a new profile picture, but had no inkling where to start. Whenever he looked in the mirror, no angle seemed complimentary. In addition to the shame of having a second chin, his nose bothered him greatly. He didn't have a large nose, but it was beak-shaped enough to cause him great anxiety. No one respected people with beak-shaped noses, and he knew this because no one had ever shown him any respect. Any amount of facial hair immediately made him look a decade older, and having no facial hair made him look like a serial killer.

When Barry directed his attention back at the screen, he noticed that the curly-haired girl had gone.

Barry's phone began to vibrate again. This time it was from Daniel, which was odd because Daniel never initiated contact with Barry. Usually, Barry had to call and text several times before Daniel responded, often two or three days later. If Daniel were calling Barry, he must have something of great importance to tell him. *Let Daniel wait for once.*

Daniel's mom was the exact opposite of Barry's. Barry's mom was the type of woman who looked like she'd always looked old, as though she'd been born a matron. Daniel's mom, on the other hand, was nearing fifty and looked better than most women in their twenties. Barry, of course, never revealed this information to his friend, but it was something that he and everyone else noticed. Something else Barry never told his friend was that the girl Daniel was currently dating looked just like his mother.

Daniel's girlfriend, who was annoying among other reasons for having the name Chelsea but insisting it be pronounced with a hard k sound, was an attractive girl. She had fake breasts, something even Stevie Wonder would have been able to see, but Daniel revealed it to Barry as if handing over top-secret CIA documents and made Barry swear an oath of secrecy. Why someone as good looking as her would be so unhappy that she'd be willing to permanently change her body confused Barry, but only at first. Barry understood all too well the desire to change. In Chelsea's case, all it took was putting silicon in her breasts and life was good.

Barry wanted to change his name—no one cool had ever been named Barry. Even less cool was his surname, Schnitt, which was just begging to be made fun of in school. Barry was Italian but somehow ended up with the last name Schnitt. What was the point of being Italian if he didn't even have a cool, melodic, vowel-ending last name? He couldn't very well go around reminding people every day he was Italian. A last name was supposed to do that for him. He'd often studied lists of Italian surnames, trying to find one to adopt that wouldn't just be arbitrary but would make some sort of sense.

He hated his beaky nose and wished he could change that too. He wanted to get rid of the fat under his chin and in other places, but mostly under his chin. Even if he changed all those things, he still would have been forced to deal with the fact that at five foot six, no girls would pay him any attention. In a girl's eyes, five foot seven might as well have been three foot seven, and he was five foot six. So, changing his last name to something with a vowel in it seemed like the least of his problems.

Everyone assumed he was Jewish, and he was getting really tired of people he'd already explained this to asking him time and again, "Wait, you're Jewish, right?" Why did it matter to people? Would it be beneficial to them just to say he was? Often, Kenneth didn't even refer to him by his name and simply called him "the Jew."

On the way to the bus after the movie, Barry was swiping through Tinder profiles, neglecting the missing button on his shirt as well as passersby, when he saw that he had four voicemails from his mom. He entered his password to listen to them, but the background was so noisy and his connection so staticky, he realized the futility of the attempt and decided he'd see what she wanted when he got home.

The bus always depressed Barry. In a city where everyone had their own car, the only people who rode the bus were those unloved, poor, unfortunate souls left behind by society. Most were transients and people who looked like they'd soon reach their hundreds. Any one of them could have been a mirror showing Barry his future.

The bus ride lasted about twenty minutes, with an additional ten-minute walk to Barry's house. As he approached his building (the only one-story house in a two-story-house neighborhood), he was greeted by the strange sight of his dad's car in the driveway. His father wasn't due home from work for another five hours.

After struggling a bit with the key in the faulty lock, Barry stepped inside to a silence he'd never before experienced. He made his way to the living room, where his mother nearly jumped out of her skin at the sight of him and turned ghostly white. Then she broke down in hysterics, the likes of which Barry had never seen before. He felt sick to his stomach.

She jumped from her chair and charged at him, causing him to jump a bit himself. He wasn't sure whether she was going to embrace him or devour him. She held him tightly in her arms, squishing his head into her collar as tears flowed down onto him.

After the downpour of his mother's tears, his father got up and joined them in the embrace. Barry was utterly confused until he saw Kenneth's face on the TV.

Hugs and tears and kisses lasted for twenty minutes. By

the twenty-first, Mr. Schnitt was ready to watch TV. Watching TV for Mr. Schnitt consisted of choosing the most boring program possible, then spending ninety percent of its runtime glued to his computer monitor as opposed to the television screen, but fuming if anyone dared touch the remote to change the channel.

During dinner, the news was on, and both Mr. and Mrs. Schnitt took turns commenting on which politician was a crook and which was an asshole, or feigning outrage at something they'd already feigned outrage over the previous day. It was remarkable how fast his parents had gotten over the news about Kenneth.

Barry escaped to his room as soon as he could. He felt guilty—not because he'd survived a shooting that killed people he knew, but because part of him wished he could have been there. Kenneth and Barry often had talked long into the night about how women love wounded men with war stories and scars who they could nurse back to life. Barry didn't want a wound that was fatal, but a bullet to the shoulder or leg—or even one that grazed his face, giving him a scar straight out of an anime artist's sketchbook—would have done wonders for him. Instead, he wasn't even there. When he went back to school, he wouldn't be able to relate to those survivors who had gone through the trauma together. Further, he was pissed at himself for not foreseeing Kenneth taking such a measure.

Barry's stomach began rumbling. He'd barely touched his dinner. He felt intoxicated, as though deadly toxins were taking over his body and making different parts ache and screech. On the forums, he attempted reading several posts but stopped after two or three lines. This went on for ten minutes, maybe an hour, maybe two. Everyone was talking about Kenneth. While no one was outright saying they supported him, no one was calling him a murderer. They were acting as though Kenneth's actions had been a natural course of events. At that moment, Barry didn't want to be an incel. No incel wanted to be one, but he didn't want to have anything in common with those guys.

Barry had last seen Kenneth during a student committee meeting for a film studies class. The professor had been ousted from the school for showing insensitive films. Weeks of protests from various student groups finally had forced him to leave, and an entirely new curriculum was being put together. The students demanded that as part of their reparations for the hardships they'd been put through by being subjected to such horrendous films, the administration would allow them to dictate which films would qualify as appropriate viewing on campus.

Barry had had no intention of joining the committee. He'd been conned into it. He wasn't even in the film studies course. Kenneth wanted to show Barry a girl he'd been following on campus, and that led to Barry's name being added as a committee member.

Kenneth's girl hadn't even shown up for the meeting. Besides Kenneth and himself, the committee included Black Barry, whose full name was Barrion. Black Barry, being the only non-white member of the group, loved watching all the white folks in the group squirm as they struggled with figuring out how to refer to him. He insisted on Black Barry, but none of them were brave enough to bring themselves to do it. Black Barry always kept track of the time. It wasn't for the sake of records or data input. It was so no one wasted his time and kept him longer than need be.

The committee also included a girl named Michael and a

guy named Michael. Barry once called Girl Michael "Michelle" by mistake and had been lectured for it. After that, Barry made it a goal to never speak at committee meetings. Kenneth despised Guy Michael. He was a New England trust fund baby who somehow had forgotten he was attending a community college and not Harvard or Yale.

The final member was the group's de facto leader, Ainsley. Ainsley was as cruel as she was fat and miserable.

The Frenchman who enjoyed staring at Barry from across campus sat at the table next to them, loudly eating a mayonnaise sandwich. His impossibly shiny head looked freshly polished. Even through Ray-Bans, Barry felt the odd foreigner's gaze penetrate him. He'd never heard him speak before, but no one from Barry's neck of the woods looked the way he did or wore the clothing he wore. Barry decided he was French because it was as good as any other ethnicity.

Barry had been tasked with the list that week. The list contained not only films screened as part of the course curriculum in semesters past but all the films that had been nominated for or received the Best Picture Oscar.

"Next," Ainsley demanded, fixing her pale gray eyes on Barry.

"Uh, hold on," Barry said, consulting his notes. *"Call Me by Your Name."*

"What's that?" Black Barry asked, looking confused.

"It's a movie about a young man living in Italy who falls in love with a grad student working with his father," said Michael (the one with breasts). "The two love each other and have a passionate relationship. It's a beautiful love story between two men."

"Um, actually, I find this film to be problematic," Ainsley said.

"Oh my gosh, you're so right," said Michael (the one without breasts).

"Oh?" Black Barry asked. "I haven't seen it. But Rotten Tomatoes says it's a beaut—"

"I can't believe I have to explain," Ainsley said. "Do we really need yet *another* movie featuring two white males in the lead roles? I think they've monopolized movies about queer people enough. Because that movie was made and became so successful, it takes away from stories about queer people of color. Remove it from the list, Barry."

"Wow, I totally agree with you," Guy Michael said. "It is problematic, you know? Like, would it have been so hard to cast the movie with people of color, right? Like, did they have to cast two straight white male actors? Did they even seek out queer actors? There are literally millions of them, yet they chose two straight, white males."

Barry picked up his sharpie and crossed out *Call Me by Your Name*.

"What's next?" Ainsley demanded.

"*Schindler's List*," Barry said.

Black Barry nodded.

"Great mov—"

"Hold on," Girl Michael said. "I think that movie is a little problematic."

"You're, like, so right," Guy Michael said.

Black Barry raised his hand to speak.

"How is it problema—"

"Um, hello?" Girl Michael said. "I think it's highly irresponsible of us to allow our school to screen movies like *Schindler's List* when literally millions of Philistines are getting killed and ravaged by Jews every minute. How can we subject our peers to a film like that when what we should be doing is promoting all the films made by Philistine women and Philistine non-binary people?"

"Great point," Guy Michael said.

"Barry," Ainsley said, "make a note that we demand films made by Philistine's non-binary community be added to the curriculum."

Barry wasn't sure where to write it, so he simply wrote it over the words *Schindler's List*.

"Next?" Ainsley seemed determined to keep things moving along.

"*Lord of the Rings: The Return of the King*," Barry said. An hour of discussion had passed, and this was the first film on the list Barry had seen. He glanced at Ainsley for approval.

"Absolutely not," she snapped.

"Why not?" Barry asked.

"Um, could you, like, please dial back your toxic tone?" Girl Michael asked. "Your cadence is threatening, and I feel very uncomfortable right now."

"Oh, I'm sorry," Barry said.

"Hey, don't, like, condescend," Guy Michael said.

"Why can't we watch *Lord of the Rings*?" Black Barry asked.

The question went unanswered until Kenneth reiterated it.

"I don't even know where to start," Ainsley said, shaking

her head.

"The whole portrayal of the Hobbits in the film is questionable," Guy Michael said.

"Wow," Girl Michael said. "Ugh, can we please not be so blatantly offensive by calling the little people in the films Hobbits? They're called dwarves."

"They're actually called Hobbits," Kenneth said. "Dwarves are a different race."

"*Oh em gee,*" Girl Michael said. "I can't even with that statement right now."

"The race of people in the film are referred to as Hobbits," Black Barry explained. "Dwarves are a different race of pe—"

"I think what Michael is getting at," Ainsley said, "which is way more important than these semantics, is that the proper term is 'little people.' These films had ample opportunity to cast little people to play these prominent roles, but instead opted for straight, white men and shrunk them down. How offensive is that? Don't tell me there aren't little people actors out there. I can name seventy-two off the top of my head. How is that any different than making a film about Japanese culture and casting a white guy in the lead role?"

"I'm also triggered by the fact that little people are treated as a separate race," Girl Michael said.

"I'm offended that there are literally no female speaking roles in that film," Ainsley said.

"Yes there are," Kenneth said.

"Um, don't interrupt me," Ainsley said. "I wasn't finished speaking. Tolkien was a huge, outspoken racist, and so is the white male who made the movies. Do you really think it's appropriate to show our peers 'White Power' the movie?"

"How is it 'White Power' the movie?" Black Barry asked.

"Barry, thank you so much for your contribution to this topic," Girl Michael said.

"Where are the people of color?" Ainsley asked. "Where are the speaking roles for women? How are we supposed to watch these movies when none of the characters on-screen look like us?"

"I mean," Black Barry started, "I suppose they could've put a black dude or two in there, but I like the mo—"

"It's a fantasy world!" Kenneth yelled. "It's supposed to be a parable for medieval England or Europe."

"That's, like, a really bad argument, right?" Guy Michael said. "It's a lazy excuse for whitewashing the story. I haven't heard one compelling reason why they couldn't have cast people of color and non-cisgendered people."

"Exclusively," Girl Michael said.

"No, equally," Ainsley said.

"Very cool," Guy Michael said.

"How many people are in that movie?" Ainsley asked.

"Oh, I don't know. It's a big cast. Hundreds. Thousands even."

"How many main characters?"

Barry thought back to it. "There was Frodo, and Sam, and Aragorn, and Gandalf . . . Around twenty prominent characters."

"All white," she pointed out. "For us to show a movie like that, there'd have to be representation of equal parts men and women."

"Don't forget gender non-binary," Girl Michael said.

"Very true," Guy Michael said.

"Right. Equal parts male, female, and gender non-binary."

"How do you count that?" Kenneth asked.

"Don't interrupt," Ainsley said.

"Not cool," Guy Michael said.

"You'd also have to make sure there was equal representation of people of color within those groups," Girl Michael said.

"Very true," Guy Michael said.

"Don't forget differently-abled people as well," Girl Michael said.

"Very cool," Guy Michael said.

"And make sure for each of the actors portrayed by little people, there is an appropriate level of representation that includes gender non-binary, people of color, queer people, and people with disabilities."

Barry's head began to hurt as he tried to keep things straight. "Do we put Chinese and Japanese people in one category, or do they get separate categories?"

"Is this amusing to you?" Ainsley asked.

"What about Jews?" Girl Michael asked.

"Pffft," Ainsley said. "Do Jews really need any more representation in movies? As if they aren't overrepresented enough."

"So true," Guy Michael said.

"Barry," Ainsley said, "when you go home tonight, take the twenty lead characters from *Return of the King* and make a list representing an equal number of gender non-binary actors, male and female, queer male and female, people of color, and people with disabilities. Also, movies with *king* in the title ought to go."

"I don't think anywhere on Earth looks li—"

"African Barry, we appreciate you bringing your insight on this matter," Guy Michael said.

"I don't think anywhere on Earth looks like that," Kenneth said.

"Excuse me," Guy Michael said, "but as a straight white male, I don't think you really have a say in the matter."

"I think you should leave," Ainsley said.

"I do too," Guy Michael said. "Bye. Why don't you take this time to educate yourself?"

Kenneth stormed off, red-faced. Barry remained seated, wondering how in the hell he'd accomplish the task he'd been given.

Girl Michael was in tears.

"Did his violent outburst hurt you?" Guy Michael asked gently.

"Yes, but that's not why I'm crying," Girl Michael said. "I'm so upset that my friend's ex-boyfriend is such an insensitive asshole. She broke up with him because he's white. She's Asian. She told me how he didn't understand why she was breaking up with him. She told him it was precisely because he didn't understand that he was part of the problem."

"I'm so sorry the two of you had to go through that," Ainsley said. "White guys need to learn it is not okay for them to try to date women of color. They don't know how much damage they're doing."

"So true, so true," Guy Michael said. "Michael, that reminds me of this great poem I read. Let me read it to you after this—maybe at your place, since it's not far from here."

~~~

Now, in his room, Barry wondered if things would have been different if he'd walked out with Kenneth. He had no way of knowing what Kenneth was planning to do. Could he have prevented it? The memory faded, just as Kenneth's face had faded from Barry's mind. He was back at home with his family. He thought about Daniel. A true friend.

Barry pulled out his phone and wrote him a text. *Hey, Daniel. Sorry I missed your calls. You can imagine it's been a wild day. My parents have been holding me hostage for a while. Why don't we meet up and have some drinks? I could use one or twelve.*

Daniel didn't reply until the next afternoon, writing: *Oh, I was with my girlfriend.*

That's cool, Barry wrote. *How about today?*

Daniel didn't reply.

~~~

Mrs. Schnitt had allowed her son to stay home from school on Tuesday. On Wednesday, she entered his room without knocking to find her son still in bed past eleven a.m.

"Barry, I understand you've gone through something horrible, but we've given you time. You need to get to school."

"I don't think I'm ready yet," he mumbled into his pillow.

"If you lie there in bed all day, you'll never be ready. What about a job? Are you ready for that yet?"

"I've been looking."

"Oh really? Where? We're happy to give you money when you need it, but at some point you're going to have to get a job."

"You guys barely give me any money anyway."

"And we'll give you even less if you keep spending it on movies."

"What? How did you know?"

"I get an email alert for every time you swipe your debit card. So not only are you spending my money on movies, you're doing it while you're supposed to be at school. It may be a big joke to you, but it isn't cheap. Your father and I aren't paying for you to skip classes and waste all our money on movies. What time does your next class start?"

Barry cast a bleary eye at the bedside clock. "In about thirty minutes."

She sighed dramatically. "Fine, you can stay home the rest of the day, but you're going tomorrow."

"I don't think I can."

"Why not?"

"Because what can I say to them? They all know I was friends with Kenneth. They're all going to hate me and look at me like I'm a bastard for not being there when *it* happened."

"Well, if they think that, then they were never your friends to begin with."

"They weren't my friends to begin with."

"You're going," his mother said. "Get up. Your father has something he needs to talk to you about."

"What's he doing home?"

"Just go out and see for yourself."

Barry emerged from his bedroom in his pajamas, hair unkempt, and with a five o'clock shadow turning into a six o'clock shadow.

"Barry," Mr. Schnitt said. "Come outside with me."

"Do I need to get dressed?"

"I wouldn't think so."

His father led him to the car, and the two took off on what turned out to be a fifteen-minute ride. At each red light, Barry felt the eyes of every driver and passenger in the stopped cars next to him staring right at him, and when he turned to test this, he confirmed that they were.

They stopped in an industrial district, far from any place Barry would have spent his time, and not a place he wanted to be while in his pajamas. "Do I have to get out?"

"Yes."

"I'm in my PJs! I asked if I needed to change."

"Oh, well, it's really no big deal. You should've thought about that before sleeping in until past eleven."

Barry opened the door and heaved himself out of the car. The cool breeze went through the fabric of his jammies, and he could feel his balls shriveling.

They stood there while his father periodically checked his watch. One thing he didn't do was speak to his son. If Mrs. Schnitt wasn't around, Mr. Schnitt could have gone an entire week without saying a word.

Several years later, when Barry's poor little berries were frozen stiff, a car finally pulled up next to them. A man in his late fifties, who looked as though he'd begun drinking before Barry had woken up, struggled to get out of a Honda Accord that was at least twenty years old.

"Hey!" yelled the drunk, who Barry finally recognized as his father's old friend Ray, a man he hadn't seen in over a decade. "What do you think?" Ray asked with a giant grin, addressing Barry.

"About what?"

"The car! It might not be a pussy magnet, but it beats riding the bus, huh?"

Mr. Schnitt laughed and looked at Barry with a big smile. Barry turned red all over, not wanting his dad to know he knew the word *pussy*, and not ever wanting to see his dad acknowledge that word ever again.

"Pussy magnet," his father said, laughing at such a concept. "It's all yours, son. Ray's practically giving it away. I know taking the bus everywhere sucks, and you'll definitely have more luck with the ladies with a bad boy like this, if you know what I mean."

Barry wanted to run to the nearby underpass, lie down, and let the first passing eighteen-wheeler run over him.

"So, what do you think?"

"It's nice, Dad. Thank you."

"Well, don't thank me yet. I'm getting it for you, but you're going to pay for it. Ray isn't just generously giving us one of his old cars. Do you remember that café we sometimes went to for breakfast, the one by five-points?"

Barry didn't.

"Ray's mother-in-law owns the place. He got you a job as a dishwasher. You don't even have to interview!" His father smiled as if delivering the greatest news anyone could possibly hear.

It seemed Ray had caught wind of Barry's pouty

expression. "My son is an ungrateful little shit too. I give him everything: a car, a job. The damn kid can't even sit with us for dinner. Little shit. But when he wants money to spend on some broad, suddenly he's the kind, loving son. I swear puberty hit him at eleven, and he's been a sex-crazed fiend ever since. He brings so many girls back to the house, thinks his mother doesn't notice, and then acts like he's not banging their brains out. Never seen the same girl twice, neither. Some of them are ugly as sin—even uglier, I tell you. He sure does love ass though. I mean, who doesn't? But he really loves it. What's your boy prefer, tits or ass?"

Both the dads stared at Barry, waiting for him to contribute to the conversation and spill out stories of his own conquests. His father spared him the chance to embarrass himself by embarrassing him for him.

"Yeah, Barry doesn't bring any girls back, unless he's doing it quietly. He never even seems to really express any interest in them, at least not around me."

Barry could bear it no longer. He walked over to his new car and pretended to inspect it.

His dad gave Ray a ride home while Barry took his new Honda for a test drive. He was given two keys, one for the ignition and one to open the door. He nearly broke both keys, as neither seemed to want to open the door. After five minutes, the lock decided to work. The inside smelled of cigarettes, sweat, and stale vodka. The lining had several staples inserted into it to keep it from falling and blocking the rearview mirror. The car didn't have a CD player, nor even an AV jack. Before driving off, Barry spent over ten minutes trying to find a suitable song to listen to, and even the one he settled on wasn't ideal, some inane classic rock song.

~~~

The following Monday would go down in history as the most momentous day in Barry's life. It was the day that would set the remainder of his life in motion. All of Sunday and Monday morning, the only thing on his mind was the upcoming crucifixion his surviving classmates would bestow upon him. It wasn't only that he'd skipped school the day of the shooting. He was the murderer's friend, and therefore guilty by association.

Barry decided to wear his nicest button-up shirt, which was two sizes too small and revealed his stomach rolls every time he sat down. The only remedy would be to wear a white T-shirt underneath. He looked normal enough, but the extra clothing caused Barry to sweat profusely. To make matters worse, he discovered that the AC didn't work in his new car.

A replacement still hadn't been found for Mr. Sandoval, so that early-morning class had been postponed indefinitely. Now Barry's first class began at 10:30, but he arrived early to get himself a parking permit for his new pride and joy.

He walked up the hill to the student service center, a building he'd never had any reason to enter before, to waste fifty dollars on a parking spot he didn't want for a car he wanted even less. The walk was strenuous enough on its own, but it was made even worse that day because it was being blocked by a student protest.

At the head of the protest was Ainsley with a loudspeaker, both Michaels by her side. She was screaming her lungs off about a recent incident everyone was talking about. At a university not too far from their own school, audio had leaked of a white female student casually saying she didn't think she could date a black guy. The clip caused outrage among many of the students at Barry's own campus. The matter didn't end there, as it wasn't enough for the girl to be expelled from her school. In an act of solidarity, Ainsley demanded that all white people should be required to stay home from school that day and the following day.

"I don't care if you're Jewish," Ainsley said. "You guys seem to have done pretty well for yourselves, haven't you? Why don't you go home and take this time to reflect on what's happening in Palestine?"

Barry was prevented from using the front entrance by Ainsley and the two other whites, so he walked all the way around to the back entrance, where the protestors couldn't be bothered to protest.

Inside, he spotted the creepy French guy—at least Barry thought he was French. He walked around campus all day long, occasionally stopping at the library or cafeteria to give death stares to people. He always wore a leather jacket with a black turtleneck. Indoors or out, he wore thick-rimmed shades, and he always carried a briefcase. One day, this mysterious bald Frenchman left his briefcase in the cafeteria while he spent several hours in the library. Barry had been tempted to open it, positive he'd find anything from diamonds to payments for hits on politicians, possibly even nuclear launch codes or body parts.

The mysterious murderous Frenchman was in the student service center, staring at various people as they passed. Most bizarre of all was his perpetually moist face. Several times a day, he'd go to the washroom to splash water on his face. His black leather gloves never came off. This had earned him the moniker of "The French Face-Washing Murderer," which eventually became "French Murder Face." Not far from the Frenchman was a man of sixty watching porn on one of the school-provided computers in full view of all eyes, and without an ounce of shame. Cholos and gangster-looking types waddled in and out of the building with various forms and paperwork.

The only thing linking all these people was their current geographic location. Barry couldn't imagine what any of them were actually studying there. He'd been told that the old man watching the porno had been coming to campus for a decade. This wasn't a college. It was a place for those left behind by society to congregate and waste their days until they themselves wasted away.

There was no conceivable way that real universities could have had such a colorful cast of characters. Barry was certain he'd never know. He hadn't even chosen a major, and the longer he didn't choose, the less appealing they all seemed. Transferring to a four-year university hadn't even entered his wildest dreams.

Although there were only two others in front of him in the line for parking tickets, he'd been standing there for half an hour already because some guy in his forties with an impossible-to-decipher accent was arguing with the poor bastard behind the counter over a payment of five dollars and seventy-five cents. The young man behind the counter, who had a beard, dark eyes, and long, black hair tied back in a ponytail, explained to the mysterious foreigner that if the payment wasn't made, his grades would be put on hold. The heated conversation finally came to an end when the foreigner angrily threw folded one-dollar bills at the man, then meticulously went through his pocket to find seventy-five cents in exact change in nickels and pennies.

After this exchange, the bearded man behind the counter

disappeared. The person who had been waiting directly in front of Barry, a middle-aged woman with tired eyes, turned back several times, either looking at Barry for answers or at the empty space behind him. Barry tried desperately not to meet her gaze. He was terrified she might begin speaking to him.

Luckily, the counter was once more open for business. Gone was the frustrated bearded guy, who was probably in the break room complaining about his job. In his place was the most beautiful woman Barry had ever seen. She was so beautiful, in fact, he felt embarrassed to even look at her. The sudden outburst of embarrassment added a new load of sweat into his already sweat-stained clothes. As long as he didn't move his arms, he couldn't smell the stench emanating from his body and clothing.

He stared at her as she did her business with the tired-eyed middle-aged woman. She was tall, and not just tall for a girl, but tall. She was easily five foot ten, perhaps even taller. She had a round face, not in a fat way, or in any way that would indicate a shortcoming, but it was clearly and distinctly round. Her eyes were strikingly large and blue. Not a bright blue, but a blue that invoked an icy coldness. Besides being large, her eyes were quite far apart. If one were to shave her head, Barry thought, with its roundness and large-eyedness, she might resemble an alien. With hair, though, she resembled a beautiful young woman who looked like she might be only slightly older than Barry. Her hair was light brown. Her skin was pale, almost to the point of looking sickly, and Barry was absolutely crazy about it.

"Next," she called.

Barry waddled up to the counter, trying not to move his arms too much, and making sure his stomach rolls didn't come out through any of the openings in his shirt. "Hello," he said, making sure he didn't sound too excited.

"What do you need?"

Barry was shocked. Was she this abrupt with everyone, or only with him? Maybe she was trying to get rid of him as quickly as possible due to his horrid stench. "I'd like to buy a parking permit, please." He put in extra effort to make sure he enunciated every word.

"Give me your driver's license."

He went through his wallet to pull it out of its sleeve, but his sweaty hands prevented that process from being an easy one. He fumbled around as she looked on in boredom. He handed it over, hoping it wasn't too sweat-marked.

She wrote down his information. He grew even redder than usual when he remembered how stupid his hair looked in his ID photo. It had been taken right after his seventeenth birthday, when his hair was much longer, back when he'd fancied himself a metalhead and wasn't self-conscious about what he looked like. Now, he was always self-conscious about what he looked like, in general and especially in that specific situation.

Whether she thought his photo looked as stupid as he knew it did, her eyes gave no indication. She scribbled down his contact info as quickly as her hand allowed. Would she even remember his name the moment he walked out the door? Should he ask for hers?

"Fifty dollars," she said, her hand out waiting for the money.

He pulled the bills out from his back pocket. They were damp from sweat and close proximity to his body. She quickly put the money in the register and handed him his permit. Before he could even utter a thank you, let alone ask for her name, she called out, "Next," and the next customer shoved forward.

Barry exited the student service building in a state of confusion as his roiling mind tried to process the fact that he'd just come face to face with the most beautiful woman he'd ever seen. Halfway down the hill leading to the cafeteria, he realized he didn't know her name and would therefore have no way of looking her up on social media. He paid no heed to the shouts and abuse from the angry protestors. He contemplated going back inside, but going back without a reason would look insane. Would it have been plausible to claim he'd lost his permit and needed a new one? No, he couldn't do that, because he didn't have any additional money to pay for it even if they gave it to him.

He thought of every reason he could come up with to be in that building, settling on how they had open computers for all the weirdos on campus to use. He went back inside from the far exit and sat at a computer. The computer lounge was separated by a wall from where people paid for parking permits. So that idea failed immediately.

She had an accent—from where or what kind, he couldn't guess, as one foreign country was just as mysterious to him as another. Her accent was soft, but there was a definite sense of aggression to it as well. He wanted to believe she was French. Were French girls typically that tall? He'd heard French men were impossibly handsome. Even if they weren't, they spoke French, and that already upped their looks by about five notches.

Barry realized that laying eyes on her was a defining

moment in his life and that he'd crossed a threshold, where everything that had happened to him before that moment no longer mattered. This was a new era.

Like the person he had once called friend but who was now a dead murderer named Kenneth, Barry had naively believed college would represent a new beginning. Perhaps that would have been true only at a real college. Community college was no new beginning at all, but a mere extension of high school. Barry's idea of reinventing himself as a new person had gone out the door the moment he stepped into his first class and saw all the familiar faces who couldn't fail to remember all the times Barry had embarrassed himself in high school.

The first two decades of Barry's life had been full of embarrassment, to the point that he felt both firsthand and secondhand embarrassment just from thinking about his own experiences and sharing them with none other than himself. He knew he didn't have the worst life in the world, but it was far from the best. Even though most of the people he'd gone to high school with were quite nice to him now, that didn't change the fact that they'd actively participated in many of the moments that stuck out to him as particularly embarrassing and shameful. He couldn't decide which was worse, for these people to remember those moments or for them not to remember them. Whatever the case, he'd never forget.

After laying eyes on the impossibly beautiful, tall, blue-eyed, round-faced, possibly French girl, Barry decided his life needed a drastic change.

Capitolo 4

Miranda

Sitting on bench was what Miranda had written in her notebook. That was over an hour ago, and within those sixty-plus minutes, the girl on the bench had remained right there. Being on a bench in one stationary period for that amount of time wasn't the odd part. The part that truly struck Miranda as strange was that the girl wasn't wearing headphones, wasn't reading a book, wasn't eating, and hadn't checked her phone once. She merely sat there, motionless. A statue.

Miranda desperately had to pee, but she knew that the moment she got up, the girl would move from her position on the bench. When Miranda was finally on the verge of tears and could no longer hold it, the girl got up from the bench, stretched her arms, looked in both directions, and then moved over two feet to sit on the grass with her back against a tree.

I could kill this bitch, Miranda thought.

The girl Miranda had followed into the park looked to be about twenty-eight years old. She had quite homely features but was nonetheless cute in Miranda's eyes. However, any charm Miranda had seen in her had gone forever due to the bench incident.

Miranda had been experiencing many such days of late. She found herself following many people, only to find out that most of them led even more boring lives than she did.

On a Friday three weeks and five days previously, she'd come home from work at the café crying. The tears weren't due to one event or person, but came from several factors teaming up to beat her over the head until all that remained of Miranda was a sad, shallow shell.

On that particular Friday, she'd planned to do something she hadn't allowed herself or been allowed to do in a long time: go out and get shitfaced drunk. Christian, her best friend since the age of three, was back in town for the weekend and was assembling the girls to go to Main Street and drink till the early hours of the morning. Miranda couldn't even remember the last time she'd gotten truly shitfaced drunk, especially with friends. It had been at least since before Miranda's other best friend, Sabrina, became no longer her other best friend.

The moment the friendship ended was still raw in her mind. It was just past eight a.m. when Miranda had returned home from taking her ex-best friend to the airport. It wasn't only that Sabrina had gone without Miranda, it was that asking Miranda to be the one to drive her to the airport was like rubbing salt in the wound. Miranda had dreamed of Italy and Italian dinners and the Italian language and Italian romances for as long as she could remember. As she already spoke Spanish, the language came to her quite easily. She'd been playing Italian audio lessons and listening to podcasts in Italian every time she got in her car for months, much to the annoyance of her friends, who pleaded to listen to something they could understand. She'd fallen in love with the music of Mina and Bocelli and Tozzi and Ghali.

Senior year of high school, she and three friends had made a pact to travel to Europe, mainly Italy, after graduation. One by one, each girl backed out of the plan, and hell would freeze over before her own father would lend a penny to such an endeavor. The dream faded to the back of Miranda's mind, but never fully disappeared.

Then Sabrina sprang the news on Miranda that she was going to Italy for ninety days. She hadn't even given Miranda warning or time to process it. Her grandfather had died, she'd inherited a big chunk of his money, and she'd bought herself a ticket to Milan. She hadn't even consulted Miranda. They were supposed to have gone together.

To make matters worse, Sabrina had the audacity to ask her friend to give her a ride to the airport. For reasons unknown, she couldn't buy a ticket for a flight leaving from LAX, and instead would be departing from the Santa Ana airport, meaning Miranda would have to get up at an ungodly hour and spend extra time in the car with her.

She arrived at Sabrina's shortly after four in the morning. Sabrina took her sweet time to come out and get into the car. The entire ride over, she went on and on about all the places she'd looked up on TripAdvisor. She referred to several Riccardos and Alessandras who'd be hosting her from Couchsurfing as though they were already longtime chums. If Miranda had been a different person, she would have thought Sabrina had intended to make her jealous.

The ride home, Miranda couldn't bear to listen to her Italian lessons. She nearly teared up on hearing the phrase *Vorrei andare a Roma*. Sabrina the spoiled brat. Sabrina the bitch.

Sabrina, who insisted on pronouncing the *ci* in the Italian word *cinema* like *si* as opposed to *ch*. Sabrina, who couldn't even roll her fucking r's.

At least Miranda still had Christian. She plopped onto her bed and decided to sleep until it was time to go out. She'd never wanted a drink more in her life. The day before, she'd planned exactly what to wear and was going to make sure she got enough rest to be ready for the night of fun.

Those dreams spiraled to the ground in a fiery crash when she answered the phone on Friday. She never answered unknown numbers—not because she was trying to avoid strangers, but because an unknown number was usually someone from work trying to coerce her into taking more hours. Either due to negligence or to her newfound good spirits, she answered.

"Hello?" she said, answered only by silence. The silence was cut through with slight hints of breathing, indicating that she was more than likely dealing with a telemarketer, whose tactics always included a delayed response.

She wasn't about to say *hello* again, but was too slow to end the call when a familiar voice said, "Miranda?"

Miranda recognized the voice but didn't want to acknowledge it.

"Yes?" she said finally.

"What a surprise! We finally got through to you." It was the unmistakable voice of Lisa, the overworked night manager Miranda would have loved nothing more than to help in real life but then never see again in work life. "We need you to come in for this evening's shift."

"I wish I could help, but I can't."

"You need to. David requested the day off three weeks ago, and for some reason, we printed an outdated version of the schedule. Everyone else is either working or has also requested the day off."

Miranda bit down on her pillow. *All you have to do is say no, Miranda. They can't put a gun to your head.*

Within minutes, she was changed into suitable work clothes and on her way.

"You're too softhearted," Christian said after she told her friend she wouldn't be able to make it out.

Her car seemed to will itself to the bookstore's parking lot. She'd taken that path so many times she could never actually recall how she'd gotten there. With one blink, she'd be there, saddened that the ride hadn't taken longer. Miranda was always frustrated by California traffic and the incompetence of its drivers, but she would have desperately embraced a delay on her way to work that evening.

As she got out of her car, she caught a glimpse of herself in the rearview mirror of the sedan parked closest to the store. Her hair was a wreck. It was too late to go back and do anything about it. Lisa had already seen her from inside the store. Miranda rubbed her hand through her stubborn bit of cowlick to no avail.

As she entered, a father (one of those in their mid-forties but impossibly good-looking in a dad-like way) was walking out with his two young daughters, who had big smiles, likely due to whatever was inside the giant bags they carried. The hot dad's smile was nearly larger than those of his daughters. Miranda remembered a time when the store also made her smile, back when she used to shop there up through her first week working there when she was still gung-ho and ready to impress.

There were two entrances to the bookstore: a general entrance and a café entrance. Miranda preferred to take the main entrance. Despite only extending her freedom by twenty-odd seconds, it allowed her to assess the situation from a distance.

Shit! He's here! Miranda knew all her regular customers, though only by face and not by name. Headed toward the door was a customer she referred to as Melvin. The name made sense once you met him. There was a reason he could only be Melvin, not Lenny or Benny. He was just Melvin. And Melvin was generally a pleasant person. His biggest flaw was that he seemed incapable of reading when the conversation was finished. He'd talk on and on about absolutely nothing and everything. There wasn't a topic in the universe he didn't have a million badly thought-out opinions or comments on. Worst of all, when you thought the conversation was finished and you could go on living your life as he took a step backward, he'd take two steps forward with a, "Have you heard about the Starbucks Christmas cup controversy?" Even when Miranda had three blenders going and music on full blast, he'd stand on the other side of the counter, flashing his pearly whites, yapping away.

Miranda was relieved when Melvin came through the door but started browsing through the bookstore. Maybe he'd already had his caffeine hit.

That small bit of relief was annihilated seconds later when Rudy appeared out of nowhere, glanced at her, then pretended he hadn't and hid behind a shelf. *Doesn't he work morning shifts?*

Life proceeded as usual. Customers came in, they sat, they ate, food fell on tables and the floor. There was a mess.

Trash cans were strategically placed to never be more than five steps from customers. There were three in the café. Customers didn't believe in trash cans. Customers believed in leaving messes on tables and the floor. New customers complained about the messes. Miranda cleaned the messes. Customers ate, leaving messes on table. Trash cans went unnoticed. Customer demanded decaf coffee. None was brewed. Whole pot brewed for one customer. Customer drank decaf. Complained it was too hot. Or too decaffeinated. Customer complained when three-months-expired coupon was rejected.

Miranda's hair somehow managed to get even more untamable as the night progressed. She could feel Rudy's eyes on her neck. Customer ate an entire banana split before complaining it wasn't any good and asking for money back.

Even worse than feeling Rudy's eyes on the back of her neck was seeing them look at her face. Unlike other guys who were at least subtle, Rudy went from looking directly at her breasts to staring at her lips, as though she couldn't notice. Miranda tried to make her transactions with Rudy as quick as possible, but Rudy was a Melvin himself (a less-articulate Melvin). Miranda couldn't remember the last time she'd had a smooth, let alone coherent, interaction with Rudy. If he were going to stare at her, she'd stare at his perfectly round head and his ridiculous baggy shorts with his ridiculous key chains hanging out of them.

"Oh, hey, I didn't even see you here," he said, trying to be smooth. "I guess you're, like, working nights now, or something?"

"What can I get you?"

"Oh, I don't know. Whatever. What do you like here? I'll have one of those."

"One of what?"

"Oh, like, I don't know. What're you having?"

"I'm not having anything. I just clocked in."

"Oh, well. When's your break? Maybe I can join you. I also have breaks. Remember my card I gave you? I can, you know, tell you about my business, or whatever. It's not a big deal. When's your break?"

"I like black tea. How 'bout I give you a black tea? I have to study on my break."

His round head bobbed up and down. "Oh, studying is cool. That's cool. What are you studying?"

Miranda swore if she ever saw David again, she'd murder him in the most vicious way possible. What angered her most was that she knew for a fact the moment she saw David he'd make her laugh, and that would be it. David would take her laughter as approval to continue with his horrendous attitude.

At that moment, Melvin shuffled up to the register, holding three coupons and ready to share five opinions about the most recent episode of *Grey's Anatomy*, which Miranda had never watched.

She had held off, but she could bear it no longer. She pulled out her phone and looked at the wonderful scenery of Cinque Terre. The perfectly blue-green water washed gently onto the shores. Above on the rocks lay the brilliant yellow, pink, and red buildings, impossibly beautiful, and the humans unworthy of living in them. Her feelings betrayed her, and tears flowed.

At the forty-five-minute mark of fun time with Melvin, Lisa asked Miranda to run upstairs for more paper towels. Miranda ran. She ran out of the café, out the front door of the store, and into the parking lot, swearing she'd never return. Her moment of triumph quickly turned to dread, and she melted into the driver's seat of her car, the weight of what she'd done sinking in. She began to sob.

It wasn't too late. She'd only been gone for three minutes. She could easily run back to the café and make up any number of excuses for why she'd run out. But no, she couldn't. She was halfway home already, tears flowing down her face. She had nothing she could say to her father to make him understand.

There was only one thing to do: get drunk with her friends. And she did it all in her work uniform.

~~~

The next day she decided to visit Alexei.

Alexei's office did indeed exist. For once, a business card led to something real, but where it led was a strange place in a strange part of the city Miranda hadn't even known existed. Once past the train tracks, the buildings and homes became desolate, tumbleweeds grew to enormous proportions and outnumbered cars, and vagabonds appeared out of the shadows, ready to stick their hands through your open car window when you least expected it.

Feeling as though she'd been transported to 1965 Saigon, Miranda warily entered the rundown office building. Most of the offices were barren. The numbers on the doors had fallen off, making it nearly impossible to navigate through the maze of white hallways. Eventually, at the far end of the building she found a distractingly red door with *CoinciDATE* written in innocent-looking letters.

Miranda told herself that behind that red door could only be a shady sex club, or worse. She was convinced that at any moment masked men would burst through the walls to kidnap her and sell her into the human-trafficking trade. Then she remembered how she was much more scared of her father, and rang the buzzer.

The door opened. She didn't know why she was expecting to see Alexei standing there smiling his boyish smile. Instead, a cute, meek-looking receptionist with a ponytail and childish bangs greeted her.

"Welcome to CoinciDATE," she said without looking up.

"Um, hi."

"Do you have an appointment?" she asked, clearly uninterested in the answer.

"No. Was I supposed to? I'm here to see Alexei."

The woman finally looked up to scrutinize the person who'd thought she could simply walk in and talk to the boss. "I don't know how you think things work around here, but in order to speak to Alexei or any of the staff, you have to make an appointment. All appointments must be made either through our Gmail, Dropbox, or via WhatsApp. You cannot make an appointment here."

If you can't make appointments here, then what's your big, fancy desk for, cunt? Miranda wanted to say. Instead, she stammered, "Oh, I didn't . . . "

The receptionist cut her off with her best insincere smile. "Alexei is incredibly busy and isn't taking any new appointments at this time. Bye-bye."

"Nonsense!" a voice boomed as though coming from the walls. Alexei had appeared out of nowhere. He was dressed in a dark purple and blue polo that, despite its casual cut, clearly was expensive. "Miranda," he said, all smiles. "I see you've met our wonderful receptionist, Judy. Judy's the best you could ask for. Come on back!"

Miranda smiled and followed him down a dimly lit hallway. The walls were bare, she noticed, devoid of photographs or documents. There was nothing to indicate the place was occupied or that the company had any certification of legality or proficiency.

"I'm glad you're here," Alexei said. "I've been sitting here all week thinking, 'Where's Miranda? Is she ever gonna drop by?' Well, here you are."

Alexei's office had his name printed on the door in big, blocky letters as though shouting at everyone who approached. All the photos missing from the hallway seemed to be hanging in Alexei's office. There he was, shirtless on some tropical beach. Thailand, maybe Bali. Another picture showed him, once again shirtless, parasailing over impossibly clear waters. Another photo showed him arm in arm with a gorgeous woman with the Eiffel Tower in the background. Cinque Terre . . . The photos were endless, each one depicting Alexei in some extreme or picturesque environment with even more picturesque women at his side.

"You like to travel?" Alexei asked as she lowered herself into the offered chair.

Miranda felt inadequate just sitting in that room. She'd never left the country and had only been out of California twice. Alexei grabbed a picture of himself taken on an African safari in an open-canopy jeep. He smiled and let out a small half-sigh, half-laugh. The mechanisms in his head indicated he had a story to tell about that picture, a story he'd probably told a thousand times to a thousand people sitting where Miranda sat now. He looked at her and seemed to decide against retelling the tale.

"So, Miranda. What brings you here?"

"I quit my job," Miranda blurted out, deciding to bypass foreplay altogether.

"Did you?" Alexei's eyes lit up.

"I did. If I'm being completely honest, I did it rashly and without much thought. At the same time, it felt really good."

"I'm sure it did."

"What is this place?" She wasn't sure what had gotten into her, but ever since quitting, she'd found herself skipping all niceties and small talk in favor of getting straight to the point.

"This place is my baby. This place has made me a stupid amount of money. It's also made a stupid amount of money for the people who work for me. Instead of boring you with details, how about I just show you?"

Miranda didn't like it when people beat around the bush. She'd asked a question and wanted a straight answer. If Alexei wanted to make a game of things this early into the conversation, she felt every inclination to leave.

Alexei stood and walked to a shelf, then picked up an envelope from it. He pulled out two photographs and handed her the first. "What do you see?"

"I see a boy. Well, a man."

"Very good. Details, adjectives. Please."

"He looks like he hasn't exercised a day in his life."

Alexei cracked a smile.

"He's not fat, per se, but he's pudgy. He looks like he'd

have the potential to be decent looking if he lost some of that neck fat and learned how to comb his hair. The peach fuzz on his face doesn't do him any favors. He looks like his mom dresses him. He looks boyish and old at the same time."

"Does he look confident?"

"Not really. No."

Alexei handed her the second photo. "Okay, now tell me about this guy."

The man in the second photo was much better looking. He looked like a businessman or professional. He wore a gray suit and looked like he could be a minor character on a show like *Suits*. There was some gray in his jet-black hair, but it only added to his attractiveness. He looked like he was in his mid-thirties. There was no mistaking the fact that he was a man, whereas the person in the first photograph was a boy.

"What do these two guys have in common?"

"Honestly? Nothing that I can see."

"Looks can be deceiving," Alexei said. "What they have in common is that they're both clients of ours."

Miranda still felt none the wiser about what services were being provided to these clients.

"I'd like you to meet one of our most talented staffers. He's going out into the field in about half an hour. I think the best way to get a feel for what it is we do here would be to tag along and watch him do his work."

Alexei led Miranda to a lounge where the expensive, futuristic, impractical chairs were all empty save one. Slouched to the point of sliding off was a guy no older than twenty-one, typing furiously on his phone. He had one of those floppy emo haircuts Miranda hadn't seen since the end of high school. She couldn't determine whether he was white, Hispanic, Middle Eastern, or Chinese. Everything from his eyes to his hair to his skin tone was ambiguous. What wasn't ambiguous was his disdain and disinterest for anything and anyone not currently on his phone. If he hadn't come from the same seed that had spawned Judy the receptionist, then the universe lacked all rhyme and reason.

"Adam," Alexei said, "this is Miranda."

Silence.

"Miranda is going to tag along on your assignment today."

Adam continued to type away at his phone.

A half-hour later, Miranda found herself in the passenger seat of Adam's Mercedes-Benz C Class. The inside presented her an evil concoction of new car smell, peach-scented air freshener, and at least two different colognes. The air blasted far too cold for anyone to enjoy, and the music—some sort of awful Eurotrash synth whose genre Miranda was too out of the loop to know the name of—blasted harder than the air conditioner. Adam still hadn't said a word.

"How long have you worked for Alexei?"

"What?" Adam asked, pointing at the speaker to indicate that it would be foolish to ask him a question.

"I asked how long you'd worked for Alexei."

"A while," he said, not turning down the music.

He never put down his phone while driving, even as he shifted gears. Five times he came scarily close to running into other cars, curbs, and trees.

They arrived at a small outlet that had some clothing shops and stores with names that made it impossible to guess what they sold. Adam grabbed his keys and got out of the car without a word to Miranda. She followed.

"You stay in the car," Adam said, walking toward a small booth that sold smoothies.

"You didn't say anything about me staying—"

"I'm saying it now. Stay in the car."

Miranda got back in the car. Shortly, Adam returned with a smoothie. Despite not being in the mood for one, Miranda was annoyed that he hadn't even offered or asked. He drank in silence until reaching the bottom of the cup and making ever-so-annoying suction noises as he searched for every last morsel of fruit.

Now that the ignition was off, it was getting stuffy. When Miranda rolled down her window, Adam rolled it back up.

Ten minutes passed, and the small outlet grew busy. Japanese tourists passed with giant shopping bags while small children cried and begged their mothers for smoothies. At that point, Miranda began to think a smoothie might be the greatest thing in the world.

"See that girl right there," Adam said in a tone that made it impossible to know whether it was a question, statement, or command.

"Which one?"

"The one coming out of Glenn's. In the gray slacks."

"The blonde?"

Adam sighed. "No, the *gray* slacks."

Miranda noticed a thin girl with a serious face half obscured by wavy hair. She walked quickly, and nearly bumped into an elderly Japanese woman on her way to the parking lot.

"What does the time say?"

Miranda looked at her cheap watch, wondering if there was something wrong with the gold one on Adam's wrist. "Six-thirty."

"Looks like she works from noon to eight p.m. Mondays and Wednesdays. Today is Tuesday, so it looks like she works from ten-thirty a.m. to six-thirty p.m. on Tuesdays, Thursdays, and Saturdays. She goes to the gym after work on Thursday and Saturday, so I'm assuming that's where she's going now. We still have to follow to be sure. When she has the eleven a.m. shift, she takes her lunch break every day across the street at that bullshit health food place. When she works the ten-thirty shift, she switches it up from the sub place to eating in her own breakroom. There doesn't seem to be much consistency between when she does what on those days. Sometimes she'll go three weeks in a row eating at that sub place. Sometimes it's every other day. Sometimes it's every other week. Hard to tell. On weekdays, she tends to go home after the gym. On Saturdays, she sometimes goes out for one cocktail with friends at Hardy's."

Miranda turned to stare at him. "How do you know all this?"

"That's the job," Adam said.

"Your job is to stalk girls?"

"Not only girls. Men too. Transgenders and everything between. If you pay us enough, we find them for you."

"People pay you to stalk people?"

"Why do you think it's called CoinciDATE?" he asked. "Someone has a huge hard-on for a girl, but they're shy, fuck ugly, awkward, or just too damn busy. They come to us. We find out this person's daily routine. Where do they work? How often? Where do they shop? What shampoo do they buy?

Where do they spend their free time? Do they read books at cafés or at the beach? How often do they go to the movies? What parks do they run at? Who are their friends? What are their dietary habits? What bars do they go to?

"Once we've collected any and all information you could want to know about a person, we give it to the client. Now desperate John doesn't have to think of anything clever to say when he sees her sitting at her favorite café reading Tolstoy. Because it's also his favorite café, and Tolstoy happens to be his favorite author. Wouldn't you know it, they strike up a conversation. It turns out John has just taken up Pilates, which is what she does twice a week. They love all the same things. Now she's thinking, 'Where has this John been all my life? He has all the same interests I have. Coincidence? Or maybe fate.' They discover they're soulmates."

"It's like a weird, pervy version of that movie *Hitch*."

"Huh?"

"*Hitch*, that Will Smith movie. He goes around helping shy guys get the girls they want."

"Don't watch movies." Adam went back to fooling around on his phone.

"What's her name?"

"Jenna."

"And who's your client—the guy who wants to know what kind of toothpaste Jenna buys?"

Adam pulled up a photo on his phone. A man in his forties popped up. While not bad looking *per se*, he wasn't what Miranda would have described as a catch. There was no way a girl like Jenna would ever notice him.

"You're thinking there's no way a girl like Jenna would

ever notice him, huh? That's the point. That's why he was willing to pay so much for us to collect this information. This poor sap saw her for the first time at the health food place. He went back every day for a week hoping to see her there. He came to us to find out where she worked. Now he doesn't have to let his lackluster looks hold him back."

"What if she's not interested?"

"So what? Happens all the time. We aren't hypnotists. We can't force anyone to do anything. All we promise is to provide information. The clients are happy to pay for information. Even if things don't work out for these guys, a lot of them are lonely. They like the excitement of the chase and the confidence boost it gives them."

"Isn't it *wrong*?"

Still staring at his phone, he asked, "Why would it be wrong?"

"Well, it just seems . . . " She couldn't quite find the right words.

"Whatever." Adam either didn't care or didn't care to defend the job. It had provided him with a car with the coldest AC in the world and a phone he could swipe his life away on.

An hour later, they were sitting in the parking lot of the community college. Community colleges depressed Miranda to no end. To her, they represented a black hole of ambition, a place for people too lazy and unmotivated for real college. But then she felt depressed because she remembered the students here had been just as successful at finding careers as she'd been.

"Do you go here?" she asked.

"Nah," Adam said.

Despite seeing a diverse age range in the students they

passed, Miranda felt old as she and Adam emerged from the car and walked onto campus. She didn't belong.

They entered a two-hundred-seat lecture hall. They sat down easily enough and were able to avoid any suspicion about whether they belonged. No one paid them any heed. The lecturer, a small man in an oversized suit, droned on about Roman archeology. Maybe he'd once expressed passion for the subject, but it was impossible to tell from his droll delivery.

"Who are we here for?" she whispered.

Adam stopped texting long enough to pull up a photo of a girl sitting in a chair in the same lecture hall. The photo had been captured as she was turning her head, getting a good view of her in mid-profile. It looked as though Adam had taken the photo from the same chair he was sitting in now.

Miranda looked around and saw the same girl sitting two rows in front of her. "Don't tell me the teacher wants you to stalk one of his own students."

"Nah, he's not our client," Adam said much too loudly for Miranda's comfort.

Other groups of students were talking even louder as the lecturer prattled on about aqueducts.

Miranda looked at the photo and then at the girl herself. "Who is she?"

"Some girl. Named Misty."

"That's really her name?"

"Guess so."

"Who's the client?"

"A teacher here. Guy in his mid-thirties. Thinks he's younger than he is."

That was all Adam was willing to say before returning to

the pressing matters on his phone. Miranda would have to wait until she returned to Alexei's office for the rest of the story.

~~~

"Oh, Austin Nash," Alexei said with a smile when she asked him later. "One of our repeat customers. This is the third girl he's had us tail. All of them students, by the way. None of them his, though. He complained that he doesn't have any hot students. Says his boring colleagues get all the hot ones. Apparently he saw this girl, Misty, waiting outside his lecture hall several times to meet up with one of his students. He had no other info to go on."

"Which is when he came to you."

"Bingo! At first we had less to go on than he did. He said to us, 'Guys, this girl is way too fucking hot. I see her all the time waiting for one of my stupid fucking students. I swear to Christ if she were in my lectures, I'd have to constantly be standing behind the podium to make sure no one saw my raging hard-on. She is too sexy.' I told him we'd be more than happy to help. He'd already gotten a head start, though. He got buddy-buddy with one of the guys working in Admissions and was able to get access to all of the students and their addresses. As of now, we know where she lives and what classes she takes. Tomorrow, we're going to see where she goes in her free time. Interested in going out and tailing her? If you say yes, it means you're under my employment."

Before she could answer, Alexei wrote down a series of numbers on a piece of paper, preceded by a dollar sign.

"That would be *just* for tomorrow's work." He smiled.

Miranda let out a more violent than expected choke-laugh.

"What can I say?" Alexei asked. "When people are desperate to get the one they're longing after, they'll pay almost anything. Especially when we do all the hard work for them. Also especially if the person has no social media presence. Our clients are extremely grateful for our help in those cases."

There was a knock on the door.

"Yes?"

A man about the same age as Miranda entered the office. His face reddened when he saw her sitting there. Miranda racked her memory and finally recognized him as a high school classmate, but was certain they'd never spoken to one another.

Before allowing the situation to get awkward, she said, "I'm Miranda. Pleasure to meet you."

"Yeah," he said, offering his hand. "Likewise."

"Jimmy!" Alexei said. "Everything is all set. You ready for this?"

Jimmy nodded.

"Excellent." Alexei consulted the screen of his phone. "Sarah has night classes on Tuesday and Thursday at the community college from five p.m. to nine-thirty. On Wednesdays—not every Wednesday, but often enough— she studies at the campus library. She divides her time about fifty-fifty between the study rooms on the third floor and the computer lab on the first. The longest she's been there is three hours. On average, she's there for around two hours. She usually arrives at two p.m. Occasionally, she'll grab a bite to eat at the Mexican place across the street.

"She lives next to the harbor and often swims at the beach on weekends. She goes to the gym five days a week— always Monday through Friday and always in the morning. The twenty-four-hour gym next to the old movie theater that's a church now. She shops at Whole Foods once a week, usually a Monday or a Tuesday. Sometimes she stops at the bar there for a drink. She's a slow drinker. Sips it. Sometimes doesn't even finish it. She likes to browse at the used bookstore on Main Street. She almost never buys anything, but she'll spend an hour looking through what they have. Typically in the science fiction and fantasy section. Sometimes YA.

"Fridays, she doesn't usually go out, but she almost always goes out on Saturdays. She goes in quite large groups, too, sometimes with as many as seven people. There's one guy who's always there. We believe he's nothing more than a gay friend. She and her friends frequent the same three places. She's quite a dancer. Their last spot of the night is usually the club, but sometimes they finish the night—well, early morning—at Henri's Diner." He tapped his phone, flicked a finger across the screen, and said, "I just sent all this to you."

Jimmy glanced at his phone and nodded. "Got it."

After Jimmy departed, Alexei stared across the desk at Miranda. "I'm not the type of guy who's going to put you on the spot and force you to say yes right away. Take your time, honestly. I, we, think you'd be a great fit here."

Miranda didn't know what to say. In the past, for all the jobs she didn't want at all, she was still compelled to call the supervisor multiple times to remind them of her application. Yes, she had in fact sent them the application because she did indeed want to work there. Now she was practically being invited by a smile and a stupid amount of money.

Miranda's mother, unlike her father, was able to understand her interest in literature and writing. She claimed that a friend of a friend worked in the industry and would be happy to meet with Miranda. The woman was nice enough. On their second meeting, it turned out the whole writing thing was just a pretext to get Miranda to come to a pyramid scheme presentation at a hotel. Five months on and the calls hadn't stopped.

At Alexei's office, she was waiting for that *aha* moment to pop out and give her a reason to leave and never come back.

"Let's grab dinner," he said. "Don't worry, I'll keep the work talk minimal. Think of it as two high school friends catching up."

~~~

She had no appetite that evening. Despite hating it, in all of her recent memories of working behind a counter, she'd been a slave to routine. She knew what her life was and what she had to do. Nothing had ever been offered to her on a silver platter before. She couldn't tell what was more overwhelming: the fact that she'd followed strangers around all day in a stranger's car, the too-good-to-be-true salary, leaving her previous job in such a dramatic fashion, or the fact that the guy in high school she had a small crush on for a minute back when he was ugly was properly handsome now.

What to wear for the occasion was added to the list of things she couldn't make her mind up about. She called Christian. No answer. She knew her friend couldn't choose for her, but she still wanted to hear her voice and thoughts and just be reminded she was there.

The restaurant Alexei had chosen was rumored to be owned by a washed-up actor and to transform into a nightclub on weekends with strictly enforced face control. She wondered if her face would be acceptable enough to eat there on a

Wednesday evening.

Without uttering a word, the maître d' led her to a table where Alexei was sitting and typing away on his phone. With the exception of Alexei, the clientele all seemed to be from Middle Eastern countries. Fat men and old men and ugly men and ordinary-looking men all sat beside trophy wives. Some of the women feigned smiles while others looked openly bored.

Alexei nearly leaped out of his seat when he saw Miranda and gave her an awkward hug. "So happy you came," he said with a big smile. "Great place, right?"

"Actually, I . . ."

Before she could finish the sentence, he was on his feet again, eyes beaming and pearly whites as well. They were joined by a tall redhead in a black dress. She was Miranda—except she was graceful where Miranda was clumsy, modelesque where Miranda was gangly. She was Miranda 2.0, new and improved. The girl radiated class and elegance. Miranda didn't radiate at all.

If the girl was as confused as Miranda, she didn't show it. Alexei's face, on the other hand, went through various stages of happiness and confusion. His head jerked back and forth between the two redheads before he decided who he should introduce to whom.

"Charlotte, this is your stunt double." He indicated Miranda. "Meagan . . . sorry, Miranda . . . this is Charlotte. This is somewhat embarrassing. I've been so busy I lost track of days and forgot I invited both of you to dinner at the same time. But, as we'll all be working together, this is good. Let's get to know each other."

Miranda 2.0 happily sat down, so Miranda did the same.

"I'm actually so happy the two of you are here together," Alexei said. "Isn't it great how these mistakes turn into blessings? I was just about to order this great Chilean red they've got."

"That sounds great," Miranda said.

The intimidating young waiter walked over and mentioned the wine. Ready to impress her potential new boss and happy to drink, she ordered the wine.

"I'll have water," Alexei said.

"Me too," Charlotte said.

"Excuse me," Alexei said, getting up to go to the restroom.

That left the two girls. Perfect strangers. Even with guys Miranda had been enthusiastic about going on dates with, she'd always had moments of hesitation where she'd think through every scenario and excuse to give herself a reason not to go out that front door. This was worse. She was already at the restaurant, stuck with someone she hadn't known would be there.

Charlotte smiled as Miranda sipped her Chilean. "How do you know Alexei?"

Miranda drank even more. "We went to high school together. You? Are you from here?"

Charlotte shook her head.

More wine. "Everyone kind of knows everyone here. Even if you haven't seen someone in years, they always manage to pop up again. And you? Where are you from?"

"I'm from the Midwest, but I'm going to school in LA."

"Is that where you know Alexei from?"

"Actually, I don't really know him at all. He was at my campus handing out business cards and fliers. When he offered me the job, I didn't think it was real. I wanted to see for myself."

"You're studying at the moment?" Miranda asked.

"Mmm."

"What do you study, if it's not a secret?"

Charlotte smiled. It was a hot-person's smile, one that looked practiced and perfected. "You won't make fun of me?"

Miranda smiled. "I might."

"Literature," she said. "And currently I'm taking part in a writing workshop I got a scholarship for."

Miranda emptied her glass and was desperate for another.

"Did I say something wrong?"

Miranda realized she'd been making a face. "I'm sorry. No. I think that's great."

"With the risk of sounding pompous, I'm proud of myself. I'd never won anything in my life. It got pretty demoralizing, seeing all these people around me going off to do these amazing things and being handed money to do it. I've loved writing ever since I was a little girl, but I was never so naïve to think I could ever do anything with it. When I got the notification I'd been awarded the scholarship, I swear I nearly shit myself. I'm sorry, I'm talking too much."

"Not at all," Miranda said. "Again, if it's not a secret, what are you writing about?"

"It's not a secret at all. I'm finishing the final draft of my second book."

At college, every second person Miranda met was a writer. People couldn't shut up about how they had the next big mind-bending idea, but when asked what the idea was or if she could read it, they'd feign modesty or make up any number of excuses to not share. Charlotte, without hesitation, pulled out her phone and emailed Miranda her manuscript.

"I say it's the final draft, but I'd love another pair of eyes to take a look and give me some feedback. Let me know if it's truly ready."

"I'd love to," she said, "and those aren't empty words. Give me two weeks and I'll have it done."

Alexei was all smiles when he returned. "This is exciting. Looks like you guys have a good rapport. I love it when the crew is all on the same level. The crew was already a solid bunch, but with you two joining, I think we're going to have something truly special."

He had come down with the sniffles, and blew his nose into a napkin.

"Can I ask you something?" Miranda asked.

"Only if it's about Argentinian beef."

"Huh?"

"Have you ever had beef from Argentina?"

She shook her head.

"Well, as we're here, it'd be a crime to order anything else." He called to the waiter. He'd left Miranda with no choice, so she ordered an eight-ounce steak and more wine.

"I'll have the Caesar salad," Alexei said.

Charlotte ordered a salad as well.

"If you don't mind my asking, how did you come up with the idea for the company?" Miranda asked.

Alexei beamed. "Wow, that's such a fantastic question, but actually, I have something to do real quick."

Once again, Alexei's seat became empty. It didn't matter. Miranda almost felt like this was a dinner between her and

Charlotte. They had more in common than not. Miranda had been ready to put her foot down and decide that she no longer had it in her to make new friends. She'd gone into this dinner with every intention of turning down the offer and leaving early. She hadn't had friends at her last job. Those were merely people put together by fate. Maybe here, just maybe, she'd finally found something she'd be proud to be part of. If this was the extent of team-building exercises, she decided she could live with it.

Her would-be employer returned as the two girls discussed why *Book of Numbers* by Joshua Cohen was the worst thing either of them had ever read.

Miranda, no longer caring, took an enormous bite of her steak. Alexei played with his salad.

"Are you going to tell us how you came up with CoinciDATE?" Charlotte asked.

"It all really boils down to the economy and the ever-shifting dichotomy of elastic and inelastic products. You see, an elastic product is . . . well, it doesn't matter. It's all technical. I don't want that to be what we're about. It's about the economy, sure, but not simply our economy. Think of it as a web of economies. A web of connections. A big web in which everything is intertwined and nothing can function with the removal of any component. Us not being here at this restaurant tonight wouldn't have any long-term effect on its success as a business, right? Right. Wrong. No, wrong. If we're not here today, then we aren't here next week, and we're not here the eight times we would have gone this year. We decide whether this establishment stays a stable part of the world money-exchanging machine by coming here. Young people aren't eating out as much as they used to, even with these Argentinian steaks being as good as they are. They're busy taking out loans they can never pay back. I met a girl the other night who only listens to artists whose names begin with the letter M. Let that sink in."

Miranda tried.

"Brilliant, isn't it? She's an artist. She only paints using colors that begin with the letter B about themes based on the vibes she gets from the people she meets. She sees people's auras in color and paints them. Her mother used to sniff paint. Yes, we need to live in a world where people know what they want and spend money on it. My goal is to make the world less cynical. Just imagine if that kid who shot up that school had a little bit of hope in his life, what might have been? Pretend, if you will, we have no salaries here, and think about how many people you're making happy by doing this service for them."

"How many employees work for you?" Miranda asked.

Alexei sniffled and blew his nose. "Sorry, allergies. You and Charlotte would make us eleven, not including our lovely receptionist. Excuse me." He was off to the bathroom again.

Miranda realized she'd never known Alexei at all, but with a belly full of steak and Chilean red, there was still enough instinct left in her gut telling her she very much wanted to know Charlotte.

~~~

She got home a little after eleven p.m. and called Christian, but it went straight to voicemail.

"Hey, boo, guess who just accepted a new job offer? Even bigger than that, there's a girl I'll be working with who is beautiful and has written two fucking books. I've started reading one, and it's so fucking good. She's my new girl crush.

Hope you're not jealous. I assume you're sleeping like a normal person. I'm going to drink and read. Just wanted to share my good news with you. Love you."

Miranda had a job. One day of work would be equivalent to what she'd made slaving away for a week at the café. She couldn't help but wonder if there were guys out there—guys she'd never met or even seen—who had as much information about her as Jimmy had about some Sarah. Was there a guy out there who knew the frequency of her trips to the toilet?

Chapter 5

Barry

Barry wondered why he wanted something so badly despite never having had it. He'd never tried escargot, but that didn't make him desire it more. He'd never taken part in a marathon, and never would. He'd never jumped out of an airplane, and no force in this universe could convince him it was something that would change his life for the better. Barry had never kissed a girl. He'd never touched a breast, and had never put his penis inside of a woman.

He jerked off daily. He'd never been able to recapture the magic of the first time he'd come. He was thirteen and had taken off all his clothing when he went to bed. His raging hard-on had been present since he'd gotten home from school. Twisting and turning, desperate to fall asleep, he realized how good the sheets felt as they rubbed against his dick. He began to move back and forth, gyrating his body, the cool sheets rubbing against his swollen cock. His mind shut off. Eyes closed, he began to ferociously fuck his bed. He paid no mind to the fact that the bed creaked worse than the floorboards of a haunted nineteenth-century mansion. The pleasure became unbearable, to the point that he was frightened. He was frightened at what he was feeling, but he had to keep going. It couldn't possibly get any more intense.

It did. He kept going until it became so unbearable his legs tensed up, and suddenly his dick was throbbing and pulsating and giant torpedoes of white goo shot outward. He couldn't believe what had just come out of him. The feeling of extreme pleasure was soon overshadowed by dread as he looked at the white, gooey mess he'd made on his blue bedsheets. He ran to the bathroom, wetted a towel, and lathered it with soap. Try as he might, he seemed to only make the stain in his sheets worse. He'd never know whether his parents figured out what he'd done.

From that point on, he masturbated every day. Each time, the pleasure was less and less, but he never stopped. He couldn't imagine that an orgasm from sex could possibly be *that* much more pleasurable than an orgasm he could achieve simply from using his hand or rubbing against his bed. If that was the case, why did he need it so badly?

It was a Thursday, and for some reason, Daniel had invited Barry out with him. Despite having lived next door to one another for nearly twenty years, they'd spent little time together of late. Barry had been texting Daniel daily to hang out, but after receiving negative responses more often than not, and soon enough no responses, he'd gotten the hint. Because Barry had no pride, he jumped at any opportunity to hang out when Daniel sent a text his way.

The time they spent together consisted of two variants. The first was when Daniel would call Barry over late at night. Everyone at Daniel's house would be fast asleep. Barry would watch his friend smoke weed, and Daniel would soon be so gone that whatever movie they put on would go unfinished. Daniel almost never called Barry to hang out at normal hours, and he was certainly never sober when he did. The second variant consisted of subjugating Barry to hanging out with his friends. Barry didn't like any of Daniel's friends.

Like Daniel, Eddie was handsome. More importantly, he was tall and had big arms. Barry made the mistake of thinking that Eddie shared the same sense of humor that Daniel and Barry had grown up with. Barry did an impression that used to put Daniel in stitches, but when he acted it out in front of Eddie, he received blank stares from the both of them.

Adam, Daniel's other friend, wasn't tall, but he was handsome and had great hair. Adam was either Chinese or Irish. They were always polite in the beginning when they saw that Daniel had brought Barry along. Barry knew, though, that they disapproved of him. Their eyes gave away their true feelings whenever they saw him walk through the doorway.

That Thursday, they were at an establishment Barry couldn't comprehend the appeal of—especially to the likes of Daniel and his friends. It was a kitschy restaurant with loud music and an even louder clientele of families, out-of-control children, and cougars on the prowl. The only thing Barry could think of was that the happy hour appealed to them. It didn't appeal to Barry. The only time he touched alcohol was with Daniel. He was babysitting his first beer while the others were well on to their second or third.

Barry had tried and failed for the third time to start a conversation, so he sat back and grew invisible in his accustomed manner. The others spoke about mutual friends, weed, music, things he had no knowledge of. There were two subjects Barry always avoided: sex and his hair.

Despite being in his early twenties, his hair had begun to thin and recede noticeably. It seemed to happen overnight. His hair had always been untamable and uncooperative, but he'd been able to find compromises. One ordinary morning, he woke up, looked at himself in the mirror, and came to the horrible realization that no matter what he did with any comb or brush, he could no longer hide his big forehead with his hair. His hair was betraying him. He'd been willing to handle being overweight, but losing his hair was a blow so unbearable he started to weep. Even worse, people who knew him had made comments about it, as though they didn't think it was the one and only thing constantly on his mind.

One time when he was with Daniel and Eddie, Eddie had asked him if he was going to the beach the following day with everyone. Barry made the mistake of saying, "Can't. I'm getting a haircut."

Eddie had burst out laughing. "Haircut? What hair is there to cut?"

Why had Eddie said that? Couldn't he see what a pathetic creature Barry was? Why remind him of what was already causing so much torment? As usual, the subject eventually turned to sex, and then Barry truly wished he were invisible.

"Why are you being such a little liar?" Eddie asked.

"I'm not lying," Daniel insisted. "I just think you're wrong. Simple as that."

"Adam, back me up here?"

Adam looked up from swiping right on his phone. Barry spied that Adam had over ninety matches. Most of them looked attractive, but that didn't stop Adam from swiping right on every girl whose face popped up on his screen.

"I'm with Danny on this one," Adam said.

"You guys are so full of shit," Eddie said.

"We're not full of shit. You've just been fucking women with monstrosities for vages."

"Look," Eddie said, visibly frustrated. "I'm the master of fingering. No one loves it more than I do. Hell, I make women come fast with my fingering. Instantaneous like. Girls could take every measure not to come, but my fingers are impervious to their defenses. That's not the point I'm getting at. I feel like what I'm saying is quite simple and you're not listening. I'm not saying I dislike it or don't want to do it. What I'm saying is the first time I stuck my finger in a woman, it was weird. It didn't feel how I expected it to feel."

"What did you expect it to feel like?" Daniel asked.

"Smoother. I don't know. Just not like *that*. It's fucking small and has, like, ridges. It's ridged. Like . . . like there are mini canyons down there. I'm not saying I don't enjoy it, and I'm not saying I won't do it. I'm simply saying it's a weird sensation, and no matter how many times you stick your finger in a woman, it's still a strange feeling. It's not something fingers get used to feeling."

"I disagree," Daniel said. "It's not strange."

"Okay," Eddie said. "You're just too fucking macho to admit it. Nothing weird about the pussy. What do you think, Barry?"

Barry's invisibility cloak had fallen off. "Nah. It's not weird," Barry lied. He knew nothing about what the inside of a vagina felt like. Truth be told, vaginas terrified him.

Once Daniel had told him about how pussies were

oily. Barry didn't know what that meant. He knew they were supposed to be wet, but oily? Like olive oil? He'd heard others say they had a fishy smell. That scared Barry even more. He hated seafood, and he was especially susceptible to strong odors. He remembered a time when one of Kenneth's farts had been so rancid it caused Barry to empty his stomach all over the kitchen floor. If his face, and more importantly his nose, ever came into close contact with a pussy, would he be able to handle the oily, fishy smell?

Daniel loved to show Barry the nudes sent to him by the girls he was fucking. Often, they were girls Barry knew, had spoken with, and considered friends. One girl, Des, was someone Barry considered really intelligent and friendly. She wore glasses and was always nice to him. And there on Daniel's phone were photos of her with her tits out and bending over, spreading her pussy and cheeks. There was even a video Daniel showed him, without warning, of Daniel fucking her from behind. Was it that easy to get girls to send nude photos? Was being a handsome guy all it took? If Barry had Daniel's looks, would it be as easy as simply saying, "Hey, Des, show me your tits"? Was that how it worked?

"There are no nice girls," Kenneth had said. "They're all sluts. Every single one of them. If she's so nice, why isn't she sucking your dick instead of his? He's got a big dick and a pretty face. She's *nice* to you because she knows you're so far removed from her radar that saying kind things to you and giving you a smile or two won't lead to a goddam thing. Any girls who send naked pictures of themselves have no right to be shocked when those pictures end up online. A female requires no skills or talent to bed a man. If she's opening her legs for multiple partners and sending nudes, it means she's a whore. The male seed isn't a valuable resource. When a man shoots his load, millions of sperm will never reach that egg, and the human race goes on. Seed can be spilled and wasted. A woman's egg is much more valuable. Therefore, it's scientifically proven that it's okay for men to have multiple partners and not women. Stupid fucking sluts."

Barry couldn't argue with science.

Wouldn't life be so much easier without a penis? Barry often asked himself this question. It only caused him grief. He wasn't using it, so why have it? All it did was distract him with constant boners. If it were painless, he often thought he'd simply cut it off. With no dick, maybe he'd have time to finally be good at something. Maybe he was good at guitar and never even knew it because he never took the time to apply himself. Maybe he was apt at tennis or golf. He'd never know because he never tried. He never tried anything. He blamed his penis.

Barry thought of his dog. He'd pitied the poor creature when they took him to get snipped. The pup had gone into the car so hopeful and energetic, oblivious to what was about to be done to his balls. Barry had been against the idea. But looking back on the past five years of the dog's life, there had never been a happier creature. Perhaps having a pair of balls would have prevented the beast from experiencing such joy in life. Barry wanted to be that happy too.

He imagined the melodies and rhythms he'd create on the guitar. His own creation. Something to be proud of. It was then that it hit him. Why do men learn musical instruments in the first place? Why do they take up a hobby or learn a skill? Sure, there has to be an initial interest, but at the end of the day, didn't it all simply boil down to attracting female attention and fucking them? How many eunuchs played in successful rock bands or fought for the UFC? What motivation did a dickless man have to become the next Hendrix?

Barry loved porn. He watched it first thing in the morning, before going to bed in the evening, and often in the bathrooms at school. Porn was the best thing ever created. It presented you with everything you could possibly want to do to a woman. Any category you could want, any combination of threesomes.

The best part, though, was there were no smells. The women on screen were perfect angels whose breath always smelled of fresh mint, who had nipples that tasted and smelled like strawberries, and pussies that were even sweeter. When guys would eat girls' pussies on film, Barry always paid extra close attention to see whether they winced or were holding back any disgust or discomfort. Often the men ate them from behind, and the only place for their noses to go was directly into the girl's asshole. Did they smell bad? Barry imagined a woman's asshole was made of the exact same material as his, and he recalled how ripe Kenneth's farts had been, but in porn, the asshole is filmed to look like a perfect, clean, rose-smelling hole, just waiting to get filled. Porn didn't have smells.

He wanted his first time to be like the porn he saw, where the woman had the perfect body, did everything he wanted her to do, seduced him, danced for him, rode him, sucked his dick, and stuck out her tongue as he came all over her face. Having said all that, he still feared the vagina. He knew if he were to have sex, it would be expected that he'd stick his finger up there. That's how it was done. He didn't want to show that he was inexperienced, let alone frightened of putting his finger in that.

Barry's opinion wasn't required again for the rest of the night. Adam left early to meet up with a new Tinder match.

Daniel and Eddie eventually left for a party. No invitation was sent Barry's way, and he was more than happy not to be invited. He wanted to go home and masturbate. He was going to watch scenes of guys going down on girls and try his damnedest to imagine the smell and the taste, and to work out a scenario in his head in which he'd like it.

Odds were that Daniel had gotten laid. Daniel always got laid. The rare times they did meet up, Daniel never failed to mention his conquests. Barry couldn't tell if Daniel was after validation, or simply rubbing it in by giving him all the gory details.

~~~

Barry rolled out of bed. The previous night, he'd sworn an oath to God, or whoever was listening and held the power, that he'd put some effort into being healthier. He'd start each morning with some push-ups, sit-ups, and bicycle kicks. Nothing too drastic. Perhaps fifty of each, just to get used to it, and each consecutive day, he'd do more. He told himself that once it became habit, it would no longer feel so awful.

He eyed his hard wooden floor and thought, *Perhaps I'll start tomorrow.*

He put on a hoodie that was two sizes too big, even for him, and covered his head with a baseball cap he'd owned since he was eleven. He got in his car. The heater seemed to do nothing to counteract the cool morning air. He shivered and shook as he started the ignition and drove to school. He wasn't sure why he even bothered. Due to his fruitless night of hanging out with Daniel and his friends, he'd done none of his homework.

He found himself on the familiar trek up toward the

student service center. He had no reason to be there. He was already five minutes late to his first class, which was on the opposite side of the campus, yet he continued with heavy feet.

Before he knew it, he'd entered the building. He passed students and transients sitting behind computers and arguing with staff. French Murder Face was whispering something sinister in one person's ears while molesting Barry with his eyes. *What the hell am I doing in there?* He only ever had one reason to be in this building—to purchase a parking permit. He already had one. Yet he kept walking toward the counter.

There she stood. The girl who'd left him thunderstruck. She was chatting with her coworker, a tall and tan guy with a goatee and a floppy head of hair pulled into a ponytail.

Barry froze. The two of them glanced at him before continuing their conversation. Barry couldn't move. He couldn't do a damned thing. Several people bumped into him as they moved past him to make their way to the counter. He remained where he was.

When she finished serving her customers, she glanced up and saw that strange guy still there, pretending not to look at her. When it became unbearable, he walked straight up to the tan guy with the goatee, refusing to let his eyes wander in her direction. He was there to buy a parking permit, plain and simple. His mission was to complete a transaction. Her being there was completely incidental.

He bought a parking permit and walked with his head held in shame back down the hill toward the cafeteria. Five hours of dishwashing were gone—time that his life would never give back to him. He had no willpower to attend any of his classes that day.

Fortunately and unfortunately for him, the usual

suspects were sitting on the stone chairs spread out in front of the cafeteria. They were always there. The time of day made no difference, nor did their course load. Most of them had stopped attending classes several semesters ago, but they nevertheless showed up to campus like clockwork to sit in front of the cafeteria, where they slowly rotted away.

The first to look up from his phone and inane conversations was Sonny. That wasn't his real name. No one knew his real name, nor how old he was. Rich, Barry's cousin, remembered seeing Sonny hanging out in front of the cafeteria when he'd attended school twelve years earlier. His origins were as mysterious as his age. His dark skin was only bested by his long, flowing hair, which was darker than any eclipse. Some said he grew up in the Philippines. Others said he was an ancient Mayan king who refused to die. The only thing definitively known about Sonny was his love for all things metal. That day, he had on his worn-out "Ride the Lightning" T-shirt.

Next to Sonny sat Bert. Barry liked Bert because Barry felt bad for Bert, and if Barry felt bad for someone, it meant that person had it pretty bad. It was difficult to discern exactly what was wrong with Bert because nothing was right with Bert. His nose wasn't large, but its shape was odd enough to make it instantly noticeable. It managed to be small and pointy all at once. He had a weak chin, which made him look both like an old man and a baby simultaneously. Barry had never known him to have short hair. His hair fell past his shoulders and was always tangled and knotted. Maybe Bert had once believed that adding pink and purple to his dark hair would distract from how ugly it was. It only enhanced the ugliness. Bert was extremely kind to everyone he talked to, and that made Barry sad.

A girl Barry didn't recognize was sitting on top of the table wearing a sleeveless black shirt and strumming a banjo. Barry only hoped she didn't start singing. When she did, he took solace in knowing at least he didn't have to talk to Aimee and Sonny for a few more minutes. Aimee was the fattest person Barry had ever met who could still walk. She was as mean as Bert was kind and as fat as he was ugly. Cartoon characters. Every one of them. Was Barry any different? Was he not also a ridiculous caricature of a human being? Did he not fit the role of the virgin splendidly? He wondered if the others talked about him while he wasn't there. He wondered if the way he thought about them was how they thought about him. Would it be worse if they didn't talk about him at all?

One day, Barry had woken up and understood he was ugly. He'd never believed himself to be handsome, but for years, he grew up with an image in his head of how he believed he looked. Then one day his reflection in the mirror taunted him with its hideous face. In Barry's head, he was five foot eleven. He wanted to be slightly above average, but not so tall that it called attention to him. He had broad shoulders and was lean but not buff. He could take his shirt off without being embarrassed. He had short, dark-brown hair that grew thick and was tamable but also had that purposely messy look. He'd get out of bed, and his hair would be messy in the most perfect way. He had white teeth that made his smile to die for. He looked normal, but because his looks were absolutely fine, it was his personality and talent that would make girls flock to him.

Instead, he had no looks, no talent, and no flocks.

Sonny was deep in conversation with some guys about gun control. Ever since the incident, none of them had mentioned Kenneth by name, yet if there was ever anything being discussed, Sonny always had an opinion. Sonny had gone as far as to say that the shooting hadn't even happened and that everyone involved was a crisis actor. Barry was certain Sonny had been sitting exactly where he was on that bench when the shooting occurred. Was it possible that the sounds of gunshots hadn't been audible at that distance?

Sonny argued about everything. If someone brought up the moon landing, he claimed it had never taken place. The next day, he'd go as far as to say that space wasn't even real. When he couldn't defend that claim, he'd resort to saying, "Well, it's real, but because there are such high levels of radiation, you can't send ships up there. It's so simple and obviously impossible. Even in spacesuits, astronauts would melt away. Why do you think aliens have never come to Earth? You can't travel in space. Radiation, man."

A week prior to that, Sonny had talked for hours about a documentary claiming that aliens were responsible for most of man's achievements and technological advancements.

Making the rounds were the representatives of various groups, clubs, and organizations, some of them campus-based while others were infiltrators ready to bestow the gift of whatever wisdom they bore. Ainsley's fliers condemning Israel were followed by leaflets for a seminar inviting white men to accept that they had privilege and learn how to atone for it. Other handouts were more boring—glorified tutoring sessions, auditing classes, coding classes, and the like.

French Murder Face collected fliers from everyone who had them. He stopped to chat with Ainsley about something that Barry couldn't hear. Then he pulled out a sandwich containing only mayonnaise and made quick work of it.

Sonny's attention was distracted by one colorful flier featuring incredibly attractive men and women, handed to him by an attractive young woman in an impossibly tight dress. Her big smile was only surpassed by his.

"Beatitudinem," he read. "It means 'happiness' in Latin." He skimmed the details of the club before he was distracted by the next attractive woman to walk by. This one also was dressed in something very tight, and more importantly, short. It looked to be some kind of slutty version of German traditional dress. It came as no surprise that she was trying to recruit students for the campus's German club.

"I'd learn German for her," Sonny said as she walked away. His eyes followed her ass up the hill.

Barry had never put any thought into learning another language. It made no difference to him. Languages were a useless skill, as far as he was concerned. He had no plans to go anywhere. Be it Italy or China, far-off lands had no place in his imagination. As long as they remained where they were, he paid them no mind.

Then it hit him. Perhaps the tall beauty in student services was German. Maybe that was the key. Maybe learning a language had a purpose after all.

Chapter 6

Doug

Doug woke at six, as he always did. In the kitchen, his wife was already active, making some sort of protein shake. With increasing frequency, she was eating things that contained less and less real food. But he figured as long as her body remained as tight as it did, she could put whatever the fuck she wanted into it.

"Are you going to talk to Gendo today?" she asked from the kitchen.

He examined his torso in the mirror. "What's that?"

"Are you going to talk to your boss today?"

"Am I less fit than I used to be?"

"What's that, babe?"

Doug took a shower and examined his torso once more. He had nothing to worry about. It had merely been a case of morning eyes.

"Lunch today?" she asked as she finished up the knot on his tie.

"Lunch." He kissed his wife and left for work.

Doug and Sandra had gotten married their freshman year of college. They'd started dating their sophomore year of high school, and had become a star couple overnight. You couldn't flip through the school yearbook without constantly running into their perfect smiles. The cuteness of their relationship could have killed. It almost did, as one of Doug's best friends had been extremely jealous of Doug and Sandra and had given Doug the cold shoulder for five months. His jealousy eventually manifested into attacking Doug in front of everyone at school. Doug swiftly won the fight. That only made Doug and Sandra more popular.

Now, at thirty, Doug's jealous and admiring classmates had been replaced by jealous and admiring coworkers. Moving from Small Town, Vermont, to Medium-Sized City, California, Doug had left most of his friends behind. His new friends were the people Sandra told him to hang out with. He was indifferent. It made her happy, and they weren't entirely insufferable. His wife was hotter than theirs were, so he enjoyed that perk.

At work, Doug tolerated Joey above the others. Joey was on the wrong side of thirty, whereas Doug looked better than most guys at twenty. Joey was pudgy and had a soft, sympathetic face. Doug had asked him once to bring him some coffee. Joey had been fetching coffee for Doug ever since. Doug was keenly aware that Joey was not-so-subtly in love with Sandra. That amused him.

Doug was in his cubicle reading one last email when Joey approached. "Doug! O'Leary's?" Joey seemed far too excited, like a dog who heard his owner grabbing the leash to take it for a walk.

"No, I don't think I can tonight," Doug said. He was

distracted. Gendo Yagami, the company's president, had been spotted several times in the office. He almost always delegated his affairs to the vice-president. If he was in the office, it meant something big was about to go down. Perhaps a round of promotions. For a month, Sandra had been asking her husband if he planned to talk to Gendo. She didn't understand what an inscrutable bastard Gendo was.

She also wasn't aware of Kale's ability to suck up. Of all the people who could be a threat to Doug, it was the one with the dumbest name in the world. Kale routinely went around the office asking people if they needed anything. The answer was almost always no, but on the rare occasion someone said yes, he'd disappear. More importantly, he'd been with the company longer than Doug and had gotten in tight with the vice-president. While Joey was talking to Doug, Kale hovered over Karen's desk, fiddling with his tie.

"Ah, come on," Joey said. "Everyone's going. Even Karen, and she never goes out."

"Ah," Doug said. "Karen. Sounds fun. Go on ahead."

Truth be told, Doug could no longer go to O'Leary's. Not since he'd fucked the bartender with the tattoos. It was a decent place and conveniently located to both the office and his home, but fucking the bartender made it impossible to return. Every time he passed it with Sandra, she hinted at wanting to go. Whether or not she'd been there, he couldn't say. He couldn't go with her. The bartender was far from Doug's type. She was thirty-two and had tattoos on her arms. Doug didn't mind that. He didn't love it either, but arms weren't so important. He was less accepting of the tattoo that covered the small of her back and the top of her ass. She had a great body, but years of smoking showed on her slightly stained teeth and gave her a voice that sounded as though she'd been swallowing glass for a decade.

She was a good fuck, but after that, Doug was aware he needed something different. Unlike Joey and his other single acquaintances, Tinder wasn't an option. He had a profile anyway (obviously not containing any photos of himself) and used it merely to see what was available. His friend Timothy from back home had gotten caught by his wife using Tinder. Doug had heard all about it from Sandra the evening it happened. Having Tinder and seeing the menu made him incredibly depressed. He was tempted on several occasions to whet his appetite and use the app, but Sandra was simply too popular and had too many friends. His chances of getting caught were between ninety and a hundred percent.

Joey kept distracting Doug. He wasn't interested in anything Joey had to say. He was interested in finding a way to talk to Gendo about his role in the company.

"What're you up to that you can't go out with us?"

"Going to grab a smoothie before going home. Movie night with Sandra."

It wasn't movie night, and he didn't like smoothies. He couldn't figure out why he'd chosen that as his excuse. Excuses came easily to Doug.

"Great," Joey said enthusiastically. "I'll come grab a smoothie with you before going to the bar."

Piece of shit, Doug thought.

The smoothie place that Doug hadn't actually planned on going to was a ten-minute walk from the office. Doug normally appreciated quiet walks alone, but Joey seemed to be afraid of silence. If Joey had nothing to say, he'd point out anything and everything he saw around them to make conversation.

"You ever notice how beer commercials aren't as funny as they used to be?"

"Dear God," Doug muttered.

"Like a rock!" Joey sang, laughing. "Remember? Are you insured?" He laughed even harder. "Remember that guy? He turned down the ride because the hot chick in the car wasn't insured. Hero!"

The smoothie place was brimming with activity. The sound of the blenders was overpowered only by that of aggressively noisy teenagers.

"Oh, so many choices," Joey said. "I ought to get a protein shot in there."

Too late for your pudgy ass, Doug thought.

When the two of them had finally made it through the sea of people, they were greeted by the cashier, and Doug's heart nearly exploded. He was perplexed that Joey could be seeing what he was seeing and not have exploded as well. Doug had to relearn English and screw his head back on before he could even find the words to describe what he was seeing.

In high school, Doug had been obsessed with Becky, a girl on the swim team. He even joined the swim team to get closer to her, despite finding the sport tedious. Most of all, he despised the smell of chlorine. But it had been worth it because after a month on the team, she was taking his dick in her mouth. Sometimes they wouldn't even shower the chlorine off and would go straight from the pool into the locker room, and she'd suck him off right then and there. Since then, he couldn't go near chlorine without getting an erection. Fourteen years later, and he still hadn't found a girl that sucked better dick.

Her pussy was disappointing, though. As a swimmer, her body was naturally phenomenal. She had a nice face with a nice head of blonde hair to top her off and make her pretty, but her pussy was all wrong. Once inside her, it didn't matter, but he hated to look at it. The lips were big and meaty, the kind that made him turn the video off if he was watching porn. It was tight enough, but the meaty floppiness of it always gave him a millisecond of hesitation when he pulled off her panties. He never went down on her, and even fingering her required a bit of effort on his part. Thank God she could suck a dick. He loved her for that.

Not all the women he'd been with could do it. Lacy hated sucking dick. It was only fair, Doug supposed, as he didn't have the desire to go down on anyone after experiencing the swimmer's wreck of a pussy. Lacy had the biggest tits of any girl he'd been with. They were big to the point of nearly being ridiculous, but it was that fine line, the almost being off-putting, that made them all the more appealing. He could bury himself in those tits and live there forever. As long as his face was buried in those massive bags of flesh, he didn't even need sex. He could suck on them all night long and run her nipples along his lips and nose. He loved rubbing them on his nose.

The best lay he ever had was the girl who worked at the pet store. She loved animals and reeked of dog. Doug hated her own dog, a stupid little shit that wasn't so little. It barked like a retarded maniac every time he came to her place, even though it had seen him so many times it should have been well aware of who he was. The dog would leap forward, planting its front paws on Doug's chest while slobbering all over the place, trying to connect its tongue with Doug's body. Pet-store girl would always respond with, "Oh, how precious. He loves you."

No matter how many showers she took or how often she brushed her teeth, the stench of dog was always there. It was worth it, though, because she fucked like a raging beast. The way she could contract her pussy was commendable. Doug once tried to explain to his wife how he wanted her to contract her pussy, and she got angry at him for using that word. Pet Store's tongue was also commendable. It would go back and forth trying to connect with his body the same way her dog's did.

It gave Doug intense anxiety that a girl with perfect tits might have a nasty snatch or vice versa. When he thought back to those amazing blowjobs, he thought about how it would have been if she'd had Lucy's tits or Anna's ass. All of those on one woman. Sandra came close. She wasn't great at sucking dick (and had no love for the act), but still would do it. She had a flat, white girl's ass but made up for it with big breasts and a pretty face. Her pussy, while not perfect, was tight enough and didn't have offensively large lips.

Doug also got anxiety while walking around in his daily life. One time he shared the elevator up to his office with some young girl in a smart-looking suit who must have been a new intern on an upper level. The way her hair was pulled back made her look like such a fucking bitch, and he loved it more than his own wife. Her glasses only cemented her hard and bitchy demeanor. Her lips were smeared in ridiculous amounts of lip gloss that gave them a nice wet sheen. Then he imagined that her pussy lips (which in his head were small and perfect) were wet as well. Her ass was small but had enough fat on it to feel good in his hands. Her skin was olive and her eyes were dark brown. He wanted her more than he'd ever wanted anyone.

That was until he got on the escalator taking him to the food court in the mall. Going up, he saw a brunette bombshell going down. He smiled at her. Her long, wavy hair hung all the way to her ass. She was nearly as tall as he was, with her impossibly long legs inside her tight yoga pants. She wasn't wearing a bra. She was perfect.

But there was a problem. What about the girl in the elevator? The girl in the elevator worked in his building. If he was patient and played his cards right, he had a good chance of bedding her. But how could he think about her when a girl as wonderful as the girl on the escalator existed?

To make matters worse, there was the girl in the parking lot. She had to have been a model. She walked like one and dressed like one, and her indifferent demeanor to everything around her proved that she was one. If he bedded the model, it meant he wasn't bedding the girl on the escalator, and that thought depressed him. So many beautiful women around him depressed him rather than encouraged him. Even if he got with one, it meant there were ten others he wouldn't have. How to cope with that, he didn't know.

The girl standing behind the register at the smoothie place added an entirely new and unexpected layer to Doug's conundrum. The girl from the parking lot disappeared. The one in the elevator vanished from his memory, and the escalator girl was a mere piece of passing debris. The only thing that mattered was the girl who was about to take his order. He purposely hesitated to give it, using that time to take a good look at her. He knew that once he walked out the door, her image would fade in his memory, and he wanted to remember every last piece of her.

She was about five foot five and had a slim frame. Her neck was long. Almost too long, but, like everything else, it was those *almost* moments that drove Doug crazy. Long enough to be noticeable but not long enough to be a defect. Her bottom lip stuck out slightly more than the top one, giving the impression that her face was pouty, which made Doug incredibly hard. She had light, slightly olive-tinted skin and dark brown hair that fell past her shoulders. Her eyes were big and brown but retained an Asian quality. She had to be mixed race. Part Asian, part white. Oh God! Doug could die. Her firm tits pushed her white work shirt forward. They weren't particularly big, but dear God, the shape of them made Doug want to take her back there behind the counter, rip her shirt off, and fondle them forever.

Her lower body was concealed by the counter. *Please walk away so I can see.*

When she took his order, she smiled at him.

"What is that?" Doug asked, pointing to something he knew very well was a box containing different protein powders.

"Protein powders."

"Can I take a look at that?"

She walked away.

My God, her ass is magnificent, Doug thought. *It's beyond magnificent. It's so wonderful, a superlative that could do it justice hasn't been invented.* He wanted to stick his head between her legs and suffocate. He wanted her to sit on his face so hard that while he ate out her wet pussy the only place for his nose to go was up that small, tight butthole of hers. He made a pact with God. He would lick Joey's dirty, crusty asshole for five years straight just to be able to stick one of his fingers in her asshole.

When Doug made love to his wife that night, he came within two minutes because his mind was racing with memories of the girl from the smoothie place. He would die if he didn't fuck her. It was a fact.

After the short performance, his wife got out from under him, laughed it off, and turned on some brainless show on Netflix. He was already hard again within minutes. He went to the bathroom and rubbed himself raw to the thought of her.

"God," he said as his cum began to crystallize on his pubes. He hadn't shaved in a while. His wife said she preferred him with some hair, but he felt like a Neanderthal. "God, I swear to you. I swear. I know we haven't talked much recently. In fact, I don't think I've ever asked you for anything. But I don't know if I can do this one on my own. Today, I saw something, someone, so wonderful that I will die if I don't have her. I will die. Can you let one of your children die? Please, take me at my word. Take the fact that I don't ask for much to mean that I am not a selfish man, and I don't ask you for things carelessly. I need this girl. I need her with every inch of my body. I won't jerk off for a week if you give her to me."

~~~

Doug left work early the next day. Gendo had disappeared, and with him his chance to put himself out there for the promotion. He also couldn't bear to listen to any of Joey's inane nonsense when such a beautiful creature was waiting for him.

The line at the smoothie place was long. When Doug finally made it to the counter, he was greeted by an ugly, pimple-faced ginger.

"What can I do for you?" the ginger asked with too much confidence, as though he didn't realize how fucking hideous he was.

"Hey, I was here a couple of days ago . . . "

"Oh, nice. Welcome back."

"Yeah," Doug said. "Anyway, I was here and I had a special drink made for me. It was made by a girl, about five foot five."

"Oh!" the ginger said. "Long neck? Yeah, that's Talia. She's always going off the menu making drinks that the register doesn't have buttons for."

"Yeah, I think that's her," Doug said.

"Ah, too bad. Yesterday was her last day. Our supervisor has gotten a lot stricter about us making special drink orders that aren't on the menu."

"Fuck!" Doug screamed, startling the ginger.

"Do you want to try the strawberry delight? It's deeeeelightful."

"Yeah, give me your strawberry bullshit."

That night, Doug couldn't sleep. He regretted little in his life. If he wanted something, he did whatever it took to get it. When he wanted to go to school on the West Coast even though his parents were firmly against it, he pulled every link, article, and statistic to prove why it was the best course of action. When he wanted to go to a certain restaurant and his wife desired another, he created fake Yelp accounts to write negative reviews to sway her opinion.

But now Doug was at a loss. He had seen her for a brief moment, and she was already gone. Her face was in his mind, but if he didn't see her again, his vivid image of her likeness would disappear. He couldn't jerk off to a phantom.

Sandra lightly licked the back of his neck and let out a

soft giggle.

Fuck off, you cunt, he wanted to scream.

She slipped her hand down his leg and grabbed his flaccid cock. She began yanking the thing as though trying to uproot a weed in the garden. Doug had never been more depressed.

"I love you, baby," Sandra said as his limp cock stretched in her hand. "I love you so much."

He knew it was true. She did love him. She also loved the terrible shit she watched repetitively on Netflix. She loved jazz too. Doug had no idea how much value there was to what she *loved.* Doug loved Talia's bottom lip. He loved what he imagined her asshole looked and smelled like. He loved that her name was as exotic as her face. What did Sandra know about love?

~~~

"Okay, so this is what you do," Joey said the next day, all smiles at O'Keefe's.

It seemed that Joey was capable only of going to Irish bars that began with an O followed by an apostrophe. He'd been all smiles ever since Doug finally agreed to go out with them.

"Each one of you takes a piece of napkin. Really, it should be a card, but all I've got is napkin." Joey tore jagged pieces of napkin and distributed them to the five people at the table.

Doug would gladly have wiped his ass with the shitty napkin shard Joey had given him and then smeared it on Joey's upper lip.

"You write down the name of someone famous. It can be anyone . . . well, not *anyone,* but any well-known figure from history, cinema, music, the arts, etcetera. Anyone famous. You can't say 'my uncle Bob.' It should be someone guessable."

"Yeah, we get it," Donovan said, stealing what Doug would have said. "Someone famous and guessable."

"Right." Joey smiled. "Write down the name of someone famous and pass the napkin to the person on your left."

Doug was livid. When it was time to drink, he wanted only to drink. When it was time to socialize, he smiled and answered accordingly, but these parlor games were an inane waste of time. The person to Doug's left was Cedric, who happened to be the most boring person Doug had ever met, and he liked him immensely more than he liked Joey. Joey was likely to write the name of whoever was in the headlines or the star of various memes circulating around the office.

Joey smiled and giggled like a fool as he scribbled the name down on his napkin. It was *SpongeBob SquarePants*.

"Once you've written the name, you pass it down to the person on your left. Don't look! Don't look, and hold the napkin over your forehead so the rest can see."

Doug wrote *Joseph Goebbels* and passed it to Cedric.

"To play, you can only ask questions where 'yes' or 'no' are the answer."

Doug wondered if Talia had a meaty pussy or a tight, perfect pussy. How much hair did she have down there? Did she suck a good dick? Did she use her tongue to lick around the tiny hole at the tip of the head of the dick? Would she continue to suck and lick his head once he'd already come? That, he knew, would drive him crazy to the moon and back.

Her face was nearly visible. He could make out her pouty lips, but then her face morphed into Kale's. How long had he been standing there?

"Well, doesn't this look like a good bit of fun. Hi, guys. Cedric. Douglass."

No one ever called him Douglass. Two tables away, Kale had been sitting with a group of friends. An attractive blonde—who wasn't his wife—sat next to Kale. Doug had definitely had better, but he couldn't forgive the fact that an attractive woman sat next to Kale. While Doug was mostly satisfied with his list, the idea that Kale's could be comparable was worrisome. He'd have to get Joey to find out how many women Kale had slept with and who they were.

It was one thing for Kale to sleep with women Doug wasn't sleeping with, but to also take a job away from him? No, that wouldn't do.

"So, I can ask, 'Am I white?' but I *cannot* ask, 'Am I white *or* black?' Got it?"

The game lasted three hours and four rounds. Joey, who set up the game and was so adamant about playing, was absolutely useless, came in last every single round, and couldn't guess the easiest people chosen for him.

"How's Sandra?" Karen asked during the third round.

Why does she give a shit? Doug thought. Karen and he were hardly chums at work. What did she care about Sandra?

"Talia's fine," Doug said.

"Great," Karen said. She was struggling to guess that *Jackie Chan* was scribbled on her fucking forehead.

At the end of the useless night, Doug helped carry Joey's heavy, drunk ass to the Uber, then returned to the bar, planted himself behind the counter, and ordered whiskey on the rocks. The bar was gradually clearing out. In the far corners had matriculated those who were fifty and older, those who had made this place their second (and possibly first) home and drank themselves silly. They were usually blond-haired, for whatever reason, and seemed to have stopped mentally developing in 1975.

Doug was working on his second glass of whiskey, looking forward to chewing on the ice cube, when a drunk patron sat down next to him. Normally, Doug would have been perturbed if someone had chosen to take the urinal directly next to him in an empty bathroom or sat next to him in an empty theater, but on that day, only one thing mattered.

"Cheers," the drunk said, smiling and offering up his glass for Doug to clink.

Doug clinked. He'd pegged the man for much older when he sat down, but on closer inspection, realized he wasn't much more than thirty-five, though years of drinking had taken their toll. He wasn't fat, but he was on the verge of having two chins. If he wore the right jackets, he could have hidden his developing gut. His hair was greasy and receding. He looked harmless.

Of the two television screens on the dark wooden walls, one showed highlights of the night's baseball games. Doug had played baseball as a child but no longer followed the sport. This was the type of bar where the sunburnt, blond alcoholics pushing fifty and above would come to watch the games. They'd cheer in excitement when their team scored a run and would scream in louder disappointment over bad calls. For Doug, sports were only a means to keep his body in peak condition, not a form of entertainment.

"Married?" the man asked, somehow sounding even sloppier than minutes earlier.

"Yup," Doug answered. "You?"

"Twice." The man smiled. "I'm Paxton. I was married twice. One stole my heart, and the other stole all my money." He ordered a shot and downed it before it even touched the counter. "Don't ever get married."

"Well, I'm already married."

"How's that going? You love your wife?"

"I'd say I do."

"I believe you believe you love her. But no matter how much you might love her, part of you wants to fuck every hot piece of ass you see, right?"

Doug took a sip of his drink.

"I'm right," Paxton said. "I loved my wife, the last one. I did. Just not as much as new pussy. You ever use Tinder?"

"No."

"Good. Don't. It's useful for women and women only. They get to choose any dick they want for the night. All it's done is made dating and finding a piece of ass even harder for normal guys. Also, if you're married, Tinder will only betray you. Your wife's friends and colleagues will find you."

This drunk was reading Doug's mind.

"I've had a lot of fun with this here," Paxton said, pulling a business card out of his wallet.

"CoinciDATE," Doug read. *What the fuck is this?*

"Give these guys a call. They'll find you all the ass you could ever want."

"I don't pay for sex," Doug said.

"To each his own," Paxton said. "But they aren't an escort service. Give them a call. You won't regret it."

Doug examined the card. Any time a stranger handed him anything, he was skeptical. But all he could think of was Talia. If this card could bring her closer to him, he'd give it a go.

"Can I also interest you in Beatitudinem?" Paxton pulled another card from his wallet.

Doug was no longer listening. It didn't matter, though, because Paxton just kept ordering more drinks and prattling on.

~~~

Doug's consultation at CoinciDATE was with a girl named Miranda. Before seeing her face, he knew she'd be a looker— every Miranda he'd met had been sexy. Some names could only belong to attractive people. He'd never met an attractive Joanne or a smart Tiffany.

When Miranda sat him down at her desk, he wasn't disappointed. As she explained the ins and outs of the company, he felt as though he were committing a crime. Not a serious crime, but as though he'd just come upon a hack that would make his life a whole lot better. His excitement grew as he watched the words flow from Miranda's mouth. She had a nice mouth.

"All I have is a name," Doug repeated, trying to figure out how legit the company was.

"A name is a lot more than many of our clients can provide," Miranda said. "A name is a great start. We also have a previous place of employment. We'll be able to find everything you could ever want to know about this girl."

Doug had to contain his excitement. He couldn't show just how giddy and optimistic he was. During the consultation, he'd kept his wedding ring in his pocket. When meeting women, regardless of what their relationship to him was or in what capacity they were meeting, he wanted to keep all options open. Miranda wasn't model-hot, but she was cute. Sometimes it was the simple-looking girls who drove Doug the craziest.

Capitolo 7

Miranda

The excitement of a new friend was like discovering a great new book after thinking there was nothing left to read. Miranda had gone as far as to write down a list of questions and comments concerning Charlotte's manuscript. She hadn't seen Charlotte since the dinner with Alexei, but two weeks later, she still couldn't stop thinking about her.

Charlotte had given nothing in terms of a synopsis, leaving Miranda to go in totally blind. There was no way she could have known what sort of writer Charlotte was, but it still caught her off guard that Charlotte's novel featured a dark and funny tale about a woman working as a translator for a mail-order-bride agency in Eastern Europe. Where the idea came from and how much of it was based in fact were among Miranda's questions.

Miranda's office was small, especially compared to Adam's or Alexei's. There was little in the way of personal mementos or décor. Were it not for her red hair, it would have looked like a white void, impossible to determine where wall met ceiling. Her desk towered as a futuristic monstrosity, like all of the furniture in the office. Her first client for the day was scheduled for nine a.m., and at 8:45, there was a knock on the door. She'd been waiting for her coffee to cool and hadn't even taken a sip.

"Come in," Miranda said.

A man in his mid-fifties with a tan complexion walked in wearing an expensive suit. He had a comb-over and a pencil-thin mustache. He didn't wear his thinning hair with shame. On the contrary, it seemed to empower him. Miranda recognized him immediately.

"Frank Sanchez," he said. "You probably recognize me from the commercials."

In fact, Miranda recognized him as the customer who'd forced her to remake his blended drink three times until he was satisfied with the consistency of the ice-chunks-and-drink-to-whipped-cream ratio. She never forgot the face of a rude customer. As she stared, she realized that in addition to being rude, he was one of the wealthiest attorneys in the city, and the star of a series of tacky commercials that had run for decades. Naturally, he didn't recognize her.

"How long have you been working here?" he asked.

"Sorry?"

"How long have you been working here? I was expecting to meet with the other guy, Adam something. He had a much bigger office."

"I assure you I can provide the same results as anyone else here."

"We'll see."

Frank sat looking at Miranda, waiting to see if she'd

break. Maybe he did remember her. Maybe he came here all those months later simply to berate her again.

"I'm here on behalf of my client. Do you know John O'Flannery?"

Everyone knew John O'Flannery. Besides being brother to the mayor, he was one of the city's wealthiest citizens and a prominent Catholic. He generously donated to many different charities and city events.

"Remind me your name," he said.

"Miranda."

"Are you discreet, Miranda?"

"That's what makes our business thrive."

"Mr. O'Flannery has a son around your age. Though he might not be able to show it publicly, Mr. O'Flannery knows the pressure his son is under, having to keep up appearances, be the poster child of a good Catholic, be seen doing the correct things with the correct people. Clean as a whistle. His son is all those things. He's a good boy. He's a homosexual."

"I see."

"No, I don't think you do. Mr. O'Flannery is aware of this. Though his son has never told him, he's aware. He loves his son more than anything. All he wants is for his son to be happy, but he's scared. Maybe in a place like Vermont, or maybe even LA, this is something the people would be able to accept, but in a backwards town like this one? The people aren't ready. Last year alone, two men Mr. O'Flannery knows personally lost their sons to suicide. They'll never admit that their sons killed themselves due to being tormented for their sexuality. Mr. O'Flannery wants his son to be happy. He wants his son to know he can be who he is. He wants him to find someone. There is a someone, in fact."

That someone was a handsome twenty-two-year-old Italian in town as part of a work-exchange program. He worked in the same building as O'Flannery's son, and all the signs were there that O'Flannery Jr. had an enormous crush on the young man.

"Money isn't an issue here," Frank Sanchez said. "You make this happen, we'll double your fee."

He left her his business card before exiting.

"You're doing really well," Alexei told her after the meeting.

Miranda smiled. She never knew if he meant what he said. Was it an empty compliment, sarcasm, or genuine encouragement? Miranda was never confident of her skills when it came to a new job. She wasn't lazy, for sure, but she always second-guessed every aspect of what she did. It was that way at the café and every other place. If she kept a job for more than a month, it meant she must be doing something right; she only wished she could determine what that was.

She was coming up on her one-month anniversary at CoinciDATE, and the stats showed she was one of the top earners. She could doubt herself all she wanted, but numbers don't lie. She was nowhere near the stratospheric income Adam earned, but she was miles beyond the rest. The company didn't keep average employees who did decent work. You were either a top earner or a two-week wonder. There were so many of the latter that Miranda never bothered to learn most of her colleagues' names. At any moment, there were eleven to fifteen employees.

Miranda did so well because she was hungry for it. She'd never been handed anything in her life, nor been allowed the luxury of dreaming big. Nice clothes and cars and meals had been a fantasy until the money she was earning opened her eyes to the reality that she could indeed obtain these things.

"Join me in my office a moment," Alexei said.

Miranda came. Adam stood in the corner on his phone.

"I try to avoid formal *meetings*," Alexei said, quoting the word with his fingers. "They're really just power plays by managers to say things that can be summed up in a three-sentence email. So don't take this as a meeting. Take this as you guys educating me. While we're a relatively young company, I'd still like to hear your ideas on how we could improve. Adam?"

Adam shrugged his shoulders.

"Actually," Miranda said, "after my morning meeting, I was thinking, we really ought to expand. We've got some pretty high-profile clients, and that's just for our small town. Imagine if we opened up branches in LA or San Diego. I think expansion is the way to go."

"That's cute, Miranda," Adam said.

"Let's hear your idea then," she said.

"We should just keep doing what we're doing."

"Thanks for your feedback, Miranda," Alexei said, "but Adam is right. The reason we're so effective is because we're a small operation." Alexei looked at his watch. "Excuse me, Miranda. I need to talk to Adam privately."

Miranda left Alexei's office to find herself face to face with Charlotte. It took Miranda a moment to articulate her thoughts in a way that was coherent, but she didn't entirely succeed.

"I'm happy you liked my book," Charlotte beamed. "It's always so nerve-wracking when someone reads it. You never know what they're going to say about it. Tell you what, as a token of my appreciation, let me buy you lunch after I have my talk with Alexei. Deal?"

"Sounds great," Miranda said.

Miranda waited impatiently while Charlotte had her meeting. Unlike at the café, no one yelled at you here for being idle. Often, she found herself scrolling through social media, reading, and scrolling YouTube in her downtime. That downtime was often accompanied by Adam loitering in her periphery, although he rarely engaged in conversation with her.

"I hear she's not going to be here much longer," Adam said, not looking up from his phone.

"Who?"

Adam tipped his head toward Alexei's office.

"What's that supposed to mean?"

"Just something I heard."

"You're talking nonsense."

"Whatever."

Not five minutes later, the door to Alexei's office burst open violently, and Charlotte stormed off, tears in her eyes. Miranda got up and tried to catch up with her, but the girl was already out the door by the time Alexei had grabbed Miranda by the shoulder.

"What happened?" she asked.

Alexei sniffled and rubbed his eyes. "Yeah, that was unfortunate. I believe in giving people chances, but Charlotte wasn't a team player. I'm usually spot on about who to hire too. This reflects poorly. Not on me, it just reflects poorly. Well, the silver lining here is you get to take on all her clients."

"Congratulations," Adam said.

Miranda ran out to the parking lot. It was empty. No clouds or birds or people to make Miranda feel anything other than empty. She immediately wrote Charlotte an incoherent email. Two days passed with no reply. Then a third and a fourth.

They'd only had one dinner together.

~~~

Charlotte's former clients were fascinating. On Saturday, Miranda followed a girl with a high forehead and broad shoulders. Her name was Gabby, and a classmate was desperately in love with her. Miranda liked the guy well enough. He was even cute, but as soon as he began talking about his unrequited love for Gabby and how he was destined to be with her if she'd only give him a chance, he became a weak, pathetic worm. If he ever talked to Gabby the way he'd spoken to her, he'd be remaining celibate for quite some time.

The following Monday, Miranda arrived at work to discover that her new client meeting was with none other than Gabby herself. Gabby, as it turned out, was desperately in love with a close friend of the man who was desperately in love with her. Obviously, Miranda couldn't disclose any of that information, but the prospect of actively observing people involved in a love triangle ignited a fire within her. She'd be an unseen observer in a melodrama unfolding before her very eyes. Eventually, there'd be some sort of three-way confrontation between the parties, and depending on what information she gave and when, she could be directly responsible for how the climax unfolded.

Another target Miranda had been following was a man in his late twenties. He had light brown hair and was a tad below average height. She followed him into a small mom-and-pop coffee shop where he planted himself behind a table. There were comfortable-looking chairs with cushions all around, yet he chose the wooden chairs with the wooden backs. He sat there and pulled out a pile of books. He read one for twenty minutes before switching to the next to read for an hour. Then he pulled out a third. He rotated between the three for about four hours before finally heading out.

Miranda followed him to the exact same café the next day, where he did the same thing. On the third day, she followed him to a different café, where he sat with his pile of books. He never checked his phone, and save for the baristas, he never spoke with anyone. He never lifted his head to see what was taking place in the world around him. His eyes were glued to his books.

He did this four to five times a week, always beginning in the early morning. Did he not work? Miranda couldn't believe someone was paying money for this information. She couldn't believe someone was obsessed with this person.

But, strangely enough, Miranda soon found herself slightly obsessed with him. She didn't worry about him catching her staring. He never looked up. What was it about him? He wasn't particularly good looking. He was dressed decently enough. Why couldn't he read at home? Why was he reading so many books at once? The baristas didn't seem to mind him. He gave them money, seemed to always put his spare change in the tip jar, and showed gratitude for their service. Other patrons were noisy, rearranging chairs and speaking at obnoxiously loud levels. He merely sat and read. On her drive home, Miranda's head ached from being unable to get such a forgettable person out of her mind.

She stopped at the shopping outlets to treat herself. She

used to go to the outlets often, though she never knew why. She was never able to afford the things she wanted, but she tortured herself all the same. Now, thanks to CoinciDATE, she could. She swiped her card in three different stores without even bothering to look at the price tags or receipts. Cinque Terre, the Amalfi Coast, Rome, Tuscany . . . Did she dare consider that one day these places would no longer be only dreams for her?

Miranda watched people, gave the information she collected to desperate people, and those desperate people walked out with profound optimism and hope. Meanwhile, Miranda walked away rich. Like the food or gas industry, Miranda found herself working in a business that would never lose its customers. Sure, some would come while others would go, but as long as the human heart pumped emotions and desires along with blood, people would come to her.

Adam had told her not to worry about the success rate, as they never promised customers they'd end up with their objects of lust; all they promised was to lay the groundwork. But after spending so much time getting invested in these peoples' lives, Miranda couldn't simply stop at delivering her findings to her clients. She felt a deep desire to know what became of them. How many ended up in happy relationships and how many ended in disaster?

Most of all, Miranda wondered what would become of Ethel. Ethel was a woman of seventy-six, because no one named Ethel had been born after 1950. On a good day, Ethel stood at five feet and was so small and fragile a light breeze would blow her away. She wore little old lady pants that complemented her old lady slippers. Like an old lady, she dragged her feet across the floor with an awful scraping sound every time she approached.

Ethel, as it turned out, had as much lust and longing in her heart as anyone else. Her husband had died twenty years earlier, and she hadn't been with another man since. After hearing that story, Miranda desperately wanted to help the old woman. When Miranda found out that the man of Ethel's desires was a twenty-year-old boy named Jake who worked at an electronics store, she wanted nothing more than to get her head examined.

She remembered when Shaun had walked in. He was five foot eight, had short, dark hair, and wore a Puma jacket. His style seemed like he was trying to embrace a Eurotrash look despite being from the same town as she was. Perhaps he wasn't happy with his identity and thought if he dressed a certain way people would think he was more interesting.

"What can I do for you?" she asked.

Clients always had a different way of answering that question. Some got straight to the point. Some beat around the bush, clearly embarrassed to be there and searching for a tactful way to get to what they wanted. Some gave their whole life stories. Others talked about how great they were, particularly in the field of love, and about how they were only doing this either to try it out or because they were bored. When clients walked in and sat down before her, Miranda tried to ascertain what kind of response they'd give just by looking at them.

"We went to high school together," Shaun said.

"Did we?" Miranda wasn't trying to be dismissive or to pretend she didn't know him. She simply didn't remember.

"We did. I was a year above you. Don't feel bad if you don't remember me. I don't forget faces. You were on the track team, right?"

"I was."

"I did track for a year. Primarily, I was a swimmer."

She looked at him. His shoulders were broad enough, but when he sat down, his body betrayed him as his beer belly pushed his shirt outward.

"Do you like working here?" He scanned her office. What was he looking for?

"Are you here for a job inquiry?" Miranda asked.

"No, I'm here because I'm desperate," he said.

Miranda was surprised by his bluntness. All the clients were desperate, but they never just up and said as much. A part of her admired him.

"I've been in love only once in my life," he said. "That was three years ago. Have you ever been in love?"

Miranda feigned a smile. "Let's talk about you."

"I was in love. Before her, I'd had two girlfriends. I thought they were pretty in the beginning. Obviously, they had qualities to make me want to go out with them, but do you know what happened on both occasions? Within days of dating, you know, being an official item, I was utterly bored. I felt absolutely nothing toward them. I didn't hate them or wish them any ill will, but I had no passion. I thought then that maybe I just wasn't meant to love anyone.

"Then I met Melissa. She was so goddamn beautiful. I have ridiculously high standards as it is, but she was beyond beautiful. No other girl could compare. I spent a month just looking at her, not daring to talk to her. What could I say to someone so beautiful? Do you know what I did? One day I said *fuck it* and added her as a friend on Facebook. She'd seen me before, but it would be a lie to say we were anything resembling acquaintances, let alone fucking friends. She had no reason to engage in conversation with me, but she accepted my friend request nonetheless. So I messaged her and asked, 'Why don't we get acquainted sometime?'"

"What did she say?"

"She told me to fuck off. And why not? What did this girl who knew nothing about me have to talk to me about? You don't have to answer, but I'm sure you get dozens of messages a day from random guys you've never met, insisting that they're nice, that they've read your profile and think you have a lot in common. How was I any different from any of those other guys? I don't know. The girls you send messages to on Tinder are strangers, too, but it's okay there. Write the same exact thing and send that to a girl on Facebook, and suddenly you're a stalker. A psychopath. A creep. I was upset when she told me to fuck off. Well, her exact words were, 'I see no reason why we should get acquainted.'

"I didn't stop thinking she was beautiful, though. But what could I do? I can't force someone to love me. So I looked at her pictures every morning and every evening, worked myself up and got depressed, and found it hard to think about other girls. But eventually, about two months on, I was able to continue with my life. Of course, I still thought she was beautiful, and I remembered just how beautiful she was, and that was a depressing reminder, but I had a life to live."

He paused. Miranda was a good listener, and she did just that, but there was a limit to how much she could listen to. When her friends would ramble on and on, she'd hurry them to the point. The kindest thing a human being could do was not waste someone else's time. She had gotten used to tuning out boring stories and BS background, as it was the majority of her job, but they were more often than not mercifully brief.

"Like I said, two months went by. It was my birthday, actually. I was out drinking with friends. Got home pretty late, appropriately smashed. Before knocking out for the night, I got on Facebook to see which people I don't give a shit about wished me a happy birthday. Those were all there. All the people I went to high school with and was never friends with and couldn't give less of a fuck about. But among all that trash was a message from Melissa. It said, *Happy Birthday! Sorry for my rudeness before. It was uncalled for. I hope you have a great birthday.*

"I must've read that message five times over, not believing it could possibly be true. How could it be? I'd made my attempt and failed miserably. She was right. She had no reason to get acquainted with me. We hadn't spoken in two months. When we did speak, it was only that one exchange. What had motivated her to wish me a happy birthday? Pure human kindness? I was nothing to her. I wrote her back. She wrote back almost immediately. Turns out, she'd had a boyfriend at the time I'd written her. She didn't when she wrote me happy birthday. We talked until four in the morning. Back and forth. All my stress and fear had gone out the window. I talked to her about pure and utter nonsense, and no matter what I wrote, she kept responding. I did the only thing there was to do and asked her on a date."

He perked up in his chair. During the storytelling, he hadn't looked Miranda in the eyes. He twiddled nervously with his fingers. But he gave a slight smile after the word *date*.

"The date happened four days later. We met for the first time, officially, face to face. And guess how it went? It was a train wreck. The girl I'd spoken with on Facebook certainly wasn't present that night at the restaurant. Every attempt at making her laugh was a failure. She saw right through me. My suggestion for getting drinks afterward was crushed immediately. I walked her to her Uber, and before she got in the car, something came over me. I'm not sure what motivated me to do it, considering how the date had gone, but I asked if she'd be interested in seeing a movie with me. She was.

"After the movie, we walked around a bit. I tried to kiss her. She rejected that. I went home. Obviously, I was disappointed, but at the same time, I was just happy to be around her. She was different. She laughed, smiled, and joked. It was great. She agreed to meet for a third time. That time, I didn't plan anything. No fancy dinners, no movies, just one another's company. We walked, sat, drank coffee, and talked late into the night. We were near her place, so I walked her home. I was ready to give her a hug and walk myself home. When I hugged her, she held on. It was tight. When I pulled my head back, she was staring right at me. I stared, too, perhaps a little too long. I leaned in and kissed her. She was mine.

"The next six months were the happiest I'd ever known. She was quite busy, being a med student and all, but when she was mine, she was mine. I'll never forget the first time we made love. Believe me, she made me wait. The longer she made me wait, the more I had to have it. When it finally happened, good God it was wonderful. Even better than that, though, was afterward when she got cold. She went to my closet, pulled out one of my T-shirts, put it on, and snuggled up next to me. I'll never forget seeing her walking around my apartment the next morning with my big T-shirt on and nothing else. I'd never seen such a beautiful sight in my life. I had won. Life couldn't possibly get better.

"I told her I loved her, and she told me she loved me.

I'd never told a girl that before. I'd been in love before, but it was never reciprocated. When she said those words back to me, that was it. I could die happily. It was too good to be true. Literally. Two days after she told me she loved me, she sent me a message on Facebook, 'We won't be seeing one another anymore.' And she deleted me. I called her a million times, wrote her, showed up at her house, messaged her friends, I even wrote to her mom. I got no response. Nothing. Not a word.

"Weeks went by, then months. Still not a single word. I can't speak for everyone, but I think it can be agreed that getting dumped sucks. It depends on the seriousness of the relationship, but no one likes to get dumped. I've been dumped before. I've dealt with it. What I don't know how to deal with is the most important person in my life simply vanishing without explanation. A sick part of me thinks it would be easier if she were dead. But she isn't. She's alive. I'm just not in her life anymore, where she remains my life. I don't know how a human can do that to another human. An explanation wouldn't ease the pain, but it'd be a helluva lot better than nothing at all."

"So you've found another girl, are finally moving beyond Melissa, and want us to help you?" Miranda asked, a tad tactlessly. It wasn't how she intended to ask, but the story was starting to make her feel uncomfortable.

"On the contrary," Shaun said. "I haven't found anyone. How could I? She's the only one I ever loved. The only one I ever will. I can't replace her. I haven't seen her in years. She's married now. Got married a year ago."

"That sounds pretty definitive then," Miranda said.

"It does. But does it have to be? I've realized something.

I will never love again. I can't. I don't believe in fate, but it was fate nonetheless that she wished me a happy birthday two months after telling me to go fuck myself. It's fate she left me without warning or explanation; it's fate she got married; and it's fate that after years of no communication and moving, I've discovered the gym she goes to. This is all God's way of teaching me something. I don't know what it is, but my time away from her was meant to teach me something. I needed to grow. I needed to be better. I want you to follow her and find out as much information as you can."

"Shaun, this might sound counterintuitive on my part," Miranda said, "but this seems like a terrible idea."

"You don't have to tell me. She's married. I get it. People change. She's changed. So have I. I need her back in my life. I need to show her that I'm the man she wants to spend her life with. I'm going to give her everything she's ever wanted."

"If I take you on as my client, you do understand that I don't guarantee she gets back with you?" Miranda asked. "The only thing I can do is provide you with information. The rest is on you."

"I'm aware. I'm willing to do everything it takes to get her back. I have to, because if I don't, I'm going to kill myself. I swear it, I'll end myself."

Miranda thought about that as she drove home. *Io vado a Roma per trovare un amico*, she repeated after the audio. A friend. She had a friend who couldn't even roll her fucking r's.

She stopped at a bar. She wasn't ready for sleep, or to be alone. She didn't want to be with friends either. She wanted humans around her. She wanted to hear their voices and know that they were there. A bar.

She ordered a gin and tonic and rested her head on her

arms on the hard wooden bar top. She'd never liked threats, especially when it was friends or family trying to guilt-trip her into doing something for their benefit. With Shaun, it was different. His eyes didn't show any indication that it was a threat. She believed it was the simple truth. The world he'd created for himself was unlivable without Melissa. Despite Shaun's affirmative nod that he understood her job was only to provide information, a part of her felt he depended on her to get him back with Melissa. Otherwise, he'd be dead. It was her responsibility, whether anyone else was willing to call it that or not. Ethel had a better shot with Jake.

She ordered a second gin and tonic.

There were several couples at the bar, young and old alike. Some were sitting close and seemed nothing but teeth and laughter, the kinds of couples lonely singles scorned. Others sat across from one another with their eyes and fingers glued to their phones.

Miranda's anger at what Shaun had put her through turned into sympathy. He wasn't bad looking, and clearly had a good head on his shoulders. What a tragedy that someone so young and kind should waste so much time on sadness and loss. How many people out there were like Shaun? How many future authors and filmmakers and musicians would never unleash their potential because they lived in a pit of despair, longing for love?

She'd never loved anyone as intensely as Shaun loved Melissa, and she was quite certain no one had ever loved her that much either. Was Melissa worth it? If she met Melissa, would she see in her what Shaun did?

On her second gin and tonic, she got so sad she nearly cried—not for love lost, but for love never had. Her longest relationship had been with Chris. They'd dated a year and a half. They had a lot of fun. More good moments than bad, yet it ended anyway. And the saddest part about the relationship ending was how not sad Miranda was. She felt guilty for feeling so little sadness about the whole thing. Within two weeks, Chris had found someone else, and other guys had caught her attention as well. She didn't even know where Chris was now.

She needed to fuck something. No emotions, no romance, only pure flesh pounding flesh. She needed to get drunk and fuck something. Most of the handsome candidates were already taken, she noted as she scanned the bar. Perhaps a third gin and tonic would turn the average-looking candidates into handsome ones. She was worried about what would happen if she had to drink a fourth.

"Mind if I order a gin and tonic before you drink them all?" a voice behind her asked.

She looked up to see a smiling face covered in beard. It was one of those perfectly styled and trimmed beards, the kind guys have when they want to show you how rugged they are without putting in the effort. His perfectly messy head of slightly curled hair complemented his perfect beard. He would have been a beanpole if it weren't for his broad shoulders. He was a picturesque JC Penney model. Everything about his face and wardrobe seemed as though it had been cut from a catalog and glued together to make the perfect, rugged, handsome boy.

"You been watching me?" she asked.

"Most of the people who sit alone at this bar and drink as much as you do are women in their forties or fifties, looking for young meat, or else homeless. You're not homeless, are you?"

"No, but I just celebrated my forty-fifth birthday," she

said.

He smiled. "Let me buy myself a gin and tonic, and when I safely have mine, allow me to buy you one as well."

"By all means."

"Wonderful."

"Cheers."

They clinked their glasses. He removed the cucumbers from his drink. Before he could discard them, she took them for herself and ate them, savoring the remnants of gin she tasted on them. He seemed like the type of guy whose diet consisted entirely of e-cigarettes. To Miranda's surprise, he didn't have the musky smell she expected. He smelled like fresh laundry.

"What do you do?" he asked.

"Something more interesting than what you do, I'm sure."

"Are you sure?"

"I'd gamble that I do."

"I'm a sex therapist," he said. "Well, a consultant really. I counsel individuals and couples who are having trouble satisfying their partners, or receiving satisfaction themselves."

Miranda raised her eyebrows. She didn't care what he had to say for the rest of the night. She'd already decided she was going to fuck him, and all he had to do was not fuck it up by saying something ridiculous or inane. Perhaps he did; Miranda wasn't listening all that attentively. A sex therapist had to be good in bed.

His apartment was small. There were clothes on the floor and unwashed dishes in the sink. She let it slide. Perhaps he wasn't expecting any company, and besides, she wasn't planning on moving in.

His lips tasted like e-cigarette, and he shoved his tongue into her mouth far too aggressively. His kisses were sloppy, and she didn't see how he could enjoy them, but she liked how his body felt pressed up against hers. When he took his shirt off, he was hairless and even skinnier than she was.

Once he was inside her, she wanted to close her eyes and feel his body thrusting into hers. That hope was short lived, as he wouldn't stop kissing her. That was fine at first, but he kept grabbing her head and looking her in the eyes.

"You're beautiful," he said, his face inches from hers.

She rode him harder, closing her eyes.

He grabbed her face and once more said, "You're beautiful."

"Thanks," she said.

He kissed her, soft and slow. "I'm not just saying this. You're really beautiful."

She stopped riding him and got on her back.

"What're you doing?" he said. "Everything okay?"

"Christ, everything is fine. Are we going to fuck or talk?"

"Did I do something wrong?"

"Jesus fucking Christ," she said.

He put his head down, looking like a sad, silly dog, defeated and ashamed. She could have laughed. For all his beautiful curls and perfectly trimmed beard, he looked ridiculous in that naked and sad position.

"Come on, let's keep going," she said, even though she didn't particularly want to finish. She wasn't close to climaxing, but screwing him at least was better than listening to him talk.

After he finished, she dressed quickly and gave him a soft hug goodbye. His sex skills were sorely lacking for someone in his profession. She wondered if his clients ever asked for a refund.

When she got home, she felt as though the opposite of getting laid had happened to her. It was time she'd never get back.

Chapter 8

Barry

❝A female can never love a man as much as a man loves a female," Kenneth would say.

"Really?" Barry once asked. Barry felt stupid, aware that he always answered Kenneth with a silly question. Kenneth was the most intelligent person Barry knew, so he felt bad for constantly throwing silly questions at his wisdom.

"Of course it's true. Think about it. If women loved men as much as men love women, why don't women put even a quarter of the amount of work men do into courtship? Why is it men who always have to do everything? You can't even call it a relationship. A relationship implies something mutual or equal. Men bust their asses to win the affection and attention of women. Women just have to sit there and look pretty. It takes no effort on their part. A guy like you or me could spend years trying to win a woman's heart. We could do everything right and by the book, but she'll always choose the guy with the bigger cock, or the more handsome face. Loving females is a curse. They get to sit there on their pedestals, all high and mighty like the cunts they are, and choose from dozens of suitors. Could you imagine if we had it that easy?"

"I can't," Barry said.

Kenneth had been right. He always was. The girl behind the counter (the possibly French one) probably saw nearly a hundred guys a day. She could have anyone she wanted, whereas Barry sweated and shat just thinking about her. How was he expected to actually go up to her and introduce himself? He couldn't very well buy another parking permit. Barry cursed his cock, the useless appendage that did him no favors and remained unutilized.

He saw no point in going to class that day. He saw no point in being on campus. The same faces in their same positions only depressed him. The thought of being in the same vicinity as the girl at student services but not being able to do a thing about it saddened him. He bought lunch from the vending machines (a bag of chips and a Cherry Coke) and returned to his car.

While his car was an embarrassing pile of junk, it was the only place he felt truly comfortable and secure with his thoughts. It was stuffy, the roof liner hung loose, the AC didn't work, and there was no auxiliary port, but nonetheless, he liked being inside the car. Thoughts of loneliness, useless cocks, and unobtainable girls disappeared whenever he sat in the death trap that was his '98 Honda Accord.

He pulled forward, not going home but not quite sure where he was going. That often happened when he got into his car. His mind turned off. He'd listen to dull music or radio DJs and drive for miles without understanding how he'd arrived at his destination. He drove down one street that had three Subways in less than a mile.

His car ended up in a parking lot. Surrounding him were the usual establishments—a Taco Bell, a grocery store, a donut shop, and a mom-and-pop-looking café. He didn't particularly like coffee. He'd finished his bag of chips but felt too guilty about getting himself Taco Bell. Feeling hot and stuffy inside the car, he got out and found himself in line at the café.

The girls working behind the counter were all cute. *Great,* he thought. That was the last thing he needed. His hometown wasn't known for being a plethora of beauties, but of late, it seemed like more and more beautiful girls were coming out of the woodwork. At least at Taco Bell, he most likely would have been surrounded by people as ugly as he was.

He ordered a drink with a ridiculous name that contained more calories than the chips he'd just eaten. It turned out to be some chocolate monstrosity with caffeine and whipped cream and chunks of ice. He found a seat in the corner of the store and planted himself there.

Around him, people were studying, working behind their laptops, and reading novels. He hadn't brought his backpack inside. He checked Facebook on his phone. No new messages. He scrolled through some of Kenneth's old messages. Then he checked out different girls' profiles. Kenneth used to add random girls to his friends list just to see what would happen. Barry couldn't bring himself to do that.

Next to him, a guy dressed like a cowboy butted into the conversation of a pair of middle-aged women. They laughed loudly at his cheesy jokes, and he laughed the loudest of all.

Barry's attention rested on the redhead sitting alone in the opposite corner. Like him, she had her eyes glued to her phone. Barry didn't usually pay attention to redheads, but something about her was radiant. That night, he decided, he'd imagine a threesome with her and the possibly French girl. He played out in his mind how it would go down. He'd introduce himself to the possibly French girl, and she'd greet him with a big smile. She'd say she'd noticed him around campus and was waiting for him to approach her, as she was too shy to do it herself. She'd be friendly, but wouldn't put out immediately. That would make her a slut, and Barry had no interest in sluts. He'd win her affection by demonstrating his value, and she'd see what a great guy he really was through his actions and kindness and character.

She'd be walking at night, alone and defenseless. Out of the darkness, two thugs would approach with sinister intentions. She'd try to fend them off, but given that she was a woman, they'd easily overpower her. At the last minute, Barry would emerge from the shadows—the last person she ever expected. He'd hold them off just long enough for her to gather her strength and run away. In his fantasy, he'd suffer several serious blows to the face. Even with blood in his eyes and his muscles weakening, he'd continue to fight. At last, bystanders would come to his aid and drive off the hooligans.

When all was safe, the possibly French girl would see who had saved her and what it had cost him. At a loss for words, she'd walk him back to her place. She'd tenderly wash and nurse his wounds. With each towel dab to his cut and bruised face, she'd lean in closer to him on the couch. He'd smell her perfume and feel her heartbeat. She'd thank him endlessly for saving her life. Being as modest as he was, he'd laugh and say anyone would have done it.

"No," she'd answer. "They wouldn't. My boyfriend wouldn't have."

"Oh, you have a boyfriend?" he'd ask.

"I did, but he wasn't brave. Not like you."

He must have been French, he'd think. *They aren't known for their bravery.*

"Thanks," she'd say, then kiss him softly on the cheek. "Does it hurt?"

"It's okay."

"Let me see the bruises on your back and stomach."

"You really don't have to." Barry was modest and humble.

"I can help."

She'd gently pull off his shirt. Eyeing his wounds, she'd slide her hands ever so tenderly over his black-and-blue parts. Her touch would be light, almost tickling.

"My ex-boyfriend wouldn't have saved me. Not like you did," she'd say, kissing his cheek again. But this time, she wouldn't remove her lips from his face. As her hands massaged his stomach and worked their way down, she'd take his earlobe in her mouth and suck on it. Then she'd kiss his neck while her hand went down his pants.

Before he could comprehend what was happening, the door to her place would open, and the redhead from the coffee shop would be there. Staring at the situation on the couch, she'd be at a loss for words, but the possibly French girl would explain.

"Barry, this is my best friend and roommate. We share everything together."

Before Barry could fully take in the possibly French girl's words, Redhead would be on her way to the couch. She'd sit down in Barry's lap and begin kissing him. As he kissed her, the possibly French girl would slide her tongue down along Barry's dick. Slow, so slowly in the beginning, to the point that Barry would think he was going to explode. She'd use her tongue to lick around the hole at the tip of Barry's dick. They'd alternate between sucking his dick and kissing him and then kissing one another.

While he was sat down, they'd stand so he could see every inch of them. That was one thing about sex that always worried Barry, the fact that if the action started while they were already lying down, he'd barely have a chance to see all the glory of their bodies. He needed to be able to see what they had before he could stick it in them.

One, probably the possibly French girl, would remove her top while facing him so he could see her tits, while the other would have her back to him and would take her pants off so he could see her ass. Once their respective articles of clothing were off, they'd switch positions so he could see everything they had. That was another thing that saddened Barry, that if he was looking at a chick's tits, he couldn't also see her ass unless there was a mirror involved. No problem. The possibly French girl's walls and ceiling were covered with mirrors.

They'd touch one another and lick each other, driving him crazy as he sat, watching everything. He'd fuck them for a good thirty minutes before shooting his load all over their faces, an equal amount for both.

Barry had barely touched his drink, but when his fantasy ended, there was wet residue on his jeans, seeping through his boxers and reaching the surface of the denim. His dick was so hard he could have shot his load right then and there. He nearly did shoot a load, not out of erotic excitement, but out of fear, as the redhead he'd pictured with her mouth around the tip of his cock was hovering above him. Had his thoughts summoned her to him? Was she a clairvoyant who knew what a pervert he was?

He looked down. He didn't know what else he should do. Women never approached him, not on purpose. He couldn't think of anything he could possibly have to say to her. She was even prettier up close, so he didn't mind that, but he did mind her being so close and making him feel uncomfortable. *Please say something*, he begged.

"Can I sit?"

Barry looked down at his pants. *Idiot!* he thought to himself. *Why make it so fucking blatant?* He wasn't subtle at all, and she followed his eye movements. Red in the face, he nodded, and she sat down next to him.

"Hi," she said.

"Hi," Barry said, looking in her direction but not quite capable of looking her in the eye.

"I'm Miranda. What's your name?"

"Barry."

"Don't meet a lot of Barrys," she said. "Barry, can I tell you something?"

"Okay."

"Barry, you've been staring at me since you sat down. It's not even my intuition or something like that. You've been blatantly staring at me."

"I, uh—" Barry was done. He had absolutely nothing to say. He had been staring at her, and any lies or excuses he could have conjured up about why escaped him.

"Do you find me attractive, Barry? Is that why you were staring at me?"

Barry put his head down. He tried to will her to disappear.

"Barry," she said, "I'm not here to chastise you. I'm not mad. It's just something I noticed. You were looking at me. I assumed you were going to come up to me and say something, but you didn't, so I came up to say something to you."

"I'm sorry," he said.

"It's okay. So, do you think I'm attractive?"

"Look, I uh . . . " He was visibly sweating. "I'm sorry."

"Stop saying you're sorry."

"Sorry."

"There ya go. You know, if you stare at a girl and don't go say something to her, it's a little weird."

"I'm, uh . . . "

"I know," she said. "You're sorry."

"I *am* sorry," he said. "I didn't mean to make you feel uncomfortable. I didn't realize I was staring."

"I don't mind," she said. "Do you come here often?"

"No. Not at all, actually."

"What brought you here today?"

"I don't know, really. I just kind of ended up here. I wasn't really thinking about why."

"What do you do for a living?"

Barry wanted to lie. He wanted to invent something cool, something that painted him as a mysterious lone wolf that would pique her interest. Something that would inspire her to ask questions about him. But that wouldn't work with her. She'd already caught him staring at her, on the verge of shooting his load.

"I'm a dishwasher at my dad's friend's place," he said.

"I've washed dishes," she said. "I worked in customer

service at a café. I didn't love it."

"Oh."

"Yeah, 'oh,'" she repeated.

There was a pause. Barry played around with the straw in his drink.

"Do you have a special someone in your life?" she asked.

She's read my mind, Barry thought. *She's testing me. If I say no, it's a fuck-up, because it means she was interested and I ruined any and all shots by saying no. If I say yes, it's a trap, because there's no way a girl this beautiful could ever be interested in me. I can't win this one.*

"I don't, but—"

He wasn't sure why he said but. There was no but. There was only no.

"But?" She tilted her head.

"Nothing."

"No, come on. You can tell me. What's with the *but*? Is there a special girl in your life?"

"It's stupid, really," he said.

"Try me. Nothing you can say could surprise me."

Barry looked at her for the longest he had since she'd sat down. There was something she was concealing from him, but he was blind as to what it was. All things considered, he didn't see what he could say to her that was weirder than what he'd already done in her presence.

"There is a girl, but, well, she doesn't know I exist. She works at my school. I only see her in passing. Because she works in student services, I really have no reason to ever see her or talk to her. I want to, but I don't know how."

She was smiling. It made him uncomfortable. Had he

said something amusing? He was embarrassed simply thinking those thoughts, let alone sharing them with a stranger.

"If you stare at her the way you were staring at me, then she'll definitely have noticed," Miranda said.

Would she? Barry began to panic. He wanted to swallow himself and implode, to be forgotten by the world. He could no longer bear the torment and embarrassment.

"How often do you think about this girl?"

"Often."

"I think today is your lucky day, Barry. I can help you."

"How?"

~~~

That night, Barry plopped onto his bed and tried desperately to recapture his fantasy from the café. When he jerked off, he never liked to imagine things out of order. Even if his mind tried to force him to imagine having sex doggy-style, he couldn't allow that before the girl had given him head for several minutes. The fantasy was so explicit and overwhelming that Barry shot his load before Miranda had even taken off her panties. Barry was disappointed, but the load itself was one of the biggest and most potent he'd shot in a while. Well, he'd just have to continue the fantasy the next day.

Now that his hard-on had been tamed temporarily, he could consider what Miranda had told him. Barry didn't believe in God. He didn't believe in much of anything. But he didn't think it possible that it was sheer coincidence that Miranda had sat at his table and offered him a solution to the problem that had been tormenting him. Miranda, who looked like an angel, was an angel sent specifically to help him get what he wanted. If

Miranda had been sent to help him, it therefore meant that he was meant to meet the girl who worked at student services, and she was meant to be his. All the pieces were falling into place. This was the work of gods. Gods of fate and coincidence.

Miranda would do all the hard work. All he had to do was memorize the script and not fuck it up. He also had to save money. Miranda wasn't cheap. Washing dishes wasn't the worst thing ever. No one bothered him. He didn't have to work with customers, but the days were long and tedious, and his father's friend was a bit of a cunt. Barry often found himself working an hour or two after his shift ended, with no extra pay. He was being paid under the table, so if he wanted the little money he was entitled to, he had to be an obedient little dog.

Barry was terrible at saving money. He'd have to cut out all the McDonalds before and after class, no more in-between-class sodas from the vending machines, no more buying video games he'd only play once and relegate to some shelf to collect dust. *She's worth it*, he told himself. Was it worth it to lose a chance with the most beautiful woman ever just so his fat ass could drink Cherry Coke four times a day?

Since he was up, he walked to his fridge and grabbed himself a Cherry Coke. The burning sensation he felt in his throat as he gulped was comforting. By that point, his erection had returned, and he decided to finish what he'd started.

Capitolo 9

Miranda

Miranda stood in line to buy a parking permit she didn't need. She wouldn't lose sleep over fifty dollars, as the money coming in from Barry would more than cover it.

Her phone vibrated. It was the attorney, Frank Sanchez. She knew without looking. Twice a week for the past two weeks, he'd been texting her one-word messages: *Update?*

Barry's girl towered over most. Miranda considered herself tall by girl standards, but this woman had legs for miles. Miranda couldn't see what all the fuss was about. The woman before her wasn't bad-looking, but she didn't see how a guy could lose his mind over her. *To each his own*, she thought.

Miranda was next in line, and the girl gave her a small smile. Miranda noticed her big, cat-like eyes. Perhaps that was enough to enchant a guy.

"That's a really cute bag," the girl said.

Miranda was proud of her Louis Vuitton bag. It was one of the most expensive items she'd ever purchased. "Thank you."

"I've always wanted one like that," the girl said. "Did you get it at the outlet?"

"I did," Miranda said. "Do you go there often?"

"I go to the gym near there."

"I've been looking for a new gym. The one I go to is close, but it's ridiculously busy, and the staff leaves a lot to be desired. Do you like your gym?"

"I love it. It's small and cozy. I usually go late at night when no one is there and people can't see how awkward I look when I run on the treadmill."

"Well, maybe I'll see you there sometime. I'm Miranda, by the way. What's your name?"

"I'm Nastya."

Miranda didn't want to push it, but the girl was giving away information about herself freely. Almost too freely, it seemed. Perhaps she was looking for a friend. Miranda couldn't allow herself to get too close, but so far, things were panning out quite nicely.

One of the reasons Miranda was so good at her job was that she rarely lied. She truly did need a new gym membership, so if she happened to see Nastya at the gym, it was because Miranda had genuinely needed a membership, and the friendly girl who worked behind the counter at the community college had recommended that one to her.

After leaving campus, she was set to track down Italian boy. She'd save Melissa, the love of Shaun's life now happily married to a man not named Shaun, for last. Throughout school and university, Miranda had always tackled her most difficult assignments first. This was different. She was dreading starting her profile on Melissa. As long as it remained last, she could pretend she didn't have to do it.

She climbed to her third-floor apartment. She passed her neighbors, whose door was open, and gave the slightest hint of a smile. She never spoke to them, and they never spoke to her. Judging purely by appearance, they were a young, conservative couple who didn't like Miranda because they didn't understand her. She didn't fit into their worldview of who should be sharing a wall with them. They were no different than the customers she'd wasted hours of her life being subservient to. The look her neighbors gave indicated that she belonged behind a counter serving, not living for herself. At least they were quiet.

The same couldn't be said for her upstairs neighbors.

She'd signed the lease on the place and begun moving in her things before even telling her dad. While proud of how much money she was making, he was still shocked that it had all happened without his knowledge. After being on her case for so long about getting a good job and a good place, she finally had all that, and it had left him in a state of confusion.

Her apartment was less than two miles from her parents' place, but as she lay on her bed and stared up at her fresh new ceiling, it might as well have been in Morocco. Her place was spacious enough. It wasn't the most luxurious place she'd ever been in, but it was hers.

Growing up, being able to afford a place of her own before thirty had seemed impossible. Most parents, excluding her own, seemed to be aware of this, given that their kids were living with them well into their thirties. Now, even thirty was an overly optimistic number. If you were thirty-five living in this small Southern California city, you'd be lucky if you'd finally picked your major and were finishing up your BA. The fact that Miranda had her own place before twenty-five was remarkable in and of itself.

The apartment complex had a communal pool. She told herself she'd get down there one day, but the noisy crowds of families and friends convinced her that one day would be a long way away. As a kid, nothing had sounded more appealing than having a pool, but her father never budged. Miranda still had years of unpacking to do, but until then, she sat on her balcony and thought about her ever-growing list of clients.

The people who came to CoinciDATE were afraid to make that initial contact with the objects of their desire. All it required was saying, "Hey, what's your name?" but it was much easier to hand over their paychecks and let someone else do it instead.

The person Miranda most feared starting a conversation with was her father. She'd always been a daddy's girl, but once she got old enough to express herself, their conversations became briefer and briefer. Despite living under the same roof, they'd become strangers. Did she even know what his favorite movie was? He certainly didn't know hers. She was twelve the last time they'd gone to the movies, just the two of them. She and her mother had lunch and movie dates all the time.

Before moving out on her own, Miranda had worked up the courage to ask her dad to dinner. She had every intention of paying. He refused, but drove them to dinner anyway. She wasn't sure how they ended up where they did. There was no prior discussion, and it wasn't a place they'd ever gone to before. Did he think this was a place they used to go to?

Whatever it was, it was safe. Anything she ordered was sure to be bland and adequate. Her father sat in silence, face in the menu. It would be up to her to initiate conversation. Before that, she ordered water. He ordered a vodka martini, so she thought *fuck it* and ordered a gin and tonic.

Tired of the silence, she asked her father, "How did you and Mom meet?"

Papa Enrique sipped his martini. He looked taken aback. "You know the story."

"No, you've never told me. Maybe you told my brother, but I don't know it."

"That can't be. We talk about everything."

"Used to."

Her father ordered another drink.

"After high school, I worked as a longshoreman. For four years, I was a stevedore. Not exactly the best environment for meeting women. But we'd go to the bar every night. And for guys like us, you can only imagine what kind of bars we went to."

The waitress came with her dad's drink. He thanked her and smiled. Considering his bushy mustache, it was a smile that required more than usual effort to be seen. The waitress smiled back. When she left for the next table, his eyes not so subtly tracked the young woman's movements.

It shocked Miranda. For that instant, she wanted to launch her drink at her father's face. She'd caught every one of her guy friends checking out girls in public, and usually she'd been able to laugh it off. Though she was sure it happened, she'd never seen her father look at another woman before.

"Mm?"

"You met Mom at a dive bar?"

"No, flaca. She was my nurse. A pallet crushed my leg on

the dock, and I was rushed to the hospital. When they brought me in, I saw her and told her she was the most beautiful woman I'd ever seen."

"And after that, the two of you were dating?"

"No, the two of us were not. She was happily married to a doctor."

"What?"

"Your mother was married."

Miranda felt sick. In twenty-two years, she thought she'd heard everything about her family. The man sitting in front of her with his bushy Stalin mustache was a stranger, and her mother even more so.

"He was a doctor. Persian guy. I know his name, but don't feel like saying it. They dated for half a year before getting married. She was twenty-two. We married young back then. After she dealt with me there in the hospital, I asked for her name and she flashed me her ring. I told her I'd be back with another injury."

"Dad . . . "

"Nothing serious. Unfortunately, more than one nurse worked at the hospital. The one that time was an unpleasant Polish woman. But after walking around a bit, I found Elena."

Miranda couldn't remember him ever calling her Elena. She was always *Mom* or *Your mother*. Her father's eyes lit up when he said her name, only slightly, but Miranda saw it.

"Elena was no fool. She had no reason to do anything for me. She was a married woman. But I told her I'd come by once a week to see how she was doing and thank her for her part in saving my leg. After three months of this, she gave in and let me buy her a coffee. After the coffee, she said she was hungry. So, I cooked for her."

"She came home with you?"

"She did."

"And?"

"Let's just say Mr. Persian couldn't compete with my cooking."

"Gross."

"It wasn't a euphemism."

Miranda's parents had met in the '80s. The plot of nearly every '80s romantic drama featured a guy lusting after an unavailable girl. But those movies taught men to never give up. Because despite how married she was, or repulsed by said guy, the true way to a woman's heart was persistence. Keep doing the same thing every day, and eventually her forcefield would wither away and she'd be defenseless to stop you. Take that same strategy and transplant it to the 2010s, and the situation became problematic.

But Miranda viewed her father's situation as something sweet. Despite impossible odds, the heart won. Her parents had been people once, and young. She wanted to help Shaun. Perhaps his case wasn't so hopeless. Sure, Melissa's current husband looked like Brad Pitt, but she definitely saw how Shaun and Melissa could have been cute together.

For so long, she'd viewed Enrique as the father and not as the man, Elena the mother and not the woman, but they were both. They'd been men and women and lovers. Despite his bushy mustache and graying hair, Enrique was the man that evening. She told him she worked in an office. For Enrique the father, that was enough.

~~~

"Have you ever noticed your dad checking out other girls?" Miranda asked Christian.

It was nearly two in the morning. Typically, Miranda respected others' desire to sleep, but she also knew regardless of where the hand was on the clock, she could call Christian.

"I'll do you one better," her sleepy friend replied. "I found what porn he watches."

"Eew!"

"I mean, do you think your dad doesn't watch porn?"

"I can remain an ostrich with my head buried in the sand for the rest of my life if it means I never have to think about that imagery again."

"I don't want to think about it either, but is it really that weird? Do you believe any guy who says he doesn't watch porn? Sure, I didn't expect to be confronted with it, but there you go."

"Does he know you know?"

"Hell no. I wasn't going to go tell him. I was on his laptop, and because he's an old-ass man, he doesn't know about clearing his search history."

"What kind of porn was it?"

"Oh, God. I feel gross saying it. All I did was type the letter *j* and 'Japanese Upskirt' showed up in the search bar."

"Eew!"

"I know. So specific. But I guess, I don't know, is it really that bad? I guess if you go under the assumption that every man you ever see watches the same shit."

The conversation with Christian momentarily eased her

conscience. Still, this was her father. He was supposed to be more than that. Better than Japanese upskirt videos. Had he checked out her friends who'd come to the house? Miranda couldn't reconcile those feelings.

She also couldn't reconcile just how fucked the Gabby love triangle was. Gabby, despite having a large forehead, was quite cute. Neither the guy after her nor the guy she was after were good matches for her. Eddy had no job, no car, and no personality of any kind. Jordan fared better, which was probably why Gabby noticed him in the first place, but God almighty was he a weasel—one of those guys who had little to be cocky about but was boastful and brash all the same. Jake, on the other hand, had been taken from Gabby's deepest subconscious and could not have been a better match, if only she knew the young man existed. But then who would there be for poor Ethel? The coffee shop where Miranda had met Barry had a group of old-timers who met regularly in the morning hours. Surely one of them would be a young enough old person for Ethel.

Something was ticking inside Miranda's brain. Ethel, Gabby, Jake, coffee, John O'Flannery, the lawyer Sanchez, her dad, Japanese upskirt . . . sleep.

~~~

Working in an office gave Miranda a place. She liked being in her own place because she could be alone. But she was never truly alone. Her notebooks were filled with pages and pages of other peoples' lives. Strewn about were the details of seven women and three men. She knew more about them than her dad knew about her.

Maria lived an eventful life. She'd been in the Peace Corps

in Senegal before an internship on the East Coast. By twenty-eight, she'd been working for a non-profit, then made the move to Southern California, where she became an entrepreneur. She followed her schedule like clockwork, which made Miranda's job easy. Sergio, the guy who wanted to date her, was punching so far above his weight that Miranda almost felt like she was robbing him. Miranda worked in a fantasy factory, where they mostly gave false hope to those desperately in love and lust, but this was the most skewed case she'd seen. Sergio would never be with Maria. Even poor Barry had a better shot.

Sergio smelled like a rotten animal carcass, which was the first thing Miranda noticed when he stepped into her office. Adam and Alexei noticed it as well, and nearly gagged on the lingering stench when they came in afterward. It had seeped into the chairs and carpets and walls, seemingly the very foundation of the building. Despite intensive spraying and cleaning, the stench never completely left.

Then there was Helen, whose mother had died when she was thirteen. Helen took up drugs and hard drinking to cope, and had lots of promiscuous sex. She had a strained relationship with her father, hated dogs, and seemed to have had sex with just about every man in the city, save the one who so desperately wanted her.

Aubrey had extreme OCD and worked tirelessly to hide it with her professional and positive demeanor. Miranda considered Aubrey was the most boring human being she'd ever witnessed, but all the same, there was someone out there who thought she was the sun and stars.

Miranda often looked at these people and wished she could manipulate them into being interested in one another. Gabby and Jake were completely unaware of one another's existence, but she was certain they'd be much happier together than they'd be with the respective people paying to have them followed.

Miranda slept, but her dreams were filled with visions of faces and beating hearts, loneliness, yearning, and desire. They swirled around without rhyme, reason, or end in sight. The only thing left to do was embrace the abyss and give into those emotions.

She began touching herself, slowly at first. But she wasn't allowed to go slow, as the visions running through her mind refused to slow down. She went faster. There were faces, but she couldn't make them out. One face stood out among the others, but she didn't want to admit nor accept whose it was. The more she thought about that face, the more intense the pleasure.

When she woke, it was three p.m. She'd been asleep three hours. She was exhausted. She never liked taking naps. She never felt refreshed afterward, and this was worse than usual.

She showered, then grabbed her things and rushed down to her car without offering a smile to her neighbors. She headed for the smoothie place. Due to her disorientating nap, she still hadn't quite recovered from the realm of the unconscious. She still had no game plan when she entered the shop.

The scent of fruit was enticing, but the sterile smell of the store's interior nauseated her, especially in combination with the noise of blenders and teenagers. To her surprise, standing directly ahead of her in line was David. It struck her as odd, given that she'd never seen him anywhere but the bookstore. Seeing him in a different environment and out of work clothes felt wrong. He turned slightly in her direction and turned back around.

"Hey, don't pretend you don't know me."

"Oh, hey, Miranda."

"Aren't you supposed to be at work right now?"

"You're one to talk. I respect leaving without notice the way you did, but still, you could've at least given me some notice. You stole the way I was planning to quit."

"You're planning to quit?"

"Well, not anymore. Not for the time being anyway."

"So why aren't you at work?"

"The car was ninety percent parked when I looked through the window and saw the café was swamped with kids and families. It was some event they didn't feel the need to tell me about, so I drove away and called in sick."

"You're not worried about anyone seeing you here? Don't the supervisors come here on breaks?"

"Fruits and proteins are the best cures for sickness."

"Got it."

"So what do you do now that you've left our lovely place of business?"

For a moment, she considered telling him the truth. She also wondered briefly whether David could be a good fit for the company. His blank slate of an appearance enabled him to blend in almost anywhere. He hated customers and possibly even people, so she didn't see him having any moral conundrum with the job. She realized that after working with him for such a long time, she knew absolutely nothing about the guy. She knew he complained a lot, sure. But she didn't know his last name, where he was from, what school he'd gone to, or what he liked. In a way, he frightened her—not because she thought he'd ever do any harm to her, but since working at CoinciDATE, she liked when peoples' lives fell into place. She understood the people she followed. Their lives had order and made sense. What was David's life? She almost wished a client would come to her with David as their object of lust so she could follow him and find what it was that made him continue living his life.

"I do office work," she said. "Boring stuff."

"Well, probably suits you. Boring work for a boring girl. Don't look upset. It's a compliment."

Miranda stared at the counter. Though the girl she needed to find information on wasn't currently there, it seemed that nearly half the girls she followed were girls who worked behind counters. What was men's obsession with these girls? Was it the added risk factor? The fact that they were so close, but out of reach? Was it because, as she knew all too well, a girl behind a counter was required to be friendly and smile and be welcoming?

It was her turn. "What can I get you?" asked the pimple-faced ginger behind the counter.

"I was here about two weeks ago, and the girl who served me made my drink a really specific way. She was really friendly. I think her name was Tania."

"Talia," the pimple-faced ginger said. "Why is everyone asking about her? She doesn't work here anymore."

"A pity. Why did she quit?"

"Got a job somewhere else."

"Oh, where?"

"Why are you so interested?"

"Is it somewhere else making smoothies?"

"If you must know, it's as a lifeguard."

"Oh, at a pool or a beach?"

"Are you writing her biography or something?"

"Oh, can you tell me, please?" she asked, batting her eyelashes and smiling in a way she'd never done before.

It seemed to have some small effect on the ginger. "Hey," he yelled back to a stocky coworker. "Do you remember where Talia went to work?"

"Over at that yuppie community center pool."

"Yuppie community center pool," the ginger said.

"Great," Miranda said, turning to leave.

"Aren't you going to order anything?"

"Nope," she said, walking briskly out the door.

That narrowed things down considerably. While there were quite a lot of public and private pools in the city, there were only three community pools that could have been considered yuppie. Normally, Miranda would simply look up the girl on social media. But no matter how many variations of the name Talia she'd searched, she'd found no results. Talia was one of those rare girls who stayed off the grid, just like Nastya. Miranda had her work cut out for her.

Nearly half the people Miranda followed posted every detail of their lives on Instagram. Her clients could get all the info they wanted for free simply by following their crushes. They'd find that the Marcia they so desperately wanted always posted pictures of her cappuccino at Starbucks. And if they paid attention to the décor and the buildings in the background through the window, they'd be able to narrow down which Starbucks it was. In reality, the clients simply weren't as smart as Miranda. The day they became smart was the day they no longer needed her.

~~~

That weekend, Miranda signed up for a gym membership. The gym was small and cozy. It had all the necessities and none of the extra nonsense so many modern gyms have. No saunas or massage rooms. No movie-theater-sized screen for an audience of fat treadmill joggers hoping to lose weight watching *Forrest Gump* for the fiftieth time. Just basic, almost quaint equipment.

After changing into her workout clothes, she eyed a treadmill. She climbed on to run with her headphones in and the music loud. Not one minute into the workout, she felt a tingle on the back of her neck—a tingle that could only mean one thing.

She turned to her right and saw a big, goofy face with its mouth agape, smiling at her.

"Miranda?" Rudy said. "Oh, cool. You, like, come here, huh? That's cool."

"Hi, Rudy," she said, then turned forward again to resume her workout.

Twenty seconds passed and her neck continued to tingle. She knew he was still staring at her. He mouthed something that she couldn't hear. She nodded as politely as she was physically capable of doing and carried on. That didn't stop Rudy. He stood where he was, his mouth continuing to move.

"What?" she asked, pulling out her headphones.

"Did I tell you I run on the track team?"

"You run on the track team?"

"Ranned," he said. "I mean ran."

"When would you have told me that?"

"Oh. Well yeah. I ran all through high school. I can give you tips. Show you some things." He smiled.

"I know how to run."

"Oh. So, you come here too, huh?"

"Jesus, Rudy, what do you want?"

"I can't remember. Did I ever give you my business card?"

The gym was empty enough. She looked around at all the different weights and various things that could easily smash in a head. If there had ever been a moment when Rudy's infatuation had been charming or cute, that time had passed.

"What business card? What are you even talking about? I have my headphones in for a reason." She turned back to the treadmill again and ran, refusing to glance in his direction. Let him stare; it wouldn't get him anything.

After her run, she went to catch her breath before continuing her workout. The door opened and Nastya walked in, already in her workout clothes. Before Miranda could conjure up something to say, Nastya was already smiling and greeting her.

"Look at you," Nastya said. "I should be a salesperson, I'm so good at convincing people."

"I hope you don't think I'm stalking you." Miranda smiled but thought wildly to herself, *why the hell did I say that?* It wasn't like her at all.

"I don't mind. Want to spot me?"

"Yeah, sure."

"Who's that?" Nastya pointed.

Miranda didn't even have to look up to know who the finger was aimed at. "A guy who's been stalking me, and only a dumbbell to the brain will help him get the hint."

"Oh dear," Nastya said. "Well, imagine being behind a counter all day and unable to move. I can't tell you how many guys I see come in and out and then run away as soon as I turn my head and make eye contact."

"It must be your accent," Miranda said.

"I thought I'd lost my accent," Nastya said, feigning offense.

"Your English is amazingly good," Miranda reassured her. "But you still have a slight accent. It's quite beautiful. I can't pinpoint what it is."

"It's Russian. Nastya is a common Russian name. Really, in Russia, it seems like there are only four names for girls and four names for guys. Every girl is a Nastya, an Anya, a Masha, or a Katya."

"Sorry."

"Don't be. What was your name again?"

Miranda worked out with Nastya harder than she ever had. After showering and changing, she walked quickly through the parking lot. She was proud of Barry for falling for Nastya. After getting to know her at the gym, Miranda began to see the appeal of the long-legged, big-eyed girl.

Rudy was sitting on a bench across the street, pretending not to notice her as she made her way through the parking lot.

Her body was killing her. She was feeling aches in muscles she didn't know she had, but she was inspired to keep working. As much as she loved living alone, home was lonely, and she wasn't ready for that. Going to the bar three days in a row was pushing it.

She was angry at how much space Rudy took up in her

mind. She tried thinking about Adam, Alexei, David, anyone but Rudy, but Rudy's big stupid face kept popping up. She had half a mind to buy a gun.

Some days, she was lucky, like with Nastya, where targets would voluntarily supply every bit of information about their lives. Miranda was hoping that streak of luck would continue and she'd find Talia at the first pool she went to. She did not. She didn't find her at the second or third either. It turned out there was an elite, and expensive, fourth pool she'd never even heard of, in a part of the city she didn't know existed.

This job, just as when she'd found the CoinciDATE office itself, made her aware of how little she knew about her own city. She could draw a perfect map of Rome, including all the restaurants and cafés she'd never been to, but her own city? The two to three restaurants and three stores she frequented represented a small, walled-off, and sheltered community that didn't reflect the actual nature and essence of where she lived. Whereas CoinciDATE was located in a dingy industrial district, the community pool was nestled in an area that led her to believe she'd been transported to somewhere in Tuscany.

Miranda didn't know what Talia looked like, besides being described as "some kind of half-white, half-Asian." That didn't help matters when Miranda spotted a middle-aged white man as the lifeguard on duty. The Olympic-sized pool had swimmers in each lane. No one was there for leisure. The swimmers zoomed by before turning end over end to swim the return lap, seldom stopping to catch their breath.

Miranda certainly wasn't getting in the pool, but she had to at least pretend she might at some point. She took her time pretending to prepare herself. She adjusted her clothes, pulled on a pant leg, and then put it back in position. Mainly, she eyeballed all who got out of the pool.

Most of them were men, and most of them were middle-aged to elderly. After about forty-five minutes, legs completely numb, she saw a girl with an incredible figure pull herself out of the pool. Even without any makeup and with chlorine-drenched hair, the girl was amazingly pretty. Miranda could see how a guy could go crazy over her.

"See ya next time, Talia," said the lifeguard on duty.

Once the girl was dressed, Miranda kept her distance and followed her to the parking lot. The girl didn't walk to her car but stayed put and played on her phone. The parking lot was nearly empty, and if Miranda stayed where she was, it would look odd. She pulled out her phone and pretended to converse in Spanish.

Fifteen minutes passed before a car pulled up and a woman in her forties picked up Talia. Miranda ran to her own car and followed. The car entered a suburb that was interchangeable with a million other suburbs and pulled into the driveway of a two-story house. Miranda made note of the address and headed home.

~~~

Next morning, Miranda woke up early. It was doubtful that Talia would be anywhere before six a.m., but all the same, Miranda needed to know what time she got up and where she went. She parked her car outside Talia's house at 6:45. At 7:20, the door opened. Talia emerged wearing a backpack and started down the sidewalk.

Miranda trailed behind in her car. At that hour, there was little traffic in the suburbs. Occasionally, she'd spot old men or women who'd most likely been up since five a.m., walking dogs who looked as old as they were. Five minutes later, Talia turned a corner and was joined by two girls and a boy, also all wearing backpacks.

One girl was quite pretty, but paled in comparison to Talia. The other girl was chunky and had a childish haircut. In fact, everything from her clothes to her backpack to her face was childish. The boy looked to be an actual baby—a baby inflated to half a man's size. What Talia could have been doing with such a group of people, Miranda couldn't guess. They seemed to stay in place for several minutes, laughing and sharing stories. Miranda was forced to park her car around the corner so she wouldn't be seen.

Eventually they took off. Miranda followed and watched as they entered a high school. *That explains the babyfaces*, she thought. When she looked at the boy again, she thought he looked eleven, not between fourteen and eighteen. Had Miranda's peers looked that childish when she was in school? She could only see them as they were now, twenty-two-year-old adults transplanted back into high school. These kids were too little, and they looked it. It made Talia seem all the more out of place. She truly was beautiful, but looked mature beyond her years compared to her friends.

Still, once Miranda understood that Talia was indeed in high school, her face began to take on a childlike quality. The girl was a child. She went to PE and most likely hadn't even chosen a college yet, let alone a major. Three years earlier, she'd been out of elementary school for a year, and hadn't even had her period yet.

Miranda considered the possibility that Talia was a senior. Maybe she was eighteen. Did that change anything? Miranda didn't know. Even eighteen in college and eighteen in high school meant a world of difference.

Still conflicted about what to do, Miranda found herself pulling into the parking lot and leaving her car behind. A golf cart was racing between cars and kids, the driver shouting at any students who dared get in his way, and even those who didn't. Miranda remembered her own school gatekeeper who'd also proudly ridden around in a golf cart. Miranda had been the first of her friends to get her driver's license, and she'd been generous with her car. They'd always escape from campus to enjoy the much better fast-food offerings nearby. Their campus guardian, Louie, was unsuccessful at stopping their escapes, nor capturing them upon their return every time. But no one had ever tried harder.

At the entrance to Talia's school, kids handed over skateboards to an ancient man who served as a different type of gatekeeper. Miranda avoided him by going directly to the administration building. Despite not being her old school, it smelled the same. She was immediately pulled back to the time when she was pimple-faced with slightly chunkier cheeks, and the idea of stalking someone for cash hadn't entered the dark depths of her imagination.

What did schools smell like? Usually, she was good at placing smells with their respective places. The locker rooms certainly reeked of BO, but this wasn't that smell. Was it the smell of desperation? Of hopes and dreams and untapped potential? Idealism and the lack of cynicism? Was it paint? It was the smell of youth. Not youth in a broad sense, but youth as in, "This person is too young for you to be doing this."

Please be eighteen, Miranda thought. If Talia was eighteen, Miranda would bite the bullet and cash that paycheck. *Please be eighteen*. How many times had guys thought that same thing when they saw a cute girl smile their way? *Please be eighteen.* She didn't want to know how many guys knew a girl wasn't yet eighteen and didn't care.

Miranda walked up to a man at his desk behind a giant, ancient computer. He couldn't have been more than thirty, but his hair was already thinning in the most unfortunate of ways.

"What can I do for you?" he asked.

"Hi. I just dropped off my cousin, and she left her textbook in my car. I tried to catch up with her, but I don't know where her first class is." Miranda said all this despite not having a book, a backpack, or anywhere else to store a book.

"What's her name?"

"Talia."

"Talia what?"

Fuck me, she thought. But before she was forced to surrender the fact that she didn't know her last name, the thinning-haired man was typing away at the keyboard.

"Ah," he said. "We've only got one Talia. Talia Lew. Mr. Flint's sophomore English class."

"Sophomore," Miranda whispered to herself. "Thanks."

She walked back out the door.

"Where are you going?" he asked as she left.

"Sophomore," Miranda repeated as she got into her car.

It meant that at the oldest she was sixteen. Miranda remembered that her sophomore year had contained the occasional student who had just missed the cutoff and was fourteen on entering the year. Could the girl be as young as fourteen?

When she was fourteen, Miranda had a crush on Dylan.

Dylan also was fourteen. Looking at him now, Miranda couldn't understand what she'd ever seen in him. It certainly wasn't his shaggy hair or his rosy cheeks or his harelip. It didn't have to make sense. The things fourteen-year-olds think and desire often don't make sense, but being fourteen, it's forgivable. At thirty, however, such desires aren't as easily forgotten.

When she was sixteen, Miranda had the biggest crush on her uncle Roberto's wife's cousin Johnny. Johnny was thirty-one, and every night for two months straight Miranda imagined what it would be like to lose her virginity to him. Johnny reminded her that all the boys at her school were simply that—boys. Nothing ever happened between her and Johnny, but it didn't mean her sixteen-year-old self hadn't wanted it. Were sixteen-year-olds excused for what they wanted?

Chapter 10

Doug

Doug could never forget the first time Sandra farted in front of him. It was the night they'd gone on a double date with Jeremy and his wife of four years, Ari. Doug and Sandra had only been in California for three months. Sandra still insisted on double dates. Doug acquiesced.

Jeremy and Ari were one of those couples that thought they were far cuter together than they actually were, and Sandra was inclined to indulge them. They shared an Instagram account and knew one another's Facebook passwords. They had a dog that slept on their bed and which they brought to restaurants and stores with them. Doug always wanted to kick it. In fact, once, when everyone else had left the room, Doug did kick it. Not hard enough to cause any damage, but hard enough so the dog knew that Doug despised it. It was important to him that the dog knew that.

Doug tolerated them because it was what Sandra wanted of him, and back then, she was still nearly perfect in Doug's eyes. After dinner, they saw a movie and then had drinks, and

Doug paid for everything. After that, the cute couple insisted that Doug and Sandra join them for board games at their place. Doug declined, insisting he had to be up early the next morning. He was in bed reading an article about translucent deep-sea worms while Sandra was in the bathroom, door open, washing her face.

Despite the splashing and dripping of the running faucet, Doug had heard the distinct sound of a sharp, wet fart. He was ready and willing to pretend he hadn't heard it, and that would have been fine with him, had Sandra not begun giggling like a fool.

"Oh my God, did you hear that?"

"No. Hear what?"

"I farted so loud. I thought you heard it." She laughed again.

Why is she so satisfied with herself? What does she want from me? To tell her good job, I'm so proud of you? Does she think we're that kind of couple now? I've never farted in front of her and don't plan to. It's those fucking friends of hers, making her think what she did is okay. Is this going to become habitual?

He could see it clear as day, fucking Jeremy and Ari, sitting beneath the blanket on their couch, watching some terrible movie, dog in their laps. One of them would fart and laugh as though it were the height of comedic wit, and moments later, the other would fart in response.

"Isn't it adorable?" one would say, it didn't matter which, as their thoughts and words were interchangeable. "Isn't it adorable how close and comfortable we are with one another?"

Doug had done everything in his power not to become that couple, even if his future wife was pushing in the opposite direction. She didn't fart in front of him again that week, but the following week, she did.

All of that was on Doug's mind when he entered the pub. He feared he was beginning to make a habit of stopping there, but he couldn't bear to be with Sandra. When he told her he had to go out, she shrugged it off and said she'd call some friends to go to the movies. *That's fine*, he'd thought.

Not a soul seemed to have moved inside the pub since he'd last been there. Everyone was right where they'd been, nursing the same drinks. Despite the law banning smoking inside such establishments years back, the stale smell of cigarettes still lingered in the walls and rugs. Doug plopped himself down next to Paxton.

Doug was delighted when Paxton introduced himself. In fact, Paxton was the only person Doug wanted to converse with. He didn't need the man to remember him.

"Did your wife ever fart in front of you?"

"Sure," Paxton said. "Would shit with the door open too."

"Didn't that bother you?"

"That's what happens when you get married, kid. All those hearts and rainbows and blowjobs go away to get replaced by dirt and shit and smelly farts."

"Does it have to be that way?"

"Whatcha mean?"

"I mean, who decided that all the stuff that made being in a relationship great has to either disappear altogether or slowly degrade over time? Who said five months or five years into a relationship it's suddenly okay to let farts slip out?"

"No one said it," Paxton said. "It's just what happens."

"Why, though?"

"Who wants to hold in farts?"

"No one. But is holding in a fart really so hard that you can't find a restroom, go somewhere else, or just be a goddamn adult and hold it in for a few more minutes?"

"One time when I was young, younger than you are now, a girl from college flew across the country and stopped by to visit me. I must have angered the gods or done something evil in my past life, because as we were getting into bed, the vilest gas anyone had ever had began to creep out of my body. I could feel it. All it would take was one loud and long fart to let it out, but that would kill the mood, and ol' Paxton wouldn't be getting his dick wet."

"So what did you do?"

"I held it in, of course. And each minute I held it in, it only got more painful. She didn't know what exactly was wrong, but she could see by the faces I was making and how tense I was that something was up."

"Must have been strenuous sex," Doug said.

"Are you listening?" Paxton said. "Of course there was no sex. I was Chernobyl waiting to pop. One thrust and I'd be spilling radioactive gas all over the bed. I never thought I'd be in a situation where I was happy to hear a girl say, 'I'm not ready. I really like you, but let's wait.' I almost applauded right then and there. We lay down together, and she rested her head on my shoulders."

"She stayed over?"

"She did, but the urge to fart never left. When we were both good and tired, I tenderly lifted her head off my shoulder to go to the bathroom. It was close enough to the bed that

I wasn't confident enough the sound would be muffled, so I started the shower. While in the shower, I let loose the loudest and most painful fart anyone has ever farted."

"That the end of the story?"

"Unfortunately not."

Doug hadn't planned on getting wasted, but he was going to need another drink.

"I got back to bed," Paxton said. "As soon as I was settled down and her head was back on my shoulder, the urge to fart was back and stronger than ever, as if I hadn't released anything at all. I cursed and prayed and closed my eyes and wished for sleep. But I couldn't sleep. Less than an hour went by when finally I got out of bed and ran back to the bathroom. I couldn't very well take a shower again, could I? She was asleep as far as I could tell. I ran the faucet and sat on the toilet. I thought maybe I could shit out whatever evil was stirring in my body. After struggling for about ten minutes, I farted out the absolute most minuscule little pebbles. Perhaps that had been the bastard blocking up my system. I went back to bed. Like clockwork, the urge returned. Every twenty to forty minutes I had to get out of bed, run to the bathroom, and fart."

Doug sat, rubbing his finger along his cold mug, watching the condensation on the glass break away as his finger touched it. There was dust on his glass.

"So, you're probably thinking, if it was so bad, why not just bite the bullet and fart in bed and get it over with?"

Doug remained quiet. Now there was dust on his fingertips.

"I didn't, of course, because I still wanted to sleep with her. I was willing to let her think I was a little odd by constantly running off to the bathroom as opposed to being a fart machine in bed before we'd even had sex."

"There's a point somewhere," Doug said.

"There is. Imagine if that hadn't been a one-night thing. Imagine if that happened every time I was with her. What am I to do, run away every time I have to fart? Eventually, you have to do it."

"I can't speak to your situation, as I've never been in such a predicament, but I think nine times out of ten, it's possible to hold it."

"Maybe, but sometimes it isn't."

"But doesn't it bother you? It doesn't bother you when not just a woman, but *your* woman does that in front of you?" It was too difficult for Doug to get out the word *fart* when it followed the word *woman*.

"I mean, it's not like it made me happy when she did it. I wasn't waiting for it eagerly, but what was I to do? Tell her not to fart? Tell her it's against the rules? If the worst thing to ever happen to me in my relationship is that my woman farts, I think I could look past that."

Paxton never looked directly at Doug. His eyes were always on his drink, which was good, because if Paxton had looked, he would have seen a man of thirty squirming in his seat like a child wrestling with a ridiculous internal conflict.

"What the hell you two complaining 'bout?" asked a third voice. A man, older than both Doug and Paxton, sat down between them. He reeked of vodka-tainted sweat and looked as though his skin was hidden under several layers of muck and filth.

Doug had no inclination to answer, but Paxton seemed

right at home talking to the filthy old drunk.

"Who's complaining, old-timer? Just talking 'bout life and love."

"Yeah, I heard ya," the old man said. "Two of yous talk loud enough for the whole damn bar to hear. It's either listen to you or listen to the shit music they got playing. You're complaining like a buncha fucking women."

"Kid seems to be upset that his wife farted in front of him. I explained to him that old bit of wisdom from the Bible, 'Better Out Than In.'"

"Tell him my whole life story, why don't you?" Doug muttered.

The old man grunted, a sound full of phlegm and booze and disinterest.

"What's your take, old-timer?" Paxton asked.

"Who gives a rat's ass?"

Why'd you sit down then, asshole? Doug thought. Instead, he said, "My dilemma is this . . . " He'd been thinking it through the whole night but was still finding it difficult to vocalize exactly what was pressing down on him. "I've never understood that whole 'my wife is my best friend' thing."

"What do you mean?" Paxton asked.

"Who gives a rat's ass?" the old man asked.

"I believe a significant other, lover, wife, whatever you want to call it, shouldn't be put into the same category as a friend. They should be special. Someone you desire. They should be perfect for you, and you should be perfect for them. When you got married, why did you do it? What drew you to your first wife in the first place?"

"She put up with me." Paxton chuckled.

"That's it? It wasn't because out of all the women, she was the one you wanted to sleep with more than any other? The one you wanted to hold tight because she was so utterly perfect?"

"Nah," Paxton said. "Her sister was the better looking of the two. She was fun, had a nice rack for sure, and put up with me."

"Maybe this doesn't apply to you," Doug said, "but my philosophy is if you're going to get married, it's because that person is as close to perfect as a lover can get. They have all the things you need to satisfy your desires. I never bought this load of crap that once you become a couple, suddenly you become *comfortable* with each other, and then all effort to be what initially attracted them goes out the window. You begin to relax, you gain weight, eat like a slob, don't shower, fart, become lazy. Why is that the accepted behavior among so many couples? Why isn't it the other way around? Why isn't it, 'You were attracted to me because I worked out, styled my hair nice, dressed nice, and worked hard. Wouldn't it be better if I kept that up?' Once I'm hers, isn't it my duty as a husband to keep that up? To give her more of what she desired about me in the first place? Save your farts and gross eating habits for your friends. Let them see your weird sides and your flaws. If you can't be perfect for your significant other, then who the hell are you supposed to strive to be perfect for?"

"Crock of shit," the old man said.

"Why?"

"You're too young and too stupid to hear how young and stupid you sound, you goddamn fool."

"Let's hear some wisdom, gramps," Paxton said.

"Buy me a drink, you cheap sack of shit, and I'll give you

wisdom," the old man said.

Once obliged, he continued. "Your ideas make you sound like a little boy. Okay, let's play your game. Two pretty little twenty-somethings get married. They're perfect, whatever that means. They fulfill your little philosophy you just pulled out of your ass. They don't stop trying to look good for one another. They don't fart in front of each other. No flaws. No farts. He married her at twenty-three, and goddamn it at twenty-eight she's still looking great. Hell, she's looking great at thirty-eight. But at fifty-eight? At fifty-eight, no one is looking great. They had a good twenty years or so together, but eventually, her tits will sag, her face will sag, her legs that he used to love wrapping around his head so much will no longer be so appealing. So whatcha left with? Sure, you fucked each other's brains out for a while, but now you're left with a skeleton inside some floppy skin. So much for having no flaws. Now you can't stand looking at each other. You no longer even know the person standing before you."

"So what then?" Doug asked. "Farting in front of each other from the beginning saves the marriage?"

"Didn't hear a damn word I said, did ya? I said you weigh your options. At the end of the day, we all age into ugly, unbearable shits. What's more important? Some bullshit fantasy of being perfect for your spouse, or farting and eating comfortably in your own house? No matter how hot your wife might be, eventually she won't be, and it's worse for us than it is for them, because women age much worse than we do. Why do you think so many older guys marry younger women? They can't bear the thought of living with a wife who looks as old as they feel." The old man, with his skin clinging to his bones, made no expression except for the occasional grimace.

He looked like the living embodiment of stale vodka. In a bar like this one, it was only people like him who didn't look out of place.

"So that's the key to a happy marriage?" Doug asked. "Marry a hot twenty-something when I'm a fifty-five-year-old man?"

"If a nice pair of tits is enough to make you happy, sure," the old man said. "Never in history has there been a happy marriage between an old man and a young wife where they actually loved one another. You really think some twenty-something dumb blonde loves her geriatric husband? She loves comfort, a nice house, and money. But him? No, she doesn't love him. He loves firm tits and a pretty face. But does he love her? How can he? What love can there be between two such people?"

"There are no happy marriages then? That's what you're implying."

"You young fool, are you listening to a word I say? You're still naïve. You think there is happiness, and if there is, you think you're entitled to it. There is no happiness and there are no happy marriages, you dumb prick. There is only settling. You settle for the least terrible option that presents itself. You find someone who is full of flaws and drives you crazy, but you settle because they do enough for ya that ya don't want to blow your brains out. Imma shit myself."

"Hear, hear," Paxton said, chugging the rest of his drink.

~~~

He's wrong, Doug thought as he pulled his car into the garage at home. The lights were off. Sandra hadn't returned yet. Odd as it was, he didn't mind. He sat down on the sofa without bothering to turn on the lights. So often lights and TV and radio were on, not because anyone actually cared about what was on, but because they couldn't bear to share the silence with one another. The silence only reminded Doug that he was sharing his life with a woman he could no longer stand.

The old man is wrong, Doug thought again. *Talia is perfect.* He felt it when he laid his eyes upon her. He didn't simply desire her, he needed her. She was the necessary cure for the black hole in his heart. The details of her face became fuzzier as he tried to recall them.

Doug didn't want to imagine Sandra at fifty. He didn't want to imagine her a day from now. He wanted Talia. Talia in his arms. Talia kissing his neck and taking his whole ear in her mouth. Talia sitting on his face. Talia, Talia, Talia . . .

Chapter 11

Barry

For most, it was simply Tuesday, but for Barry, it was set to be a momentous occasion. Mrs. Schnitt had made another mediocre meal in her long, sad history of mediocre meals, but Barry had lapped it up happily and quickly all the same. Mr. Schnitt was busy doing God knew what in the garage with another new toy he'd bought for himself that Mrs. Schnitt couldn't stand. The week prior, Mr. Schnitt had bought new gardening shears that were abnormally large and even more comically sharp. Mr. Schnitt had forbidden Barry to touch them, as though Barry had been planning to take up gardening.

None of that mattered to Barry. He had news of his own. But even his news would have to wait, because more momentous news was coming his way from one of his online brethren. This incel brother in arms was known as DukeRedPill. His real name was Benjamin.

Benjamin, aka Duke, Barry, and six other brothers in the struggle had joined in a private chat to listen to his tale.

"Hey, guys," Duke said. "I thought about making a video about this, but because you guys are my brothers, I figured it was only honorable to fill you in first."

Barry wasn't sure what Duke was getting at. Duke was one of the few on the site who wasn't afraid of showing his face, and had made several videos he posted on his YouTube channel. His videos didn't hold anything back, and Duke seemed to feel no shame or embarrassment about his attempts and inevitable failures at trying to meet women and not be an incel. He even filmed himself at bars trying to talk to women—and their reactions when they shot him down. His videos usually contained several minutes of his attempts plus a half hour or so of his own commentary.

What troubled Barry most of all was that Duke was nowhere close to bad looking. His brow ridge was slightly enlarged if you looked closely enough, but with his thick, floppy hair mostly covering it, it was hardly noticeable, just as his occasional bright red pimples were hardly enough to deem him ugly. If Duke couldn't get anywhere with girls with his completely adequate looks, then what hope was there for the Barrys of the world?

At least, that's what Barry thought before Duke became the bearer of momentous news.

> I'm twenty-six years old, as most of you know. For twenty-six years, I've lived a lonely existence. I have hobbies, as I'm sure most of you do, but still, I was really lonely. I've never had a girlfriend. It's weird to want something so bad that you've never had.
>
> When I was nineteen, I was convinced I was

going to die alone. I was so sad and angry and hurt that I resolved to kill myself then and there. I mean, I was a useless human being. I didn't see things getting any better. I couldn't go through with it, though. I don't know if it's because I was just that weak, or because I was naïve enough to think that there was a glimmer of hope that one day I'd actually be able to connect with someone.

Seven years passed. Still a virgin and still single. I asked myself so many times, "What is wrong with me? Why can't I be with someone?" Then I realized I wasn't to blame. I'm a good person. I'm healthy. I work hard. But if it wasn't my fault, then whose fault was it? It had to be somebody's fault.

I tell you this: it's the fault of feminists, liberals, and professors who teach lies and evil practices at their liberal cults we call college campuses. These devils have been at work for years demonizing men, particularly straight, white men, and doing everything in their power to make females hate us. For normal guys like me and most of you, we don't have a say in the matter. The females of our country are being turned against us, to the point that in their eyes, only one percent of men are desirable. Those one percent are the Chads.

That leaves only two types of females in this world: the manipulated and brainwashed feminists who hate men, and the sluts who have never had to work a day in their life or feel what it means to be lonely or undesirable. All they have to do is spread their legs, and they get everything they want.

My sadness at being alone turned to anger, my brothers. Anger at what the world has done to our women, and what that has inadvertently done to us normal guys. This situation isn't going to get better for us, only worse. The feminists will only be indoctrinated into hating us more and more, while the sluts will only grow more and more beautiful and their standards for men higher and higher.

So what can we do in this world that's been created without our input? Sluts are awful people with no morals. Do you want to have a meaningful relationship with a slut? The feminists are even worse! What are we to do? What are we to do when, even with that knowledge, the hole in our heart remains?

Barry contemplated that. He had a big hole in his heart, but he still hadn't given up on the notion of having a meaningful relationship with a woman. In fact, he'd only recently entertained the idea that a meaningful relationship with a woman might actually be possible.

Duke continued.

There is no longer a third option to choose from regarding females. Even ugly chicks fall into one of the two categories. What can be done about this? I looked at myself in the mirror and said, "You are too good for them—for either. Perhaps fifty years back, a guy like you could have had a perfect wife, but that option no longer exists in the world the cunts have created. The world our fathers enjoyed won't exist again until my brothers and I rise up and take it back. Until that time, what's a guy like me got to do to get laid?"

So I got a part-time job as a waiter. It was humiliating, but I needed money. I saved that money. For three months, I didn't buy video games, didn't treat myself to good food, ate only Cup of Noodles, and saved every penny I could. I drove to Nevada and spent four nights there. The brothel was a stone's throw from my motel. I'd looked at some of the girls on the website, but I was pretty sure the actual girls would look nothing like the pictures.

When I got there, I was greeted by the madam. She sat me down and told me to wait for the girls to come out and present themselves. I don't know how many there are in actuality, but six came out. Truth be told, most of them looked pretty beat. Even the ones with good bodies had messed-up faces. Most were blonde. I'm not that into blondes, but I wasn't there to be picky. There was one Asian girl, though. She was older than me, and her tummy was a bit flabby, but she was still nice to look at. I chose her, and she took me to a dimly lit room.

I gave over the money right away. I tried to kiss her, and she told me she didn't do that. I asked how much it would be to kiss, because I'd never kissed a girl before, and I wanted to at least have my first kiss before I lost my virginity. I handed over a hundred dollars more to kiss her.

A user named MoadDeeb interrupted to ask how much it cost in total. Duke replied: $280. Barry wondered if that was a reasonable amount for such a service. Then again, if he had a thousand dollars, he'd have paid it just to see the girl Miranda had told him was named Nastya bend over.

So we kissed. To be honest, I don't think I liked it much. It was really warm, and all I could think about was how I could taste her breath, and her tongue seemed a little rough. I don't think I liked having somebody else's tongue in my mouth. But I did it anyway because I wanted to know what it was like. It became hard to breathe after a bit, and I was glad to stop.

Then she got naked. She was embarrassed to take off her top because she said her breasts got messed up after she gave birth. I told her I'd paid, and I wanted to see everything. Her breasts were deflated, as though everything had been sucked out of them, leaving only the floppy flaps of skin. All the same, I needed to suck on them. I had to. I had dreamt of sucking on tits my whole life. When I finally did it, I didn't feel anything new. I was expecting some burst of pleasure or ecstasy, but I didn't get any of that. I was just sucking on skin.

After that, she sucked my dick for about a minute. I was scared of bursting then and there, so before it became too much, I asked her to stop. After waiting for a minute, I told her to ride me. I lasted about two minutes. With all said and done, it was okay. I was glad to get it over with, but it wasn't the amazing experience I was expecting. With a condom on, I couldn't really feel what a pussy felt like. It was like tugging on your own dick but slightly warmer and wetter. I guess I expected sex to feel ten times better than jerking off, but really it was kind of just more of the same.

The next day, I decided that I owed it to myself to try one more time. Perhaps I'd have a different experience. I didn't like beer the first time I tried it, but after the fifth, I began to see the appeal.

I returned to the brothel and saw the lineup of girls. This time, there were ten. Some were the same from before, including the Asian girl, but there were others. Two genuinely cute brunettes were there, and both looked younger than me. I would've had them both, but I didn't have enough money. I chose one. I chose not to kiss her this time, but I did lick her asshole. She rode me and I did her doggy-style. I lasted about five minutes that time.

All in all, I didn't have the best experience, but the second time was marginally better than the first time. I think I've figured out how to achieve happiness. I'm never going to have a meaningful relationship with a slut, but if I keep working and save my money, I can at least fuck them from time to time. The girls Nevada had to offer weren't the highest quality, but I think if I save enough money and have patience, I can find higher-caliber hookers and call girls. I encourage you all to do the same. In fact, I even thought about the possibility of all of us chipping in money to a general fund that we can distribute among ourselves to use for this purpose.

Duke was the first person on Incel.me to lose his virginity. All of them had contemplated it and even taken bets on who would be the first. The fact that Duke had to pay for it meant there wasn't much hope for the rest of them losing theirs without emptying their wallets. Barry wanted to be the first to lose it without having to pay. Firstly, he didn't have the money for it, and secondly, he was going to make Nastya his or die trying. After Duke's epic story, Barry felt like a child in comparison for the news he was about to deliver to his comrades.

MoadDeeb shared a story about how a girl who sat next to him in class let him have a lick of her Popsicle, and that excited him until Duke told him it was the most virgin statement he'd ever heard.

Perhaps Barry's statements were destined to sound just as virginal. No matter, his head was bursting, and if he didn't share it then and there, his chance to share would be lost forever.

Guys, I've got some news too, Barry wrote.

Barry's got news? MoadDeeb asked.

I thought Barry was dead. Didn't Kenneth shoot your ass? another asked.

Barry paid it no heed. *My news isn't as momentous as Duke's, but—* he stopped himself and contemplated his options. Did he truly want to reveal the existence of CoinciDATE to them? They claimed to be his brothers, but several weren't even aware he was still among the living.

I have a girl too.

What? gasped Enlightened Celestial, who also happened to be the only person remaining in the chat. Thank God for that, as Barry wasn't sure what had compelled him to say it.

Okay, let me explain.

Please do, Enlightened Celestial wrote. *Because if Duke and then you have found girls before I have, I'm going to kill myself.*

It's because I'm Russian, Barry wrote.

You helped elect the president?

What?

I'm the one asking questions here. Start making sense, damn it.

Barry took a moment to regroup. Then: *Remember a while back I told you about the girl who works at the student services center of my school?*

No.

Oh, well, for the longest time, I assumed she was French or something. Turns out she's Russian. I never would've guessed. So, in order to get her attention, I'm going to introduce myself and tell her I'm Russian as well.

That's the stupidest plan I've ever fucking heard, Enlightened Celestial wrote.

What? Why? I thought it was a pretty good idea.

She'll know you're not Russian because you aren't Russian, dumbass.

Obviously, but she doesn't know that.

She'll know it as soon as you open your mouth and don't speak Russian. In fact, she'll know it just by looking at you.

What do Russians look like?

Scary, intimidating. Like gangsters. Your name is Barry. There's nothing Russian about that.

It'll work. I know it will. I have a plan, but if you're going to question everything I say, I don't think I'll bother telling it to you.

I'm only saving you from embarrassment, Enlightened Celestial wrote.

Barry left the chat without saying goodbye. He had a plan, but Enlightened Celestial had decided to be a jerk instead of an encouraging friend. Barry would never tell him of the wonders of CoinciDATE. Thanks to Miranda and her wonderful service, he not only knew that Nastya's name was Nastya, but that she was twenty-two, and from some city called Ufa, which Barry was convinced was made up until he looked it up. She lived with her father and brother, went to the gym, liked hiking and surfing (more importantly, liked surfers), and was studying biochemistry. While Miranda was in the field gathering more information about Nastya, Barry was growing impatient.

After two years in college, Barry was no closer to selecting a major, and he was retaking algebra and geology. No force in the universe would help him prevail in math, but he'd gone into geology this year with optimism—short-lived when two weeks into the semester, during a mandatory field trip, his three group-mates iced him out, leaving him to wander, clueless, holding a hand lens and a pencil magnet, feeling as useless as an asshole on an elbow.

He had no idea what he wanted to be. In adult life, he'd paid little attention to that question. When he was five, he wanted to be a dinosaur. When he was six, he more specifically wanted to be a velociraptor. At seven, he wanted to work at Sea World. At nine, he went to Sea World for the first time and was bored silly. After that, he lost all ambition to ever choose a career.

He still had no idea what he wanted to be, but he knew what he wanted. He wanted Nastya. He wanted her so bad that he taught himself the Russian alphabet. It took him time to accept that the capital B-looking letter, in fact, produced a *v* sound. He even bought himself a notebook, in which he wrote down the alphabet numerous times. First, he wrote it with the English letters next to their Cyrillic counterparts. After doing that half a dozen times, he tried to write the alphabet from memory. He was never quite able to get it. He always mixed up the sound the spider-looking letter made with the one that looked like an O with a line through it. He also could never remember which of the two letters that looked like the number four made a *ch* sound and which a *ts* sound.

He even went as far as to book a Skype lesson with an online tutor. His teacher was humorless, and nowhere near as cute as Nastya. Her teeth were blackened from years of cigarette smoke, and Barry thought maybe he could smell them through his monitor.

Barry felt embarrassed when the teacher, Albina Ivanovna, asked him why he wanted to learn Russian, and he couldn't think of an answer, so he stated he had heard the literature was good. He was certain he had heard that somewhere before. When she'd gone down the list of at least a dozen supposedly famous Russian authors, he was too embarrassed to say he hadn't heard of any of them, so he merely shook his head, stating he thought they were all great. When Albina Ivanovna asked him which works were his favorite, he stumbled and merely said "all." Albina Ivanovna, in all her inscrutability, would have none of that.

After she'd chastised him for his ignorance of the Russian literary giants, he made a note to get Dostoevsky from the library.

When she began speaking in Russian, it sounded nothing

like the phrases he'd written down in his notebook. She was inventing syllables where they didn't exist and dropping them when they were needed. Barry could barely make out a single sound she uttered, and try as he might, he couldn't roll his r's to save his life.

~~~

Barry had promised himself he was going to introduce himself to Nastya on the first of the month. Despite having had only two online Russian lessons and no surfing lessons, he had to do it. It was then or never.

Before leaving his house, he shat twice, and shat a third time upon arriving on campus. Praying his bowels were empty, he made the long walk up the steadily inclining hill to the student services center. Halfway up, he felt a new shit brewing inside him. *Goddamn it. Not now. Either I go up now, or I don't go up at all.*

The shit grew heavier with each step. He was sweating through his nice shirt. When he lifted his right arm, it was drenched to the point of looking like a small pond. *Shit*, he thought. *No matter, she won't be able to smell me behind the counter. You've got this, you bastard. Shit, maybe I didn't.* He'd forgotten to do push-ups that morning. He'd told himself that doing a minimum of fifteen push-ups each morning would mean he'd earned her. Perhaps if he did thirty when he got home, it would be okay.

He stepped inside. In the blink of an eye, he was standing in line, not quite aware of having made the journey there from the entrance. Three people stood in front of him. She made eye contact with him. Once again, she was standing next to the tall, long-haired guy with the beard. One person left the line, leaving only one ahead of him.

You got this, he said to himself. *You got this because no one has ever wanted anything more than you want this.* It was his turn. He looked at the bearded man and looked back at Nastya. It was time to buy a third parking permit, and this time he knew who was going to give it to him.

"Hi," he said. "Parking permit, please."

"Sure," she said. "I just need your driver's license."

He handed it to her, and as soon as it left his hand and transferred into hers he realized she'd see his name and would know he wasn't Russian. *Think, Barry, think.*

She handed it back to him.

"Fifty dollars," she said.

He handed over the cash.

"Next," she said.

Barry turned around. The line had already grown with four people behind him. *Act, Barry. Act, goddamn it.*

He turned back to the girl and said, "*Kak dyela?*"

She looked up, confused. "What?"

"*Kak dyela?*" Barry asked again, raising his voice this time.

"Come again?"

"*Kak dyela?*" Barry asked a third time. He could smell the sweat coming from his right armpit. "You're Russian, aren't you?"

"Yes," she said. "Why do you ask?"

"I could tell. I can always spot another Russian," Barry said.

"Another?" She looked questioningly at him. "Were you trying to say, '*Kak dela*'? I couldn't understand what you were saying."

Barry stood for a moment, trying to gather his strength and figure out what to say. His ID was still in his hand. Without warning, her arm shot out and grabbed it.

"Barry Schnitt," she read. "That's not a Russian name. You said another Russian."

"My grandparents are Russian," Barry lied. "I grew up hearing a little of the language but never had real practice. *Menya zovut* Barry. *Kak tebye zovut?*"

"*Kak TEBYA zovut,*" she corrected his pronunciation. "*Menya zovut Nastya.*"

"*Ochen priyatno, Nastya.*"

"A pleasure," she repeated. "Last name Schnitt and Russian grandparents in California. You must be Jewish."

Barry panicked. "Wha? No, I'm not Jewish at all."

"Hmm," she said. "You don't look Russian. You do look Jewish. My grandfather was Jewish."

Barry, you idiot, he said to himself.

"What part of Russia were your grandparents from?"

All Barry knew was Moscow. Was Prague in Russia? Was Czechoslovakia a city or a country? "They're from the southern part," he said, hoping that would suffice.

"The south?" she said. "Do you mean the Caucasus?"

"Yeah, that's it, the Caucasus," Barry said. He'd never heard the word before.

"Hmm, you don't look Caucasian either."

Barry was confused.

"So you're Caucasian?"

"Definitely, just like you."

"What? No, I'm not Caucasian. I'm Russian."

Barry was even more confused.

"Can I help you with anything else, Barry?"

"No, I think that does it. Thanks for the conversation. Always nice to chat with other Russians. Maybe you could help me out if I see you on campus, with pronunciation and all."

"Yeah, sure."

"*Spasibo*," Barry smiled, "*Do svidaniya.*"

"*Poka*," she said.

He had to stop himself from running down the hill, his adrenaline levels were so high. As soon as he slowed down, he realized shit was on the verge of plopping out of him. He was covered in sweat and his leg was shaking, but once he got to the toilet, he took the most satisfying shit of his life. He'd had a full conversation with Nastya! She gave him her name and, more or less, seemed to believe his story. He'd flubbed it in the beginning, but he was confident that his Russian had worked enough to get the job done.

He loved her even more up close. He loved her big, cat-like eyes. He loved the roundness of her face. Her face wasn't fat or big, but round, in a way he hadn't seen on other girls. He loved her small, button-like nose compared to his larger beaky one. He loved her voice.

He couldn't wait to get online and rub it in Enlightened Celestial's stupid face. He eventually wanted to rub it in Duke's face as well. While this was only the beginning, it was the beginning of more conversations that eventually would lead to a relationship and then sex—sex he wouldn't have to pay for.

He wanted to tell Daniel everything. He wrote him a quick, *Hey, what's up?*

His leg ferociously jolted up and down. The shit was beginning to take a turn from pleasant and satisfying to stressful and painful.

The difficult part was over. He'd made contact. But now he had to keep up contact. He needed a consultation with Miranda. No one had ever told him what came next. In all the movies he'd watched, it always seemed that the guy only ever went through two steps in courtship: meeting the girl and bedding the girl. Everything in between always seemed to be left out.

You just have to keep being Russian, he thought. Barry had never known that all it took to find his way to a girl's heart was to have an identity. Throughout his life, the only identity he'd ever had was that of a Jewish kid, despite not being Jewish. In the beginning, sometime around second grade, when he still wasn't quite sure what a Jew even was, he went along with it when the other kids called him one. At the very least, it made him different. Soon enough, no one called him Barry at all, but rather "the Jew."

"Hey guys, let's go play kickball," one kid would say. "Hey, Jew, what team do you want to play on?"

A little later, Barry realized it wasn't much fun being the Jew. He just wanted to be Barry. But what was Barry? Barry had no hobbies and no talents. Barry's dad signed him up for karate at nine. After two lessons, Mr. Schnitt pulled the plug on that. Mrs. Schnitt signed him up for piano. After Barry's first lesson, the piano instructor informed Mrs. Schnitt that Barry was the most hopeless pupil he'd ever taught. Mr. and Mrs. Schnitt got the hint.

Barry was surrounded by people with identities. He didn't know what to do with himself. Most of the people he knew were Mexican, and their names proved as much. There also were plenty of white kids around boasting about their Irish heritage. Barry was confused by that one because as far as he knew, most white people were of Irish descent anyway, so they were simply boasting about how white they were. Were they proud of their commonness?

Once upon a time, being Italian made you interesting. Being white wasn't cool, no matter how much those of Irish descent (no matter how faint) tried to cling to the belief that it made them cool. Italians, on the other hand, were in a category of their own. Unlike other white people, they'd only recently become white. So while they were counted as part of the greater white census, they were still considered ethnic and distinct enough to be a category of their own. They had their cuisine and distinct looks and hand gestures and emotions and wonderful names that ended with vowels. Barry cursed his father. What kind of an Italian was born without a last name ending in a vowel? And what the hell kind of a last name was Schnitt anyway?

Barry gave up early on trying to convince his friends he was Italian. They never listened. Even if they had, Barry didn't talk with his hands (they were always in his pockets). He didn't have big family dinners and was certainly not exotic or sexy. His last name, more than anything, was the final betrayal. He no longer had any fight left in him to try to convince his peers he was Italian. He barely even believed it himself. That was then. Now Italians weren't special anymore either. They'd joined the ranks of the oppressive privileged class.

The only people who were special anymore were those who weren't privileged, particularly those who identified as gender non-binary or were an oppressed ethnic or religious minority. Their identities mattered. Barry's didn't. That was until he decided he'd be Russian. If people could change their identities and be a different gender on Thursday than they were on Wednesday, then why couldn't Barry be Russian?

Barry sat outside of the cafeteria for the better part of an hour, waiting for Daniel to respond. He was certain Daniel had read the message. Daniel never set down his phone. Would it be so hard for him to simply write "hey" back? Another part of Barry wanted to write Miranda. What he would say, he hadn't a clue, but without Miranda, there would be no Nastya. Were those really his only friends? One never responded to him, and the other he was paying.

He looked across at the table next to him. Bert was sitting there with his purple-pink hair, crumbs on his black shirt, staring off into nothingness. Barry didn't want to be alone.

"Hey, Bert," he said.

"Oh, hi, Barry. What's going on?"

"I decided not to go to class today. Was wondering what you were up to."

"Really?" Bert's eyes lit up.

"Yeah."

"Oh wow," Bert said. "That's great. I've actually been wanting to ask you about something for a long time, but I wasn't sure if you'd be interested."

"What is it?"

Bert smiled. "It's the greatest thing that's ever happened in my life."

"I'm happy for you."

"Oh, Barry, I want you to experience it with me. I've already signed you up. My acting class can't wait to meet you!"

Capitolo 12

Miranda

"She's fifteen," Miranda repeated.

"Hmm," Alexei responded. His face didn't betray what that meant to him. He began to play with his tie. "I can see how that might come off as unfortunate."

"Might? Alexei. The girl is fifteen."

"Yes. Fifteen."

"You don't seem all that bothered."

"Miranda," he said, "I don't like to feed people's egos. I also don't like to criticize too harshly. When people do a good job, it's no benefit to tell them so. Stay silent, and they'll keep doing what they're doing. Miranda, I never doubted you. I always knew you were smart. Even having said that, I'm so thrilled by what a fantastic job you're doing. Even Adam took longer to get the hang of things than you did. I can't stress enough what a valuable team member you are."

"She's fifteen," Miranda said.

"We're still on that? Look. It's not up to us to age-check

or set age limits. So she's fifteen, and what? We aren't forcing her to do anything. As with most of our clients, the most likely outcome is that nothing will happen between her and the guy after her."

"But what if something does happen between the *girl* and the grown man twice her age who's after her?"

"That's not on us. It's not on you. You didn't force them. You didn't kidnap or brainwash anyone. All you're doing is providing information. There's nothing wrong about that."

"I don't know . . . "

"Look, Miranda. If it makes you feel any better, we can charge him more for this."

"It doesn't."

"Well, one way or another, we're going to give our client what he's paying for. Nothing more, nothing less. Having said that, for clients who have unusual needs such as this one, I'm starting to think we might need to offer additional services."

"I'm not following."

"Well, in a situation like this one . . . Thirty-year-old men aren't often in the same environments as fifteen-year-old girls. We might have to manipulate events to go in his favor. I was thinking of starting a new service—ManipuDATE. Or maybe I might even make that a separate entity altogether. Anyway, this Doug will be our test run. If only you knew how much he'd be willing to pay for these additional services."

Alexei went on at length about what breakthroughs would be made with ManipuDATE. Eventually he forgot Miranda was in the room entirely after congratulating himself on a brilliant idea for the sixth time. She felt sick and left.

In the car, her Italian audio lessons provided no comfort,

so she shut them off without even repeating any of the phrases. She knew the job had been too easy and that eventually she'd run into a situation like this where she'd have to call it a day and go back to working as a human punching bag.

She was naïve to have believed that good things last. Love didn't last. All good TV shows turned to shit once they overstayed their three-season welcome. So why should this job be any different? Was it because she was making money more quickly than ever before? Was it because for once she was not only playing an important role but being recognized for it?

Christian had graduated university as Miranda had. Unlike Miranda, Christian would soon be entering grad school. After grad school, she'd become a teacher. That was her plan from day one, and nothing had changed. The rest of her life was written out for her. Miranda had been jealous back then, back when her father had been on her case to find a real job. Was CoinciDATE not a real job? The money felt real. People would always be desperate, especially when they were lonely, wouldn't they? Maybe it wasn't about the money at all. Maybe focusing on the lives of her clients allowed Miranda to forget her own. She couldn't remember the last time she'd had a conversation of value with anyone. Maybe Shaun? The Talia situation reminded her that not only would she be out of a job soon, but she'd have no idea what good she was to anyone. What kind of headhunting agency would like to see CoinciDATE on a résumé?

On top of all her tormenting thoughts, Miranda had completely forgotten she had to pick up Sabrina from the airport. She wasn't sure why she'd agreed to speak to Sabrina in the first place. In the ninety days she'd been gone, they'd shared two conversations. Each consisted of Sabrina boasting of the places she'd seen (including all the gorgeous Italian men she'd met), and Miranda consistently responding with an enthusiastic, "Oh."

By the time she got to the airport, it was already 6:30 p.m., a full hour and a half later than Sabrina's arrival time. Watching the planes take off made Miranda sad. Her obsession the past couple of years had been to fly off to Italy, but once she'd started working, she thought perhaps she'd be able to treat her parents to a vacation. They earned enough to make ends meet, but a vacation was out of the question. Miranda had money. What was stopping her? Would she have to beg her father to accept the money?

She waited impatiently as sons and daughters and mothers and fathers and significant others ran into the arms of those who were waiting to greet them. Miranda had been forced to change her spot three times already, as a middle-aged Sudanese guy wouldn't stop asking her questions.

Not that Miranda had experienced it herself, but from the looks of it, most people got off of long flights exhausted and not looking their best. Often, she'd see people unshowered, unshaven, teeth unbrushed, hair unkempt, and clothes spoiled by sweat. When Sabrina came to baggage claim, she looked as though she'd been transported from Milan Fashion Week. Her bright red dress was matched by her bright red lipstick. Her high heels made her even taller than Miranda. Miranda could only wonder how long Sabrina had spent in the minuscule bathroom on the plane making sure her makeup and hair looked just right. No doubt a long line of impatient passengers must have formed behind her. Sabrina would have paid them no mind.

On the car ride home, Miranda barely spoke. Just as she'd predicted, Sabrina had come home with a new and profound sense of sophistication and arrogance.

"No one drinks cappuccinos after eleven a.m. You just don't do it."

"Mmm."

"They don't eat spaghetti and meatballs over there. It's such an Americanism."

"Oh."

"They eat pizza with a fork."

"Really?"

"Oh my God, I just looooove siesta time. It's so great. If we had that here, I feel our workers would be so much happier."

"Mmm."

"People are just, I don't know. They're like, more real over there. If someone invites you to come out, they mean it. There are no empty gestures. If someone says they're your friend, they mean it."

"Oh."

"Did you know that people don't even eat dinner over there until like, ten p.m.? Isn't that random?"

"So random."

"People dress well over there. They put effort into looking good. And it pays off. I don't know how I'm going to be able to go back to American guys after what I saw over there."

"So, no more American guys?"

"I mean, I hooked up with like, two, no, three American guys while over there, but only because it was random. They got me, though. They were real travelers, not tourists."

It went on. Even as they got stuck in deadlocked traffic,

Sabrina never stopped yapping. Miranda tried but couldn't recall what she'd ever seen in this girl that made her want to befriend her. Miranda also couldn't believe that after two layovers and thousands of miles sitting on a plane, Sabrina was showing no signs of falling asleep and letting her mouth shut down.

"We should totally get drinks tonight," Sabrina said.

"Aren't you tired?"

"No way. I want to drink."

"I'd love to, but I already agreed to meet Christian tonight."

"Oh, I looove Christian. Let's all go out together. I haven't seen her in forever."

Miranda knew that Christian didn't looove Sabrina and would be less than thrilled to see her, but she had no fight left in her.

~~~

Christian was already sitting at the bar when they arrived. Her simple white top not only stood out among all the dark objects of the dimly lit bar but looked quaint and modest next to Sabrina's red attire. Christian's expression gave no indication as to whether she was annoyed by Sabrina's presence.

Miranda had chosen the bar. It was the same one where she'd met the perfectly shaven, nice-smelling, basic-bitch fuccboi whose name she couldn't remember. She didn't know why she'd chosen to meet her friends there. Yet there they were.

Miranda ordered a gin and tonic while Sabrina regaled Christian with tales of Italy. Christian, unlike her gin-and-tonic-loving friend, was diplomatic and enthusiastic in her responses. In the past, Miranda had always been apprehensive and often embarrassed about bringing someone from one group of friends to meet one from another. All too often, the two worlds didn't mesh. Still, she never seemed to learn her lesson. It was similar to when the movie she'd suggested watching turned out to be a dud. Despite having no part in the filmmaking process, she knew her friends had blamed her for the movie failing to deliver. As Miranda couldn't care less what Sabrina thought of Christian, she'd been waiting all night for Christian to send her a text in secret chastising her for being friends with such a person. But that text never came. Not only were Sabrina and Christian deep in conversation, they were smiling, laughing, and completely oblivious to Miranda even being there.

Let them talk. The watered-down gin and tonic was the only friendship Miranda needed. After listening to Christian encourage Sabrina to prattle on with all of her ill-formed knowledge of Italy, Miranda decided she hated all things Italian. She'd start learning French tomorrow, or Mongolian, for that matter.

When Sabrina finally stopped talking about herself, she asked Miranda, "What's new with you?" It felt like an afterthought because it was an afterthought.

Miranda, no longer caring about being tactful, told her two friends all the gory details of her job, up to and including her new client's desire to bed a fifteen-year-old girl.

For the first time that night, she looked her two friends in the eye. Sabrina's red outfit shone in the dimly lit bar. Miranda had red hair, but Sabrina's entire essence was red. Had she even heard a word? After chewing loudly on an ice cube, she put her attention on her phone. Miranda turned to Christian, noticing for the first time how pale her friend was. Pale, but not sickly. Well, just nearly not sickly. Pale in an annoying way where her shortcomings only added to how beautiful she was. Pale in a way that no other skin tone could ever suit her. It helped emphasize the blackness of her eyes.

If no one wanted to talk, Miranda would chew her ice cubes as well.

"What's it called again, Collaborate?" Sabrina asked. "Collabodate?"

"CoinciDATE," Miranda said.

"I don't get it."

"What's the guy look like?" Christian asked.

"Does his appearance change your views on the situation?"

"No. But it helps to paint a picture."

"I'm not supposed to reveal who our clients are."

"But you're going to show us a picture anyway, right?"

Miranda showed them Doug's photo.

"My God, look at those cheekbones," Christian said. "Looks like a *90210* stunt double, and I mean that as a compliment."

"He's okay," Sabrina said. "He'd be like a six in Italy."

"Well, he's a ten here."

"I'm waiting for words of wisdom," Miranda said.

"Here's your wisdom," Sabrina said. "Do you want to go to jail?"

"Why would s*he* go to jail?" Christian said.

"Hello, by being an accessory to pedophilia."

"Don't you think you're skipping past a lot of steps there? Right now, we're just talking. This Doug, does he have a shady background?"

"We ran a background check," Miranda said. "Clean as a whistle. Not even a speeding ticket."

"And he's thirty?"

"He's thirty."

Sabrina frowned and said, "And she's fifteen."

"How much is he paying?" Christian asked.

Miranda showed her the amount on her phone.

Christian laugh-choked on her drink. "All you do is follow and collect information?"

"Right."

"You're not actually encouraging her, are you?" Sabrina asked, no longer smiling.

"Technically speaking," Christian said, "she hasn't done anything illegal."

"Are you fucking kidding me? What about morally?"

"Okay," Christian said. "You open your phone and see an ad for McDonald's."

"Doubtful. I've never consumed fast food in my life, so you'd never see that shit flooding any of my social media pages."

Christian sighed. "Just hear me out. You see a billboard for McDonald's while driving on the 101."

"I wouldn't pay attention."

"Miranda, help me."

"Choose something else," Miranda said.

"What kind of bag do you have?" Christian asked.

"Michael Kors," Sabrina said.

"It's cute. But what's your dream bag?"

"A Gucci Ophidia."

"Wonderful bag."

"I could never afford it."

"Doesn't matter. You wake up in the morning and check your phone. On Facebook, you see ads for the Gucci Ophidia. Later on, you're scrolling through Instagram and you see ads for this bag. Maybe at work, you even hear your coworkers talking about it. You see a woman walk by wearing this bag, and while you think it looks good on her, you know it would look great on you. Now, it might seem strange that everywhere you turn around, there's that bag. It might even seem like a sign you were meant to buy it.

"You consider this. You think, 'Maybe the fact that everywhere I look I see this bag means I'm meant to buy it.' Or, despite everything pointing you in that direction, you still say no. You don't buy it. The choice is *yours*. No one put a gun to your head. No one shoved the bag into your hands. No one said that if you don't buy it, fifty kittens will be murdered."

"What if he rapes her?" Sabrina asked.

"What if your parents never met?" Christian asked. "What if Coke was Pepsi? What if this bar got shot up? What if we'd chosen to go to a different bar tonight? Are we responsible for those who got shot up in this one? What if this Doug guy had never heard of CoinciDATE? He'd still know of this girl's existence. What if he found her and raped her? What if it's thanks to CoinciDATE he doesn't do that? Whatever happens between these two isn't under Miranda's control. Things are already set in motion. The only thing under Miranda's control is whether she gets paid to feed some stalker trivial information."

Miranda wasn't certain at first if the bag metaphor had

worked on Sabrina, but finally she nodded. It had. Despite attempts to lighten the mood, all other conversations failed to take off. At least the budding friendship between the two girls had been put on hold.

~~~

Miranda was happy to be rid of the two of them when she got home.

Then, just as she was on the verge of sleep, as though on cue, her upstairs neighbors began going at it again. They were screaming and either body-slamming one another into every shelf and stack of plates in the universe, or else having the most calorie-burning sex ever. She could never tell. She was worried that one day they'd be going at it so hard the ceiling would cave in and they'd come crashing through on top of her.

She opened her laptop. She looked at her bank statement, and for the millionth time, her bank statement stared back at her. Never had she had so much money. And she could have even more. She could even buy the heel from Italy's boot.

Miranda thought of her parents. What difference did it make what they thought? Wasn't her dad always on her case about getting a job?

After checking her bank statement, through no will of her own, she found herself watching videos of Chris Hansen catching predators on YouTube. Each one was more pathetic than the last. Besides the blatant creepiness, the one thing they all had in common was that they were liars. Even when presented with the photographic and video evidence of them attempting to sleep with girls as young as twelve, they lied every single time. They never remembered sending pics of their genitals, and none of them knew why they'd driven ninety miles to spend time with a thirteen-year-old. It certainly wasn't for anything sexual. None of them looked like Doug.

The worst thoughts and feelings always happened at night. Right on the verge of sleep, eyes closed, head comfortable, the temperature just right, when images of all the bad things she'd ever done or said would plague her. Flooding feelings of guilt crashing down on her, lies she'd told her father, something as small as saying she'd done her homework when she hadn't to forgetting to pick something up at the store for him to lying about drinking and driving. She'd remember all the classmates she'd made fun of behind their back while smiling to their face. They were completely oblivious that this girl, who didn't even know them, could be capable of thinking such nasty thoughts about them.

One face stuck out more than any other. It was that of her high school volleyball coach. Coach R. was loved by students and parents alike. All the dads, hers included, never failed to mention what a real man he was. Every time the varsity team won a match, credit was given to Coach R. first and foremost. The girls' performance was a secondary matter.

When the team was playing at its peak performance, its star player had gone missing in action for a week. Miranda eventually found the girl, looking sickly and disheveled. Coach R. had been sexually abusing the girl. Without hesitation, Miranda knew she must tell her father. The girl begged and pleaded for Miranda not to say anything.

"Someone needs to know," Miranda had insisted.

"*You* know," was the girl's response.

So Miranda had remained silent.

A month later, allegations from other girls regarding the coach surfaced. When her father saw it on the news, the first thing out of his mouth was a declaration that he would kill him. Miranda wished she had told her father. Coach R. escaped any punishment, brushed off the allegations like they were annoying gnats, and found work in the next county over. Miranda knew that if she had just told her father right then and there, his declaration to kill the coach would not have been mere words, but a fact, and she would have been proud of him. That poor girl had to suffer, knowing so many people didn't believe her and knowing Coach R. was more than likely continuing to do what he did in the next county over. It really did boil down to his charm and good looks, and that was enough to make him feel entitled. In his mind, he deserved to do what he wanted to these girls. These children.

Doug, as handsome a product as a small town like this could produce, was also entitled. Deep down in the recesses of his soul, entertaining the idea that he had one, he felt he was entitled to this girl. Miranda blamed her earlier inaction as to being young. This time she had a choice. Her boss couldn't force her. With his constant sniffles, she was certain he was coked out of his mind and couldn't remember what he said or who his clients were on a day-to-day basis.

Please, just let me sleep. She was past the point of desperation. The sun would be up in a couple hours. *It's not all bad. Think of the gay couple you made happy. The young Catholic boy was happy in the arms of his Italian lover and also had the love and approval of a kind father.* Even praise from that arrogant lawyer, Sanchez, felt nice. It didn't stop him from having a big head, but seeing as those as self-centered as him rarely throw out praise so freely, it meant it was real coming from him. Some things were good. Some things. Wasn't that enough? Or was she truly her father's daughter? The way he would focus on her one B instead of all her As. Perhaps they were more alike than she was willing to accept.

Italy could wait, Miranda decided. If Doug wanted help manipulating a teenager into sleeping with him, he could look for help elsewhere. She thought of her father trying to woo her mother, and how he'd called her Elena. Those were the type of people Miranda wanted to help. Getting paid to help scumbags was dirty, and she no longer cared to have that on her conscience.

As much as the future terrified her, she felt she had only one course of action. Ideas began running through her head. Maybe she could start her own company where she only helped the most-deserving people. It would probably take a while to get going, but it was certainly a better alternative to what she was currently doing.

She wanted to reach out to Sabrina and apologize, not just for the night, but for harboring so many nasty feelings toward someone who was supposed to be her friend. She felt she owed Talia an apology, too, and while she was at it, her father, and Charlotte . . . She'd have to make a list.

Her upstairs neighbors' endurance had not let up forty minutes later. She could only imagine what condition their bodies were in. Whereas others used white noise or music to soothe them into sleep, Miranda decided to make do with what she had: body slams and Chris Hansen.

~~~

It wasn't yet eight in the morning when Miranda exited her building. She loved the cool morning air and quiet streets. She loved seeing people taking their dogs on morning walks.

Her phone vibrated so violently in her hand she nearly dropped her thermos full of hot coffee. It was from an unknown number and merely said: *Good morning, Miranda. Look up.*

Chapter 13

Shaun

Shaun didn't hate him, and that was the most difficult pill to swallow. His name was Spencer. Shaun hated that, but he didn't hate him. His own friends he hated. Himself, he mainly hated. But not Spencer. He'd met Spencer for the first and last time the previous day.

Make someone laugh more than once, and you're the comic relief. He'd never seen himself as funny. Self-deprecating, sure. Cynical, absolutely. But funny? How many times at parties had he been told by girls, "Oh my God, you are so fucking hilarious"? Only Melissa's laughs had mattered to him. Especially the way she'd inevitably start coughing after laughing too much. She could spot a fraud a mile away, and none of his jokes had worked on her. The first time he made her laugh had been a hard-fought victory.

Once dubbed the clown, you can't escape it. They expect wit and sarcasm and irony, and when you fail to deliver, they cast you out like a leper. Any moment of sincerity or vulnerability makes them uncomfortable.

He was out with friends the evening Melissa left him. He'd spoken for less than two minutes before they told him to get over it. "You're ruining the mood," someone had said. No one has sympathy for the clown. Everyone else is allowed to spill out their lives' sorrows, but not silly clowns. They must stick to their assigned role. It was then that he realized his relationship with his friends was as dead as his relationship with Melissa.

He preferred to be alone anyway. It allowed him to reflect on how miserable he was. His friends would have to look for entertainment elsewhere.

The redhead, Miranda, had delivered in a big way. Not only did he have results, he couldn't believe how fast they'd been delivered. The most shocking development was that Melissa frequented a bar twice a week. In all their time together, Shaun had gotten her to drink with him once, maybe twice. But she'd never gotten drunk in front of him. That part hurt. He had photographic evidence of her drinking with friends. She gave him her body and her heart yet wouldn't drink with him. Perhaps the heart had never been involved at all. *She drank, just never with me. Why couldn't I let that go?*

She drank with her friends. She drank with Spencer, her husband. Sometimes they all drank together. When she wasn't drinking, she went to the gym. That was nothing new. What was new was that she walked her dog every day. When she was with Shaun, she'd been a dedicated cat lover who abhorred dogs. Shaun had debated it mercilessly with her. Yet there she was, walking a beautiful canine. Shaun had always pictured the two of them walking a dog together in the cool, early-morning air.

Drinking with her friends at a bar. He'd never met her

friends, not really. He met a cousin once.

He didn't act immediately. He couldn't. He had to make sure he chose the right words to say when he faced Melissa.

The gym she frequented had big windows facing the parking lot where the runners on the treadmills and ellipticals could gaze outside, and the perverts outside could stare at the runners.

From his car, all he could see through the gym windows were amorphous shapes. Luckily, he was wearing a hoodie. With his hood covering his head nearly to his eyes, he got out of the car and made a pass by the gym windows. Impossible. Up close, the amorphous shapes were indistinguishable objects while he was in motion. He turned to make his way back, knowing he'd have to stop at the window to make anything out.

Already a few passersby were staring daggers at him, the man with the concealed face on a bright sunny day. He made his pass once more. This time he stopped for half a heartbeat. Half a heartbeat was all it took for him to see his Melissa jogging along gracefully on the treadmill, her ponytail bobbing back and forth in perfect slow motion. Her tight shorts ended well above her knees. Her shirt stopped before her ribs. Her stomach had never been tighter. How was it possible that after all this time she was more beautiful than ever? She looked out briefly, not seeing Shaun but some transient stopping a tad too long.

Back in his car, he had the urge to jerk off immediately. He had her image clear in his mind, clearer than it had been in years. He couldn't bear the idea of losing it. The way the sweat glistened down her body. He often wondered if girls knew when a guy was jerking off to them, just as they had the psychic power to know when guys were staring at them.

He decided against having a wank in the car. He was going to confront her at the bar, and he couldn't decide if jerking it was the best course of action. Would it be better to be tense in order to be more alert?

He chose alert. No matter how intense his desire grew, he wanted to feel it. Now and always. He wore the dark purple dress shirt he'd worn on their third date, the one she'd complimented him on.

He entered the bar. It was packed. That didn't matter. He knew she was there. He ordered a cocktail to calm his nerves, and recited what he was going to say. He'd been practicing all morning, had written it out, then rewrote it again from memory.

He could no longer delay. The bar was getting more crowded, and the body heat was beginning to bear down on him. If he ordered another drink, he'd get sloppy, and she'd see him as a drunk.

Shirt was straight, hair good. Shoes polished. Wasn't sweating too badly. Shaven. Breath, while having a hint of booze, was fresh. He made the trek over to her table. The closer he grew, the more people got in his way. Every patron seemed to want to bump into him. There were three others beside her at her table. Two girls and a guy. He didn't see her husband anywhere.

One more step. This was the closest he'd been to her in years. This time, there was no glass wall to divide them. No barriers. He imagined he could smell her. Her neck was so long and sensual. He was getting hard.

Nearly there. He only had to make his way through one more group of people. No more obstacles. She was laughing animatedly at something the guy had said. Her two friends seemed bored and were glued to their phones. The song on the

Jukebox changed to "Didn't I Blow Your Mind This Time?" by the Delfonics. No matter how much passion he put into describing why it was such a beautiful song, she'd always laugh at how he could like such an old song. He couldn't convince her of how universal the appeal of the melody and lyrics were, about how the second the song started, it grabbed hold of your heart, squeezed mercilessly, and took hold for the rest of your life. Was she listening now? It didn't look like it. She was listening to the guy who wasn't her husband and had the cheesy haircut. But she had to hear it, right?

She hadn't looked up yet. Not a sound in the universe could take her eyes away from Bad Haircut. Suddenly, Shaun found himself hating this man and felt the urge to defend her husband. There were no longer any patrons blocking the path to her table. All she had to do was look up.

No, the time isn't right. I can't recall the order of the things I was supposed to say. He needed one more drink. That was all. One more, and he'd be unstoppable. He turned abruptly, right into a waiter carrying a tray of margaritas and other cocktails. The ones that didn't spill on his dark purple shirt crashed onto the floor. All other sounds ceased aside from the Delfonics.

Melissa looked up. For a moment, she didn't quite know what she was seeing. When her expression turned into one of horror, he didn't know whether to run to her or away from her. It didn't matter. A strong hand had grasped his shoulder. The manager would be asking him to leave. When Shaun looked up, he didn't see the manager, but Spencer.

"Let's go outside," Spencer said.

Words were impossible. Everyone was staring, Melissa most of all. Shaun saw her one last time as his own legs betrayed him, pulling him outside. What Spencer wanted didn't matter. He could beat the living shit out of Shaun, and it would be all the same.

Outside, he was finally able to size up Spencer in person. He was about five foot ten. He didn't have a muscular build but certainly had broad shoulders. His tight-fitting shirt accentuated his body. He had perfectly shaped black hair that complemented his tan complexion. His Brad Pitt-esque smile made him either the most handsome normal person or the most normal-looking handsome person. If Shaun had met him in any other circumstance, he wouldn't feel threatened. It was the guy telling Melissa jokes at the bar he'd always kept an eye out for. Not Spencer.

"Are you okay?" Spencer asked. "The glass didn't cut you?"

Shaun looked down. No cuts, just soiled clothing.

"I'm really sorry we had to meet like this," Spencer said, "and I'm sorry for the conversation we're about to have."

Shaun waited for the inevitable punch to the face.

"Why don't we sit?" Spencer gestured toward a backless bench.

Outside was much quieter than inside. Even the crickets were mostly keeping to themselves.

"How are you doing?" Spencer asked.

Shaun was at a loss. What could he say? He merely looked up at Spencer.

"It wasn't a trick question," he said. "I mean it. Is everything okay?"

Shaun stared down at his shirt. "Does it look like everything is okay?"

"It looks like you're hurting," he said. "But this has to

stop. For your own sake. What were you hoping to achieve here tonight?"

"I wanted to see her again," Shaun said. "Someone who was such a big part of my life."

Spencer didn't look angry. "You have to let it go. I know it probably feels horrible, but doing this isn't going to help things any. It's that old cliché, man: if you truly care about her and want her to be happy, let her be."

"Is she happy?"

"Very much so," Spencer said.

"Can you allow me five minutes? Just to talk to her."

"You cannot talk to her. We really don't want to do this, but she will file a restraining order if we see you again."

"I want closure. Is that too much to ask?"

"Yes. It's too much to ask."

"Why did she leave me? Can I get at least that much?"

"She met me."

They sat in silence for a while.

"She cheated on me?" Shaun asked, instantly recalling those times she was busy every day of the week.

"She was never in love with you. She said your mind was one of the sharpest she'd ever come across, but you never utilized it. She expected a lot from you, but not a future with you. Look, I used to hear all the time about how funny you were. Every time I suggested watching a movie, she'd say, 'Oh, Shaun showed me that one.' How do you think that made me feel? She thinks you're a great guy, but that part of her life is finished. She has a new life now. In order for you to move on with your life, it has to be a life without her. That's not meant to sound cruel. It's for your own good. If you want her to be happy, be the man she thought you were."

The man she thought I was. I was. I was a writer who had never written anything. I was a fraud. Be the man she thought I was.

Shaun nodded and walked to his car, repeating those words. He started the engine and drove home, repeating those words the entire drive. Spencer was a better man than he was. Shaun was nothing. A writer who didn't write was no one. A good idea meant nothing if it never became more than an idea. One Wright brother didn't say to the other, 'Wouldn't it be cool if we could fly?' and left it at that.

Shaun didn't bother turning on the lights when he walked inside. He threw his soiled shirt on the floor. He sat at his desk and opened the drawer. Inside was a chaotic mountain of papers. Abandoned stories, novel outlines, ideas and fantasies all lumped together. He'd never finished anything. He always seemed to hit a wall around forty or fifty pages and could never get past it. Why the ideas couldn't travel from brain through vein to finger to pen to page he didn't know. He wasn't being asked to cure cancer or land a man on Mars.

He remembered Melissa's birthday, when he'd bought her half a dozen books and slipped the first ten pages of his "debut novel" into the pile. Watching her smile and play with her hair as she read it was the happiest he'd ever been.

After she left him, he'd planned to finish it, become renowned, maybe even dedicate it to her, or use it to spite her. Was it too late to finish it? Had too many years gone by for him to have any meaningful attachment to that story?

How often he'd written with booze. An excuse so common among "writers" to help them believe they were being productive. No booze this time.

He put on the Delfonics' "Didn't I Blow Your Mind

This Time," pulled out a piece of paper, and began writing like never before.

~~~

The morning was fresh. He'd slept and didn't even feel the need for coffee. It was only a little after six a.m. He showered and put on a light polo. The morning air felt great on his body. Outside, dew clung to cars and plants. Birds began waking, soon to be followed by people. In the apartment courtyard, an old man was walking at a glacial pace. When the man passed, Shaun greeted him with a friendly hello. The old man smiled.

Shaun triple checked that last night's writing was secure in his left pocket while his pen was in his right. He got in his car and took off.

His destination was much closer than he remembered. Finding where Miranda lived hadn't been hard. All he'd had to do was wait until she got off work, follow her as she ran a couple of errands, then eventually to her home. The next morning he'd parked his car at her apartment at five a.m., unsure how early she left. At eight a.m. on the dot, she was out of the apartment complex. It was the same every morning.

On this day, he arrived at the complex and used a service ladder to get onto the roof. The sun was up, but the air was cool and there were only a few clouds. His hand tapped his left pocket, ensuring his writing remained secure. He put his headphones in to listen to the Delfonics.

At five stories up, it was hard to make out the details of faces and bodies below. He looked down at the courtyard for a redhead. Perfect. He saw her just as the Delfonics belted out, "I tried so many times and that's no lie." He sent her a text message. It looked as though she'd gotten it, as the petite redhead looked up in his direction.

"Hey, Miranda!" he yelled. He closed his eyes, let the music take him, and jumped.

PART II

Глава 14

Барри

"Is that an Adidas tracksuit?"

"It is," the other said, as surprised as the first.

"Why would anyone wear that?" a third girl asked.

"You don't see that too often," the first said.

All their eyes were locked on the mysterious tracksuit-wearing stranger.

"But, if I do say so," the first girl chimed in, "he looks pretty damn good in a tracksuit."

"Absolutely," the second said. "Not many people could pull it off, but he wears it well."

"It must be because he's exotic," the third said. "And it makes him look even more exotic. Sketchy and dark, but in a hot kind of way. Everyone around here is either Mexican or some boring white-bread type of white person."

"I heard he's Russian," the second one said.

Though the name Barry didn't sound Russian, he

explained to curious ears that his ancestors had to anglicize their names upon coming to the United States. He wore his tracksuit with confidence and made sure to be seen smoking. One morning at school, Nastya had asked him if he had a lighter. He was determined never to be without a lighter or cigarettes again. That was his second interaction with her. He also was determined to make new friends, but for the time being, he was stuck with Bert and his ridiculous purple hair. Barry had thought himself done with embarrassing things, but it was taking a lot longer than expected to get there.

"That was the most embarrassing thing I've ever sat through," Barry said.

It was true, and he felt happy that it was someone else's embarrassment for once.

"Why?" Bert asked. "I thought it was fun."

"Dude, you were soaked in sweat. I could see it coming through your shirt. You stuttered and mumbled your way through every single line. Why do you put yourself through that? Wouldn't you rather not make a complete ass of yourself?"

"It's the only way to get better."

Barry didn't get it. Watching Bert act on stage in front of a dozen people had caused him more embarrassment than most things that had actually happened to him in real life. Most of the would-be actors were terrible, but Bert was atrocious. The words *charisma*, *talent*, and *charm* could never have been used to describe him. The acting teacher had tried to force Barry to take the stage and perform. When Barry refused, the teacher said a tracksuit was too anachronistic for *A Streetcar Named Desire*.

The appeal was missing for Barry. Why anyone would put themselves out there only to embarrass themselves in front of others, reading words written by others for other, more talented people, left him confused. To him, they amounted to nothing more than a group of weirdos.

When the acting class let out, several members went out for drinks. Among their ranks, to Barry's horror, was French Murder Face. It turned out that French Murder Face wasn't his real name. His true name was Rocket Jizz. At least that's what he insisted they call him. Also in attendance were Black Barry, who was the best actor of all of them; Rudy, a short guy with a round head and baggy shorts who was incredibly inarticulate but spoke more than anyone; Lilly, a cute Japanese girl who was the second-best actor; and Debbido. Debbido's name was David, but he insisted on being referred to as Debbido because he was learning Japanese. At six foot two, his large, pear-shaped body gave him the appearance of a lumbering ogre. He wore sandals, and his feet looked the same as they smelled. His mouth was always slightly agape, and he never smiled. When Barry was about to sit down next to Lilly, Debbido used his stomach to shove Barry aside so he could sit next to her instead.

Debbido was a weeaboo, a white person who had convinced himself that if he watched enough anime, he'd become Japanese.

"Actually, this isn't real sushi, is it, Lilly-chan?" Debbido asked, pointing at their plates.

"What do you mean?"

"You can only find real sushi in Nippon, isn't that right?"

"Oh, I don't know," she said. "I've never been to Japan."

"I think you must go to Nippon to honor your ancestry," he said, with a slight Japanese accent on the word honor.

"I don't have much of a connection, to be honest," she said. "I'm learning French because I want to study there junior year."

"My Japanese is excellent," Debbido said. *"Watashi wa Debbido desu. Watashi wa Evangelion suki desu."*

He stared at Lilly.

"Anata wa Evangelion sukidesuka?"

He continued staring.

"Did you hear what I asked, Lilly-chan?"

"I told you, I don't speak Japanese."

"I asked if you like *Evangelion*."

"I have no idea what that is."

"It's basically the best thing ever. Next year, I'm going to move to Nippon. Because my *Nihongo* is getting so good and my dad has a lot of money, I'm going to direct a live-action version of *Evangelion*. Once I show Anno my script, he'll know I'm worthy of adapting it. I'm also going to play the part of Kaji so I can be in the love scene with Misato-san. That's why I'm taking acting lessons. Maybe I can come to your house to practice some scenes with you."

"Hey, Barry," she said to Black Barry, "I ought to get going. See ya later. Bye, guys."

Mouth agape, Debbido watched her leave. He was the poster child for why CoinciDATE was an absolute necessity. Debbido had done everything wrong. Had he done his homework, he could have avoided embarrassing himself in front of his acting class.

Barry recalled his most recent consultation with Miranda. Instead of meeting at the office, they met at the café where he'd seen her for the first time. Something about her demeanor had changed. She didn't take her sunglasses off, and despite looking the same, she seemed older and more robotic. She laid out a bullet-point list before him.

"She goes to the gym a minimum of three times a week. She tries to do four or five, but a minimum of three. The days vary, but this graph shows sixty-five percent of the time the past two months she goes at seven p.m. She's also really into surfing but doesn't do it enough for it to be habitual.

"She smokes Marlboro Gold cigarettes. She uses matches, not a lighter. She smokes one cigarette at lunch, one after work, and one before bed.

"She can't stand spicy food. She once commented that teriyaki sauce was too spicy for her. She rarely eats out. She makes her own lunch every day. She doesn't drink much, but every once in a while, she goes to the Blue Door Lounge with friends. Not frequently enough for it to be habitual.

"She mainly reads science journals and doesn't have much time for literature. She hasn't been to the movies in over a year, and she doesn't own a TV. She doesn't have a driver's license.

"She lives with her dad and a younger brother. Her brother is into PC gaming and her father is an engineer. Her mother left the family when she was still in Russia at age fourteen.

"Her favorite music is basic top-40 radio stuff. Her favorite movie is *Eyes Wide Shut*. She prefers cats to dogs. The only caffeine she drinks is tea. She likes masculine men and said any man she dates has to be smarter than she is. Her last boyfriend was a Marine pilot, but they broke up because he was too career focused. She also likes guys who can make her laugh.

"She likes going to that store, Cost Plus, where the old mall was, that sells trinkets and useless junk from around the world. She goes two or three times a week after work but rarely buys anything . . ."

Miranda talked on for another five minutes.

"Any questions?" With her glasses on, it was hard to tell if she was even looking at him.

"No, I don't think so," he said. "Just, uh, is there some way I can thank you for all this?"

"Your payment is sufficient," she said.

"I know. I mean, can I buy you a coffee or something? I enjoy talking with you and want to show how appreciative I am."

"Let me know when you've received your bill." She stood. "Looks like this is our final meeting. Goodbye." She walked away without waiting for his response.

She must be on her period, Barry thought. He knew girls tended to behave strangely on those days and often said things that shouldn't be taken seriously. Debbido needed Miranda in his life. Had the weeb consulted with Miranda beforehand, he might have actually known how to speak with Lilly.

"Barry," French Murder Face, aka Rocket Jizz, said in a truly bizarre accent. He was addressing Black Barry.

Rocket Jizz had the smoothest face Barry had ever seen. It was almost devoid of features, making him resemble a badly rendered CGI character from the early 2000s.

"The girl, she is some kind of Chinese? Are you having the sex with her?"

"Jesus Christ, man." Black Barry laughed. "I'm not even talking about that with you."

"Oh, come on, it's what guys talk about, right?"

"I just don't know how much I want to tell a guy called Rocket Jizz," Black Barry said. "Where are you from, anyway?"

Rocket Jizz, who hadn't removed his gloves when the food arrived, answered, "Well, you see, I mainly am from outer space. I come from a planet that worships trees, but now mainly I want to be actor. Also I very much like the sex. What about you, Rudy? Do you like the sex?"

"Yeah, well," Rudy said, "I'm probably seeing two chicks right now. One's really cool. I don't want to lead her on, but I definitely could if I wanted to. The other one I hooked up with."

"Oh, very nice, Rudy. What she look like?"

"She's pretty. Tall. Redhead."

"Very, very, very cool, Rudy. This girl, does she has a name?"

"Yeah, her name's Miranda." Rudy sat back in his chair, smiling behind the sunglasses he was still wearing even though they were indoors.

Could it possibly be true? Barry thought. Rudy didn't seem like her type, but then again, what was her type?

"You hooked up with Miranda?" came a stranger's voice.

Barry turned around to see an unassuming-looking guy dressed all in black with slightly expensive-looking clothing. He was probably only a year or two older than Barry. Rudy looked distressed at seeing this newcomer.

"Oh, hey David," Rudy said.

"It's Debbido," Debbido said. "Respect the culture."

"I was talking to him," Rudy said, pointing at the newcomer whose name was also David.

"You hooked up with Miranda from work?" David asked.

"I thought you don't work there anymore," Rudy said.

"No, I don't. You had sex with Miranda then?"

"Well, we fooled around a bit. She said she wasn't ready for sex yet."

"Oh, so you guys made out?" David asked.

"Well, we totally could have, but she knows this other chick is into me, and I don't want to make Miranda jealous."

"Forgive me," David said. "I'm a little confused. What exactly did the two of you do together?"

"We've hung out a bunch, and she's totally down to hook up. I'm just, you know, playing it cool."

"Right," David said. "I don't even really give a shit about any of that. I came here to hand these out." He pulled a box seemingly from nowhere and removed several fliers. Each flier he handed out was, upon closer inspection, several pages thick.

"What is this?" Black Barry asked.

"It's called Beatitudinem," David said. "All the info is in there. Check it out sometime. It's really cool, really open, and completely free to come. Nice tracksuit," he said to Barry before walking away.

"That guy doesn't know anything," Rudy said. "If he were more smarter, he would have handed out a business card."

Barry flipped through several pages without reading any of the content. On nearly every page were photos of gorgeous women. Barry couldn't get distracted. He had Nastya to think about. Before even being asked by Rocket Jizz, Barry volunteered, "There's this really hot Russian girl I've got my eye on."

"Oh wow, Russian, very cool, White Barry," Rocket Jizz

said. "You think you have good chance with her?"

"I do because I'm Russian, and we've chatted a bunch of times."

"I thought you were Jewish," Bert said.

"No, damn it," Barry said.

At that moment, Barry felt the sensation of being watched. He scanned the bar but didn't find anything out of the ordinary. He did see Daniel sitting with some friends, but Daniel not coming over to say hi was ordinary.

"What do you do for a living, Mr. Jizz?" Black Barry asked.

"Well, you see, mainly I am massacre many peoples. You can say I am doing genocide and possess weapons of mass destruction, but also I can reduce people on a smaller scale if you need me get rid of someone."

"Good to know," Black Barry said.

"And I mean it. I help you any time. Don't be shy, boys."

"What do you think of acting class?" Black Barry asked White Barry.

"I don't know," Barry said. "It seems pretty stressful."

"You're goddamn right it's stressful. Especially because they make me do everything to make up for the lack of brothas here. Eventually, I'm going to be playing every goddamn part. It all started with that damn *Lord of the Rings* poster you made with all the black and brown and gay midgets and shit."

"I didn't want to make that poster," Barry said.

"Doesn't matter. Now the department is restricting new white members from joining and wants me to play every lead role until more brothas come in. But they can't find a single one who wants to. And you know, Mr. Hawthorne had the nerve to ask me to go out and recruit as if I know every fucking black person in the city."

"Want me to kill Mr. Hawthorne?" Rocket Jizz asked.

"Shit, maybe," Black Barry said.

Barry didn't have time to be sorry about stupid movie posters. He had to start going to the gym. He needed to work more to afford a gym membership, but also to make sure the hours he worked allowed for him to go to the store that sold useless trinkets so he could run into Nastya. He needed to start drinking tea instead of Coke. He needed to buy more tracksuits and some other clothing. He had to start reading science journals, whatever the fuck those were. He was going to start his morning with twenty-five push-ups and twenty-five sit-ups. That was the rule. If he couldn't stick to that every day, then he'd no longer have any right to Nastya in the eyes of the gods of fate.

Eventually, everyone began to disperse. When only Bert and Barry were left, Barry declined the invitation to go to his place to rehearse lines. Barry stepped outside and imagined how he'd look standing there holding a cigarette.

"Hello, Barry the Russian," a voice called out.

There was only one other person standing outside the bar. He was tall, skinny, and had greasy blond hair and enormous googly eyes struggling to stay inside his skull. He was almost as ugly as Bert.

"Oh, hi," Barry said.

"You talk very loudly," the stranger said. "I heard your entire life story in there. Even if I hadn't, it wouldn't have taken me long to figure out who you are. There aren't a whole lot of Barrys in this city."

"Wait, who are you?"

"My name is Christopher, but I believe you know me as Enlightened Celestial."

"Oh shit," Barry said.

"After your friend Kenneth became famous, I was shocked to see he lived in the same city as me. I looked through his friends list on Facebook and found you. You think you've got yourself a girlfriend, eh?"

"Well, I can't say for sure, but I think something could happen."

"Have you learned nothing? You can learn as much of this stupid language as you want and feel good about yourself because she smiled at you once, but you're never going to sleep with her. I'm saying this as a brother, to save you from embarrassment. Don't waste your time."

"You don't know what you're talking about," Barry said. "I have to get going."

Christopher texted him as soon as he'd reached the car, and continued all night. Barry regretted giving him his number. It might have been more disturbing if not for the fact that Rocket Jizz also texted him all night, and he'd definitely not given him his number.

Chapter 15

Miranda

Miranda bought a gun. She'd never fired a gun in her life, nor had she any desire to, but after buying it, having it was the only thing that made sense to her. Alexei had been adamant that it wasn't necessary to hire security for the office, but recent events had convinced her otherwise. In any case, she loved how the Glock 43 felt in her hands.

Her office was beginning to stink. She'd bought some scented candles and sprayed the room down in advance of their meeting, but once Sergio sat down opposite her, his stench overpowered everything else.

"I think I know where I went wrong," Sergio said, pulling a bag of corn nuts from his pocket. The smell of corn nuts nauseated her. Everything about Sergio nauseated her. The way his lips smacked when he spoke, the way bits of spittle constantly dribbled out of his mouth, his horrendous odor, the fact that he was there for a fourth time.

"Mind if I eat in here?" he asked, opening the bag.

"Yes."

"Oh." He pulled a handful out and shoved them into his mouth anyway. "I think I know where I went wrong the first three times."

Miranda knew where he'd gone wrong the first three times—no matter how valuable the information he possessed, nothing could change how awful he smelled.

"Considering the distances that have to be traveled on this one," Miranda said, "it's going to end up costing quite a bit more. But, as they say, fourth time's the charm."

"Exactly." He smiled. "It would be easy if these girls were clients of mine. Then I wouldn't need you guys' help. Well, I might, but not as much."

Miranda wasn't certain she wanted to know what kind of profession attracted someone like Sergio.

"Are you going to ask me what I do?"

"I'm desperate to know."

"I install surveillance. Well, I don't just install it. My uncle manufactures and patents it. Not cheap shit either. Really high-tech stuff. Cameras that capture HD-quality feed. Cameras so small, they're invisible to the naked eye. Microphones that pick up sound with little to no interference. You guys ought to look into it. Plant some of our equipment in these peoples' house and your clients will think you're psychics! You could charge ten times more than what you're charging now." He laughed.

Do you have equipment that detects smell? Miranda bit her tongue. The idea of someone so revolting installing spy gear in some innocent woman's house without her knowledge made her feel ill. "How much would this type of equipment cost?"

"You scratch my back, I scratch yours."

"I didn't say I was interested in a purchase, just interested in the price."

"How 'bout a discount?"

His stench lingered long after he'd departed. She was caressing her pistol when Adam walked into her office without knocking.

"I have something to take care of, so you're going to talk with my client today," he said, then quickly turned and left.

"Wait, what?" Miranda stood and ran after him, but he was long gone. Miranda, taking a cue from Adam, barged into Alexei's office without knocking.

"Why does Adam think it's okay to drop his clients on me?"

"Oh, hey, Miranda." Alexei looked as though he'd been caught masturbating or snorting cocaine. "You look nice today. New sunglasses?"

"I don't have time to do someone else's shit right now."

"Hmm. Well, Adam is quite busy helping me. Actually, yeah. I was going to tell you later, but we're expanding."

"What?!"

"Yeah, business is good, so why not branch out? We're looking to set up shop in a couple of other cities."

"Alexei, that was my idea."

"Was it?"

"Yes! You dismissed it."

"I don't recall. In any case, back to the subject at hand."

"I can't. I have too much going on already."

"Come on, it won't take that long. He's already here, waiting. You can spare ten minutes of your time and show off some of that classic all-star charm of yours, no? In any case, Mr. Santillano seems a bit nervous. I think you could help ease that for him." He paused as though something had just occurred to him. "Hey, Santillano is your last name. Hmm, I hadn't even connected the dots. Any relation?"

"What's his first name?"

"Enrique."

Miranda's heart turned to ash. She grabbed for her pistol, but only grasped air. "No relation," she forced out, then walked out of the office without another word.

Marching down the hallway, she prayed she wouldn't see what she knew she'd inevitably see. She reached the door separating the waiting room from the back offices and peeked through the window, doing her best to conceal her face. Finding out she'd die within the next five minutes couldn't compare to how she felt seeing her father there. She could have run out and strangled him right then and there. Instead, she went out the back exit to find the nearest bar.

Drinks, she'd texted both Christian and Sabrina. She hadn't seen either in weeks. With the exception of Nastya at the gym, her interactions of late were increasingly male. And most of these men were weak and pathetic. She'd come to the conclusion that weak and pathetic men comprised the majority of the male sex. The only things they were good for were paying her bills and funding her gin and tonic diet.

Miranda found herself in a joy-sucking bar with a joyless cunt of a bartender. She downed the first gin and tonic in seconds. When ordering the second, she received a judgmental stare from the bartender. "Just keep the fucking drinks coming, hold your judgment, and you'll get a good tip."

Her sunglasses had to remain on. She fought back tears

thinking about her father back there. Miranda hadn't truly believed her parents had loved each other romantically since she was thirteen, but as long as she didn't see any evidence that proved otherwise, she could live in bliss. Her parents were a happily married and loving couple. Her father was supposed to be a good Catholic, whatever the hell that meant. He was supposed to work hard, drink beer, provide, and have no sex drive after fifty. If the woman he was after was his own age, did that make it better or worse? Would that mean he was looking for love he couldn't find in her mom? If she was some twenty-year-old Instagram slut, did it make it more acceptable, as that was what all old perverts were after in any case? Was her father in love with this girl? Did he want love from this mysterious woman, or was he just looking to shoot his load? Was her mother to blame? Every thought was as disgusting as the next. Could her mother have done more to prevent this, or had she caused it? What would Miranda do when she met this woman?

She'd brought along a copy of David Foster Wallace's *Infinite Jest*, a book she'd owned for years and never opened. At the office, she'd managed to get through five pages, but immediately forgot everything. The bar didn't make reading it any easier. There were words, but they meant nothing. They were merely inkblots on a page. At home, Miranda had finished Nabokov's *Pale Fire* and would be damned if she could recall a single thing about it. Whatever point books once served in her life was gone. They made better paperweights or door blockers than anything else. The fact that Wallace had killed himself made the book all the more unpalatable. It seemed like a huge waste to make others suffer through your work when you got a free pass to fuck off and die.

Miranda pulled out her notepad instead. She nearly snapped her pen in half when it failed to leave any ink on the blank page. It finally surrendered to her on the fifth attempt. *Gabby*, she wrote. Neither Gabby nor Jake drank, so having them meet at a bar seemed unlikely. Gabby drank coffee, but Miranda wasn't sure Jake did. Ethel needed to be happy with the outcome for any of this to work, so she couldn't be left out of the equation. If Miranda could just find a way to get each of them what they wanted.

Why she cared specifically about these clients, she didn't know. Her job was to encourage dreams, not provide actual solutions. She woke up and went to bed with that knowledge every day. But if she could make Gabby and Ethel happy, it would provide her with the smallest quantum of relief. She'd get to determine who won or lost. Maybe if she could get Jake, whom Gabby should have wanted to be with, and Jordan, whom Gabby thought she wanted to be with, in the same building at the same time, she could guide Gabby away from mediocrity and toward her destiny. Miranda wasn't inebriated enough to work out this scenario.

On her third drink, several other people wandered into the bar. She didn't look up to see who was there, but she did feel a strange tingle on the back of her neck. Sabrina hadn't responded to her text and probably never would. Christian was on her way.

Since Miranda last saw her, Christian had cut her hair quite short. Miranda was immediately jealous, knowing she'd never be able to pull off that kind of style with her ears. She was on drink number four. She decided not to tell Christian about her dad. That had to remain unspoken. Instead, she told her about Shaun.

"How are you holding up?" Christian asked.

"I refuse to shed a single tear for him. That's why he

pulled that whole stunt, isn't it? For me to feel sorry for him. Because I wasn't able to end her happy marriage and reignite their relationship, right? Pity points are all it was. I hope he got five seconds of pity elsewhere. He won't get any from me. After this conversation, I'll never acknowledge his existence again."

"Choosing to put guilt on you was unfair, but I can only imagine what pain he was going through to do that. I saw his photo. Good-looking guy."

"There's a saying about good-looking people and good-looking corpses, but there wasn't much of a corpse left. He was weak. Weak men put all their failings and insecurities in the hands of women. They want us to feel the burden of all their wrongdoings and feel as bad as they do. But when did their failures become our responsibility? Why must we have to feel bad too? What the hell was I supposed to do? I'm not helping weak men ever again, or feeling sorry for them. I'll take their money. Just like I took Doug's money. Whatever does or doesn't happen between him and a teenager is his responsibility alone. And now, thanks to his generous donations, I get to do this." She ordered another drink.

Christian was silent for a while. That was okay, because she didn't try to dissuade Miranda from ordering more drinks, which was what made her such a good friend.

"That guy's been staring at you all evening," Christian said, pointing.

Miranda turned around and locked eyes with Rudy. "Oh, for fuck's sake."

Rudy took that as his signal to approach.

"*Buongiorno*," he said.

"Come again?"

"Buongiorno. It means 'hello' in Italian. I don't know if you heard me talking on the phone over there. I dabble in languages."

"I don't know anything about Italian. Maybe if you spoke Farsi, we'd have something to talk about."

"You come here often? That's cool. What's your drink of choice? Let me guess—gin and tonic? Let me buy you one."

"Wow," Miranda said. "Very good."

"Gin and tonic is my favorite drink as well," he said.

"That's amazing. Seems like a pretty big coincidence, doesn't it?"

"Or maybe fate."

"Or maybe you've been spending time with Adam."

"How did y—" He caught himself. "Who's Adam?"

"Either you think I'm fucking braindead, or you are. You show up at my gym, you show up at the bars I go to, you show up here. I see you every time you think I don't. Every corner I turn and every parking lot I pull into, there you are. If that's fate, then fate is a cruel bitch. Or maybe you know where I work, and since you know our services, you clearly know what I do. So, Rudy, are you fucking kidding me right now?"

The stupid grin he always wore finally faded. His olive skin began to turn shades of green. "Wait, let me explain. I . . . j-just give m-me a chance."

"What chance? What explanation? Try formulating a coherent sentence first. Try actually making a movie before you hand me your business card. God! I hate that I even know that about you. Rudy, there is no chance here. You creep the shit out of me. Even before you ever opened your mouth, I hated your big fucking shorts and your round head and had no interest in you. See that balding guy over there? He has a higher chance than you. In fact, I'm going to take him home and fuck his brains out."

Miranda got up to take him home and fuck his brains out.

Christian got up as well. "You will do no such thing," she said.

"I can fuck whoever I want."

"Sure, but you're in no condition to drive. I'm taking you home."

"I can take her home, you know, as, like, a way to show I care about her—"

"Holy shit, fuck off!" Christian shouted.

~~~

Christian didn't stay. After plopping Miranda onto her bed, she left her with a bottle of water and a bucket before heading out.

Weak men are the bane of this world, Miranda thought. *I'll never feel sorry for them again.* Rudy was probably out there right now complaining to his friends for hours about how some girl had led him on and then shat all over his heart. That was fine.

In the morning, Miranda woke up without a hangover. In fact, she woke up back at her parents' house. When she went downstairs, she found her parents eating breakfast together. Normally, the smell of eggs and chorizo would fill the house, but she couldn't smell a thing.

"Good morning, mi flaca, have some breakfast." Her mom smiled.

Both her parents were smiling. Miranda wanted breakfast

but couldn't stay. She had to be somewhere. She hugged her parents, her father especially hard. "I love you both."

Outside, Miranda thought about how lucky she was to have the new train station right next to her house. She took the train to the bar where she was meeting David for a drink.

David never showed up. Typical. He never showed up to work either. Instead, she saw Shaun. That couldn't be right. Shaun was dead. Or maybe he hadn't died yet. Maybe he wouldn't die at all if she could warn him.

"Shaun," she called out. "Shaun."

Why did her voice sound like it was underwater?

It took several attempts before he finally noticed her.

"Oh, hey, Miranda," he said, all smiles. "What's up?"

She couldn't find the words to explain.

"You look awful. Who died?" he asked with a small laugh.

"You did. You do. Please listen. You're going to die. Don't go to CoinciDATE, and forget about Melissa, and please, please, don't kill yourself."

Shaun was dead. Miranda saw his face every night before falling asleep. She wondered if Melissa did too.

Chapter 16

Doug

Doug couldn't remember the last time he'd taken a walk just to take a walk, especially so late at night. Several of the streetlights were out, and the only sound came from crickets and the occasional car. Doug stamped out his cigarette and lit a third. It was perfect. Walking and smoking. The night was perfect. Everything was perfect, yet he felt uneasy. The euphoria had lasted for about an hour before giving way to dizziness and an upset stomach.

He lifted his fingers to smell them for the hundredth time. There was nothing. He wished he could have remained unshowered so that her smell could linger on him a little longer, but then how would he have explained that to his wife? In any case, he could imagine the smell.

He came upon his car, the only one in the parking lot. He'd parked near a minimart several blocks away from the house. He checked his watch. He had time enough for another lap around the neighborhood before Sandra would suspect anything. He needed the time to relive the evening's events once more.

She had a cute suburban house. No one was home except for Grandma, who was out like a log. It was miraculous how easily everything had fallen into place, to the point that Miranda's involvement was almost, but not completely, unnecessary. She'd set the ball in motion, but once Talia had become aware of his existence, all he had to do was exist.

He'd taken on a part-time job as a calculus tutor. He had five students, four of whom didn't exist and one of whom was Talia. One lesson a week became two, and then three. The first time he shared a small study room with her, he couldn't believe how perfect her body was. He let himself get hard under the table. Soon enough, innocent texts about homework became selfies with childish emojis. He wasn't going to tempt fate. He had to allow things to take their natural course. Soon enough, she was sending selfies in new outfits she'd bought. He hadn't felt that level of excitement over receiving a message from a girl since high school.

Can I see a picture of your wife? she wrote one day, adding a smiley face.

Against his better judgment, he sent a picture of the two of them at the beach in Cancún from the previous summer.

Oh, she replied three hours later.

Oh?

Nothing, she wrote. *She's pretty. Not what I expected. Doesn't seem like your type.*

And what's my type? he wrote. He also included a smiley face and LOL.

I don't know. She looks like the girl-next-door type. I pictured something else. It doesn't matter. I wanted to ask you, could you please help me study?

It's a little late, he wrote. *I think all the study rooms are closed.*

You can come here. No one is home except my grandmother. I'm really stressed about this test I have tomorrow. Please? I'd feel a lot better if I had one more chance to study with you. Please? She sent a selfie with pleading puppy dog eyes.

Grandma was indeed a heavy sleeper. Nothing stood between him and Talia. Doug knew she was a virgin and realized this might be the only chance he'd ever have, so he had his way with her body, doing anything and everything he wanted. He didn't wear a condom, nor did she ask him to. He wanted to feel everything. And for thirty wonderful minutes, the hole in his heart was filled. The missing pieces of satisfaction he couldn't get with other women he found in Talia. There was no Sandra, no job, no insufferable fucking Joey, no promotion—only those thirty minutes.

He took a big risk not wearing a condom, but he had to, or else the whole endeavor would have been for nothing.

When he got home, Sandra was feeling frisky and immediately started tearing off his clothes. He closed his eyes and fucked her hard, imagining her moans were Talia's. He was lasting forever and getting tired. Try as he might and pretend as he might, she could never compare to the thirty minutes he had earlier. He flipped her over, fucked her doggy-style, then pulled himself out, jerking it for ages, Talia in his head. He finished finally and weakly on Sandra's back.

Once she was asleep, he went to the living room to watch some TV. It didn't matter what was on. He couldn't cope with the silence. Now that time had passed and the euphoria had worn off, he decided it was best not to see her again. He'd achieved his goal. It was done. But thinking about her made him hard again.

She texted him the following day, and he ignored it. Five days later they had sex again, and it was even better the second time.

This can't go on, he said to himself. *You were supposed to get it out of your system*. But like smoking crack, once he had a taste, he needed more.

At work, Doug found himself actively participating in conversation with Joey. If anything could kill desire, it was Joey.

"And that's why I add the milk after, and not before," Joey said. "Anyway, I bought these beautiful ribeyes and some nice scotch. What do you say about coming over to my place for a man dinner?"

"Absolutely," Doug said.

"Really?"

"Yes," Doug said.

"That's fantastic! You're going to love it."

It was fantastic, and it allowed Doug to spend the rest of the day thinking about Joey's house and what kind of useless information he'd learn there. Joey was definitely someone who would refer to a room in his place as a "man cave." Doug also had lunch with Sandra to look forward to. She was going to meet him outside the office, and they'd walk to the bullshit health food place that was expensive and terrible.

Another thing occupying too much space in his mind was Kale fucking Crispins. His name was almost as stupid as his appearance. He looked like a stretched-out but not grown-up version of the kid from *Leave it to Beaver*. He was Doug's only competition for the upcoming promotion. Doug was superior in the looks department and had a more-beautiful wife, but Kale Beaver Crispins had been with the company two years longer and was tight with Argyl Stokeworth, the vice-president. Try as he might, Doug hadn't been able to charm the president, Gendo Yagami, yet. Gendo was an inscrutable little bastard. Doug had let him win every round of golf they'd played and had nothing to show for it. He wasn't even sure whether Gendo knew his name. Doug's sole advantage was that everyone wanted to be him, whereas everyone thought Kale was a cunt.

A little past noon, Doug took the elevator down to meet his wife. He wasn't hungry at all and would have preferred a cigarette instead. Then he felt as though an anvil had fallen on his head while a donkey repeatedly kicked him in the balls. Before him was the most impossible of all impossibilities. Sandra wasn't alone. Standing next to her was an olive-skinned, thin, big-eyed, dark-haired girl of fifteen. They were talking and laughing. Talia saw Doug before Sandra did, which also meant she'd seen him freeze. When Sandra saw him as well, his only course of action was to carry on forward.

"Doug." Sandra's eyes lit up. "This is Talia. Isn't that such a pretty name? Talia, this is my husband, Doug."

Don't you dare, Doug thought. *Don't say it. Don't you dare fucking say it. I swear to Christ, bitch, don't do it.*

Talia smiled, her eyes undressing him. "Hello, Doug."

Doug nodded politely.

"Babe, why are you sweating?" Sandra asked.

Doug touched his forehead. He was drenched. "I was running around a lot up there, babe, and you know Joey hates turning the A/C on."

"I was walking to the office when Talia complimented

my bag. I turned around and saw she had the exact same one. Isn't that funny?"

"Yes," Doug said.

"And we just started talking. Are you ready, babe?"

"Yes."

"What direction are you guys headed?" Talia asked.

"We're going to Larsen's for lunch."

"No kidding? Me too. You wouldn't mind if I walked with you for a few minutes?"

"Not at all!" Sandra said. "That would be great."

Doug pulled out his phone and began reacting to a nonexistent caller. "Yes, no . . . hold on a second . . . I'm going to lunch with my wife. Yes . . . It can't wait? Okay, I'll be right there."

"Doug, what's going on?"

"It's Gendo. He's got to see me right away. I'm so sorry, babe."

As he was apologizing to Sandra, he was texting frantically, telling Talia: *Walk the fuck away from my wife this instant.*

Talia read the text, smiled, and waved goodbye.

Doug waited a minute to ensure she was actually gone, hugged his wife, and ran back inside his office. He ran into a third-floor bathroom and began frantically typing away, in all caps and full of typos.

DON'T YOU DARE EVER TALK
TOVMY WIFE AGAIN. DOVYOU
DUCKING UNDERSTAND? STOP
CALLING ME AND DON"T COME
TO MY WORK!!1 WE. ARE. DONE!

Two seconds after he sent the text, his phone rang. When a full two minutes passed and his phone wouldn't stop vibrating, he shut it off.

How had he been so blind to not see this coming? At his desk, he could think of nothing else. He couldn't even work up the energy to get mad when he saw that chode Kale speaking to both the vice-president and the president.

"Should I pick up some beer and snacks for tonight as well?" Joey asked.

Doug didn't respond. If word got out about his affair, losing his wife and job would be the least of his worries. Could she be pregnant? He'd put the pills in her mouth himself, but still. The thought of him putting his fingers in her mouth made him hard. *No! It's not supposed to be this way.*

When he turned on his phone, he saw more than a dozen messages from Talia. Most of them contained pictures. One was of his house, one was of his car, another was of Sandra walking down the street. The rest were selfies.

He wrote:

> This has to end. I'm sorry I yelled at you, but this must stop. What we did was a mistake. You deserve better and I know for a girl as pretty as you, it won't be hard to find a good guy out there, but this is the end. Don't call me anymore. It won't do either of us any good.

Again, his phone was vibrating.

After work, Doug accompanied Joey to pick up some beer and inedible snacks. His phone vibrated the entire way. Once, purely out of foolish hope, Doug looked at it thinking it might be an email from Gendo. No, it was a picture of Talia bending over.

Joey had a decent-sized apartment on the ground floor that was much tidier than Doug expected. It was unsurprisingly tacky though, with several movie posters and neon beer signs on the wall. Doug downed his first glass of scotch and demanded another.

Two hours passed without a message from Talia. This time Sandra was texting him, happy as ever, so Talia hadn't done any serious damage yet. If today were the worst that would happen, Doug would allow himself to have a nice dinner with Joey. In fact, it became quite fun as they both took turns shitting on Kale. Doug was beginning to like Joey. He liked that he hung on his words, laughed at his jokes, and never interrupted.

Thirty minutes later, all the goodwill had gone when Doug saw that Joey had prepared both the steaks well-done. He hadn't even asked his preference! While he was chewing on an unbearably tough, tendon-filled piece, his phone went off. When it didn't stop, he excused himself and went outside. He wasn't sure what motivated him to answer, but he did.

"Yes?"

"Hey," she replied.

"Yes? I'm listening."

"I wanted to hear your voice."

"Talia, we really can't do this."

"I like the way you say my name."

"Please stop calling."

"You were right. I shouldn't have talked to your wife or called you so much. But I was jealous. I miss you so much. I need you."

"Stop it."

"No. Please, why can't I see you?"

"You know why."

"I won't bother you at work, I promise. I just want to see you. I want you. I want you to fuck me. Please."

"I can't. This is over."

"But I'm so horny, Doug. I want you. No one's home. I want you to come on my face. Please, I'm getting wet just thinking about it. Please, Doug. You can fuck me in the ass. I know you want to. Please come over."

Doug apologized to Joey, explained he had an emergency, and left.

~~~

"Stop calling!" he screamed into the phone. "How many times must I tell you, you dumb, devious bitch?"

"It's been three weeks," she said. "I miss you."

"You need to get it through your head: we are finished. Fuck off."

"Some man you are. Thinking you could fuck me as you please and walk away. Remember, I know where you live."

"Is that a threat?"

"No, Daddy, I just miss you."

"We'll talk about this later."

"When?"

"Later, as in not now."

~~~

At work the next day, in a flurry of trying to get his things in order, Doug was called to the reception desk.

"What is it?"

"There's a young girl waiting over there to see you."

There were plenty of windows up there. Doug could begin screaming, push her out of one, and say it was self-defense. When he turned around, Talia stood up. She was wearing the shortest skirt he'd ever seen. Several of the men in the office had definitely been alerted to her presence.

Doug put on a cordial face and asked, "Is my sister okay?"

Talia nodded.

"Grace," Doug said to the receptionist, "This is my sister's kid. They're only in town for a few more days."

"What's your name, darling?"

"Talia."

"Oh, how exotic."

Doug walked Talia down to the third floor, which was almost always empty. The entire time he had to slap her hand away as she kept going for his. Once he saw the coast was clear, he pinned her against the wall. "Is it money you want? Is that what it's going to take? Name your price."

"I'm not a fucking whore."

"Then what do you want?"

"You."

"You can't have me."

"That's a shame, Doug. Here's the thing. I'm pregnant. Things would be a lot easier if you'd just be with me."

Doug said nothing. There was nothing to say. If he hadn't known any better, he'd have thought he just died. His life was over. Try as he might, he couldn't come up with the word that meant getting rid of the little bastard before it started to look human.

"Is there anything you want to say, Doug?"

At that moment, she was the ugliest thing he'd ever seen. She had sunken-in eye sockets, crooked teeth, and quite frankly, a mannish chin. She repulsed him. He felt that the air around her was foul as well. In the past, Doug had pursued girls he had deemed attractive, only for them to open their mouths and go from eights to fives. Talia was hovering around a two right then.

"My parents are home all week. You'll get a hotel for us to stay at, right? Or should I come to your place?"

"I'll get a hotel," Doug struggled to say.

"Great."

Doug returned to his desk and sat down without looking at anyone.

"Who was that, playa?" Joey asked. His smile immediately became a frown when he saw how distressed his friend was. "Doug?"

"Joey?"

"Yes?"

"Can I buy some steaks and scotch to bring to your house tonight?"

"Doug, it would be my pleasure."

Doug began crying.

Глава 17

Барри

One, two, three, four, five . . . only twenty more.

He took a break. He was allowed to sit a few minutes. It didn't have to be twenty-five push-ups nonstop. It just had to be twenty-five. He had all morning. After he'd fulfilled his morning duties, he went to the fridge. Dozens of cans of Coke stared at him, glistening in the cool air. He didn't have tea in his house, but he did have Diet Coke, and nothing in the rules said anything about Diet Coke.

His wore his gold-striped black Adidas tracksuit. He'd just gotten ready to scout out the gym when Mr. Schnitt pulled him aside and handed him his enormous gardening shears. "Why don't you try to be useful this morning?"

Barry frowned. Being useful was hot and sweaty work. Barry hated being outdoors. The initial violent snap of the gardening shears was satisfying, but that sensation gave way to boredom soon enough. After a bee flew close to him, he ran inside, told his dad the work was done, and climbed into his car.

The gym was packed, and smaller than he expected. *Good. Easier to see her.* She wasn't there. The three-percent-body-fat specimen of a manager managed to con Barry into buying a year membership upfront instead of purchasing a monthly plan. He assured Barry that three hundred dollars was a steal.

Barry looked around at the equipment and people around him. He'd never seen those types of machines in his life. He'd seen treadmills. Those seemed simple enough. The treadmills were ideally positioned, as they were directly behind windows facing the parking lot. He had a clear view of anyone coming in. He'd walk at a slow pace until catching sight of her, and once he saw her approaching, he'd switch to jogging so she could see him mid-workout.

Two hours and forty minutes of leisurely walking later, there was no sign of her. There was no sign of her at the cheap trinket store, nor at the one bar she went to. Would he really have to wait until Monday to see her? He'd canceled his six o'clock Russian lesson because he hadn't done his homework. Sunday, he repeated his steps, and still didn't see her. The wait for Monday would hurt.

He arrived at school earlier than ever, hoping perhaps she'd want an early-morning cigarette. He lit one up for himself in front of the cafeteria. He was the first to arrive, but others came dribbling in. On his second cigarette, he saw what he'd been waiting for. Nastya walked past, but didn't see him. Her eyes were glued to the textbook she was reading while walking. Her legs were so long. Her body was so long. He loved that she read while walking. He made a note to try that around campus.

"Hi, Nastya," he said.

"Hi," she said, turning around with a smile, then continuing to pour her attention into her book as she walked toward her office.

"Care for a cigarette?" he called out, louder than anticipated.

"I can't now, but if you see me at lunchtime, sure."

He thought about her all through history and geology. He thought about how he'd completed his required number of push-ups and sit-ups and therefore whatever happened today with Nastya would work out in his favor.

Then he thought about Christopher. Despite revealing himself that night, Christopher didn't like meeting in person. That didn't stop him from texting Barry every minute. Between texts from Christopher and Rocket Jizz, Barry had never been more popular.

All morning, Barry had been practicing how to say, "Would you like to have lunch with me?" in Russian. Christopher said the idea was stupid. He said it was best to save up their money so they could go to Nevada and buy some prostitutes. Barry didn't want a prostitute. In fact, once he set eyes on Nastya, all other girls disappeared. That's how he knew his feelings for her weren't trivial. They were real. Barry had a thousand crushes growing up, but none like this.

Rocket Jizz, unlike Christopher, was supportive of Barry's prospective romance.

Way to go, Barry, my little Blueberry. I so proud of you to ask out this Russian girl. I hope you have great sex with her LOL, he wrote the night Barry told him his plans.

"Would you like to have lunch with me?" Barry practiced in Russian.

At lunch, Barry didn't sit with Bert or the others. He stood several yards away from them with his eyes glued to the student services building. When 12:30 hit and Nastya hadn't emerged, he decided he'd have to go up there and get things going himself. He reached for the handle, but it was already opening toward him, and out walked a pair of long legs. He wasn't ready to see her and began sweating.

"What are you doing here?" she asked.

"Oh, uh, just taking a shortcut to the other side of campus," he said.

"I guess that means I don't get a cigarette?"

"Of course you get one," he said, pulling out a Marlboro Gold.

"Not here. We have to go down there."

Barry walked side by side with her, trying to match her long-legged steps. She was a fast walker, whereas his legs were dead jelly from the hours on the treadmill. They walked in silence. He hadn't filled in the gaps with what he was supposed to ask her after the cigarettes and before asking her out to lunch. He'd hoped to see her at the gym or store over the weekend so they'd have something to talk about.

"How was your weekend?" he asked as he handed her a cigarette. He tried to light it five times before he succeeded.

"My weekend was great," she said. "I went on a road trip up north with a bunch of friends and got way too drunk. It was really crazy. There are photos of me being really embarrassing."

He loved her voice. He loved that her accent wasn't fully Russian but was noticeable enough to add to her character. He thought she wasn't supposed to drink much.

"What did you do?" she asked.

Barry took a deep drag on his cigarette before answering. "I went to the gym. The twenty-four-hour one that used to be the video store, on Ventura Road. Do you know it?"

"Yes, I know it. I go there, actually. Interesting. I didn't picture you going to the gym. Sorry, that came out wrong."

Barry didn't know how to react, but felt happy at least that she'd pictured him. Picturing him in any capacity meant she'd been thinking of him. Holy shit. Should he push his luck?

"Then afterward," he continued, "I went to Cost Plus to look around. I don't typically buy anything, but I like to go and see all the interesting things they have."

Nastya smiled. "If I didn't know any better, I'd say you were picking my brain. I love that place. Strange I've never seen you there or at the gym."

Barry couldn't believe how well it was going. He'd ask a question and she'd give an answer. He realized he wasn't afraid and was in fact enjoying himself. He wished he could have stayed in that moment forever. He loved her eyes and her smile, and he hadn't even stared at her tits once. He was getting ready to ask what she did for fun when she was attacked by a stranger.

"Boo!" the man yelled, coming from behind and grabbing her by the shoulders.

She jumped, then yelled, "Oh my God!" when she saw who her assailant was.

They embraced for far longer than Barry liked.

"This is Niko," she said after several minutes. "Niko, this is . . . Barry."

Barry tried not to notice how long it took her to say his name as he stared at Niko. He was about the same height as Barry, with untamed, shoulder-length hair. He had dirty facial hair, and due to his glasses and round head, he looked like

Chicken Little. Niko's eyes were pointed up and to the right and would remain that way for their interaction.

"I wasn't expecting to see you so soon," she said.

"I got back last night." His voice was high-pitched, nasal, and sounded as though he were putting in an effort to be apathetic.

"Niko just got back from a month-long trip to India."

"Oh, great," Barry said.

"Not just India. Tibet as well. I followed the path of his holiness Kundun from Lhasa on his exile to India. In India, I helped work on this bio farm. I've worked and helped set up bio farms all over the world. I taught them a lot, but really I'm the one who had the learning experience."

"I can't wait to hear all about it," Nastya said.

"How about tonight? You free?"

"Absolutely."

Barry couldn't ask her out to lunch that day. Niko and Nastya—mainly Niko—talked for another thirty minutes, all but forgetting Barry. Nastya even stayed out so long listening to stories of Indian bio farms she was late returning to work.

The old Barry would have gone into a jealous rage. The new Barry let Niko talk. He had to show Niko he wasn't threatened by him. He was going to be nice to Niko, maybe even get in tight with him. Eventually, Nastya would come around. She'd realize that there was nothing all that interesting going on in India.

~~~

Barry had a routine to stick to. The gods of Fate had to be appeased. He also decided to grow his facial hair out to match

Niko's.

His fifth day in a row at the gym, he finally saw Nastya walking in from the parking lot. He quickly increased the speed so she'd see him running. Once inside, she gave him a quick wave and disappeared. She'd seen him; that was enough. After a minute of running on the 5.1 setting, he got off the treadmill and left.

I'm going to ask her out tomorrow, he texted Christopher. It had been three weeks since he'd smoked a cigarette with her and Niko.

Barry . . . Christopher replied. It showed he was typing. A minute passed, and he was still typing. Eventually, Barry was hit with a flood of texts. He hesitated to read them. For the first time in his life, he felt a sense of optimism. That Niko guy was an unwelcome setback, sure, but Barry was doing everything right. Christopher only wanted to destroy his confidence.

> Barry, this is the worst idea in the long, sad history of bad ideas. I'm going to tell you a story about a brother of ours named Ezra. Ezra went to a nice university, better than the shithole we study at. He also had wealth. His father was some Hollywood type. Not anyone you'd know, but still, he had an appropriate Hollywood-level income. He came from money, had a nice car, nice clothes, and a good haircut.
>
> One day, he started writing all his online brothers that he had some great news. There was a cute girl in several of his classes, and after a semester of sharing glances with her,

he worked up the courage not just to talk to her, but to invite her to study with him. Wouldn't you know it, they were studying together, Barry. She smiled at him, Barry. She laughed at his jokes, Barry. They met several times. Do you understand, Barry? It's important that you understand.

One day, he thought, "Gee, we've been spending so much time together, and when a girl smiles it means she likes you, so the only logical thing to do is ask her out to dinner." So he asked. She said "Yeah, maybe," but what he heard, Barry, was "Yeah."

The day of the supposed dinner came. He sent her a text at noon. He wanted to send one as soon as he woke up, but that would have seemed too desperate. Three hours went by and no response. Barry, he still held out hope, because girls like to play hard to get and there were plenty of hours left in the day.

At five o'clock, he sent a follow-up text. At nine p.m., he had no response and wished her a goodnight, suggesting maybe they try another time.

She responded three days later: Sorry, I missed this.

He responded suggesting dinner; no response.

She'd say hi to him at school and smile. Don't you understand, Barry? You don't even have the Russian's phone number.

Now, back to the hero of our story. The same thing happened to every girl at his school he ever talked to. Despite the money and clothes, nothing could change his inferior genetics. Girls picked up on it immediately. He was doomed the moment he stepped into the classroom. No amount of charm, talent, humor, or wealth could ever change their minds. All they saw were weak chins, noses too big or not big enough, arms not hairy enough, and a torso not long enough.

So, Barry, all the wealth in the world couldn't make him desirable. He did the only thing there was left to do: he took a gun to school, killed thirteen people, and died as he lived. A sad virgin. He had more of a shot than you do. Forget this girl, Barry. I've run it by the other brothers. They beg you not to humiliate yourself.

Barry sat in silence. Reading it meant thinking it, and thinking it meant the possibility of Christopher being right. But he couldn't be. If he was, then what was the point of all those push-ups and learning another language?

Barry ran to the fridge and grabbed a Coke.

No. This makes Christopher right.

He went to the gym instead. Because it was ten p.m., there were only a few people inside. He got on the treadmill and started a light jog. He went for three minutes before slowing to a walk. Nastya came through the door. He sped the machine up to a run. She stepped onto the treadmill next to him and smiled.

Barry, he thought to himself, *this is fate. She came here of all nights for a reason. If you don't see this for what it is, you don't deserve her. You're being rewarded for being strong. Relax, be cool, and wait, but don't wait so long you lose your shot.*

Barry was determined to keep pace with her, but after running side by side for ten minutes, he could barely breathe and was ready to drop. He got off and walked over to a machine he'd never used. He'd never used any of them before. He read the instructions on the side several times. He decided to go over to a different machine. It was an ab machine. He'd already done his routine that morning, but figured doing a few more on the machine could only improve his odds.

It was forty minutes before Nastya got off the treadmill, and he'd done nearly two hundred crunches using twenty-pound weights.

Nastya walked his way. He tried to act as though he didn't notice, but she wasn't just walking in his direction; she was walking toward him.

"I know it defeats the whole purpose of being at a gym, but fancy a cigarette?"

God, he loved her voice so much.

The night air made Barry aware of how sweaty he was

when occasional gusts blew his wet clothing against his skin. A woman in her forties walked past and said, "Hi, Stacey."

Nastya waved.

"Stacey?"

"I usually tell people my name is Stacey. It's easier for them. People think Nastya sounds like a porn star name because it sounds like 'nasty.' During English lessons, I went by Stacey."

Stacey, Barry thought to himself. *Stacey*. She'd given him her real name up front.

"How old are you, Barry?"

"Twenty-one. You?"

"I'm twenty-three."

"Oh, cool."

"So cool." She let out a soft laugh. She was shivering and sunk her head into her shoulders.

"I imagine it's much colder in Russia," he said.

"Doesn't mean we don't feel cold like normal people. Cold is cold. This night is cold." She paused. "I never asked. What are you studying, anyway?"

Oh crap, Barry thought. *Think*. He couldn't remember what she was studying or what her interests were. On top of that, he was still as far from settling on a major as possible. *Think, Barry. Don't be like Debbido or Rudy.* She was talking to him. She chose to speak with him. Perhaps, in that case, being honest was the simplest answer.

"Actually, I haven't really chosen a major yet."

"Don't you think you ought to? What are you interested in?"

That had been the wrong answer. Barry was interested in porn, message boards, and occasionally watching an anime. He couldn't very well say any of that.

"I'd like to do something creative," he said.

"Like writing?"

"Yeah, like writing."

"The next Pushkin, maybe?"

"Definitely," he said. He had no idea who Pushkin was.

"Maybe I'll see your name one day at the bookstore, and I can tell people I know that guy."

"Maybe you'd like to join that guy for lunch someday," he said.

The wind blew quietly. Nastya shivered. The gym was completely empty at that point. The crickets were keeping to themselves.

Nastya took a long drag of her cigarette and put it out on the trashcan. "Sure, why not?"

"Great! You have a good night!" Barry said, trying not to run to his car. Once he sat down inside, he realized he hadn't asked for her phone number. No matter, the difficult part was done. He could get the number later. He texted Christopher his good news.

Christopher didn't respond that night. Barry got the feeling Christopher wasn't the type who liked to be wrong.

Barry tried his hardest to dream about Nastya that night but dreamt about nothing at all. While that was disappointing, it felt great to be in love. She'd initiated the conversation. He'd been on *her* mind.

The next morning, he was so giddy with excitement, he allowed himself a victory Coke. Just the one.

At school, he told Bert and the gang his tremendous news.

"Whoa, that's great, Barry," Bert said. "Where are you going to take her?"

"I don't know," Barry said. "I hadn't thought about it."

"My girlfriend and I like Olive Garden," Bert said.

"You have a girlfriend?"

"Yeah, for about four years now."

"Jesus Christ."

Bert losing his virginity before Barry was either a cruel joke or a sign that Barry's time had come. He had a couple of cigarettes before going up to the student services center. He got in line behind three others. Nastya saw him right away but didn't smile.

"Hey, *kak dyela?*" he said when it was finally his turn.

"*Tak sebye,*" she said, unsmiling. "What do you need, Barry?"

"I was wondering if you'd thought about my offer last night. You busy today?"

"Yes," she said.

"Oh."

"I'm busy for the next two weeks really. After, it's Christmas break and I'll be with my friends and family. So, sometime after Christmas break."

"Okay, sometime after Christmas break." He was about to leave when he remembered. "By the way, could I get your phone number?"

"Look, I'm pretty busy. I'll give it to you after Christmas break."

"Oh, okay," Barry said. "*Do svidaniya.*"

Not great, not terrible, he thought while walking down the hill. He'd been too eager, he realized. Daniel had always said you couldn't be too eager with girls. Christopher was getting into his head.

When Barry got home, he stepped on the scale. He wanted to see what weeks of going to the gym looked like. After struggling to decide his weight, it finally stopped at 212 pounds. That couldn't be right. How had he gained eight pounds? *It must all be muscle.* Though he couldn't see it yet, the muscle was most likely forming underneath his flaps of skin. Knowing his date with Nastya was imminent, he allowed himself another victory Coke.

~~~

Christmas break was long, painful, and lonely. It felt all the lonelier because Daniel spent the entire time with his girlfriend, and Barry preferred speaking to Christopher online. All he could think about was Nastya. All he wanted to think about was Nastya, but thinking about her made time come to a standstill. He'd rubbed himself raw jacking off and saw no point in going to the gym if she wouldn't be there.

One day, Bert wrote to Barry claiming he had an offer he couldn't refuse.

It's not another acting thing, is it?

No, Barry. You're going to love it. Mind picking me up?

I don't know, Barry texted. *I think I want to stay home.*

Are you still thinking about that Russian girl? She'll be there when you get back, man. Enjoy your break, Barry! You'll go crazy staying home and thinking about her. Have some fun. She's off having fun right now.

Barry didn't like the idea of Nastya having fun without him, but Bert was right: he had to get out of the house.

Barry picked up Bert, and the two took off. They arrived at the biggest house Barry had ever seen in a place he hadn't even known existed. Technically they hadn't left their city, but it was alien to him.

"What are we doing here?" He certainly wasn't wearing clothes suitable for a place like that.

"This place is great," Bert said. "I've been coming for about three weeks. Follow me."

They got inside with ease. No security pat-downs, but being inside didn't put him at ease. The types he expected were all there. Fancy men in fancy suits, handsome and loaded. But among them, something strange was happening. There were guys just like Barry, ugly versions of Barry, more handsome versions of Barry, more Barry versions of Barry. None of them wore tracksuits, but none of them seemed at home in this environment either. Yet there they were, talking to the fancy men and being spoken to as equals.

There weren't just fancy men, but fancy women as well. But *fancy* wasn't the right word. They were sex machines—women taken from the imagination of every Barry in the world and assembled from all the best parts of them in order to create perfect specimens. He'd known women like that existed, but it had never occurred to him he'd see them with his own eyes. Women as tall as Nastya, made even taller by high heels. Tight black dresses. Tight red dresses. Everything tight. Every single one of them a perfect ten. They were existing in the same time and space as all the Barrys.

No, he told himself. *These are distractions. You have a girl, Barry. You've put in the work. Don't look at any of them. They don't matter*. If he even thought about these other women, he'd be cheating on Nastya in his head. Barry had that superpower. He willed himself to be blind to their presence.

"Bert," he said, "what kind of place have you brought me to?"

"Is this your first time here?" a female voice asked. She wasn't wearing nearly as tight of a dress as the others. More than anything, she resembled a secretary, a twenty-one-year-old, ten-out-of-ten Filipina secretary.

"Yes," Barry said.

"How exciting," she said. "I'm Alex. Let me give you a tour. What's your name?"

"Barry."

"Barry," she repeated. His name sounded tasty coming out of her mouth. "I like that. Don't meet a lot of Barrys. If you follow me, you'll find one of our many dining halls. We have nightly specials, but our chefs can make pretty much anything you'd like. If you're hungry, stop by after the tour."

Barry smelled a blend of spices—curry perhaps. He caught a glimpse of the cooks laboring away in the kitchen.

"Next we have one of our game rooms, and when I say games, I mean all of them. Video games, tabletop games, a racquetball room, a basketball court, and a swimming pool. There's time for general play, as well as tryouts for more serious players if you'd like to compete on a team. Over there is a home theater."

She carried on for fifteen minutes. Each room was more impressive than the last. Each girl he passed was more beautiful than the last. No expense had been spared, and everything you could ever need was there. All in one place.

"What's all this for?"

"How do you mean?"

"I . . . I don't think I get it."

"Are you asking if there's an ulterior motive?"

"Well . . . "

"That's okay. Do you know what Beatitudinem means? It means *happiness* in Latin. Do you know what Latin is? It's the language spoken by the Romans, and they were pretty impressive, weren't they? Did you know sixty-seven percent of all words are Latin? That's not a coincidence. It must mean something. We're upfront with what we're all about. We provide happiness for anyone and everyone. Your friend is a welcomed guest of ours. All we ask is that you make an effort to speak with as many people as possible. Don't be shy. There is no judgment here. None. Everyone has an interesting story. See that girl over there?"

The girl over there was a slim, dark-haired beauty.

"She's an ex-Israeli army medic. Could you even imagine?"

"This, all this, for us, is free?"

"Of course, silly. We can't ask you to pay for happiness. But donations are appreciated. If you see one of us going around with a donation box, anything helps."

Barry took out a twenty and put it in the first box that came his way carried by a cute girl. He saw people moving to another room and decided he was supposed to join them. There was a small stage set out before them. To Barry's left was a Debbido type, smelly and sweaty. Several rows ahead of Barry was the actual Debbido, sitting between two Japanese beauties. To Barry's right was the opposite of Debbido, a beautiful woman. Bert sat a couple of seats down the row, talking animatedly with a couple of Barrys.

"Thank you for coming," a beautiful British accent rang out.

The stage had been taken by the handsomest man Barry had ever seen. The way Barry was looking at all the women was how all the women were looking at that man.

"For those who don't know me," said the beautiful black man with the beautiful black British accent in the most expensive suit ever, "my name is Cornwallis Kensington, and yes, I am a British person."

Everyone clapped.

"I won't waste too much of your time yapping away. I simply want to express my gratitude. Enjoy yourselves. I also ask that you write your names and phone numbers on the paper in front of you. We're not going to spam you. This is part of a brilliant contest we're running. That's it for now. Enjoy yourselves."

The crowd dispersed, and Bert went off to talk with a guy just as ugly as he was. Barry's throat was so dry it began to tickle. At least it gave him an excuse to grab a drink and stand near the table, making him look slightly less silly than standing alone in the middle of the room.

Barry filled his plastic cup with the coldest ice water he'd ever had. Then his nostrils picked up a masculine, yet impossibly enticing, scent. He turned to find Mr. Kensington, all six foot and several inches of him, standing behind him in all his glory. His enormous hand dwarfed the cup it grasped. For reasons Barry couldn't understand, Mr. Kensington's eyes were on him. Barry turned around to be sure, and when he looked back to face him, Mr. Kensington indicated with a gesture that he was indeed looking at Barry. In his previous life, Barry would have referred to this man as a Tyrone. But now that he was face to face with him, Barry was convinced he was standing opposite the most beautiful man he'd ever seen, and it was pointless to be jealous of such a specimen.

"You all right, lad?" Mr. Kensington asked.

Barry nodded.

"What's your name, mate?"

"Barry."

"And what's that you're wearing, Barry?"

"Tracksuit."

"Listen here. Some tracksuits wear the man, but you, Barry, are wearing the hell out of that tracksuit." His voice was deep and velvety. "My name is Cornwallis Reginald Johnston Kensington, but I'd like for you to refer to me as 'friend.'" He offered his hand. It swallowed Barry's like a shadow. "Was that a handshake?"

"Yes," Barry said.

"I'm disappointed. I thought it was the start of a friendship, but maybe I haven't made myself worthy of you yet. Give me time, mate. But because it seemed to me that we'd just begun a friendship, I hope you don't mind if I speak to you as a friend."

"I don't mind," Barry said.

"I'm happy you said that. Since we're friends—at least you're a friend to me—I feel like I can talk to you about things friends talk about," He leaned in. Or rather, he leaned *over* Barry, but in a close manner. "You're a healthy young lad. You wear the hell out of that tracksuit. You look good. But give it to me straight. How often do you jerk off?"

"Oh, well . . . "

"We're mates. Look me in the eye and tell me. But know I'll know if you're lying, so you might as well be straight with me. There is no judgement here."

"Daily."

Mr. Kensington nodded in understanding. "I know."

"And how often do you jerk off, Mr. Kensington?"

"I haven't jerked off since 2011. I used to be like you. A daily wanker. But Barry, jerking off is acquiescence. You're too young to be so complacent. I want you to make a promise to me, Barry. No more jerking off."

"Oh, okay."

"Oh, okay. You can say it, but it's easier said than done. This is for your own good, mate. For the betterment of what it means to be Barry. There are lots of beautiful women here waiting to be explored. I've explored many of them, and many others in many parts of the world. Do you think I did it by jerking off? Take my hand again."

Barry took it, and Mr. Kensington squeezed hard.

"This handshake is a promise. An unbreakable one. When you go home tonight, you might have the urge to have a little wank, but because you shook my hand and looked me in the eye, I know you won't."

Barry thought Mr. Kensington's plan might be to break his hand so he couldn't jerk off.

"Do you have a job, Barry?"

"I do."

"I don't need to know what it is. But, Barry, any job you have, remind yourself, it isn't you, and it isn't what will bring you happiness. I don't offer this to everyone, but I see something in you. Do you like this place?"

Barry nodded.

"I want this place to be as much your home as it is my home. How would you like to come in for morning clean-up? We have a small crew that helps with the cleaning, setting things up, washing dishes, and the like. It's volunteer only, so don't expect payment, but what you get is the knowledge that you helped make all this possible."

"That makes sense."

"In that case, let's move things forward, mate." He pulled out a piece of paper with space for a signature at the bottom. "That's for you, mate. Don't think of this as a contract. Think of it as a promise between mates. First and foremost, it's a promise that you won't have a wank when you go home tonight, and secondly that you agree to help make this place a welcoming home for all its guests by coming in the morning to help tidy up the place." Mr. Kensington placed a pen in Barry's hand and gently guided it toward the paper.

Barry didn't see the harm in putting his name on the parchment. He signed.

Mr. Kensington placed the document inside his briefcase. "I've got something for you, Barry," From his pocket, he pulled something that appeared to be quite heavy and important. "Hold out your hand, Barry."

Barry did as he was told. Once more, Mr. Kensington's hand washed over Barry's like an eclipse. When he pulled his hand back, Barry found himself holding one saltine cracker.

"If you want more, come find me," Mr. Kensington said before going off to talk to more guests.

Barry examined the cracker and shoved it in his mouth,

then watched as Debbido talked the ears off the two Japanese women. They nodded attentively.

Barry looked around again. The place seemed to have everything—games, drinks, food, and women. But there was no Nastya. He'd have given all the contents of this house to Goodwill simply to hold hands with Nastya.

Barry couldn't work up the energy to talk to any women that night. If he couldn't wait a couple of measly weeks, then he didn't deserve Nastya. While not a bad distraction, that was all Barry's night with Bert was, a distraction.

When he got home and lay in bed, his hard-on appeared like clockwork. Instinctively, he slid his hand down, then caught himself. No, he couldn't. Nastya was always in his mind and always would be, but even louder was the velvety voice of Mr. Kensington. Barry had sworn an oath. If not for himself, then for Nastya. If he was so weak that he couldn't resist jerking off just once, then he didn't deserve Nastya.

Use this as fuel for when you make love to her the first time, the velvety voice said in his mind. *Envision exactly how it will go down.*

~~~

He awoke feeling clean. His morning hard-on was potent, but it wasn't dictating his behavior. The morning air was cool, and his mind felt fresh. More so, his soul felt fresh. If he'd known waking up could feel this good, he'd have stopped jerking off years earlier.

He was feeling so good that he decided to go to Mr. Kensington's mansion and help make it presentable for the next gathering. But he decided he wouldn't go to any further gatherings until Nastya was his. Everything there was simply too much of a distraction. Work, on the other hand, was a good distraction, a way to keep his mind pure and help the long winter days pass more quickly.

He arrived at the mansion a little after eight o'clock. The door opened before he could knock. On both sides of the carpet leading into the house were men of all shapes and sizes.

"Good morning!" they yelled in unison.

"Good morning," he responded.

"Barry!" Bert called.

Barry hadn't noticed him, as everyone in the house looked so similar.

"You're a little late, Barry. We've been here since five."

"Oh, sorry. I wasn't really sure when to come."

"No matter. Ready to put in some work?"

Barry nodded.

"Follow me."

They walked into a dark lounge, where several youths were sweeping and dusting. A portrait of Mr. Kensington hung above the fireplace. On the mantle was an old wooden box with several slots cut into the lid. Bert pulled out some loose coins and dropped them into the slots.

"This is the good-faith box. We aren't required to pay any more than we wish. All we're required to give is something as a testimony of our dedication to providing happiness for others."

"I don't have any change," Barry said.

"What do you have?"

Barry pulled out his wallet to reveal two twenty-dollar bills. Bert eyed them and nodded approvingly. Barry dropped one bill in the slot. Bert was still eyeing him, so Barry added the second bill.

"Trust me, you'll feel really good about that."

A faint drumbeat permeated the walls. Everyone who'd been scrubbing or dusting froze.

"'Bolero!'" someone shouted.

"'Bolero!'" another responded. He stood momentarily paralyzed, and then began dusting frantically.

"What's going on?" Barry asked.

"'Bolero,'" Bert said. "Once it starts playing, we don't stop working. No pauses, no breaks. Work, work, work."

"How long does the song last?"

Bert smiled and shrugged.

Barry was feeling good. The sun was shining through the lounge, and the morning freshness made him feel calm and alert.

He was put to work scrubbing the floors, then was led to one of the kitchens. Even considering how many guests there had been the previous night, he was astonished by the mountain of dishes before him. There was a dishwasher that could handle a small load, but the rest he'd have to wash by hand.

All the while, "Bolero" played. The melody, repetitive as it was, became hypnotic. It went on and on and on, never changing and never reaching the level of bombast Barry expected. Whenever he thought the song was ready to reach a loud explosion of notes, it never did.

When the song finally wound down, he felt a glaring emptiness. The lack of noise frightened him. He'd been staring at a mountain of clean dishes before he realized it was he who had made them clean. It took him several minutes to regain control of his neck.

As he exited the kitchen, he saw that everyone else had

departed. He finished his honest and selfless day of work at four p.m., which gave him thirty minutes to get to the café where he'd wash more dishes for five hours. By the time he collapsed on his bed, he was too tired to jerk off, even if he'd wanted to.

Thrice more he returned to the mansion, proved his good faith by donating money to the box, and put in honest and selfless work. Then he decided to spend the rest of the Christmas break at home.

When Barry checked the scale before returning to school, it read 215 pounds. After three days straight of going to the gym and not seeing Nastya, he stopped going for the remainder of the break. He also canceled his Russian lessons. He hated his teacher almost as much as she hated him. Try as he might, he couldn't understand why one word had six different endings. His teacher corrected him so often he lost all motivation.

None of that mattered. He was in love with Nastya. Several times in high school, he'd thought he was in love, but none of those compared to how he felt about Nastya. He cherished the times they shared a cigarette, despite them lasting all of five minutes. He cherished when she'd pass by at the gym and smile. He adored her accent and the sound of her voice. He loved her gigantic blue eyes that were nearly too big. He loved how she read and walked at the same time.

Most of all, he loved that she dedicated time to him. Feeling affection from a woman was something Barry had been sure would never occur in his lifetime. There were times at night that his mind wasn't even filled with images of her naked or them having sex. No, he imagined them walking side by side, holding hands. He imagined what it would be like to sit down and hold her in his arms.

In bed with his eyes closed, all he could think about was holding her and imagining how her hair smelled. Innocent as his thoughts were, his hard-ons only grew harder. That wouldn't do. Jerking off is for the weak. Gentlemen like Mr. Kensington didn't jerk off, and neither would he. He also knew that if he didn't relieve himself soon, he'd suffer a sleepless night.

He typed "Bolero" on his phone, and the name Maurice Ravel popped up. A Frenchie. He'd been hoping the composer was Russian so he could share his knowledge of the classics with Nastya.

He pressed play, and the repetitive melody started up, a long, long, gradual crescendo that went nowhere. It put both him and his erection to sleep.

~~~

Winter break was over. School was in session. He was going to go on a date and hold the most beautiful woman in the world in his arms.

Barry bought himself a cup of flavorless tea and had a cigarette. He sat outside the cafeteria, separately from Bert and the others. He wanted Nastya to see him as she arrived on campus. Her nose would likely be in a book, but he'd find a subtle way to get her attention.

Here she comes, Barry thought, his heart stopping. He was struck by how unfeminine her walk was. She moved with long, masculine strides. Yet it didn't bother him. It didn't matter how her long legs moved, so long as they were long. It didn't bother him that she wore hoodies instead of tight tops that accentuated her figure.

Then his heart exploded. She'd arrived, but she wasn't

alone. Walking by her side was someone awfully close. It wasn't just someone, it was Niko. They weren't just close, they were holding hands. She was wearing a tight top, and her hair was down.

Niko's nasal voice carried throughout the quad as they started their ascent toward the building housing Nastya's next class. She hadn't seen Barry. He watched them as they went up and up. Once at the top, they gave each other a small kiss. Nastya went inside, and Niko returned down the hill. He walked past Barry, nodded in acknowledgment, and went into the cafeteria.

Barry remained hunched over like a gargoyle. He didn't go to class. He feared that any movement would cause him to start crying or get sick. He didn't say a word when Bert spoke to him.

Later in the day, he saw Niko holding hands with Nastya again. There was something about it that destroyed him. Kissing was devastating, and fucking would have been devastating, yet seeing them hand in hand broke him. It was irrefutable proof. Handholding made what they had real. She'd go home with him, he'd hold her in his arms, and Barry would jerk off for the millionth time imagining his hand was a different body part of a different person.

Where had he gone wrong? He'd followed all the rules. Was it the victory Coke that did him in? A horrible feeling began to sink in. Why would she agree to go on a date with him if she had no intention of following through?

Barry called out of work that day. He needed to be alone, unless Daniel was willing to hang out. He texted Daniel but received no response. Several messages came in from Christopher, both on his phone and in various forums. He couldn't bear to open them. He had yet to tell anyone what had happened. He still couldn't believe it. What had the past months meant? Why the fuck was he going to the gym? Why had he bought so many tracksuits?

The image of Nastya holding Niko's hand kept returning. Even in his dreams, Nastya ended up with Niko. Even when he got ready to jerk off, Nastya would end up with Niko. Was Christopher responsible for controlling his dreams now?

If it had been any other guy, Barry would have found a way to live with it. Barry couldn't compete with a Marine pilot or male models, but Niko? Niko, who wasn't even handsome and had the personality of a ballsack. Niko, who looked more Muppet than human. Niko, who got to make her laugh and see her smile up close. Niko, who got to taste her lips and nipples.

Barry began to cry. He didn't have a friend in the world. Kenneth was a dead murderer, Daniel was a selfish asshole, Bert made him feel guilty, and Christopher was a cunt. Was Rocket Jizz really the only person he could talk to? That thought made him cry even harder. Did Rocket Jizz even understand human emotions?

Barry hadn't planned for a future without Nastya. All his eggs had been in one basket. Every decision he'd made, piece of food he'd eaten, item of clothing he'd bought, or idea he'd had was for her. There was no plan for tomorrow. He continued to cry.

Wait a minute, he thought. *Russians don't surrender. No, they don't.*

Holding hands and a petty kiss meant nothing. Russian women liked aggressive men, and Rocket Jizz was just the man to help Barry out.

Chapter 18

Doug

"But you believed she was eighteen," Joey said for the thirty-fifth time.

Doug had just removed his medium-rare steak from the grill while leaving Joey's to burn to tastelessness. He didn't know why he'd bothered taking any care with his when he had no appetite. "Yes, she told me she was eighteen."

"I can't believe you cheated on Sandra," Joey said, also for the thirty-fifth time.

"It wasn't something I was planning on doing. It just happened. This girl manipulated me. This fucking bitch. She's evil, Joey. I'm ready to face my wife, who I love more than anything, and face the consequences. But the fact that she's fifteen means I'll go to prison. Don't you know what that means? It means I'm done. My life, my job, my marriage, all of it."

"You didn't know she was fifteen," Joey said. "She tricked you. And now she's threatening you. Doug, I don't like it."

"But you believe me, don't you?"

"Of course I do."

"Then help me. Please help. I don't know what to do. I came to you because you're the only person in the world I can trust. You're the best friend I have."

"That means a lot, Doug. I mean, I always knew it, but I never wanted to push it. I'm glad you said it. You're my best friend too. One day, I'll get married, and you'll be my best man."

"Absolutely."

"While we're being honest with each other," Joey said, "I used to sort of have a crush on Sandra."

"Thank you for your honesty."

During dinner, Doug received several dozen pictures from Talia, her ugly face glaring. He hated her ugly, crooked teeth almost as much as he hated the three hairs he'd noticed above her upper lip. The sight of her and his growing anxiety put him off eating, but he drank gladly.

Rumor around the office was that Gendo was in the final stages of giving Kale the promotion. To show how solid the foundation of their friendship was, Joey began devising schemes to sabotage Kale.

"You're pretty good at coming up with these ideas," Doug said.

"That's what I've been trying to tell people," Joey said. "It's one of my better qualities. For example, I've really been wanting to tell you about my idea for the popcorn net. You want to hear it? Awesome. When you go to the movies, what's the biggest problem?"

"I don't really know. The movie sucks or it's too long?"

"No, it's popcorn. You buy it, it costs ten bucks or more, half a handful doesn't even end up in your mouth. It ends up on the floor, on your shirt, on your pants. When the movie's over and the lights come up, there's popcorn everywhere. Your pants and shirt have butter all over them. Some poor fifteen-year-old has to spend an hour cleaning up that crap."

"Okay, so . . . "

"My idea is that when you buy a bag of popcorn, for just an additional seventy-five cents, you get a popcorn net. You wear it around your waist like a belt, and a little net extends outward, so now when popcorn falls, it doesn't land on you. It lands in the net. The pants and floor get to stay clean, and you get to eat all your popcorn. Isn't that a great idea?"

"Joey, goddamn it, what the fuck are we talking about? I don't give a shit about any of this. What I really want to know is if you know anyone who makes fake IDs."

"Doug, I do."

"And would he be able to make one using one of these images?" He showed Joey various images of Talia (clothed).

"Easy," Joey said.

"Great," Doug said. "That settles it. She showed me an ID saying she was eighteen. None of our texts indicate otherwise. I can live with explaining my infidelity to my wife."

"I'm so happy we're getting all this out in the open. There's a girl I really like and was hoping you could lend me your ear for a bit and give me some Doug pointers."

"Is it really ten p.m. already? I've got to get going, but yeah, pointers for sure next time."

Doug was pulling into his driveway when he saw a dark shape on his porch. He flashed his high beams, and the shadowy figure morphed into Talia. She waved at him with her bony hands and flashed a hideous smile. He turned off his lights. Had she already been inside? He hesitated. Sandra would still be awake, and she'd likely hear any conversation that took place in the driveway.

He opened his passenger door. For a minute, Talia didn't move. Then she got up. She motioned like she was going to ring the doorbell, giggled, then climbed into the car. Doug drove off before she could get her seatbelt on.

When Talia leaned in to kiss his cheek, he nearly swerved into an SUV.

"I'm really happy to see you," she said.

Doug said nothing. No words in any language could have described how he felt.

"Are you happy to see me too? We haven't fucked in weeks. I wanted you to fuck me tonight."

"What were you doing at my house?"

"You don't answer my calls, so I decided to come see you."

"Did my wife see you?"

"No, silly. Where are we going?"

"I can't very well fuck you at my house, now, can I?"

They drove to one of the few motels in the city that wasn't completely run down. Doug paid in cash and ignored Talia when she asked if they could go in the hot tub. Their room had a bed, an ancient TV set, and no minibar. Doug sat on the bed, but Talia remained standing.

"Before we do anything, I wanted to talk to you about something," she said. "I apologize for the way I've been behaving, but you left me no choice. You're so amazing, and when you're not around, I miss you so much. I call and call, and you don't answer, and it drives me crazy. I know I shouldn't have gone to your house, but I'm only happy when I'm with you. At school, all I can think about is you."

She looked so good when she was sad. With her guard down, she looked so vulnerable and ripe for the taking. But that was what she did. She was a master manipulator, knowing exactly what to do with her eyes and lips and hips and legs.

"Have you told anybody about me?"

"Of course not. They wouldn't get it. And you're mine. All to myself."

Only then did Doug consider the possibility that she'd shared details of their affair with others. When she spoke, Doug tried to picture her as the hideous succubus he knew she was, but her sad eyes and lips were beginning to win him over.

"I understand," Doug said. "You're young. This must all be complicated for you. I need to take responsibility for this."

"I'm happy you said that," she said. "I know if we try, we can make it work. You don't look at your wife the way you look at me."

"I've never looked at anyone the way I look at you."

"Take me, one more time."

Doug got up from the bed and moved toward Talia. She was ready for his embrace as he extended his arms. He knew she loved the way his hands felt around her waist, right below her tickle spot. She closed her eyes, waiting for his kiss.

His hands wrapped around her throat and began to squeeze. She struggled, but in the end was far weaker than Doug and was unable to get out of his grip. She'd gotten her "one more time."

Doug sat back down on the bed to catch his breath. Her open eyes were staring in his direction. Doug could have fallen asleep then and there. He'd never come across a problem he couldn't solve. The Talia problem had been averted. He closed his eyes and told himself that a fifteen-minute nap would be acceptable.

An hour later, he woke up confused. He felt as though he hadn't eaten in weeks. The body could wait, as his own began to feel weak. He got in his car and drove to the nearest hamburger joint, where he ordered two double cheeseburgers and two servings of fries. He typically didn't tolerate eating in his car, but he was willing to make an exception. The first bite was euphoric. The double-stacked beef and thick layer of crispy bacon made it almost impossible to fit it in his mouth, but he managed. Hot juice dribbled down his chin. He took a second bite before he had finished chewing the first bite. Before taking a third, he squeezed the buns toward each other, letting the juice from the beef ooze into the already greasy buns.

Even at that late hour, the streets were busy when he set off for the motel. At the last minute, he made a detour and bought a large knife.

The body was right where he'd left it. No more selfies and puppy dog eyes and duck faces. She couldn't torment him any longer. Relief—that was what he felt. He was relieved, and relief was the best feeling in the world. Not love, not sex, not narcotics: relief. The kind of relief you feel when you don't miss your flight, when you get a large tax refund, when your girlfriend's pregnancy test comes back negative, when you're stuck in traffic and have to take a giant shit and you make it home at the last minute. Doug was relieved.

He turned on the TV to watch some sports highlights. Checking his phone for the first time in hours, he saw dozens of messages from Sandra. Talia's phone vibrated occasionally as well. He texted his wife he was held up. Next, he saw a message from Joey.

I got in touch with the fake ID guy.

Change of plans, Doug wrote.

He sent Joey the address of the motel. Joey said he'd be there in fifteen minutes. That gave Doug time. He pulled out the new knife, wished he had more booze in him, put it at an angle that looked as though Talia had been holding it, and slashed himself across the chest. It hadn't been enough. He did it again, this time causing blood to seep through his clothes. It still wasn't enough, but he couldn't risk letting blood drip on the floor and unintentionally leaving evidence behind. He gave himself a small slash near his left wrist. He'd received that one trying to fight her off. He then put the knife in her hand and closed her fingers around it. If his adrenaline hadn't been so high, he would have winced at the gash. It stung more than he wanted to admit.

Doug saw Joey's car pull in. His arm was throbbing. Suddenly, he wasn't relieved anymore. He answered Joey's knock.

Joey's eyes bulged out of his face when he saw the condition of his best friend. "Doug!"

"Shhh, keep your voice down, for fuck's sake."

"Are you hurt?"

"Yeah, it hurts pretty bad."

"We have to call the police!"

"Shhh, Christ. Keep your voice down. Come inside."

Joey froze when he saw Talia's body on the floor. "Oh Christ! Oh Christ! Doug!"

"Damn it, Joey, you dumb fucking bastard. You're my best friend in the world, but stop saying my name and keep your goddamn annoying voice down."

"But . . . " Joey shook his head as though to clear it. "What happened?"

Doug explained that Talia had come to his place and threatened to kill Sandra. He'd lured her away. When Doug refused to sleep with her, she came at him with a knife, and Doug had no choice but to defend himself with force.

"Doug, I'm so sorry this happened to you."

"Thank you. From you, it means a lot. Joey, I was so scared. Not for myself, but for my wife. You realize we can't go to the police. We have to get rid of the body. Joey, this is the most important thing I'll ever ask you to do. I could have asked others, but I'm asking you because I know how strong you are, and because I trust you."

"Doug, everything is going to be okay. I'm going to help you." He regarded the corpse. "I think we'll have to cut her up. Then we can take my dad's boat out and dump the bags in the ocean. It's going to be messy, but if that's what it takes, then that's what it takes. If I can play a small part in saving your life, I will."

"Thank you."

"The keys for the boat are back at the office. I'll go get them."

"Do you have anything to cut the body with?"

"Shit," Joey said. "You're right. It's too late to find anywhere open that sells saws."

"Maybe there's another way. We can light the body on fire, then quickly push it overboard."

"Oh gee, I don't know. Maybe we should be old fashioned and stuff rocks in the bag with the body."

"Whatever, just hurry. And bring a large enough bag."

Joey left for the bag and keys. Doug's arm and chest began to sting. *Shit, I have to go out again and find shit to clean my wounds,* he thought. Luckily, there was a 24-hour pharmacy not far from the motel.

When he returned, there was still no sign of Joey. Talia's body looked stupid lying there. A part of him wanted to squeeze her tits one last time. And why shouldn't he? He'd killed her defending himself. His hands would have grabbed anywhere they could. In any case, she was soon to be fish food.

Sitting there, Doug reviewed the list of every woman he'd ever fucked. They'd all served their purpose and fulfilled a certain need. None compared to Talia. She'd been the best of them, and Doug was deeply regretful that it had to end the way it did. The idea of having to wait years to find a lay that good again made him want to cry. Judging by his current diet and lifestyle, he had fifty years of life left. Fifty years. Half a century of unfulfilling sex. Sandra would start to lose her looks by forty-two, forty-five tops. He couldn't imagine waking up to that every morning for the rest of his life—what was meant to be the peak of happiness.

It was nearly one a.m. when Joey returned. "This bag was a birthday present," he said. "I was supposed to use it for my trip to Spain."

"You never went to Spain. But it's going to good use now. I'll get you an even better bag. How about that?"

Joey's dad's boat was a cheap and beat-up little Minorca Islander. The two men carried the bag onto the boat without incident. Due to the clouds and smog, everything was black when they ventured out into the open waters. The ocean made Doug uneasy. The stillness of it all was even worse.

Once they were out far enough alone in that dark void, they decided it was time. Then they realized they'd forgotten to bring rocks.

"Let's use something else that's heavy." Doug found an ancient stereo that would get the job done.

"My dad loves that stereo," Joey said.

"I'll buy him another one."

The stereo went in the bag.

"Any last words?" Joey asked.

"What the fuck are you on about?"

"I don't know. I've never done this before. Shouldn't we at least say something?"

"Let's put the fucking bag in the water."

With some effort, they tossed the bag overboard, and Talia was gone from the world.

Joey talked about something on the ride back to the harbor. Doug heard none of it. He was yearning for that feeling of relief, but something wasn't right.

Back at the motel, Doug inspected the room eight times over, ensuring there was nothing to incriminate him. Sandra had called three more times. Talia would never call him again.

"Doug?"

"Yes?"

"I don't feel so good." Joey blew chunks all over the

floor.

"For fuck's sake."

"I'm sorry," Joey choked out between violent bouts.

The sight and smell of another person vomiting was the worst thing Doug could imagine. He started to feel nauseated himself. When Joey was finished, a yellow and red pile of chunks lay on the floor.

"I can't handle the smell," Doug said. "I'm going to wait in my car until this mess is cleaned up."

Doug gave Joey twenty minutes. He embraced the smell of his car's peach-scented air freshener. That had been Talia's favorite scent.

When he went back inside, Joey looked like shit.

"You're not going to be sick again, are you?"

"I'm okay."

"Good."

"Doug?"

"What?"

"I think nights like tonight are what turn boys into men and men into brothers. This was the hardest thing I've ever done, but I'd do it again a million times over for you. If the cops come, I'll go out guns blazing for you. Hell, if we have to, we can go down to Mexico and start new lives there. We can be Mexicans. It doesn't matter. We're in this together now. You and me, buddy. Nothing else matters."

Doug began to laugh, then Joey began to laugh, and they laughed together.

"Joey."

"Doug?"

"You're such a dumb motherfucker." Still laughing, Doug pulled out the knife and stabbed Joey in his chubby neck.

He looked like such a pathetic asshole when he saw he was being stabbed by his best friend. Doug laughed. "I always fucking hated you and your banal stories and tacky life, you little shit." He stabbed Joey in the neck again.

Joey landed where his puke puddle had been and created a new blood puddle as he gurgled to death.

Doug sat down on the floor with his back against the edge of the bed. He'd resolved two issues in one night. Why stop there? He was on a winning streak. He thought of all the people who could possibly be used against him. Perhaps he'd have to take out that Miranda girl. That was it. She was a loose end. Pity, Doug thought. She was quite good looking.

His phone rang again, and he began bawling.

"I'm so fucked," he said, pounding his fist against the floor. He didn't see any outcome where he walked away from this. Maybe going to Mexico wasn't the worst idea in the world. He'd have to go home to get his passport.

No, he wasn't walking away from this one. All his life, he'd done everything right. He ate right and talked right and worked hard and fucked more women than anyone he knew. That bitch Talia had ruined him. They'd eventually find him, and he'd spend the rest of his life in prison. At least he wouldn't have to worry about mediocre sex for the rest of his life.

He wanted to be a kid again. Just to play outside from dawn to dusk when the streetlights came on and it was time to go home. He liked that memory a lot and decided he wanted the final moments of his life to be filled with it.

There was a knock on the door.

"Douglass, open up."

The police? How could they possibly be here so quickly? Joey had definitely done something stupid to alert them.

"Douglass, open up," the man said again, repeating his knock. "It's Phillip."

"Who the fuck is Phillip?" Doug asked, knife in hand.

"Mr. Yagami's driver."

Mr. Yagami? he thought. *Driver? They exist. This is real.* He cleared his throat. "Yes. Does he need something from me?"

"Please open the door."

Doug stood and complied, and there indeed was Gendo's driver. The humorless and youthful-looking chauffeur, whose name apparently was Phillip. Behind him were two men in identical suits and earpieces. Discount Secret Service agents.

Doug allowed them to enter. The two men began examining Joey's body.

"Please get in the car, Douglass," Phillip said.

"Get in the car?"

Phillip nodded.

"But why?"

"It will all make sense soon. Get in the car."

Doug climbed into the back seat of the Mercedes, and they took off, leaving the twins in suits back at the motel. Doug didn't recognize any of the streets they passed. He didn't know why he was in the car, nor where it was going. They drove past several police cars. They didn't appear to be in any hurry to get anywhere. Doug closed his eyes.

When he opened them, he found himself in an unfamiliar room, and Gendo Yagami was sitting opposite him. It was the first time Doug had ever seen the man in informal clothing. It made him look youthful and like a grandfather all at once.

"Would you like some coffee? Maybe tea?"

All Doug could do was shake his head.

"I'm sorry we had to meet like this. When your wife couldn't get hold of you, she eventually got through to me. You've had a hell of a night. I can't imagine. Your official report is being typed up as we speak, but I still need to talk to you and make sure we're on the same page. I can see you're in shock. That's okay. Joey was a sexual deviant. We all should have seen it coming. He took things too far. It's really a tragedy, what happened with the girl, but Joey made his choice. Quite frankly, the company is glad to be rid of him. I'm sorry you had to get caught up in the violence. You did the right thing trying to stop him."

"Sir, I—"

"There's no need to speak. Do you know how I run such an effective company? I know everything about every one of my employees. I know what they do, often before they even do it. I paid a visit to CoinciDATE. After handing over a considerable amount of money to the redhead, all files and history pertaining to you have been erased. Joey, on the other hand, was a repeat customer. Now, you are to go home and get some sleep. Take the day off. When you come back, I want you to pack up your things."

"Sir?"

"Your current desk isn't suitable for someone of your stature."

"You mean, I . . . I got the promotion?"

"No, we gave that to Kale. He's better suited for it than

you are. We're giving you Argyle's job."

"Argyle's job is vice-president."

"So it was," Gendo said. "We see a lot of potential in you, and I look forward to working with you in the future."

Good things happen to good people. It was the oldest rule in the book. And Doug wasn't a good person; he was a great person. Doug was meant to succeed, and if that's what nature demanded, who was he to go against nature?

He'd received the promotion because he belonged to a superior class of people, and the events of that night reaffirmed it. Doug felt relieved. Relieved to be free, but most importantly, relieved to have been born as Doug.

He also knew the world was relieved to have him. He'd one day find himself among those who added to the pages of the history books. Joey was dead because he wasn't a good person. Doug was great.

Chapter 19

Miranda

Stop being fucking busy all the time, goddamn it! Miranda wrote to Christian. She erased it before clicking send, opting for a less-aggressive choice of words. She knew the content of her text didn't matter; Christian's answer would be the same regardless.

Hey, how's it going? she texted Nastya.

Almost immediately, she received a reply. *Hey, stranger. I thought you'd forgotten about me. How are you?*

I've been better. Mind lending me your ear and letting me vent for a bit? I'll buy you a drink or twelve.

I have a better idea, she wrote back.

"What's better than twelve gin and tonics?" Miranda thought out loud.

I'd be more than happy to lend an ear, but I don't want to drink, Nastya wrote. *Come surfing tomorrow with me instead.*

Surfing?

Yes. Nothing better for clearing the head.

What time?

Six a.m.

~~~

Six a.m., and Miranda was at the beach. It was fucking cold out, and she could only imagine how torturous the water would be. The beach itself was empty. Smart people had gotten drunk the previous night and were sleeping it off. Smart people wouldn't be diving headfirst into the harsh, cold Pacific Ocean.

Despite living her whole life in California with the beach little more than a stone's throw away, she could count on one hand how many times she'd been there. The appeal was lost on her. The only beaches that mattered were those along the Amalfi Coast or Cinque Terre, where the water was a friendly turquoise, accompanied by cliffs with warm, multi-colored buildings. The beach here was full of tar and trash and seagulls. The Pacific Ocean's color was cruel and wrong. The waves served as an oppressive force coming closer and closer to swallow her up each time they crashed upon the shore.

Nastya arrived five minutes later. She wore a wetsuit and carried a single shortboard.

"Where's your wetsuit?"

"Hadn't even crossed my mind," Miranda said.

"It's going to be really fucking cold."

Really fucking cold was an understatement. Miranda felt individual molecules freeze over. Having only brought one board, Nastya floated as Miranda lay on the board.

"Doesn't look like there will be any good waves for you today," Nastya said. "But the water is calm. You can get a feel for the board. I do my best thinking out here. I also do my best not-thinking. Great place to let the brain shut off and embrace what's happening around you. I think it's better than drinking at some bar or going to some café. Here. Just you and the ocean."

Several oil platforms stood out where the horizon dropped off into nothingness, monstrous metallic structures made puny by the oppressive Pacific Ocean. Perhaps this was a place some people could come to in order to clear their heads, but not Miranda. The dark, endless water only made her sad. The lack of people made her sad. Even if there had been a million people, they would have been mere ants. Each one of them was a potential Shaun or Barry. Each one of them would suffer and feel pain, and the ocean wouldn't give a fuck. *Fight and resist all you want, the tide always comes in.* Miranda began crying.

"What happened?"

Miranda held nothing back. Her father, her job. She revealed everything.

"Maybe we should have gone drinking, after all," Nastya said.

"I don't know what to do," Miranda said. "I've been so focused on solving other people's bullshit that it never occurred to me my own life would catch up with me. Now it seems like everything is catching up with me at once."

"We get used to viewing our parents as these idols. Perfect figures who exist only to take care of and guide us. We forget they're people, and people are disgusting, weak, flawed, and full of baggage. I've told you my mom left the family. That was so many years ago. I don't even know if she's alive. She was sleeping with another man while she was still with my father. My father is no saint. He slept with other women too. He and his sauna buddies would get prostitutes all the time. It was no secret. That's just what they did. With that knowledge, does that mean any act he made as a father is negated? My father has been wonderful to me."

"That makes cheating okay?"

"No."

"Have you ever been cheated on?"

"Yes, and it sucked."

"Have you ever done the cheating?"

"One time, two years back. I went to this seven-week intensive language program out in the middle of nowhere. We lived in a small dorm. I saw the same people at the same time every day. You'd see these people more than your own friends and family. It was an unnatural environment and, whether you wanted to make friends or not, you got really close to people.

"Back home, I had a boyfriend I'd been seeing for a little over a year. On the first day of lessons, I met another guy in one of my classes. I immediately felt a connection with him and always tried to sit next to him during lessons. He almost never talked to me in the beginning. I thought maybe he thought I sucked. Later, I found out he was just shy.

"He eventually revealed he had really strong feelings for me. The truth is, I had feelings for him too, but I couldn't bring myself to tell him that. You see, I was faithful to my boyfriend, but in my head, I'd already cheated on him. If you've allowed these feelings to manifest themselves in your head, are they any less real than if you actually follow through with them? I don't know, but I felt that just thinking those thoughts was as bad as actually doing it.

"I didn't stay with my boyfriend much longer and haven't

spoken to that other boy since, but I often think about what could have been. I really did feel a connection with him. People are complex. We date and love and hold one another to high standards and try to be faithful, but if being faithful means not allowing yourself to have feelings for any other person, is that really a good thing? Isn't loving others a good thing? Shouldn't we love as many people as possible?"

"You're advocating for cheating?"

"No, that's not it. I'm saying we and our feelings are complex. And just because they may be inconvenient doesn't mean they aren't valid. Go easy on your dad. You don't know what's really going on in his head. Maybe try to understand him."

The supposedly calm waves knocked Miranda into the water three times that morning. Once, the board ended up on top of her, and she thought she was going to drown. She never wanted to see the ocean again.

~~~

The ocean came to her that night. While on the verge of sleep and thankful that no ghosts had come to visit, a giant wave swept across the city, destroying everything in its path. She managed to get out of her building before it could get her. No matter how fast she swam upward, the water kept rising. Eventually, the water reached the moon. She couldn't swim to the moon. All she could do was drown.

When she woke, it was three a.m. The last thing she wanted was to go back to bed. She made herself a pot of coffee, pulled out a legal pad, grabbed a pen, and began writing.

All dreams must eventually die. Miranda had thought her days of complaining customers were behind her. But lonely people hunting for love got just as upset as people whose coffee wasn't made correctly. All the complaints began flooding in at once. The script Alexei had handed her for dealing with complaints was useless, and dealing with complaints was eating away at valuable time she could be spending in the field.

Her own complaints outweighed those of her clients. Listening to people whine about how they couldn't get laid seemed the least of her worries. Her father trying to bed another woman resided at the top.

Miranda looked for that woman. She found her at an arts and crafts store. Remarkably unremarkable-looking and in her mid-thirties. Nothing exciting about her, yet her father, who called Miranda *mi flaca* and *güera*, was willing to pay money for help cheating on her mom.

Miranda had a ghost problem as well. Shaun's ghost visited her almost every night, the ghost she refused to acknowledge. She hadn't known him much in life, but he was quite the talker in death.

Aside from dealing with hauntings and perverted fathers, news came to her that Alexei was expanding the business and looking for a new branch manager. Unless Alexei was going for an outside hire, she didn't see how the obvious choice could be anyone but her. No one else had as many clients. No one else listened to hours of complaints. It was hers for the taking, and why shouldn't it be? She worked harder than anyone else there. Even on her most hungover days, she could sign up more clients than Adam at his best. She didn't feel excited, happy, anxious, or worried about this. She felt nothing at all. This was merely the next logical progression her life had to take.

She looked at her appointment book. Barry was next. She was sick of Barry. He was the perfect example of a hopeless case, only slightly above Rudy in her book of abhorrence. Just slightly. He came into her office wearing his ridiculous tracksuit and looking scruffy. He also looked like he'd gained a dozen pounds. Nastya hadn't said anything about Barry, so she remained unaware of what adventures Barry had gotten himself into with her.

"Hello, Barry."

"Hey," he said, eyes pointed at the floor.

"You've got thirty minutes."

"Why does it hurt so bad?"

Oh, no, she thought. She felt Shaun hovering over her shoulder, judging her. "Tell him to kill himself and it won't hurt," the ghost of Shaun said.

"She agreed to go out on a date," Barry said.

"That's great," Miranda said.

"No, it's not great. I never should have listened to you. I never should've listened to Christopher, or to Rocket Jizz."

"What the fuck is a Rocket Jizz?"

"I am," Rocket Jizz said, coming in through the door.

The man, or entity, that stood before Miranda was far stranger than even his name suggested. He looked like a human that hadn't been fully finished, a creature born at his present age, one who had never been a child. His skin was impossibly smooth and radiated an intense shine.

"How the hell did you get in here?"

"Get the hell away from me!" Barry stood and shouted.

"Barry, I try to explain you what is happen," he said.

"The two of you have five seconds to explain before I call the police," Miranda said. That's all she needed, a Rocket

Jizz situation. "Hurry up and tell me what happened, Barry."

He sat back down and eyed Rocket Jizz as though the strange man were a dormant cobra that could wake and strike at any minute. Even Shaun's ghost seemed afraid of Rocket Jizz.

"She agreed to go on a date," Barry repeated.

"She agree to go on a lunch," Rocket Jizz said.

"It doesn't matter," Barry said.

"Yes it does."

"It does," Miranda agreed. "What was it she agreed to? It means a world of difference."

"I asked if she'd like to get lunch sometime. She said yes."

"She said 'yes'?"

"She said, 'Sure, why not?' But surely that meant yes."

"No, not quite," Miranda said. "Yes means yes. When a girl says 'sure,' it means a million different things, including yes, no, and maybe. So after she said this, did you get her number?"

"Well, no . . . I didn't."

"So there was no confirmation. No date, time, or place planned. When did you see her next?"

"At school the next day. I reminded her of our arrangement. She said she was busy and wouldn't be free until after winter break. She said we could meet then. I asked for her number. She said she'd give it to me then."

"Barry, that was it," Miranda said.

"That was what?"

"That was her way of telling you she wasn't interested."

"How can that be? She said she'd go with me. She said

it."

"She half-heartedly agreed to something vague and unconfirmed. If she'd really wanted to go, she would have said, 'yes.'"

"Then why didn't she say no and tell me to fuck off right from the get-go? Why give me false hope? Why lead me on like that? For all winter break, all I thought about was our date."

"Telling someone to fuck off is mean. She didn't want to be mean, but she was put in an awkward situation. It was better to be nice and hope you'd get the hint on your own. What happened after winter break?"

"I saw her holding hands with some fucking prick. She didn't even notice me."

"Did you talk to her?"

"Yes."

"And?"

"That's when Rocket Jizz got involved."

"Oh boy," Miranda said.

~~~

Rocket Jizz

"Oh yes," Rocket Jizz said.

Unlike citizens from this world, he was able to wake up and get to his feet without the adjustment period of yawning and eye-rubbing. No coffee was required. It took less than a minute for him to reflect on everything that had happened to him up to that point in his life.

Every morning must begin with a good breakfast. Breakfast and a good dump, in that order.

Rocket Jizz enjoyed putting on his clothes, which he always pronounced as cloth-es, because saying it the other way was difficult. He put on his fun gloves and always grabbed his briefcase last. He wasn't allowed to open it, but it was essential that he carry it.

Months back at the educational facility, he'd been digging in the trash to find half the sandwich he'd been storing for later. He did not find the sandwich; instead he found something far more valuable. It had been covered in grime and muck when he brought it home. He laid it out flat on his dining room table and smoothed out the edges. Some wrinkles were there that could not be fixed, but he delicately wiped off the dirt.

Under all the damage and smudge was the most beautiful thing he'd ever seen on this planet or any other. Black faces and white faces and strange faces and beautiful faces. People short and tall and confined to wheelchairs and other devices. The title was too obscure and far gone to make out, but it was something along the lines of *The Ring Lord King Returns*. The creator was someone by the name of Barry. Rocket Jizz desired to know this Barry, one who could create something so beautiful. So many faces represented. Everyone was together. None of them looked like Rocket Jizz, and when Jizz met Barry, he understood none of them looked like Barry either. No one in the universe looked like Barry.

Jizz desired this boy. Desired his happiness and his friendship. Jizz concluded his life's mission was this boy's happiness. If Jizz had to pay for or perform the surgery himself to turn this Barry into a real Russian, then he'd do it. Jizz was even ready to reveal what was inside his briefcase to Barry.

Rocket Jizz couldn't wait to help Barry. Barry was such nice guy with a great tracksuit with gold stripes. Rocket Jizz don't have friends with tracksuits. Most of his friends were dead far away somewhere in the galaxy. He killed some of them himself.

Like all members of his race, Rocket Jizz was capable of sucking his own dick. He did this often and out of necessity. Due to this ability, he had no concept of sexual frustration, so he could not share in Barry's pain. But pain he did understand, and when he stared at Barry, he saw a pain deep and true. If he could take it on upon his own person, he would. If he could teach Barry to suck his own dick, he'd teach him. Because Barry's physiology did not allow for this, he would make it his duty to help him get his Nastya.

Barry had come to him with some most serious sadness. The Russian had a boyfriend. Barry had been betrayed LOL! Barry spent so much time fantasizing sex with the Russian, it wasn't right. Barry asked Rocket Jizz to commit violence against fucking boyfriend. Rocket Jizz had many impressive tools. Take out Niko and Barry gets Nastya the Russian.

Rocket Jizz had committed much violence in his life. He never thought about it. But one day, he watched the wonderful movie by the Jim Carrey *Liar, Liar*. It changed him so much that he wanted to make grand surprise for Barry. Then Rocket Jizz understood there was alternative to violence.

At school, Barry had talked to Nastya the Russian with hopes of romance. Rocket Jizz had his briefcase. Where he went, it went. Rocket Jizz approached the two of them, with Jim Carrey fresh in his heart.

"Barry, I know what I must to do," he said. He turned to the girl. "Russian girl. Barry is liar. He pretend to be Russian so he can be close to you. He not Russian at all. He go to your gym because he pays a company to stalk you and give all your information to him. He has your picture on his desktop." He turned back to Barry, who looked dumbstruck. "Barry, I know you want me to commit violence against boyfriend, Niko, but Jim Carrey teach me this is not the way. Only way to happiness is truth. Let truth have its day. Now Barry, tell girl how you feel. Tell it true."

~~~

Miranda

"She started laughing," Barry said. "It would have been one thing if she'd slapped me. It would have meant she at least had some sort of feeling, but she laughed in my face and walked off. I've never been more humiliated in my life."

"No, Barry, you were more humiliated in your life, because afterward you run after her and tell her you love her, and she stop laughing and get scared. When she tell you to go away, remember how you start begging and told her she is your only hope? Remember? Remember how you say, 'If I can't have love, can I just have the sex?' You offer her three hundred dollar for sex, because you say they do that in the Russia."

"I never want to see you again, Rocket Jizz," Barry said.

"I'm sorry, Blueberry."

"Get out."

Rocket Jizz picked up his briefcase and left.

"That's all I was to her," Barry said. "A big joke. After all that time. She probably thought I was pathetic all along. I can't bear to go back to school. Not after that. You gave me false hope too."

"When you came in here, what did you think you were going to get?" Miranda asked. "Did you think I was going to wrap Nastya in a box for you and give her to you for your birthday? What you do with the information we provide you is on you. We can't force someone to love you. That company hasn't been invented yet."

"Have you ever been in love?"

"That's not important."

"Yes it is," Shaun's ghost said.

"Please, answer," Barry said. "Have you ever been in love?"

"Yes," Miranda said.

"Have you been loved?"

"Yes."

"No one's ever loved me. I don't know what it's like to hold someone or to be held. I've never had sex. I think about something all the time that I've never even had."

"Sex isn't the only thing in the world, Barry."

"Easy for you to say. Do you like it?"

She realized she'd sunk into her chair. She straightened up and regained her posture. Barry was looking her in the eye, and she didn't like it. She didn't like that his hands were clenched into pudgy little fists. Most of all, she didn't like questions about her personal life.

But she answered his question anyway. "I do."

"You sit there telling me it's great, having it yourself, but also telling me not to worry because it's not a big deal. If it's not such a big deal, then why do you have it?"

"Why do you deserve sex?" she threw back at him.

"Huh?"

"Tell me, what have you done to deserve sex? Or love, for that matter? Just wanting something doesn't make it so. What are you good at, Barry? What are some of your talents or hobbies or passions?"

Barry had no answer.

"As I thought . . . nothing. You're a blank slate. When you were learning Russian and going to the gym, at any point did you think maybe you should do more things like that for yourself? To better yourself? Or were they simply ploys to get laid? Why should anyone like you? What's interesting about you?"

"I wasn't just trying to get laid. I was in love with her."

"Maybe you were. I don't know. But what did you have to offer her, Barry? Maybe before you blame everyone else, you should find something you're passionate about without the thought of sex being a reward for having crossed out points on a list. Read a book or two, write one, learn a language, build something, pick up an instrument."

"Kill yourself," Shaun's ghost said.

"How long am I going to have to keep getting rejected?" Barry asked. "How many girls will I have to spill my feelings to before enough is enough? Is six in a row a high enough number to get the hint that I'll never be loved and will die alone? Does a pilot keep flying if he crashes his plane every time, or does he learn his lesson? And don't tell me to keep trying, or there are more fish in the sea. I've been trying. All I do is try."

"Time's up, Barry," she said.

He stood and walked to the door, then stopped. "Miranda, would you go out with me?"

"Never."

He slammed the door behind him.

She was exhausted, and she had four more client meetings. She pulled out the bottle of gin she'd stashed in her desk and took several sloppy swigs, dribbling it onto her shirt and pants. While looking for something to wipe it off with, she received a text from the receptionist summoning her to the conference room.

This was it; they were going to announce the new branch manager, and she had gin stains.

Everyone was in the conference room except for the receptionist. There were several faces she didn't recognize. Two of her colleagues she'd only ever met once, but she knew Hannah had talked shit about that Miranda girl thinking she was too good to socialize with the rest of them.

"Thank you, everyone, for coming," Alexei said at the front of the conference room. "We have some exciting news. Due to the fantastic job our team here is doing, we have the possibility of branching out. And not just one new branch, but two new branches, with a location in San Francisco and another in San Diego. I'd like to introduce the new San Francisco branch manager, Frank McGregor."

One of the new faces, a spitting image of Alexei, though a little rougher around the edges, stood up to accept his new position.

"And for our San Diego branch, I'm excited to announce one of our very own. Please give it up for Adam Leghy."

People clapped. Miranda didn't. Miranda heard none of

the rest of the announcements. She was ready to punch a hole through the wall. Before the meeting was finished, she went back to her office and killed the bottle. She calmed eventually but remained infuriated. Then she burst into Alexei's office.

"Oh, Miranda, I'm kind of in the middle of something," he said, pulling out a legal pad and writing on it.

"This is some bullshit," she said.

He lifted an eyebrow. "I don't follow."

"I bring in three times the revenue Adam does, easily. Why in the world did you give him the position over me?"

"Do you really want to do this, Miranda?"

"Yes, I really do."

He sighed as though her presence were a heavy burden. "You're a great employee, but your attitude leaves a lot to be desired. You haven't really shown me how much you want the position. Nothing's been signed yet. Are you willing to show me how much you want it?" He paused, his eyes on her. "Are we on the same page?"

"I think we are," she said. "Take off your pants."

Alexei removed his belt and unzipped his pants. He pulled them down, revealing his tight boxer briefs. He was already sporting a tower.

"Wow, you ready for this?" she asked.

"Hell yeah."

"Good." She pulled out her gun and pointed it at his face.

"Miranda, no, please wait!" He covered his face with his hands as though they'd stop a bullet.

"Don't worry. I'm not going to shoot you. I just wanted

to see what your face looked like when I pointed a gun at it. Also, I want you to look at the top shelf right there." She put her gun away. "Doesn't it look odd to you? Or what about that cabinet? I won't go through all of them. You can see for yourself." She pulled out her phone and opened an app. The two of them appeared on the screen from five different angles. "It's mic'd too. So this is all being recorded."

"You bitch."

"Careful," she said. "Also, you might want to put your pants back on."

"You're not going to get away with this. You're going to have to try a lot harder if you're going to blackmail me."

"Don't worry. I did. I've already discussed everything with my attorney. In fact, let me call him in."

Frank Sanchez entered the office wearing his best suit and carrying a briefcase.

"This is my attorney. You probably recognize him from his commercials."

Sanchez handed his business card to Alexei.

"You see, that client of ours, Douglass—his situation didn't just cause a lot of trouble for our company, but for his as well. You're off so often on coke-fueled binges that I was the only one around to take care of their problem. His employers were so grateful to me for covering up the fact that we helped him go after a fifteen-year-old girl that they gave me a generous financial reward. I used some of it to have this surveillance system set up in your office and Adam's as well." She didn't tell him that her client Sergio had set it all up for her. "The amount of cocaine you two do is staggering. And because you gave me a job where I follow people for a living, I have plenty of photo evidence and video of both of you buying your nose powder. Add that to the company being directly involved in the death of one girl and the suicide of one man—that can't possibly look good for you, can it? And let's not pretend that was the first or last time you sold information regarding minors."

"And you want to be branch manager. Is that it?"

"Wrong. I want the company."

He sneered. "You're out of your fucking mind."

"No, I'm the sane one, Alexei. While you and your coke-fiend buddy were doing blow and banging hookers—several of whom were underage, by the way—I was the only one here working. I have every bit of blackmail I could ever need on you two. I've typed up a list with bullet points. I can show it to you. Recordings as well. Frank, if you'd be so kind."

Frank Sanchez pulled out his phone, and Adam's voice rang out clearly: "I knew that blonde you hired wouldn't put out."

"Really could have saved me the trouble," Alexei's voice answered.

"I had the same vibe about her I got from that redhead you hired a long time ago."

"Miranda?"

"No, the hotter one. What was her name?"

"Charlotte."

"That one. I knew she was a prude."

"I got rid of her, didn't I? I made it clear what she had to do."

"Yeah, but you didn't learn your lesson."

"I guess you're right."

A loud snorting sound followed, trailed by deep exhalations.

"Offering job benefits in exchange for sexual favors," Sanchez said. "Then firing said employee for not agreeing to said advances. Illegal narcotics. Engaging in sexual intercourse with a minor . . . well, minors. It's an extensive list."

"You're going to hand the company over to me today, walk away, and keep your stupid fucking mouth shut. If that's not enough to convince you, don't forget I have a gun."

Alexei was paralyzed. He'd been the type of kid who'd never heard the word "no."

"Let me remind you that I have videos. Frank here will go over the paperwork for you to sign."

~~~

Miranda fired Adam and the receptionist and watched as Alexei left with his tail between his legs. That night was going to be a night of solving problems.

The docks had once excited Miranda. Once Enrique had brought her to work. It wasn't any kind of bring-your-daughter-to-work day. He simply decided to take her out of school early and show her where Daddy worked. The cargo, cranes, crates, and ships had amazed her. Before she'd known what Japan was, she knew it was far away and was amazed that a rectangular container could make the journey all the way from there to her small, unimpressive city. Enrique had taught her the names of the different ships and where they'd come from.

The sun was setting when her car pulled up. Despite the maze of containers and offices, she knew exactly where to find Enrique. Unlike with Alexei, she hadn't prepared what she was going to say. She got out and headed for his office.

The light was on, and she saw several silhouettes. The silhouettes were laughing. She wondered if this would be the last time Enrique would ever laugh. She opened the door.

He and two other schlubby, middle-aged men were drinking booze out of plastic cups. Enrique was the last to look up and see her standing there. His smile faded.

Good, she thought. That was all she needed to know.

"Miranda?"

She pulled several photos from her coat pocket and threw them on the small table in front of him. He picked them up and immediately put them back down. She wasn't going to speak until he acknowledged them. What had Nastya said? "Go easy." Then easy she would go.

"What is this?" he asked.

"I'm waiting for you to tell me."

"I think we should get going," said the schlubby man she recognized as Manny.

"Stay, go," she said. "It doesn't matter."

The two men schlubbed their way out.

"Miranda, I don't know what to say," Enrique said.

"What's my favorite movie?"

"What?"

"What's my favorite movie? It's a simple question. What's my favorite book? My favorite restaurant? Where have I dreamt of going since high school? Where do I work?"

Enrique was silent.

"I work at CoinciDATE. For such a long time, I tried to figure out who this woman was. Why was she so important to you? What did she have that Mom didn't? What did my dad see in her? But you know what? Anything that comes out of your mouth will be bullshit. I no longer care about any of those questions."

"Miranda . . . "

"You don't get to talk. All my life, you've been so hard on me. I thought you pushed me because you cared. But you don't. You don't care about anything. You never gave a shit about what I did for work. No matter what I chose, you would have disapproved. My interests weren't your interests. My interests didn't have merit because you didn't understand them and couldn't be fucked to try to understand. Look at you."

That last sentence had been more for her own benefit. His bushy mustache had once been a sign of his masculine might but now only emphasized how old he was. Sitting before her was Enrique, an old, frail man. A man who had never told the truth a day in his life.

"Everything," she said. "All those words you've ever said to me mean nothing. You always told me what to do with my life. What the fuck have you done with yours? I make more in a week than you do in a month."

Miranda reached into her coat pocket and pulled out a wad of cash. It was ten grand in hundred-dollar bills. She'd counted them five times over. She tossed it on the table where it landed next to the photos of the woman.

"That's for my twenty-two years. I'll never get the time back, but that's what paying for my peace of mind is worth. Use it as you wish. I don't care. I never want to see you again."

Miranda felt as old as her dad looked. She tried to remember what college parties were like, late-night study sessions, and hanging out with classmates. Once upon a time, getting an A on an exam meant something. She remembered when the biggest problem in her life had been a broken coffeemaker. Coffee. Nothing else mattered. All she wanted was a coffee. Everything else could wait.

~~~

Thirty minutes later she was in the bookstore's parking lot. The chasm between her and the building, her former place of employment, was larger than ever. She felt dread—the same dread she always felt before making her way inside to clock in for a shift.

But once she stepped inside, the dread disappeared. She was returned to a state of mind she hadn't experienced since before she ever worked there. It occurred to her that once upon a time she'd enjoyed shopping there. There were happy faces everywhere. Fathers and daughters, brothers and sisters, couples young and old. This place once had charmed her. It was amazing how all it took to ruin something was to become part of it.

Around her, employees were busy stocking shelves, answering calls, and avoiding customers. Did any of them remember her? Did she remember any of them? It hadn't been that long since she'd left. She remembered what it felt like to work there, the feelings in abstract—dread, pressure, and shame. But she couldn't remember anything in detail. It was all lost.

She went to the café. All the faces were unfamiliar. The girl behind the counter was just a kid. Miranda sat down at an empty table next to a homeless person playing with toothpicks. It had been the longest day of her life, and she happily could have fallen asleep right there.

"I'll take a small black coffee," a familiar voice said.

She looked up to find David standing before her, dressed all in black. He looked paler than she remembered. "I don't work here anymore."

"I know that," he said. "I thought maybe you'd treat me to coffee."

"David, would you like a coffee?"

He nodded.

She returned with two black coffees. For a long minute, they sat in silence. The coffee was far too hot to drink, even in small, quick sips.

"That guy used to work for NASA," David said, pointing at the homeless man.

"No he didn't."

"He did."

"Okay, what about the old guy over there?"

"Dunno."

"What are you doing here?"

"Initially I was looking for information about the Goat Man."

"The Goat Man?"

"Miranda, everyone around these parts knows the legend of the Goat Man. You can't tell me you've never heard it."

"I've never heard it. What is it, some kind of half-man, half-goat?"

"No, it's far more sinister than that. It's a half-man, half-goat, half-homie."

"The homie part and the man part aren't the same half?"

"Of course not." He scoffed. "Haven't you ever driven down the 126?"

"Sure I have."

"Then you'd know that if you drive past Santa Paula between the hours of one and three a.m., and if you look in your rearview mirror, you'll see the Goat Man."

"Guess I haven't been there at the right time."

"This bookstore is as ignorant of the legend as you are. Couldn't find anything, so I grabbed this." David held up a hardcover book that featured the face of the most beautiful black man Miranda had ever seen. *The Happy Zone: Cracking the Code of Happiness One Dollar at a Time* by Cornwallis Kensington.

"What the hell kind of book is that?"

"An important one."

She decided it was time to change the subject. "What do you do these days?"

"I'm debating between plastic surgery and self-exile in a far-off country."

"Oh?"

"You wouldn't get it, but some guy—if I can even call him *guy*—named Rocket Jizz keeps popping up everywhere I go. I don't know if you've ever dealt with someone who had Jizz as part of their name, but it isn't pleasant. In any case, this place—not just this building, but this place—is a black hole. You'd be doing yourself a favor to get out of here while you can."

"It isn't so bad," she said. "And I've got work to do."

But perhaps David was right. Sitting in the café only made her feel empty. Not just for herself, but for everyone around her. For people in general. Even if the building had charmed her when she walked in, it was a reminder that nothing lasts. The charm was gone. All she was reminded of was failed ambition.

"What motivates you, David?"

"Lots of things. Coffee, for one. What motivates you?"

"I don't know why, but I can't answer that question right now. Had you asked me two days ago, or maybe even two minutes ago, I could have answered right away."

"There was something I wanted to ask you, Miranda."

"What is it?"

He frowned. "Do you know where Gliese 667 Cc is? No, of course you don't. Bye then."

He was gone. He hadn't taken a single sip of his coffee. She decided she wouldn't either. Taking a sip, taking in one drop, would mean submitting to the black hole. By leaving the coffee untouched, she'd be breaking all ties with this place.

When she sat back in her car, she was exhausted. Miranda had a lot of work ahead of her, but in the meantime, she was going to celebrate. Sabrina had finally responded to one of her texts. They were going out.

Before that, Miranda decided to hit up the gym. She saw Nastya when she arrived and smiled broadly at her. Nastya smiled back, then walked up and slapped her face.

Глава 20

Барри

Barry's only friend in the world wasn't even from this world but was a space alien named Rocket Jizz. Barry didn't know how to be friends with a space alien. In any case, he never wanted to see him again. Daniel was merely a name that took up space in his phone contacts, and Christopher was a cunt. He hadn't planned for a post-Nastya world, yet he was living in one.

The past year had been a colossal, meaningless waste. Barry's existence deprived others of precious oxygen. He hated himself. His push-ups hadn't made the world better, nor had they helped him at all.

Out of spite and to show how much he hated himself, he began to drink three times as many Cokes a day. He couldn't stop thinking about Nastya. Images of her holding hands with Niko were always there in his subconscious, peeking their heads in to say hello when he tried to sleep. He couldn't imagine ever going through that again with another girl.

One day at school, after Nastya and Niko had walked by the slab of flesh that was Barry, Bert came up to him. "I hate seeing you like this, Barry. Let me help you."

"Fuck off," Barry said. "You can't help shit."

"I can. All you have to do is go with me somewhere."

"That fucking Latin thing?"

"It's just what you need. Don't you want to hang out with fun and interesting people?"

He had no fight left in him. He went where he was told or dragged. In the car ride over, Bert mentioned that his girlfriend had left him. Barry offered no words of encouragement, nor did he understand how Bert was able to carry on being his usual optimistic self. It pissed him off. He was so ugly and had no reason to be happy. She probably left him because he was so ugly, but then again, she was probably just as ugly as he was.

They arrived at the same mansion as earlier. Barry entered with every intention of being as nasty and unapproachable as possible. All the same people from earlier were there, plus a few new faces.

Something strange began to take place within Barry. There were beautiful women everywhere, and for those moments when his eyes made contact with their bodies in their tight dresses, he forgot Nastya existed. Not only did he forget she existed, remembering her existence angered him. He wasn't angry that she'd betrayed him; he was angry that he'd wasted so much time on her when the women in the mansion were far superior. Instead of the androgynous, unflattering clothing Nastya wore, every girl there wore the tightest dress he'd ever seen. He'd been such a fool to devote his life to a creature unworthy of him. He could have hugged Bert for bringing him there if Bert hadn't been so ugly.

Mr. Kensington mingled with his guests. When Barry looked his way, they made eye contact, and the beautiful black British man strolled over to him. Barry had never been so nervous around another man.

"Your name is Barry, isn't it?"

Barry nodded.

"I'm teasing you, mate. Of course I know your name. How could I forget?"

"Oh." Barry giggled.

"That tracksuit is even more dashing than the last time I saw it."

"Thank you, Mr. Kensington, sir."

"What did I tell you, Barry? I hoped you'd find it within yourself to refer to me as friend. What might have been simply a handshake to you was a momentous beginning to a great friendship to me, because I knew immediately you were someone special, mate. That handshake that felt like a momentous event isn't just handed out arbitrarily to anyone. Sometimes a handshake is simply a handshake. Are you enjoying yourself, mate?"

"I think so."

"That's no good. You should *know* so. If my guests aren't having the time of their lives, it means Cornwallis Kensington has done something wrong. Cornwallis Kensington doesn't like being wrong. What's the problem, lad?"

"There's no problem, Mr. Kensington, sir. It's just . . . there are so many people here, I don't know where to start."

"Barry, you're an interesting lad. I can see that. Everyone here is interesting, too, and they are all interested in getting to know you. All these beautiful women are just people, Barry, and any one of them would be happy to have a chat with you. Do you know how I know this?"

"Um . . ."

"I'm British, so when I say things, they have more weight to them, don't they?"

"I think you're right."

"Of course I am. People respect British accents. Now go and have a good time. Talk to some beautiful women instead of my ugly old mug."

Mr. Kensington patted Barry on the shoulder and wandered away. Bert had gone off to chat with some other ugly people. Barry was in a sea of beauty and elegance. He'd spent so much of his life figuring out how to talk to Nastya, he couldn't remember how one was supposed to begin a conversation with any other beautiful woman. It couldn't possibly be as easy as saying *Hi*. Where to even begin?

He never worked up the courage to try that evening, but he did focus his attention on a black-haired beauty with pale skin. He'd been prepared to think about Nastya for the rest of his life, but now he had new imagery to jerk off to.

~~~

The next week, he returned. In fact, it was he who urged Bert to go with him. He'd thought of the black-haired beauty with the pale skin every day.

She was standing in exactly the same spot, as though she hadn't left at all. There and alone. *Make an effort to talk to as many people as possible*, he told himself. He did just that.

"Hello."

"Hi." She smiled.

"I'm Barry."

"Wow, I love your name. I'm Francesca."

"You're very beautiful. So is your accent."

"Aw, you're sweet. Thank you. What can you tell me about yourself, Barry?"

Barry told her everything. He was a Russian immigrant who'd had his name anglicized and was working on becoming the next Pushkin. Luckily, she didn't know who Pushkin was. It didn't matter. They spent the better part of the night together.

At the following two meet-ups, she spoke exclusively to Barry. It didn't make sense. He'd abandoned the word *optimism*, but that was exactly what he felt. He was happy again. All week long, he waited for the meet-ups at Mr. Kensington's mansion so he could see Francesca. Nastya could go to hell. Francesca was the most beautiful woman who'd ever lived. She spoke with Barry because she understood that he deserved her. He deserved her luscious body. Eventually, the two would be alone, and her body would be his to do with as he pleased. His whole life had been leading up to this moment. Nastya had been a mere distraction to test his resolve. Francesca was the real deal.

During the fourth meet-up, he finally worked up the courage to ask her a big question. "Could I get your phone number?"

Before she could answer, Mr. Kensington was summoning them for another presentation. Then he was on stage once again. Several others sat behind him in chairs, taking notes. Barry recognized one of the note-takers as David, the one who'd crushed Rudy's dreams and complimented him on his tracksuit. David was scribbling something furiously on his legal pad.

"We have great news. While I was mingling with some of my pleasant guests, several of them couldn't help but ask, 'Mr. Cornwallis Kensington, whatever happened to that competition you mentioned back in December? What did we write our names down for?' Rest assured, my friends, Cornwallis Kensington doesn't forget these things. In fact, he's been bloody hard at work. The competition we mentioned isn't merely a competition, but a social experiment.

"Here at Beatitudinem, we believe in building real, meaningful relationships. Apps like Tinder and social media have ruined what it means to really connect with someone. Here, we strive to help make those bonds. Whether they be friendships, work partnerships, or romances, we are here to make connections. We're all equal here, but this experiment is about fighting for that equality. The way to truly appreciate something is to have it taken away from you and to learn how to cope without it. It all comes down to how you get it back. Now, at random, you have all been divided into five groups. When your name and group number is called, go to the table that has your corresponding number on it."

Mr. Kensington read off the list, and one by one, groups began to form. Francesca waved to Barry as she was sent to group five.

Please, group five, Barry prayed. *Please.*

"Barry Shit . . . uh, I'm sorry, *Schnitt*, group one."

Barry was joined by one hot girl, Bert, Debbido, and a collection of other Barrys. Francesca and all the fancily dressed people dominated groups four and five.

"Now I know you've probably made great connections with people in various groups, and you might think, 'Gee, Mr. Cornwallis, it's unfair that you put me in group one,' but the further you have to go, the greater the reward. Your group numbers aren't permanent. Group one has a participation fee of twenty dollars. That sounds reasonable, doesn't it?

"If you elect out of taking part in the group system, you can still use the facilities, but you won't be able to speak with any of the group members. Group one members can only interact with other members of group one. If you want to interact with someone from group two, the group two participation fee is sixty dollars, and that is per event. If you're in group two and want to move to group three, it's eighty dollars. If you want to go from one to three by means of skipping two, that will cost ninety-five dollars. Going from three to four costs one hundred and seventy-five dollars, and group five, our most exclusive, has the price of three hundred and fifty dollars. If, however, you want to bypass everything and go from one to five, you can do that for only a thousand dollars."

Debbido stood up. "I'll pay a thousand dollars in cash now to go to group five."

"Everyone give it up for this young man," Mr. Kensington said.

The room erupted in applause, and Debbido sat down not next to one of the Japanese girls but Francesca.

"All of this money goes to a good and selfless cause. The notion that you can't buy happiness . . . is a lie. You can. You can buy it for others. Those in group one are paying for the happiness of group two, who have better events and accommodations than their group one peers. Those in group five have the best events yet, including yacht parties and various vacations together. If you want to see what buying happiness looks like, take a look at these."

David turned on a slideshow that showed Mr. Kensington

in front of various exotic backdrops with even more exotic women. In several photos, he was jet-skiing in some tropical paradise. Others showed him riding elephants and rock climbing. Beautiful women were never far away.

"Look how goddamn happy I look," Mr. Kensington said. "You are the ones who made that possible. You made Cornwallis Kensington very happy."

Everyone clapped.

Barry went to the following meet-up and handed over his cash. Group one was ushered into a small room that had a water cooler, saltine crackers, a ping pong table, and two TVs showing the groups four and five events. Those were lively, with nearly everyone beautiful and drinking champagne.

Group five had a pool. Barry watched as Francesca, wearing a thong bikini, dove in next to Debbido. Meanwhile, in group one, Bert was in good spirits, enjoying the free crackers immensely. The rest of the Barrys were actively vying for the attention of the blond-haired beauty who was the sole female in the group. She seemed friendly enough, smiling and laughing, but she wasn't Francesca.

Barry had to find a way to get back to Francesca. That meant he had to get to group five. Group two wasn't much better than group one, and for the time being, he couldn't afford to get past group three. He'd been so close to Francesca. This was his chance to redeem himself.

"Come on, stay in group one," Bert said after the first group meet-up. "It's fun. The guys are nice, and you really should try and talk to Katya."

"Katya?"

"Yeah, Katya. That's her name. She's Russian. I thought

you'd like her, but you didn't even talk to her."

The next meet-up, Barry handed over his cash and was ready to talk to Katya. He hadn't paid her much mind before, but being Russian made her hotter, and now he had an icebreaker. But when he and Bert arrived at group one's designated room, they found only other Barrys.

"Where's Katya?" he asked.

"She moved up to group three," another Barry said.

That settled it. No more distractions and no more fucking around. Barry needed to get closer to Francesca. He couldn't allow lesser girls to stand in his way, Russian or not.

That night, Barry went home and collected all his consoles, video games, and his father's CD collection. His father would never notice it was gone. The fifteen CDs only got him eight dollars at the used record store, but he was able to get three-hundred-and-fifty dollars for all his games. He got thirty-five dollars for a tracksuit. Combined with his work savings, he had it: one-thousand dollars.

He arrived at Beatitudinem ready to slap a thousand dollars in cash in Mr. Kensington's big hands. He'd see Francesca again, the most beautiful woman who ever lived.

"That's great that you want to join group five," Mr. Kensington said. "But due to such a high demand of group members moving up and new members coming in, we had to turn group five into group eight. But the new group five is also fantastic."

"How much does group eight cost?"

"Group eight is . . . David?" He turned to David, who had his nose in his legal pad.

"Three grand," David said.

Barry remembered the pool party and all the girls. Maybe Francesca wouldn't be there, but if there was a girl even half as good looking, he'd call that success. He handed over his money.

He arrived at the pool and found a dozen Barrys. There were no girls. Instead, there were bottomless chicken wings. *It's simply an off day*, he thought. *Not every night can be the best night ever. Even group five might have its off days.* Luckily, he only had to pay the group five fee once. Once you were in, you were in. He'd be back the next time.

The next time, they didn't even have bottomless chicken wings. There was a new food menu, and members were expected to pay. Barry saw only confused faces. A couple of guys had decided to be confused in the pool. What was the point if there were no girls? Barry's hands began to shake. The involuntary reaction confirmed that his deepest fears were true. Numbers began to flash before his eyes as the realization sunk in of how much money he'd wasted.

Barry returned to the group one room, where they were watching group eight at a foam party on a TV.

"Hey!" said one of the group one Barrys. "You can't be here!"

"You piece of shit," Barry said to Bert.

"What?"

"You brought me to a fucking cult."

"I did?"

"Yes! And I just fucking wasted one thousand dollars because of you."

"Barry, you should've stayed in group one. Have some crackers."

"Why would anyone ever fucking want to do that?"

"It's fun. These guys are nice."

"No, these guys are ugly, gullible losers, and you're the ugliest one of them all. Give me my grand back or I never want to see you again."

"Barry, I'm sorry."

As expected, Barry didn't get a refund. Beatitudinem had a policy that you couldn't un-buy happiness.

Barry had never felt less happy. Beatitudinem was the gods' way of reminding him he was meant to be a miserable cunt. He had to accept he'd never have a meaningful relationship with a woman. His bank account was nearly wiped out, all for nothing. All for the pursuit of not being lonely. All for Debbido.

He saw Debbido at the store the following week.

"I'm really not supposed to talk about it with nonmembers," Debbido said. "But yes, I definitely had sex with Francesca. I'm only telling you because it was great."

That settled it. Barry hated women. All of them. He never wanted to have a relationship with one. They were tits and asses, nothing more. He wanted meaningful relationships with tits, and the only way to do that was to pay for it. Barry was going to take what money he had left and go to the strip club. Women were meat. They didn't have souls or feelings or desires. They were meant to be groped and ogled. More than that, Barry couldn't live another day without seeing tits. He'd gladly give all the money he had left to see some tits.

"I don't want to go," Christopher said.

"You were the one who wanted to get prostitutes," Barry reminded him.

"That's different. I don't want to pay to not have sex."

"But isn't seeing tits better than not seeing tits?"

"I guess so."

"Good. I'm picking you up."

Barry passed the place three times before realizing they indeed had found the correct parking lot. It looked like they were on the set of a Terminator movie—an industrial area full of factories, trucks, and desolation. He supposed it made sense that a place like this would be all the way out here. They couldn't very well put it in the mall food court or next to a school.

Quite a few cars were already parked in the small lot. In a sea of ugly gray buildings was a small black door with a neon sign above it.

Christopher had barely spoken a word on the ride over. He'd been against the idea since Barry had suggested it. But Barry didn't *want* to be there. He *had* to be there. For once in his miserable life, he wanted to see tits up close, even if it meant paying for it and going home with blue balls.

Outside the entrance stood two guys who looked like third-rate henchmen from a Jason Bourne movie. They were smoking cigarettes.

Barry gave Christopher the "let's get a move on" eyes. The two henchmen examined them as they made their way to the entrance. A small red rope blocked the doorway. Barry glanced inside and saw some of the clientele, but couldn't get a look at any of the dancers. What he got was a hit of perfume and cigarette smoke.

The bouncer appeared a decade later, looking like an upgraded version of the two henchmen outside. "Entry is twenty dollars, and I'm going to need to see some ID."

Christopher handed the bouncer his high school ID.

"What the hell is this?" he asked, flipping the thing over.

"It's an ID."

"What? No, I need a driver's license, kid. I can't do jack shit with this." He handed it back.

"I don't have one."

"You don't have a driver's license?" Barry asked.

Christopher shook his head.

"Hey, kid, there's a line. You coming or going?"

A line was indeed forming behind Barry and Christopher. Barry handed his ID and a twenty to the bouncer, and then gave his keys to Christopher. "Go wait for me in the car. I won't be long."

His friend hesitated before complying. Nothing was going to stop Barry, not when he was so close.

Inside, the hall gave way to a dimly lit room with a stage in the middle. There were some chairs near the stage with couches along the wall farther back. No one was on stage. A couple of waitresses chatted with the DJ. In the dark corners, Barry saw a couple of girls sitting on older businessmen types' laps. Scattered about were other guys alone or in pairs trying not to make eye contact with anyone. They were either older businessmen types or just old. All of them were older than Barry.

He took a seat up front. A waitress came by asking if he wanted a drink. He shook his head.

"If you sit up front, you have to tip the girls," she said.

"Okay." Barry had the last of his money with him, all in

twenties. Group five had decimated his savings.

Several minutes of nothing but stagnation passed. Had he picked a bad day? Was the whole thing a scam? Were the old men currently laying claim to all the available girls?

"Please give it up for Star!" came the DJ's voice.

Onto the stage came a short and stumpy girl with thick pink hair and large bangs. She performed several dangerous feats on the pole before removing her bra. Her tits were small and slightly sad, with pointed nipples. After a minute, a couple of patrons threw bills on the stage.

Barry had waited more than two decades to see real tits in the flesh, but try as he might, he couldn't get excited by the girl on stage. Was it really this boring and uneventful in real life? Would he have had the same reaction to Nastya's or Miranda's tits?

Remembering what the waitress had said, he removed a twenty and placed it on the stage. Star's eyes nearly popped out of her head when she saw it.

The next stripper was more of the same. It was hard to tell, but all the girls sitting on the couches doing nothing seemed much hotter.

He felt his phone violently erupt in his pocket. When he pulled it out, the eagle-eyed bouncer reminded him of the no-phone policy.

Barry could feel the eyes of others closing in on him, and he began to grow uneasy. He knew his best course of action was to leave. He'd already spent forty dollars and had yet to get anything out of it. Forty became sixty as he tipped the next stripper.

"All right, gentlemen," came the DJ's voice. "Tonight is

a two-for-one special, so let's show some love for our ladies."

One of the back doors opened, and more than a half dozen girls of different shapes, colors, and sizes poured into the room. Some stopped immediately to sit on the laps of eager or uneager patrons. Others found dates right away and led them to the back, hand in hand. Barry strained his eyes to see if any of the girls resembled Nastya or Francesca or Miranda. They didn't. There was an attractive blonde, but Barry wasn't partial to blondes. He decided it was best not to be picky, but she'd already been snatched away by some sleazeball in a sleaze suit.

Was it acceptable to approach one of the girls yourself? Did good manners matter to a stripper?

His phone vibrated again. It was then he realized how incredibly hard he was and how incredibly big of a mistake wearing track pants had been. Jeans would have provided some concealment, but all he could do now was place an arm over the rocket.

The first girl he'd given a twenty to was chatting with the most beautiful girl in the room. She didn't resemble Nastya or Miranda or Francesca in any way. She was Asian, petite, and had incredibly dark, long hair. The old perverts could keep their perfect blondes. Barry's erection was raging for that girl.

The first girl he'd tipped smiled, whispered something to the Asian girl, and walked over to Barry. She sat down on his lap and asked where he was from.

"Russia," he said without hesitation.

"Wow, that's why you're so cute. I'm Star. Can you say something in German?"

"Russian?"

"Yeah."

"*Da*," he said.

"What's that mean?"

"It means *yes*."

"Wow, that's so awesome. Listen, would you like a lap dance?"

Barry began to panic. Of course he wanted a lap dance. More than anything, but not from her. Several perverts were already eyeing the Asian girl.

"Um . . . " Barry began to sweat. "You're super pretty, but would it be possible to have a dance with her?" He tipped his head toward the Asian girl.

"With Stacey?" She smiled. "Hold on, sweetie."

Star got up and walked over to Stacey. Barry could smell the perfume and lotion lingering on his lap. Despite not finding her attractive, the smell intensified his arousal.

Star and Stacey consulted with one another, occasionally glancing over at Barry and smiling. Then Stacey came over and sat in his lap. His erection was throbbing.

"Are all German guys as cute as you?" She smiled, putting her arms around his neck.

"Oh, I don't know." Barry laughed.

"Oh my, you're so big," she said, squirming a little against his throbbing cock. "Are all Germans as big as you?"

"Oh, uh, yeah. I think so."

"You're fun. Can you say something in German for me?"

"*Ty ochen krasiva.*"

"Oh wow. What's that mean?"

"It means you're beautiful."

"Aw, you're sweet. What's your name?"

"Barry."

"Like a strawberry. I love it. What do you do for a living?"

"It's a secret."

"Oh, how mysterious. Are you a German spy?"

Barry put a finger to his lips. She smiled. So did he. He was enjoying talking to her. Not only was she drop-dead gorgeous, she was smiling at him and holding on to his every word. He was having a good time. All his worries had left. He had a beautiful woman on his lap, and soon, she'd be naked. More importantly, she was smiling, and smiling because of him. He'd wanted for so long for a beautiful woman to be in his arms, smiling. He wanted to wrap his arms around her and hold her forever.

"Is this your first time here?"

Barry nodded.

"Well, you're cute," she said, "and I want to make this special for you."

A waitress came by to ask Barry if he wanted to buy Stacey a drink. She ended up getting an eleven-dollar Red Bull she didn't touch.

She leaned in close to Barry. "When this song finishes, I'm going to take you in back for a special lap dance."

The song ended. She stood up, grabbed him by the hand, and led him beyond the curtains. She sat him down on a red sofa. They were alone.

"We just have to wait for the next song to start." She smiled.

This was it. Barry was going to see her body up close. The song began to play.

"Just relax," she said, removing her bra. Her tits came

loose with a tiny jiggle. They weren't big, about a B cup, but their shape was perfect. Michelangelo couldn't have drawn more perfect tits.

She leaned her chest in close to his face—close enough that if he dared to, he could stick out his tongue and taste them. He held back, not knowing how much was permitted. She smelled so strongly of lotion, it was almost overwhelming.

She pulled back just before he was able to change his mind and lick her nipples. With her back to him, she bent over and pulled down her G-string. Watching it slide out of her ass and down her legs was the most glorious thing Barry had ever seen.

She sat on his lap and put her face on his neck. "You're so fucking hard," she said.

He was never going to wash those pants again. He wanted the smell of her to remain on him forever.

"Do you want to fuck me?" she asked.

Barry nodded.

"You're so sweet and exotic. It's making me so wet." She lowered her face to his thigh, centimeters away from his erection. "I want to put your whole dick in my mouth."

She pulled his track pants down. His dick was already popping out through the front slip of his boxers, but she pulled those down as well.

"You're so big."

Barry began to pray. *Don't let me come yet, God, please no. This is all I've ever wanted. Let me have five minutes of this, and I can die happy. Please, God. Just five minutes.*

Her mouth was above the mushroom head. Just a little bit closer, and her lips and tongue would be touching him.

The anticipation was wonderful agony. Her mouth was over the head and part of the shaft, open and all without making contact. The teasing was driving him crazy.

When Barry was about to lose his mind, she pulled back, looked up at him, and said, "That's two songs, and you owe me two hundred."

"What?"

"Two hundred dollars," she said. "And it's better to pay here than up front."

"W-w-w . . . wait a minute. I don't understand."

"It's simple," she said. "You pay up, or the manager gets involved."

"But . . . I don't have two hundred dollars."

She began putting her clothes back on.

"Wait!" Barry yelled, struggling to pull his pants past his erection. Then it happened. A giant white gooey torpedo shot across the room. A second torpedo landed all over his pant leg, a third landed on Stacey's panties, and a fourth dribbled onto the couch and left a wet mark.

Stacey laughed. "Are you fucking kidding me? Oh . . . my . . . God!"

Barry started shaking.

"It's going to be two hundred and fifty now."

Barry pulled out his wallet. There were two twenties left. "Please, it's all I got. The price for a lap dance. I didn't even get one. Just take the money and let me go."

"Okay, looks like we're getting Rollo involved."

"Rollo? Who's Rollo? No, let's not get him involved."

Stacey left through the curtains. Barry tripped, struggling

to go after her. The scent of fresh cum wafted over him.

Rollo was as big and scary as his name suggested. He emerged from his office, towering over any bouncer and fitted with arms and legs as thick as redwoods. His hair was pulled into a tight ponytail. "What is it now, Stacey? Can't you handle this shit on your own?"

"That would be lovely, Daddy, but this piece of shit doesn't want to pay."

Rollo looked at Barry. His eyes immediately went to his cum-stained pants.

"He came all over the place, Rollo," Stacey said, as though it weren't already clear.

This caught the attention of several girls and clients.

"Oh shit foo, homie shot a load on his pants," one cholo said to another.

"Please," Barry said. "Here's the money. Nothing happened. I just want to go home." He held out the forty dollars, and Rollo snatched it out of his hand.

"He owes two hundred ten more," Stacey said.

"Okay," Rollo said. "Get this piece of shit taken care of in the next two minutes, or Bruno breaks his legs."

One of the bouncers nodded.

Barry contemplated letting his legs get broken. His debit card was overdrawn. He could use his credit card, but that was over the limit as well.

It was clear he'd receive no sympathy from anyone there. He walked with Stacey to the ATM and took out $220 using his credit card.

Stacey grabbed the money, smiled at Barry, and said, "Come again, sweetie."

Barry left the building with his head hanging low and was pounced upon by Christopher. "Barry, goddamn it! How many times do I have to text you *Emergency* before you respond?"

"What happened?"

"What happened to your pants?"

"Doesn't matter. What's the emergency?"

Christopher held up a key that was broken in half. It wasn't Christopher's key; it was Barry's. The key to start the ignition.

"What the fuck?"

"I tried opening the door, but it wouldn't open, so I tried harder, and . . . "

"And?"

"And eventually it broke off."

"Instead of thinking, 'Hmm, maybe I should try the other fucking key,' you just kept twisting that one until it fucking broke?"

The tall, greasy-haired incel reddened. Sweat caused his hair to stick to his forehead. He looked angry, but why he of all people should be angry, Barry didn't know. "It's not my fault."

"How is it not your fucking fault, you goggle-eyed freak?"

Christopher was silent.

"Where's the other half of the key?"

"Stuck in the car door."

"Get it out—*now*, goddamn it."

"How?"

"Think."

Barry's phone rang. It was his mother. *Fuck!* He didn't answer.

"Go inside and ask someone for help," Barry said.

"I can't get in. No license."

Barry's mom texted: *Call me back. NOW!*

Instead, he went back inside, where he was laughed at and told to fuck off before he could ask for help. His phone kept ringing. Eventually, he got another text.

I get an alert every time you use your card, Barry. Are you fucking kidding me? Do you know how fucking angry we are? Come. Home. Now.

I can't, Barry texted back.

Why not?

My car key is broken.

We're on our way.

Barry began looking for the nearest bridge to toss himself off. Maybe a truck to lay himself under.

"What's happening?" Christopher asked.

"My parents are coming."

"Fuck!" he said and took off running. He didn't look back.

Barry's parents arrived to pick up the car with the spare key. Ray was there as well to take the car back from Barry. A crowd of spectators had left the strip club to watch the far more entertaining show taking place in the parking lot.

"What's on your pants?" Mrs. Schnitt asked.

Barry decided he'd never speak for the rest of his life. He sat in the back seat, refusing to look at anyone or hear anything.

"What's that smell?" Mrs. Schnitt asked.

"Drop it, honey," Mr. Schnitt said.

"It's coming from Barry's pants. Oh . . . Goddamn it,

Barry. I've never been more humiliated, disgusted, and confused in my entire life. Aren't you going to talk to your son?"

"Don't be a pervert, Barry," his father said.

~~~

Barry's parents took away his credit cards. From then on, ninety percent of every dollar he earned would go directly to them. He'd take a bus or walk to school and work. His parents also told him he had to sleep with his door open to make sure no perversion was taking place.

Barry's life was over. Although he never heard the words, he knew the story of his shame had spread at school. The city was too small for a story like that to remain a secret for long. Oh well. Sitting alone wasn't so bad. Occasionally, he'd see Nastya walk by, and she'd ignore his existence. He kept wearing his tracksuit because it was the only thing that fit him.

He looked at all the faces around him. Fat ones, big ones, pretty ones, and ugly ones. They all smiled. Why were they happy? What code had they unlocked? Ugly people smiling. How pathetic. How disgusting. How fucking embarrassing.

After three days of torment, Barry could no longer take it, so he got on the bus and skipped the rest of his classes. The last place he wanted to go to was the beach, so that was where he went. It was a place he'd always hated. When his family still did things together as a family, he always dreaded being forced along and wasting his Sundays there. It was windy and not particularly warm out.

He sat on a bench furthest from the shore. He just wanted to enjoy the view and think about nothing, but as always something had to interfere and ruin it. There was a bench about three yards in front of him. Seated on the bench was a couple, roughly his age. He couldn't see their faces, but from their body movement and the shape of their heads, he knew they were beautiful. They sat looking forward at the grey water. Their arms were interlocked, her head on his shoulder. Who knew how long they'd already been there or what they were talking about. They were happy and in love, and that was all that mattered. Barry would stay there as long as they did. As long as it took to sink in. He would never have that. From the moment he was born, the universe decided he would never experience that.

He cupped his hand into the sand. As he lifted his hand, streams of the broken rock fell through his fingers like waterfalls that had eventually got overtaken by the wind and disappeared entirely before reaching ground. He had read once that there were more grains of sand on the beaches than stars in the universe. Or perhaps it was the other way around. He didn't remember. What he did remember was that grains of sand and stars numbered in the billions. In his hand were thousands, maybe even millions, of grains. Each insignificant speck the wind carried away was a relationship he would never have, a girl he would never be loved by. Someone had more luck finding one specific grain of sand on this beach and setting it back down next to the same grain of sand it had previously been next to. Two grains of sand could drift away in the wind and have more of a shot at finding each other than Barry did someone to share a bench with.

Barry had loved girls his whole life. With Nastya, he'd believed it had been real and not a fool's hope. Just once, he'd have liked to know what it felt like to go to bed at night and be desired back.

The couple had gone. A foul smell took hold of the air.

A dead seal, most likely.

He got home and saw a long package on his doorstep. It was addressed to him. Odd, as he hadn't ordered anything. Luckily, his parents weren't home.

In his room, he shut the door and opened the mysterious box. There was a black case inside, like one used for carrying guitars. On top was a note in almost indecipherable handwriting.

Wow, Barry, so long time since I see you. If you don't know, it's me, Rocket Jizz. I'm so sorry I leave you, Barry, but I must to return to the outer space again to take care some real business. I leave you something I don't need, because in outer space I have laser weapons. I now am understand that violence IS the answer LOL. Ciao!

P.S. Barry, have fun with this.

Barry opened the case and found himself touching an AK-47. It was glorious. He'd never seen anything like it. He lifted it up. The thing was much lighter than he'd anticipated. He ran his fingers down the barrel. It had a nice polish to it. It looked like his fingertips were the first ever to caress it. The case also contained three full magazines.

At that moment, Barry truly believed that the gift was an act of the gods of fate. Fate and coincidence, hand in hand. Every single event, victory, defeat, meeting, or accident were all the result of coincidence. Nastya's rejection was the event Barry needed to realize he had to look for girls elsewhere. Looking for girls elsewhere was the event destined to take place to solidify once and for all that Barry would never be with any of them.

All these events had to occur for Barry to end up where he was. This gun had come into his hands at that time for a reason. Having it fulfilled a purpose, and he went to bed smiling. Having a purpose made him happy.

He woke up happy the next morning and ate breakfast happy and even spoke to his parents happily. They didn't see him as he ran to his room to grab his new guitar case.

On the bus, he was just any other musician carrying his guitar around. The bus dropped him off next to the school.

Kenneth had never been anything more than talk. Barry had humored him, but deep down, he'd always known Kenneth was no wiser than he was. The only wise act he ever committed had come at the very end. Barry was going to make sure he got the job done properly. He had three full magazines.

He was going to take out Chads, Staceys, and fat, ugly people alike. He wanted the fat, ugly ones to feel the pain in particular, to remind them they never had anything to be happy about.

The quad was teeming with students. *Perfect. Fish in a barrel.* With luck, he'd be able to use one bullet per person. The fat ones might require two or three.

Once he was surrounded on all sides, he set down his case. No one looked at him, and why should they? They never had before. That made their imminent deaths all the more delicious. The only thing left to do was get "Bolero" set on his phone, or the whole thing would fall apart. There it was: the soft drums, the long, dull crescendo. This time it would crescendo into something grand.

He'd begun opening up the case when a voice said, "Hey, Barry."

Barry looked up to see Christopher carrying a similar black case. Before Barry could respond, Christopher had removed his own AK-47 and shot the two girls in front of them. Christopher marched forward, shooting everyone in his path. Screams followed, and waves of people began rushing toward the exits.

Barry forgot who and where he was. He ran and ran, and finally collapsed onto a park bench about a mile away from campus. He was covered in sweat. The neighborhood was alive with police sirens and sporadic gunfire. Barry heard none of it.

He still hadn't fully processed what had happened when he found himself at a bar with a drink in front of him several hours later. His case was no longer with him, and he had no recollection of what he'd done with it.

From various news headlines and conversations, he'd pieced together that twelve had been killed, dwarfing Kenneth's number. Among the dead were Sonny, who'd lived so many centuries, and Bert, who'd died standing in the gunman's way so others could flee.

Christopher was dead as well.

Barry was alive. How and why? What for? He'd been prepared to do one thing with his life. He'd failed at being a failure. Christopher would be remembered by every friend and family member whose loved ones he took away. Nastya didn't remember Barry. Miranda didn't remember Barry. Francesca most certainly didn't remember Barry. Stacey might remember him, but he doubted it.

What had he achieved in his life? Two dead murderers for friends, embarrassing himself at a strip club, and never being able to talk to his parents again or look them in the eyes?

He couldn't understand what anything meant. Was he happy to be alive? Should he have been? Happy or alive? He hadn't pulled the trigger, but he felt as if he had. What if Christopher hadn't shown up? In that scenario, there was no tomorrow.

He couldn't even taste the beer, but it was necessary all the same. Was Christopher's arrival another sign? Another message from the God of Coincidences? He'd wanted so much to be seen, to be remembered. Nastya didn't remember him, and neither did Francesca nor Miranda.

"I remember you," came a guy's voice.

Barry looked up and saw a pale, familiar face. Everything was blurry, and the beer was making it worse. After a few seconds, Barry recognized the face. It was that guy David from the fucking cult.

"You remember me?"

"Huh?" David said. "I was talking to the bartender. Who are you?"

"Never mind," Barry said.

"Come to think of it, you do look familiar. Are you someone's son?"

"I think so."

"That must be it."

"Actually, it's not," Barry said, then paused to order

another beer. "You conned me into joining that cult of yours."

"Did I? Did you enjoy it?"

"Of course not. It was a scam."

"Of course it was a scam. That's what cults are. I wanted other people to give me their money. Nothing I said was a lie. The money they gave me made me really happy."

"The girls, were any of them real?"

"I mean, they were real models we hired. We had to give incentive to join."

"What about Francesca? What was her story?"

"Francesca?"

"Apparently she had sex with Debbido the weeaboo."

"Right, yeah. I hadn't really considered anyone actually going straight from group one to group five, but in any case, some of the models we hired also were whores, so Francesca was on standby in case a Debbido situation were to happen."

Barry nodded, trying to absorb everything. "So are you guys still operating?"

"Not now. Not here anyway. Sometimes with ideas like these, they start off great, but it's a question of how much staying power they have. So, in the meantime, I'm working on tweaking it up a bit, introducing it at different locations, and brainstorming new ideas." David pulled out a notebook with charts, arrows, names, and notes shooting off in every direction. "I was thinking of maybe starting a company where we get paid to stalk people and give that person's information to their desperate and lonely suitors. But then I found out I was beaten to the punch."

"Yeah, CoinciDATE."

"You know it?"

"Yeah." Barry sighed. "I was in love with the owner. I'm in love with most girls I meet, but I was in love with her too. I never told her."

"Who's the owner?"

"Redhead named Miranda."

"Miranda Santillano?"

"Yeah."

"Holy shit." David said. "I didn't know she had it in her. Wow." He sat silent for some time, staring ahead. "You seem to be attracted to these cults and scams," he said at last. "Do you have any interested friends I can use?"

"I don't have any friends."

"Pity."

Barry stared. "So you set up these things promoting happiness, but have no intention of actually delivering any?"

"What's happiness?"

"Come again?"

"It's not a trick question. What is happiness?"

"It's feeling good. The opposite of sadness and misery."

"Are you happy?"

"No, I'm miserable."

Neither David nor anyone else in the bar had any reaction to Barry's misery. They continued to drink and laugh and socialize. Barry's misery didn't matter there, or anywhere else in the world. Barry believed that maybe, for a nanosecond, if someone else could understand his misery, then there would be hope for humanity. But no one understood.

David was so motionless he could have been dead. It was only when he resumed doodling on his notepad that he showed he still had a heartbeat. "Why do you think you're entitled to happiness?" he asked at last. "What's happiness for the wolf is death for the deer, is it not? But aren't deer beautiful and majestic creatures? Surely you don't want to see them torn apart and bloodied. But isn't the wolf beautiful and majestic as well? Have you ever seen a Komodo dragon eating a deer? It's horrific. Absolutely do not look it up. People buy puppies because it makes them happy. They're cute, and everyone squeezes their little faces. Then we cut off their goddamn balls and the dogs will never be able to know the happiness of sex. But at least their owners have the happiness of squeezing a cute, fluffy toy's face. They use the puppy for their own happiness, but no one is asking if the puppy is happy. The little thing never had a say in the matter."

"I've never known the happiness of having sex," Barry said.

"I figured as much. Why do you think you should have sex, though?"

"Everyone wants to have it."

"I want to know what's going on at Area 51. Doesn't mean it'll happen. Remove one brick, the whole wall comes down. Get rid of bees, and we're all fucked. Hot people exist to keep the sex drive going. Without hot people, you'll have no desire. If everyone had equal-opportunity fucking, we'd collapse into madness. Happiness is oil. It's water. It's the trees. You might not be able to see it, but happiness is a finite resource in this universe. Not everyone gets to have some. It's scarce and valuable. Once you're able to understand that, you'll live happily."

"So I'll be happy?"

"You? No. You'll never be happy, but you'll live happily.

You'll live happily knowing that you were meant to be a miserable bastard all along and never had a say in the matter."

~~~

David's words rang in his ears, even when he got home in the late hours and everyone was fast asleep. Could it really be that simple? Once he accepted his role, would it become evident?

He was ready for bed when a raging hard-on struck. He cursed it. That stupid, ugly appendage had been the cause of all his strife his entire life. It wasn't women to blame, but his useless cock. He'd lost friends over it, contemplated murder, lost his car, and made a fool of himself more times than he could count.

He yanked off his boxers and stared at his cock. He refused to stroke it. No, he punched it instead. If happiness were a finite resource, his cock was an infinite source of pain and humiliation. He punched it again, crying this time, not in physical pain, but for how much he hated himself. He thought about when he was a toddler and would play outside while his mother watched. He thought about riding bikes with Daniel when he was seven and they'd scream and mimic sound effects with their mouths, pretending their bikes were spaceships shooting down aliens. Weren't those moments happiness?

He thought of Nastya. Seeing her up close for the first time, so relieved when she spoke to him and smiled. He thought about his conversations with Miranda, thinking about Nastya while slowly realizing he was also in love with Miranda. Was it still happiness if each memory was bulldozed by a tragic ending?

Thinking about Nastya and Miranda only made his dick harder. Images of the two of them naked, caressing him, flashed in a wave. No! He wouldn't allow it.

He got up and walked through the darkened house into the garage, preceded by his bobbing dick. His dad's gardening shears were right there. Having used them himself, he knew how sharp they were.

The metal of the shears was cold against his skin. He brought them to where his cock started at his pelvis. One quick, clean cut was all it would take.

"Do it," he told himself. "Do it."

"Do it," came Kenneth's voice. "Do it. Do what I couldn't. Get rid of the source of all your misery."

Barry opened his eyes. He had to see it. He had to witness its destruction. It stood there in its arrogance, as though proud of itself.

He closed the shears shut around his cock. The appendage fell to the floor, and there was an enormous *boom*, the sound of applause coming from all the people surrounding him. Kenneth was there, as were Barry's parents. Bert and Christopher were there, Nastya and Miranda, Francesca and Debbido, David, and faces familiar and unfamiliar at once. They stood in a circle clapping and shouting Barry's name.

"You did it!" Kenneth yelled.

The sun began to beam through the garage. The garage became a cloud in the sky, a beautiful blue sky that gave him a view of the entire earth. Then he was back in his garage, but the feeling remained. They were all clapping for his achievement.

"It took a while, and there were some dark moments, but you did it!" Kenneth said.

"You're fulfilling your destiny, Barry," Nastya said.

Barry felt a wave of positivity flowing over him.

"We wanted so badly to tell you what to do, Barry!" Miranda said.

"But you had to figure it out on your own," Bert said. "That's the nature of prophecy and destiny."

Barry was beginning to understand.

"Just like Jesus before you," Bert said, "you were sent to save our world. But our deliverance from a cruel fate could only come at a great sacrifice. By removing your cock, you have freed yourself from bondage. You have freed us from bondage. You have become the god of the new world and will lead us all to a wonderful and bright future. Sex and the pleasures of the flesh are for mere mortals. You are a god, Barry. Your selfless act has saved us. Your sacrifice has assured that none of us will ever live in sadness again. You will right all the wrongs, Barry. We're so sorry it was such a struggle to get to this moment, but you did it! You weren't just carrying your burden, but the burden of all of us. Your pain and suffering were great because it was our pain and suffering. We praise you for your sacrifice!"

"Praise! Praise! Praise!" they all shouted.

The path was clear. Barry knew what he had to do. He cried tears of joy. He was so touched by the scene surrounding him. No one would ever have to suffer again. The god of the new world loved them all so very much.

Epilogue

As luck would have it, Ethel and Jake had a lot in common. Both came from theater backgrounds. Both were even reformed Mormons. Even at the ripe old age of seventy-six, Ethel could belt out a tune like no other. Despite the difference in age, the two got on like a house on fire. Jake would visit Ethel during his breaks at the café, where Ethel had been accepted by the regular old-timers who congregated there.

They had so much in common it was uncanny, including the fact that they both found the same men attractive. As it turned out, Jake was very much a gay man. Ethel didn't mind. She seemed overjoyed with the amount of attention and laughter she was getting from a handsome young man. His company and compliments were enough.

Gabby ended up working up the courage to approach Jordan. Gabby had to interrupt Jake, who also happened to have his eye on Jordan. They'd all been at a café where none of them had any inclination to order coffee. Jake actually hadn't found Jordan attractive at all. In fact, he'd been enamored with Jordan's friend Eddy and was hoping to get any info he could on the mysterious boy.

Gabby looked at Jake for only a second before giving all of her attention to Jordan. They had little in common, but with both of them being young and inexperienced, the flirtatious period of getting to know one another excited them both greatly. Whether it would last was to be determined, but the beginning was full of butterflies and bliss. In the end, everyone was happy, everyone but Eddy, who was unable to reconcile his friendship with Jordan. But four out of five wasn't bad. Miranda could live with it.

Miranda was allergic to Florence. She'd left Milan five days prior and had spent every day since sneezing her brains out. She couldn't enjoy any of the views or gardens at the Pitti Palace due to constantly wiping snot away from her face.

She'd gone to Perseus, a legendary ristorante known for serving the gargantuan *Bistecca alla Fiorentina*. It came in at a whopping three pounds, and the fat waiter nearly refused her service, yelling animatedly that it was meant to serve two to three people, and a skinny, fragile thing like her couldn't handle it. "*Posso farcela,*" she retorted serviceably. "I can handle it."

When the monstrosity arrived, she realized the waiter had been right. A table of Japanese businessmen watched curiously as the skinny girl tackled the enormous steak. She finished it, even eating the fatty bits. The fat waiter wasn't going to win that round.

She only had thirty minutes before her meeting at a nearby outdoor café. The two Benadryl she'd taken that morning were beginning to affect her. Despite the three shots of espresso she'd knocked back to counteract the drowsiness, she couldn't keep her eyes open. She was meeting a man named Lorenzo, who was in his late thirties and impossibly hot. They'd only spoken on the phone briefly, but his accent had melted her heart.

Her time in Italy wasn't purely for pleasure. She was looking to expand the business, and she felt Lorenzo would be a perfect fit.

The San Francisco branch had been a disaster. Revenue at the other two locations was steady for the time being, but Miranda was trying to avoid any further financial calamities. She had enough money to live comfortably for two or three years before she'd have to worry. In the meantime, she was looking to expand into Europe, and had written the first draft of a novel with the working title of *CoinciDATE*. The main focus was on the greatest love story ever told between a seventy-six-year-old woman and a twenty-year-old gay man. Her father had been right all along: she would end up writing a book. But she'd be damned if she'd ever talk to him again, let alone show it to him. The outdoor Italian cafés had been integral to her writing the final chapters. Luckily for Miranda, Shaun's ghost didn't have a passport and had stayed behind in the US.

Feeling slightly nervous about her meeting with Lorenzo, Miranda ordered a glass of wine. In the beginning, she'd been charmed by Italy's leisurely pace of doing things, but that charm had worn off, just like the charm of Italian men. She'd toyed with the idea of maybe marrying one, but they were far too cheesy for her liking. She was tired of waking up at eight in the morning for the restaurant she wanted to eat at to open at twelve, which really meant it would open its doors at 12:45. Lorenzo was forty minutes late. But he also was really hot.

The wine and Benadryl made her sleepy. So did the beaming Tuscan sun. A sting in the back of her neck woke her right up. She turned around and saw Rudy leap behind a pillar.

The End

Acknowledgements

A very special thanks to my dear friend, John Fleming. None of this would have been possible without you. To Matt Dubow and Anne Collette, you were both my earliest readers and were subjected to reading five different versions of the same manuscript. For your critiques and suggestions, thank you.

Thanks also must be given to Inna Turchyck, Matt Zucca, Austin Wilson, Michael Pesoli, Cynthia Parten, Katia Hernandez, Samuel Heaton, and HLK. Due to your invaluable feedback and insight, I came to believe that this little idea was starting to resemble a book.

To the phenomenal artist, Alfred Obare (Behance), thank you.

To my editor extraordinaire, William Greenleaf, thank you for helping me shape this work into something presentable and all your words of encouragement.

Finally, to my parents. My gratitude for your continued love and support cannot be expressed by mere words. Thank you for everything. Continue to love and support me by promising to never read this book.

Without these people, *CoinciDATE* would not have been possible.

CPSIA information can be obtained
at www.ICGtesting.com
Printed in the USA
BVHW080136280421
605945BV00002B/63